NIGHT TOWN

NIGHT TOWN

Cathi Bond

IGUANA

Copyright © 2013 Cathi Bond
Published by Iguana Books
720 Bathurst Street, Suite 303
Toronto, Ontario, Canada
M5V 2R4

All rights reserved. No part of this publication may be reproduced, stored in a retrieval system or transmitted, in any form or by any means, electronic, mechanical, recording or otherwise (except brief passages for purposes of review) without the prior permission of the author or a licence from The Canadian Copyright Licensing Agency (Access Copyright). For an Access Copyright licence, visit www.accesscopyright.ca or call toll free to 1-800-893-5777.

Publisher: Greg Ioannou
Editor: Alexa Caruso
Front cover image: Lisa Kiss
Front cover design: Lisa Kiss

Library and Archives Canada Cataloguing in Publication

Bond, Cathi
    Night town / Cathi Bond.

Issued also in electronic formats.
ISBN 978-1-927403-62-4

    I. Title.

PS8603.O5198N55 2013   C813'.6   C2013-901508-6

This is an original print edition of *Night Town*.

For my Mom(s) and Dad.

PROLOGUE

I've always been a fire-chaser. My Dad, Dr. Theodore "Teddy" Barnes, was a country doctor, and he had to be on the scene whenever tragedy struck. But a fire was different. A fire meant every man, woman and child had to be on hand to help. When the village siren rang, our family piled into the Oldsmobile and tore down the drive, with me clutching Dad's emergency kit full of white gauze, scissors, antiseptic and pain medication. My two younger brothers, Frank and Tedder, jammed on top of one another, bounced around in the back seat of Dad's car that was always full of medical journals, bags of forgotten cookies and drug company samples. Mom tried to ignore the mess under her feet, keeping her eyes trained on the horizon looking for signs of smoke.

The only fire truck in the area belonged to a town about ten miles off, so it was usually up to the locals to deal with the fire themselves. Neighbours would run across the fields, anxious to help a farming family save their home and livelihood. Dad, in his worn fedora, applied tourniquets and salves, while brilliant yellow flames, the same colour as Mom's bandana, licked the sky. The rest of us lined up in long bucket brigades that streamed from deep rural wells.

But a doctor's family and a bunch of friends aren't always enough to stop a barn full of dry hay from burning straight up to heaven and right down to hell. Our family, the whole community, would stand there, praying that the fire didn't flash and spread along the grass and light up the house, taking everything the owners had with them. Back then few had insurance. And even if they did, I never heard of any good luck coming from a bad fire. But even when the flames took everything I secretly looked forward to the next one. I loved them. Fires have a personality. Nobody could stop them. No person. No nothing.

CHAPTER ONE

Our family lived in a three-storey white frame house with a deep wooden veranda in a small town called Sterling in Southwestern Ontario. Dad's medical practice was on the main floor of one side of the house and we lived on the other. The day after they moved in, Mom carefully stripped the veranda floor, stained the wood, and bought matching his and hers chaises. She loved the two stately horse chestnut trees that stood on either side of the house, certain they'd keep the home cool in the summer. Instead, the trees mercilessly dropped their blossoms and nuts into the eaves and Mom spent nearly every weekend up on a ladder. There was no making Dad do the job because he always used the same excuse: "I think that sick people are more important, don't you?" Mom, on her way out the back door in her gardening gloves, didn't look so sure.

The house was located on the busiest road in the village, a murderous stretch of Highway 10 that turned into McKenzie Street as it made its way through Sterling and shot out again at the other end of town. McKenzie began at a gas station and short-order restaurant at the top of the hill that served truckers mostly burgers, fries and pies. The hurtling trucks, their drivers jacked up on instant coffee, sped by our house at breakneck speeds, and more than once an unfortunate family pet was chewed up and cast aside by a thundering eighteen-wheeler. When all that remained of the neighbour's three-year-old apricot poodle, who loved to hump children, was a smashed jewel-encrusted collar, Mom and Dad sat me down and sternly warned me to never ever leave the backyard. But back then I was only five and down the street, within eyeshot if I craned my neck, stood Comfort's Diner. A candy castle of chips, toffee and creamy chocolate milkshakes poured from frosty stainless steel blenders. It was also full of older kids doing things that were a lot more fun than what was going on at my house.

Chatty Cathy's head lay on the bed beside her body. I'd begun an operation earlier that day and was about to remove the voice box from Cathy's chest with a screwdriver.

"I love you, do you love me?" Cathy asked.

She didn't have a top on. I used to love Cathy when I first got her, but now I was more interested in trying to see what made her talk than listening to what she had to say. While I dug the screwdriver into her back there was a long howling screech of tires followed by a horrible mangled bang, punctuated by a woman's scream. Dropping the screwdriver, I ran down the stairs and followed Mom out the door, onto the veranda and across the snow-covered lawn.

Dad was already there, on his hands and knees in a pool of red, cradling a little girl younger than me in his lap. Blood ran out of the back of her head, seeping into Dad's trousers. One eye was open, staring at the sky. The other was shut. The driver had both hands clamped over his mouth while the mother screamed for Dad to save her little girl. Mom approached the mother, wrapping her arm around her shoulder, drawing her close. They were a new family who'd moved in last year.

"Why don't you come into the house," Mom said, gently pulling the woman away from the road. "Teddy will do all that he can."

I stood and stared as Dad lifted the child from the road and carried her across the lawn. Her head lolled in the crook of his arm, face tilting towards the sky with her neck twisted like Chatty Cathy's the time I spun her head around. The sidewalks were filling with grim-faced spectators, some in coats, most not, while a police siren howled in the distance. Could that ever happen to me? Running ahead, I threw open the office door as Dad carried the little girl into an examining room and carefully set her down on the table.

Glancing down at her limp body, he started to cry. My fists rolled themselves into hard balls. I didn't like it when my father cried. It made me antsy.

"Can you save her, Dad?"

"She's dead."

Gently, he closed her open eye and pulled a white sheet up over the little girl's body. Was she a ghost now? Could she fly like Casper or was she just dead like President Kennedy? Everyone was so upset when he died a few months earlier and watching the funeral made me cry. How could a man that young be dead and how could that little girl be gone? Where did they go? The neon sign from Comfort's

Diner flickered through the office window – a faint flashing of red against the blue sky of the dwindling day.

The four of us sat at Mom's new teak dining room table eating salmon salad sandwiches. Mom, who had recently gone on a diet, was eating raw vegetables.

"A woman's figure is one of her most valuable assets," Mom said, with one of her looks.

"That, a clever mind," Dad replied, taking a bite, "and a good heart."

Mom gave Dad her special smile. She didn't need to be on a diet, she was perfect the way she was. The snow was letting up and the gully at the back of our property was coming back into view. The gully was deep, a natural home for tobogganing and sledding. Beyond it stretched a mile of scrubby field, dotted only by a line of telephone poles, where it was finally disrupted by a railway track. Every day the train whistled its arrival, and colourful cars of oil, livestock and grain cars rattled by.

Dad thoughtfully chewed his food. When I asked him why he ate so slowly, he said he was ruminating.

"A fence would solve all our problems," he said.

I glanced out the window. Three kids in snowsuits appeared, dragging sleds in the direction of the diner. Were they having toffee at Comfort's?

"Fence?" Mom asked.

I asked for another sandwich. "Please?"

"Fat!" Frank yelled.

Frank was only three, but he was already a goodie goodie who got on my nerves. And besides, I wasn't fat, I was just healthy. I stuck my tongue out.

"What fence?" Mom repeated. "Maddy, eat some carrots."

Frank banged his spoon on the table. "Fat fat fat!"

"Frankly, I wish you'd never been born," I said, crunching down on a carrot stick.

"Maddy, that's not nice," Mom said. "You're to set an example for your little brother."

"A cedar job might do the trick," Dad said. "But it might not be strong enough."

"No!" Mom said, loud enough that we all looked up. She rarely raised her voice. It was a sign of poor breeding.

Dad started to spell. "I t.h.i.n.k. we need to secure the property from escape attempts." They thought I didn't understand, but I knew how to spell words. Lots of them.

Peering into the kitchen to make sure Mom was busy doing dishes, I put on my coat, quietly slid open the patio door and sprinted across the neighbours' backyard, sliding in behind their miniature barn. Panting, I looked out. All clear. To be extra sure I crouched down low, running behind a long line of cedar bushes, past two barren gardens, a swing set and then there it was – Comfort's Diner. Wooden toboggans and red sleds rested against the wall to the side of the front door and some cars and a couple of big trucks filled the rest of the lot.

Standing, I kicked my way through the drifts toward the diner, dreaming about gumballs and chips, when there was a bellow. Dad, wielding a yardstick, was roaring across the neighbours' backyards, legs pumping up and down while his striped tie bannered out behind him.

I had to make a break for the gully. There was a thick line of bramble where there was a secret hole. A quick glance over my shoulder showed Dad gaining and getting madder by the moment. Mom had joined in the pursuit, her polka dot dress and apron spreading out behind her.

"Stop, Teddy! Stop!"

But Dad didn't listen. He was all red, huffing and puffing. He looked so funny I couldn't help laughing as I dove into the hole. It was smaller than I thought. Scratching and digging, I heard a rip as my coat tore. A black freight train picked up speed in the distance. I tasted mud and ice. My body was nearly through when a big meaty hand grabbed me by the ankle, and with a hard yank, my father pulled me out of the bramble, back to the civilized side of the lawn.

Dad dropped to one knee and threw me over the other. The yardstick came crashing down. Once, twice, three times. Mom pulled on Dad's arm, begging him to stop. I knew it was wrong, but I couldn't help it. I started to laugh. Dad's face flamed like fire.

"Don't you remember that little girl?" he shouted. "That child is dead!"

Up went my coat and skirt and down came the stick. Real pain came then, followed by tears. Mom pulled on Dad's arm again.

"Teddy, stop it!"

The yardstick dropped into the snow as Dad grabbed me, holding me tight, kissing me, asking me over and over again.

"Why did you do that?" Tears ran down his face.

"I just wanted some candies," I sniffed.

Mom pulled a handkerchief out of her skirt pocket and wiped away my tears. "Oh Maddy, why are you so willful?"

It wasn't on purpose. I just couldn't help myself. Now that the show was over, the neighbours who had assembled on their back stoops slowly filed back into their houses as the three of us walked hand in hand through the snow.

Dad felt terrible about spanking me. He was still crying when the workmen installed a chain-link fence the next day. They claimed the ground was too hard, but Dad didn't care what it cost. Mom stood on the back patio, arms crossed, sadly watching as sledge hammers finally broke through the frozen earth. The neighbours tried to convince her that it wasn't all that bad, but Mom knew "the blight" was ugly. I felt bad for ruining Mom's backyard, but was just as upset that I'd lost my last chance for a sneak solo run to Comfort's.

Mom dabbed a bit of Eau de Joy behind her ear lobes. The day my littlest brother was born Dad surprised her with a bottle of French cologne. He said it was because Mom insisted on naming Tedder, short for Theodore, after Dad. I think it was because she always wanted to go to France and the cologne was Dad's way of taking her there.

The smell of the Joy drifted into the back seat of the car. I loved the scent. Tedder started jumping his stuffed animals Kanga and Roo around the back seat. Mom made them for him when he turned five and he took them everywhere. Roo hopped onto Frank's hockey cards, knocking them to the floor.

"Spaz!" Frank cried, quickly rescuing his hockey heroes from the dirt and slush of snow boots.

"Francis!" Mom said, turning around.

Then it got worse. Dad started singing their song: "Gonna take a sentimental journey."

Mom chimed in, "Sentimental journey home."

"Never thought my heart could be so yearney. When did I decide to roam?" they sang together.

"No more," I moaned, clapping my hands over my ears. Since I turned twelve I decided to hate all old time music.

Mom just sang louder as the Oldsmobile clattered over a rickety bridge that spanned a churning river below. A group of kids played hockey on a ledge of ice that shot out from the shore. Blue water rushed past them, racing down the centre of the river. Frank said it was risky playing near open water like that, but I thought it looked exciting. Would the ice break? Would you fall into the water and the fire department would come and all the townsfolk would flock around to watch and hope? Would you drown? Or would you float away on a chunk of ice like an Eskimo?

"How long can a person survive in freezing water before they die?" I asked, leaning over the front seat of the car.

"Not long," Dad replied. "First you sink, then your body starts to fill up with gases and eventually you'd float back up."

A sheet of ice slid off the top of a truck in front of us, smashing onto the road. Dad veered.

"Like that dead cat in Granddad's pond?"

Dad nodded. Ick. The cat's eyeballs were gone and the rest of it was green and foamy with bones poking out. Granddad had seen the coons chewing at the corpse.

"Morbid," Mom said, opening her compact.

A deep red spear rolled up out of the silver lipstick tube as Mom's face flashed in the compact mirror. Her eyes were green and her auburn hair was flecked with strands of gold. The Joy made my nose tingle as I reached forward, slowly running the palms of my hands down the sides of her hair – the electricity made the soft strands cling to my skin.

"You don't need any makeup," Dad said, his hand reaching for hers.

"Dad's right," I said, throwing my arms around her, nuzzling my face into the darkness of her hair. "You're perfect just the way you are."

Nothing smelled like Mom. It was home and something I couldn't quite name – something mysterious and sweeter than chocolate. Mom's hand touched mine.

"Don't muss my hair, honey."

Reluctantly, I pulled away as she dropped her head onto Dad's shoulder. That was going to mess up her hair more than I would. I rolled down the window.

"Mom, it's cold," Frank complained.

"Too bad," I snapped.

"Maddy, shut the window," Mom said, lifting her head from Dad's shoulder and turning to look at me. I pretended not to notice.

"We don't want to get those ear infections going again," Dad added.

Ignoring them all, I put my arm out and cupped the wind in the palm of my hand, letting it arc and dive with the gulls that soared over the river. The sting of the cold sharp wind felt good.

Giant spruces with snowy branches like greatcoats lined the drive as we approached Granddad's enormous, two-storey, red brick farmhouse. The shutters stood open and a wrap-around veranda hugged the house like a clean, white apron.

"The lower branches need trimming," Mom said.

Granny Gillespie had planted the line of trees when she was a newlywed. She wanted shade in the summer and a place for her children to play. Granny had died three years ago and now the trees were huge, with thick branches like ladders that my cousins and I loved to climb. We hooted like Robin Hood when we poked our heads out at the top, gazing over the acres of farmland for miles around. As the Oldsmobile made its way towards Granddad's house, I wondered what it would be like to climb up the trees in the winter and look out over the snow.

Dad pulled onto the parking pad, and I could see Hugh and the other boy cousins playing hockey on the pond out past the cattle pens. The pad was full of cars. The relatives were already there. Frank grabbed his stick and skates from the floor of the car and reached for the handle.

"Can I go?" he asked.

Mom nodded her head as Dad turned off the car.

"Me too," I said snatching my skates.

"Where do you think you're going?" she asked.

"To play hockey."

Frank grinned. I wanted to punch him.

"You know you have to help in the house," Mom said.

Throwing the skates back on the floor with a bang, I kicked the car door open. Frank was already past the pens, running towards the pond while the other boys called hello.

"It's not fair," I grumbled.

Dad said that kitchen skills were important for the manhunt.

"She's too young for that," Mom said, getting out of the car.

A shop where the men sat, smoked and spat while tinkering with tractor engines stood to the west, an open cattle pen to the south. The men talked in the shop and the women visited in the kitchen. Mom said the men talked about matters that weren't fit for female consumption, and the women talked about matters of no interest to men. That only made me desperately want to be outside all the more.

A hundred or more head of cattle shifted and mooed as we crossed the yard, staring at us through the wooden slats. Frank was already at the pond pulling on his skates as Hugh approached him. Hugh was the oldest cousin and spent a lot of time with Granddad. He was tough and liked dreaming up scary dares to test our nerve. When I was ten I had to climb into the pen with a boar. When I was twelve I had to jump into a silo full of oats. I didn't know what would come next, but there would be something.

Hugh tapped Frank on the shoulder, likely selecting Frank to be on his team. Even though Frank was younger than the cousins, he had the best slap shot in our whole family. Hugh was smart to pick him.

"Is that you, Laura?" Granddad bellowed as he swung out onto the back porch.

Granddad was a tall, strong man with a stand of white hair and a sharp, bristly white beard. He wore his pants high, held there by a thick, black leather belt, and a white dress shirt rolled up just beneath his elbows.

Since Granny had died, it fell to Mom and her sisters to take care of Granddad's needs, and he sure had a lot of them. He was a busy cattleman who couldn't boil water, so every weekend one or all of "the girls," as Mom and her sisters were known, had to come and take care of the house.

As Granddad walked towards Mom, the screen door exploded open and a scruffy brownish dog tore down the stairs and across the yard, leaping at Tedder, knocking him flat on his back, fangs snarling and snapping in his face. Terror zipped up my neck. Granddad always had mean dogs, but this one, Buster, was the worst. Dad shoved Buster off with his foot, sweeping Tedder up in his arms.

"Dad!" Mom cried. "Why isn't Buster tied up?"

"What good's a tied dog if you've got thieves and weasels?" Granddad asked. "How are you, Laura?" He gave her a light kiss on the cheek.

"Honestly," she replied, returning the kiss along with a stern look. "You should get rid of that dog."

Granddad just ignored her while Dad asked Tedder if he was okay. Tedder buried his head in Dad's shoulder and held on even tighter.

"Of course the boy's okay," Granddad said. "If you can't face down a dog you're not good for much are you?" Then he turned to me.

"How's my girl?" Granddad asked, giving me a good hard pinch on the cheek.

"Fine, sir," I replied with a smile, even though the pinch really hurt.

"And how's Tedder?" he asked, reaching out to give Tedder his pinch.

But Granddad missed because Dad had walked away with Tedder still in his arms. Granddad started pinching us when we were old enough to walk. Sometimes they were hard enough to turn into welts, but being able to take them was part of being a Gillespie. Granddad always said you had to be tough to rise in God's world and only the strong survived. Tedder hid his face in Dad's neck. He sure didn't look like much of a Gillespie right now.

"Come and get your pinch, son," Granddad said, a bit louder than he needed to.

"We should get lunch on," Mom said, looking towards the house, but Granddad didn't answer. He and Dad were staring at each other.

"He's just a little boy," Dad said quietly.

"There's no boy too young to start being a man," Granddad replied. "Go!" he said and Buster lunged. Granddad laughed as Buster leapt and snapped, trying to bite Tedder's foot. Dad walked away as Mom followed him, trying to keep the peace.

"So Maddy, are you going to help your mother make me a pie?" he asked, giving a sharp whistle.

Buster turned, trotting back to his master.

"No, sir," I replied, looking out towards the pond. Frank had just scored a goal. "I want to play hockey."

"Women shouldn't play hockey. You need skills," he said, following my gaze. "How's Frank's team doing?"

I shrugged. All anyone seemed to care about was Frank and his sports.

"Do you think he's going to win another trophy?" Granddad asked, his eyes moving between the pond and the conversation Mom and Dad were having over by the car.

Buster sat at Granddad's feet. I reached out my hand to pet him. Maybe that would get Granddad's attention. The hair on the back of Buster's neck bristled. My heart jumped, but Granddad was still watching Frank. I put my hand on Buster's head.

"Hello, boy."

Buster's tail dropped as my hand touched his coarse fur. It was gritty, and his eyes were as yellow as his teeth. He let out a low growl. I wanted to step back, but instead I gave him a scratch.

Buster's head whipped up and he gave me a sharp nip. I yelped but didn't cry. Now Granddad looked.

"Why did you go and do that?" he asked. "Silly girl. You don't have the good sense that God gave a billy goat."

Mom and Dad were still talking by the car and didn't notice. The skin on my hand was raised and bruised but there was no blood.

"Go into the kitchen and get Anne to put some ice on it," Granddad said, walking away without another look.

My hand hurt. He wasn't proud of me – he was mad, and I was only trying to show him how brave I was.

"Hi," I said, dropping my coat on the captain's chair by the kitchen door. All the female relatives turned to say hello, but none of them stopped working. A pair of twins, dressed in matching tartan jumpers with bright red socks and black patent leather shoes, looked miserable. They were on potato detail. Coils of peel lay on the table like garter snakes. I showed Aunt Anne the bite.

Aunt Anne was Mom's oldest sister. She was short and wiry with curly red hair, the silliest giggle you ever heard, and always wore crisp, white shirts and dark slacks. Aunt Anne was a registered nurse who lived in Toronto with a roommate. She said she couldn't marry because her patients were her family, but Dad told me that no man wanted a woman who worked and wore the pants.

"Oh Madeline Anne," Aunt Anne sighed, walking to the ice box to pull out an aluminum tray. "You know better than to play with Buster."

"But he tried to bite Tedder," I protested.

"All the more reason you shouldn't be petting him," Aunt Anne said, setting my hand in a bowl full of ice and water. "No wonder you worry your parents sick."

Mom and Dad didn't have anything to worry about. I was as tough as Granddad. I could see him through the window standing at the edge of the pond watching the hockey game. Granddad was only wearing a shirt. His pants rippled in the wind and his hands were cupped around his mouth like a megaphone cheering the boys on. Buster sat in the snow beside him. My fingers were going numb from the ice. The door opened as a gust of frigid air roared through the kitchen.

Mom stood there in her coat. "What are you talking about?"

"Your daughter," Aunt Anne replied, flicking her head in my direction.

Mom saw my hand in the bowl of ice. "What have you done to your hand?"

"Buster bit me," I said.

"Oh for heaven's sake," Mom said, hanging her coat on the hook. "You're going to be the death of me." Tying on her apron she opened the fridge, removing a yellow bowl filled with brown eggs. "We'd better get a move on. The men will be wanting their meal."

We all sat around the table while Granddad said Grace.

"For what we are about to receive, may the Lord make us truly thankful."

I opened my eyes halfway through to see who else was peeking. A couple of the boys were stealing Mom's devilled eggs while everyone else prayed. Frank's eyes were shut tight.

Hugh was down at the end, sitting next to Granddad – a spitting image: tall and broad, with strong arms and clear blue eyes. He looked up, caught my gaze and held it. The twins giggled until their mother cleared her throat.

When Granddad said "Amen" we all dove into the meal. Dishes clattered and everyone chattered, even the kids, until we were told to be "seen and not heard." We sat there quietly for a moment, but then we started up again. Family lunches were riotous events. The boys talked sports while Granddad lectured Hugh on cattle futures. Dad and Aunt Anne shared something about a new antibiotic. They were practically best friends, always talking about new medicines and advances in surgical technique. I dumped a spoonful of peas on Tedder's plate, laughing as he stuck one up his nose. I looked up to see if Granddad was laughing too, but only saw Hugh staring at me again with a funny smile. I wanted him to like me, so I smiled back.

I was under the blankets reading by flashlight, when the door creaked open. I flicked off the light. Another flashlight beam began to squiggle across the ceiling as footsteps softly padded across the floor towards the bed. I stayed perfectly still.

"Maddy."

The twins stood at the end of the bed in identical housecoats, holding flashlights under their chins. Matching demons.

"You have to come with us," they whispered.

Hugh. I sat up. It was time to face another dare.

Following the twins, I silently padded down the staircase, through the darkened house and out the back door. Moonlight lit the path that led to the barn. Granddad always locked Buster up with the cattle, so nobody knew we were out of the house. We ran over the snow and ice, staying close to the ground, then up the graveled rise where the tractors drove hay into the barn. Panting, I placed my palms on the big barn doors. The twins stood on either side. I heard voices as we pushed open the heavy doors. Then the light went out and the voices stopped. I was terrified.

The twins' flashlight beams danced around the barn. An old cutter rested at the back, covered in dust and feed bags. Hay bales, stacked like building blocks, covered the walls all the way up to the mow. One of the boy cousins sat on a bale near the top. Another was perched on a bale near the bottom. They'd thrown Granddad's big barn coats over their pajamas and were smoking cigarettes. It was dangerous to smoke in a barn, but the boys didn't care. It wasn't as dangerous as if Granddad caught them. The twins tittered, shining beams of light into one another's faces. They were having fun, but they looked scared too. Then a spooky laugh echoed down, followed by a flap of wings, as birds struck the rafters. Crows, angry at being disturbed, began to caw and swoop.

I looked up through the gloom to the oak beams that supported the mows. Something large shifted in the centre of the middle one. It was too big to be a cat. My stomach jumped. What was it? A flashlight shone a rotating circle of light, getting wider and wider until it struck Hugh. He was sitting in the centre of the beam, a rifle across his lap, smoking a cigarette. Twenty feet high in the air, with nothing but the bare boards below to break his fall. Another crow cawed, a black shape flying high into the rafters and swooping down towards the ground.

"Are you ready?" Hugh asked. "Or are you chicken?"

The boys made clucking noises and the twins giggled like mad.

"I'm not afraid of anything."

A cold draft cut through my housecoat making me shiver.

"You're twelve now," Hugh said, flicking the cigarette down onto the floor, the ember glowing red. "Get up here."

It was a hard climb in slippers. When one of the boys behind me pulled at the hem of my housecoat I let out a kick. I'd always been afraid of heights, but climbing into the pitch black, watching the twins getting smaller and smaller was only making things worse. Shaking, I forced my eyes to focus on the rung in front me until I reached the top and stepped into the soft straw. Hugh's giant shadow spread across the ceiling. He stood, rifle loose in one hand, the other beckoning me to step out on the beam. He didn't waver, just as steady and sure as if he was standing on the ground.

"Come out," he ordered.

I started across the hay. The boys kept clucking, "Chicken, chicken!" The twins joined the chorus down below. More crows sat in the rafters, shifting black shapes, cawing into the night.

The beam didn't look so wide and sturdy from up in the mow. It was more like a rigid tightrope. Shaking, I looked down. The twins stared up, their mouths gaping as wide as the chickens they fed every day. I remembered a hired man had fallen from here once and broken his back, never to walk again, and suddenly I didn't want to go out on the beam. Hugh rammed his free hand into his pocket. He was tall and strong like Granddad. I looked into his eyes and stopped thinking about the floor. This was about courage. This was about being a Gillespie.

My legs wobbled. Even my feet were shaking. I wanted to get down on my hands and knees and belly across like a snake, but I didn't. I opened my arms wide for balance and willed myself out onto the beam. Ahead of me, Hugh set the rifle down on the rafter, then slowly walked backwards towards the safety of the other side. His eyes never left me. A few steps later, I stood over the gun, out in the centre, all alone.

"Pick it up," Hugh said.

I was shaking so hard I was sure he could see it, could feel my trembling through the beam. But I bent over and saw the planked floor below me suddenly fly up and almost hit me in the face as I tilted towards it. Then, feeling the cool metal of the muzzle, I grabbed the rifle, clasped it to my chest and stood upright.

Hugh grinned. I grinned back. I'd done it. I'd shown him. Then his hand shot out and he released a handful of corn up into the air. Golden kernels struck my legs and head and suddenly the crows, dozens of crows, swooped hungrily down from the rafters, rushing at me, searching for food. Hugh threw another shower of corn. An enormous black shape flew past, so close I could see the red in the centre of its eye. My free hand rushed instinctively to protect my face. A bird flapped against my housecoat. The boys yelled for me to shoot.

I brought the rifle to my shoulder. We'd all learned how to fire a gun. The rifle cracked. There was a bang down below, followed by a series of angry shouts, but nothing registered. I just stood in the middle of the beam firing shot after shot into the black, hearing nothing, feeling nothing but the rush of pure adrenaline.

"Maddy!"

It was Mom. I stopped and looked down, disoriented. Her face was ghost white. Everyone else was there too, all the adults, dressed in their pajamas, sharply shaking off sleep. Aunt Anne was rigid. Hugh was nearly at the bottom of the ladder. Dad shoved him out of the way and started climbing. Granddad yelled something about there being hell to pay. My foot slipped. The rifle fell and with a bang it hit the floor. Everyone scattered.

"Stay steady!" Granddad ordered. The crows cawed.

"Drop to your knees and straddle the beam," Dad said. "I'll come and get you."

I kneeled down, putting my hands in front of me, and grasped the beam, dropping one leg and then the other. Safe.

Hugh stared at me. The other cousins too. I could see it in their faces. I'd gotten them all in trouble. Slowly, I stood back up.

"Maddy!" Dad yelled. "Stay down!"

A crow swept by, catching my housecoat with the tip of its wing. Swaying, one foot shot out while my arms wheeled. Granddad opened his arms.

"Jump!" he called.

"Stay put!" Dad yelled.

"Jump!" Granddad called again, moving right beneath me, his arms held wide and high. "I'll catch you."

Of course he would. I leapt. Granddad scooped me out of the air moments before I hit the ground as easily as a bag of seed or a bale of hay. The roughness of his white bristle scratched my cheek.

"Were you scared?" he asked, setting me down.

"No, sir."

"That's a good girl."

"Thank you, Dad," Mom said, her hand gently stroking my face. All the adults' faces looked tight and stricken. All except Granddad, who smiled and gave me a hard pinch.

"I'm sorry," I said, glancing around.

One of the aunts snorted.

"You should be sorry," Aunt Anne said, her hands clasping and unclasping. "If you were mine I'd spank you within an inch of your life."

The boy cousins were dragged out the door and the twins weren't spared any humiliation either – they were spanked right there on the spot. I heard a thump behind me. It was Dad. He was so upset I thought I was going to get it, but instead, he pulled me to him and held me fast. Then he stared at Granddad, who glared right back.

"Nobody got hurt," Granddad said.

"This time," Dad replied. He turned to Mom.

"Get the boys."

"Oh, Teddy," she replied.

"We're going home."

"You don't need to do that," Aunt Anne said.

"Get the boys," Dad repeated.

I'd never seen my father so angry. Mom and Aunt Anne ran ahead while Dad grabbed my hand and pulled me out of the barn. When I looked back, Granddad was shaking his fist at Hugh. Was Hugh going to get the belt?

We crossed the yard towards the Oldsmobile as Mom and Aunt Anne ran up the stairs and into the house. The lights flicked on: downstairs, then upstairs, spilling out into the yard.

"Are you sure you're all right?" Dad asked, as I got into the car.

I nodded my head. "I'm sorry," I said again. He closed the door. I rolled down the window.

Granddad and Hugh walked out of the barn. Hugh's face was red and he was trembling. Whatever Granddad had said to him was obviously worse than the belt. Everyone had gathered around the car but nobody looked at us.

The bottoms of Dad's pajamas were dirty with mud and snow, while the wind clipped through his hair.

"You know I'd never drop her," Granddad said.

"She could have been killed," Dad replied. His voice was firm, but his hands shook.

Mom emerged on the veranda holding a sleeping Tedder. Frank was behind, rubbing his eyes, looking confused. Aunt Anne followed with blankets and pillows, clothes, boots and coats. Dad and Granddad just stood there glaring at one another, not saying a word.

"Are you sure you won't stay?" Aunt Anne asked. "Theodore, you know he'd never hurt the kids," she added.

Aunt Anne was always the voice of reason, but tonight her words weren't enough.

"Dad, say something," she said, turning to Granddad who just spat.

"It was an accident, Teddy. No harm was done," Mom said, with Tedder in her arms. "Let's stay."

Dad got into the car and the engine fired to life. Mom looked to her sisters for support, but there was nothing they could do. What could they say? You didn't interfere in other people's squabbles. As Mom got in the car, Aunt Anne tucked Frank and me into cozy nests of blankets, giving us each a kiss on the forehead, and softly closed the door.

As the Oldsmobile carefully made its way down the lane, I turned to look at my cousins. They were all standing there, everyone, watching as if they were frozen in time. All except Granddad. He was halfway up the stairs, on his way back into the house.

The car was quiet. We didn't even see another car on the road that night. Where were all the people? The world was empty except for us. Tedder was asleep in Mom's lap. Her head leaned against the glass, their combined breath fogging the window.

Frank whispered into my ear. "This is all your fault."

"You don't know anything." I replied. Dad's eyes shifted to the rear-view mirror, settling on me.

"It's always your fault. You ruin everything," Frank repeated, more loudly this time.

"Quiet back there," Dad said.

Mom didn't speak and Tedder stirred but didn't awaken. We passed a silent abandoned barn by the side of the road, fallow fields growing wild around it. Dad would never understand what happened back at Granddad's. He'd seen too many farm boys dead and maimed. But the Gillespie dares, well, none of us were dead or hurt. Granddad would never let us fall. I looked at Frank and thought how Granddad knew now that I was as good as any boy. Frank pulled a blanket over his head. Mom and Dad would get over being mad. They always did. The lights of the car swept the road as we passed by the Sterling village limits. Drapes were drawn and everything was dark as if we were silently flying into a mysterious night town.

The boys were in bed, but I was too excited to sleep. After Dad tucked us in, I snuck out of my room and crept down the hall, settling into my hiding spot at the top of the stairs. Every night I secretly watched Mom and Dad sitting on the sofa in the living room. Normally they hugged and held hands, talking about their day, but there was no hugging tonight. Tonight their voices were raised, but hushed at the same time, as if they were trying to keep the words muzzled, but sometimes they just slipped out with a power of their own. Like a series of pianissimos followed by unexpected fortes. After all of the piano lessons Mom had made me take, I finally understood what forte meant. It meant force, and it was terrifying.

"In my family we talk," Mom said.

"He never listens," Dad replied. His voice shook and I couldn't make out the rest of the sentence. Dad drove his fist down on the coffee table. The magazines jumped.

This had never happened before. My parents were fighting. Mom always said that decent people didn't shout any more than they drank. That was as much a part of me as the fact that my hair was blond and my eyes were blue. What was going on? Should I go down and stop them or would I get spanked? Would it make things better or turn them even worse? What could I do to help?

"I don't run!" Mom said, her voice volleying around the room. She caught herself, glancing quickly up the staircase.

I held my breath, ducking out of sight. Dad's fists were clenched, pounding steadily on his kneecaps.

"The next time it's going to be Frank," Dad said, jumping to his feet, pacing back and forth out of my sightline and then back in.

"No it won't," Mom replied.

"This is no good," Dad said.

They sat there in silence for a moment. Then Dad just stood up and left. I couldn't see him. Where did he go? Something clattered in the kitchen. Then I heard the cellar door open and footsteps pad down the stairs.

Shaking, Mom tried to pour herself a cup of coffee, but gave up after some of it splashed onto the rug. She didn't even get up to clean it. Instead she rubbed her neck and began nervously shifting things around on the table. My toes dug into the broadloom. Dad had been gone a long time. The house was quiet. Then the sound of steps coming back up from the cellar and there was a clink of glasses and rummaging in the kitchen. Dad wasn't getting a snack or I would have heard the refrigerator door. There was a tinkle and a ping. He wasn't in the kitchen after all. He was in the good china cabinet and what I heard was crystal. Mom looked up.

"What are you doing?"

Dad appeared carrying two cut crystal glasses and a bottle of liquor. I stood up as he set the glasses down. We didn't drink liquor. It was more than wrong – it was practically evil. Granny Gillespie said she'd turn anyone out of her house who took a drink, and the Barneses never touched the stuff either. Shaking, Dad's fingers twisted off the cap. The bottle was full of something yellow.

"Teddy," Mom said so quietly I could barely hear her.

His hand tipped and golden liquid poured into the cut glass. Then he filled the other.

"We don't drink."

He handed her a glass. "We don't fight either."

The shadow from the church spire crawled down the carpet as Mom and Dad took a drink. The taste must have been really bad, because the second Mom swallowed it, it shot back up as she spewed vomit across the lovely white rug. Dad took the glass and touched Mom's forehead.

"You're burning up."

She pulled away. "I'm fine. I'm just not used to liquor."

Mom was pinning pieces of a dress pattern onto Dad's receptionist, while the patients in the adjoining waiting room watched. Ruth was nineteen and recently engaged. When Mom discovered Ruth couldn't afford a proper engagement outfit she insisted on making one for her. Ruth said she felt she was being a burden.

"Every woman needs a little black dress," Mom replied, her mouth full of pins.

"You shouldn't talk with pins in your mouth," I said, leafing through a copy of *Teenage Confidential*. "You could swallow them and they'd become lodged in your trachea or bowels."

"How would they get them out?" Ruth nervously asked.

I was too busy staring at a pin-up of the Monkees to answer. I'd begged for their new record, any new record, but Mom wouldn't let rock and roll into the house. It was old people music or nothing.

"Maddy, put that magazine down. It's too mature for you," Mom said, silver pins flashing between her lips.

Florence burst into the waiting room. She was a farmer's wife who came in every week or so complaining of an imaginary gut ache. Florence staggered up to the reception, seized the counter and asked for Dad. He was busy giving a local farmer a pain shot.

"Is there anything I can do to help?" I asked.

I'd been working in Dad's office since I was born. When Mom couldn't take me shopping or playing bridge, Dad parked me on top of the filing cabinet in my bassinette while he treated the patients. I'd grown up there and never really gotten into the habit of playing with other kids.

Florence seized me by the arm. "I'm feeling poorly."

"Your skin does look a little grey. Why don't I take your temperature?"

Florence sat on the edge of the examining table while I removed a thermometer from a sterilized glass jar.

"Open your mouth."

Florence did as she was told, but when Dad walked in Florence leapt off the examining table.

"Oh, Dr. Barnes, my stomach's acting up again."

"Let's check you out first."

While Dad and Florence chatted, he looked into her eyes, took her pulse and tested her joints with a reflex hammer. Up went the knee. Mom said that Florence was in love with Dad, but Dad and I knew better. Florence was in love with the attention.

"You just wait here while I get you some tablets."

Florence's eyes went wide as I followed Dad into the dispensary. The walls were covered in shelves brimming with large and small brown bottles full of all kinds of tablets, capsules and liquids. Dad removed a bottle of red pills from the top shelf and poured a handful into a white paper packet. I hopped up onto the stainless steel stool.

"What are you giving her?"

"Sugar pills. There's nothing like the power of the placebo."

Dad had every kind of medicine in the world in his dispensary. If the drugstore was closed Dad had to be able to give his patients the medication they required. I opened one of the big bottles and stuck my hand in. Tiny pills slid through my fingers like grains of sand. Dad handed me a bottle of clear liquid and asked me to give it to Ruth.

"What's this?" I asked.

"Demerol."

While Dad left to give Florence her magic pills, I opened *The Canadian Pharmaceutical Compendium* to see what Demerol did. There was the entry: Demerol: 50 mg every three hours for pain.

"I wish your father wouldn't keep this stuff on site," Ruth complained, hiding the Demerol in a drawer with the other restricted drugs. "Some dope fiend could rob the place." The pieces of pattern made her look like a scarecrow.

Ruth crinkled her nose as Florence walked out and Dad walked in. "You should bill her."

"It's only a bit of my time," Dad replied, picking up another patient file as Mom removed pieces of pattern.

"Can you talk some sense into this husband of yours?" Ruth asked.

"About what?"

"He's treating people for free again."

Some of the people Dad treated were poor farmers and had to pay in chickens, pies and produce.

"Oh, I think that's all right now and again," Mom replied. "You never know when you might need some help."

I slumped down in the chair, listlessly flipping through the pages of an old medical journal I'd already read twice.

"What's wrong with you?" Mom asked. "You've been sulky for weeks."

"I don't have any friends."

Mom and I always said we were best friends, but now I wanted friends my own age. Frank appeared in the doorway in his baseball jersey. He was lead pitcher for the Sterling Squirts.

"You have to be nice to have friends," Frank said.

"Shut up."

"We don't say 'shut up' in this house," Mom said.

"Every now and again we do," Dad replied.

He asked Mom how her day was going. Mom said she didn't get all her cleaning done.

"I had to take a nap. Can you imagine that? Me napping."

"You should have asked me to tuck you in," Dad said.

Mom smiled.

"How do you make friends?" I asked.

"Let's see what I can do," Mom replied.

The doorbell rang and I ran to get it. Betsy and Sandy stood there with their mothers. Mom came up behind me, drying her hands on a tea towel.

"Thank you for bringing the girls," she said to the mothers.

Mom asked me who I wanted to be friends with and then she'd actually gotten them to come over. Betsy and Sandy were the two most popular girls in school. Betsy already had a boyfriend, Brad, who followed her around like a collie. Sandy's mom craned her neck, trying to get a look into the living room.

"Would you two like some coffee?" Mom asked, noting their curiosity.

The mothers glanced at one another. A chance to see Laura Barnes's house was an offer not to be refused.

"If it's not too much trouble," Betsy's mother replied.

"No trouble at all," Mom said. "I'm just so happy that the girls came over to play with Madeline." She turned to me. "Why don't you show your friends your room?"

Betsy was drawing colourful butterflies with my new pencil set while Sandy leafed through *Atlas of Diseases of the Upper Gastrointestinal Tract*. Dad had given it to me for Christmas and I'd forgotten to hide it, worried that they'd think I was weird for having a book like that. But Sandy was fascinated by all the pictures of blood and guts. Betsy leaned over to take a peek.

"It is not uncommon to find a prolapse," Sandy read. "What's a prolapse?"

"It's when something falls in on itself," I replied.

Betsy painted the butterfly's wing a crimson red. "Like what?" she asked, running her fingers through her long black hair. Betsy was so beautiful. Mom would never let me wear my hair long.

"We had a sick baby in here once with a prolapsed lung. It was terrible. It was a stormy night last winter. Maybe you remember the blizzard just before Christmas?"

Sandy picked at a beauty mark on her cheek that made her look like Marilyn Monroe. "Yeah, one of our cows wandered out of the barn and died in the snow. What happened?"

They were both staring at me. I liked the attention.

"It was a night in the middle of the winter and there was a blizzard raging outside. Suddenly there was a terrible banging at the front door and a woman screamed." The lady hadn't really been screaming but it sounded more dramatic that way.

Betsy stopped colouring. I opened my eyeballs as wide as I could for effect and breathlessly continued.

"We all ran down the stairs, and when Dad threw open the door a farmer and his wife were standing in the middle of the driving snow. The wife had a baby wrapped in a blanket. And the baby was…blue."

They gasped. I shook my head in dismay.

"Lucky I was there."

"You helped?" Betsy asked. "How would you know what to do?"

"I've been helping take care of patients since I was four," I replied, and was about to continue with how I was going to take over the practice one day, but I could tell that they didn't want to hear about me.

"Dad scooped up the baby in his arms, while I ran ahead and turned on all of the lights in the office and put a sterilized sheet on the bed. The mother was going out of her mind with fear."

"So then what happened?" Betsy asked, biting her nails.

"It was a prolapsed lung."

Nobody breathed.

"The lung was collapsing in on itself?" Sandy asked. "What did you do? What did you do?"

"I called the ambulance."

"They took a call from a kid?"

I tried out a modest shrug. "Sometimes I help my Dad out. They know me at the OPP."

"Wow," Betsy said, still looking at the prolapse. "That's so cool. Nothing like that ever happens over at my house."

"What happened to the baby?" Sandy asked, returning to the book.

"It lived. Thanks to my Dad."

Sandy was eating an apple, but I couldn't finish my lunch. Betsy and Brad disappeared into the woodlot behind the school, and I was worried about Betsy. Mom always said the worst thing that could happen to a woman was to lose her virginity before she was married. If that happened, the girl would be banished from the company of decent people. It was a fate worse than death. The foliage rustled. What were they doing?

"Have you ever been Frenched?" Sandy asked.

"What's that?"

"A French is when the boy sticks his tongue in your mouth."

"Doesn't it make you gag?"

Sandy opened her mouth, sticking out her tongue for a demonstration.

"A good Frencher knows just how much tongue to use," she said, giving her tongue a flick. "They've got to slip it in, find your tongue, and then the two tongues dance."

I couldn't imagine tongues dancing.

"But you have to be sure you don't get them too worked up."

"Why?"

"Because of their penises," Sandy said. "If you get a penis too excited, a boy can't be responsible for what happens. That's why girls have to make sure they don't tease the boy too much. If they do, then the girl gets what she deserves."

"Hi." Kenneth was standing in front of me spinning his sneaker in the dirt. Kenneth was the shortest boy in our grade, but he was the biggest jock. I'd had a crush on him since Grade Two when he'd given me a red ribbon he'd won in a race. We hadn't talked much since, but after the story about the blue baby, I was part of the cool clique. Kenneth sat down beside me, leg bouncing up and down like a jackhammer.

"Are you going to the dance?" he asked.

"I don't know," I replied, trying to act nonchalant. Secretly I was desperate to go, but nobody had asked me.

"So if you did decide to go, maybe you'd like to come with me?"

"I guess that would be okay."

"Should I pick you up?"

Mom would never allow it. "I'll meet you there."

"Okay," and then he ran back to the ball diamond.

I was stretched across the bed on Mom's green eiderdown, while she sat at the vanity table rooting through her cosmetic bag. Her precious bottle of Eau de Joy was displayed against the beveled mirror. I caught my own reflection. Did liars really go to hell? It was probably too late already because I'd just lied to my mother for the very first time. The thought made my stomach hurt, but Mom would never let me go to the dance if I told her the truth. Maybe lying was a part of growing up.

Mom patted the floral, padded bench. I sat down beside her and looked in the vanity mirror again. It was no wonder Mom told me to watch my weight and stop biting my fingernails. She was the most beautiful woman in the world, and compared with her I was plain ugly.

"I need rouge."

"No you don't. Look at me."

I turned. She smiled and brought her hands up to my cheeks, quickly pinching them. It stung. Then she gave me a kiss on the nose.

"There you go."

I turned to the mirror. Mom's pinches gave me a nice rosy glow.

"What about lipstick?"

Mom twisted a golden tube and up popped a pretty pink spear.

"What do you think of this?"

It was beautiful. "Will you show me how to put some on?"

Mom nodded, pursing her lips.

"Put your lips together like you're going to kiss a baby. That's good. Now you apply just a bit. Roll your lips together to spread it evenly."

Mom pulled out a Kleenex.

"This is to dab off any that's left over. You don't want to look cheap."

Wow. I looked at least five years older. Mom pressed the tube into my palm.

"I want you to have this."

My very first tube of lipstick! I threw my arms around Mom's neck, about to kiss her cheek, when something inside made me kiss her on the lips instead.

"Maddy!" she said, pushing me away as if I'd done something really bad. When I started to cry, her face softened. "That's something you do with a boy."

"I'm sorry," I snuffled, noticing something on Mom's neck – a bump just beneath her ear that I'd never seen before. I reached out and touched it. The bump was hard.

"What's that?"

Mom turned back to the mirror to freshen her own lipstick. "Mumps, I think."

"That's a childhood disease."

"It's adult mumps. I'm going to have Daddy take a look at it."

A black thought crossed my mind – mumps was contagious. What if I was to take sick before the dance? That would destroy everything. I had a date. I had lipstick. This was awful.

I didn't get sick. Not unless you count a case of butterflies that nearly caused me to barf three times while I was getting dressed. It was the last Friday night in June. School was over for the year, and I was up in my room standing in front of a full length mirror wearing a beautiful new dress that Mom made for me. Carefully I applied the lipstick, pinched my cheeks and stood back. I never looked so grown up. Grabbing my brown purse by its long golden chain, I slung it over my shoulder, galloping down the stairs.

"No later than nine thirty!" Mom called out as I ran past the dining room.

Mom, Dad, Frank and Tedder were still finishing their dessert. Mom got up and followed me to the door.

"Let's have a look at you."

She pulled me around.

"Soon you're going to be all grown up." Her eyes were getting wet. I hoped she wasn't going to cry.

"I've got to go Mom. I'm going to be late."

"You don't have a belt."

I looked down. Sure enough there were empty belt loops hanging from the sides of the dress. I panicked, about to run back up the stairs.

"Do you think this might work?"

Mom had a belt in her hand – a handmade fabric belt that must have taken hours to sew by hand.

"Do you like it?" she asked almost shyly.

"I love it."

I slipped it through the loops as Mom did up the buckle.

"Thanks," I kissed her on the cheek.

"Have fun, sweetheart," she called as I ran down the stone steps.

Halfway down the sidewalk I looked back and saw Mom silhouetted in the doorway, waving goodbye. She fastened the top button on her sweater and turned back towards the house. It wasn't all that cold. For about five seconds I felt guilty about lying about Kenneth, but then I started thinking about the dance.

The gymnasium was packed. A bunch of girls danced together while some of the boys sat on the edge of the auditorium stage. Brad and Betsy were in the middle of the dance floor under a big silver ball. Kenneth was leaning against the brick wall by the punch bowl wearing a checkered shirt, blue trousers, a blue tie, black shoes and white socks. He'd slicked his hair back and I could smell Old Spice. "Crimson and Clover" started to play. Kenneth took my hand and led me onto the dance floor.

His chin pointed into my shoulder as he drew me close and I could hear his rapid breathing. We were both shaking, but we started to dance. First one foot and then the next until Kenneth stomped on my toes.

He began to apologize, but I didn't care. Kenneth wasn't heavy enough to hurt. I likely outweighed him by twenty pounds. I pulled Kenneth close, trying to sniff him. I'd hugged my family before, but this was different. I stopped looking at Betsy and Brad. I stopped worrying about whether people were looking at us and laughing. I just wanted to feel Kenneth. That's all I wanted.

The four of us broke the 'gymnasium only' rule and went out by the picnic tables. If we were only gone for a bit the teachers wouldn't miss us. The moment we were outside, Betsy and Brad took off. I wanted to follow, but one look from Betsy and I knew enough to get lost. She took the gum out of her mouth and pressed it against the brick wall as they disappeared.

"You want to swing or something?" Kenneth asked.

I nodded, following him across the grounds, looking back at the school, nervous that one of the teachers would see us through the windows.

"You're a good dancer," he said.

"You too," I lied.

We sat there swinging back and forth under the bright full moon. Shadows like witches' fingers beckoned from the trees as the bushes shifted. What were Betsy and Brad doing in there? Kenneth grabbed my swing, stopping it instantly. Then he leaned over and kissed me so hard I could feel his teeth behind the lips.

"Do you like it?"

I nodded yes but the teeth hurt. Then he kissed me again. His lips were tense and he tasted like salt, not sweet like Mom. I kissed him back.

"Do you want to get suspended?" Betsy laughed, scaring me so badly that I knocked into Kenneth's teeth and cut my lip.

"Very funny," I mumbled, tasting the blood in my mouth.

I was worried that Kenneth tasted it too, but if he did, he didn't seem to mind. Being a jock, he'd probably tasted a lot of blood.

Betsy took Brad's arm. "We better get back. The teachers will notice we're gone."

When I got home, nobody was in the living room. That never happened before. Mom always waited by the window whenever I went out at night. The flickering TV offered the only light. A newscaster talked about the war in Vietnam while boys not much older than Brad and Kenneth jumped out of flying helicopters, landing in a jungle. I walked across the living room, into the kitchen and down the narrow corridor towards the light of the dispensary. Hushed voices drifted down the hall. Dad was holding a bottle of pills telling Mom that she should take one to calm down, but Mom didn't want it. She shook her head, saying that she didn't want to be all doped up through this thing.

"Through what?" I asked, walking in.

They both jumped as if they'd been caught doing something bad.

"Your mother needs to have some tests," Dad replied.

"What kind of tests?"

"It's nothing worth fussing about," Mom said.

"The doctors want to check out that lump on Mom's neck."

"I thought it was mumps."

"We're not sure..." Dad replied, about to say something else, when Mom cut him off.

"I told you Theodore, it's nothing."

Mom never called him Theodore unless she was mad. Then she noticed the cut.

"What happened to your lip?"

"One of the kids hit me in the face with the washroom door. It was an accident."

"Teddy, take a look at it."

I weaved out of the way. "It's fine. What are you doing in here?"

Mom slipped her arm around Dad's waist. "We've got a surprise."

"Mom and I are going to see the Grand Canyon," Dad said.

"What?" I asked, stunned. Flying was unbelievably expensive. Mom once told me that cost was the reason Dad never took her to France on their honeymoon. He didn't like to waste money. But now he was going to fly her to the Grand Canyon. It didn't make any sense.

"While we're gone the three of you will be staying at Aunt Anne's in Toronto." Mom leaned into Dad's shoulder, looking up into his eyes. "Isn't it romantic?"

It was all so unfair. I had a boyfriend. I had plans with my friends. We were going to go to a big fish fry at Lake Erie and Betsy's brother Dave was going to drive. I didn't want to go to stupid Toronto. There was a quiet rap at the door as Frank slipped into my bedroom, just as upset as I was. We both started to cry.

"I'm going to miss the League Championship," he sobbed, crawling into my bed. "The team might lose without me. Is there anything you can do? You're bigger than me and Tedder. They might listen to you."

I shook my head. I'd tried everything.

"Why do we have to go now?" he asked.

We cried ourselves to sleep.

CHAPTER TWO

Heat waves floated over the black tarmac as two men pushed a ladder on wheels across the runway. Our family was standing outside with the other passengers waiting for the plane. Still upset about missing the championship, Frank had refused to wear his good shirt and tie and was wearing his Sterling Squirts jersey and baseball cap in protest. Tedder clutched Kanga. In all the packing excitement Roo had been left on the dresser at home, and Tedder had cried all the way to the Toronto airport. I was worried it might trigger a barf because Tedder got carsick.

"Roo can guard the house," Mom said, bending down to kiss him. "And when Kanga gets home she can tell him about our adventures. That way you can live them twice. Once for real and then again in your memory."

Mom had bought a brand new white Samsonite luggage set for the trip. It came with a round hat case and a very smart carry on makeup case. She looked like a movie star in a sleeveless black shift, matching leather slingbacks, black sunglasses and a wide brimmed hat with a white ribbon. A couple of army boys walking by saluted her and nearly stumbled. Mom's arm shot up.

"Anne!"

Aunt Anne ran through the gate and gave Mom such a big hug that it knocked off her new hat. The black hat rolled down the tarmac with Dad chasing after it. I'd never seen Aunt Anne hug anyone. Wasn't she worried about swapping germs?

"We didn't know if you'd make it," Mom said.

"I always do," Aunt Anne replied. "So are you kids all ready for a couple of weeks in the big city?"

"I guess so," Frank replied.

"I forgot Roo," Tedder complained.

A new Air Canada plane taxied towards us, brilliant sunlight striking its white wings. The door opened and two beautiful stewardesses stepped out, welcoming Mom and Dad aboard. They climbed the rolling ladder and vanished into the white plane. The propellers began to sweep, faster and faster as the plane turned, racing down the runway and up into the sky. Aunt Anne and I stood there with my brothers waving good bye until the plane became a dot and then disappeared.

"Wow," Frank said, as plumes of water rocketed up from the bottom of Niagara Falls. Aunt Anne had brought us there to forget our misery, but there was no way I was going to forget how the adults had destroyed my summer.

"I don't feel good," Tedder moaned, clutching Kanga like a life preserver.

The four of us leaned over a little guard rail, watching fast water churn, fall and then crash. It was hard not to be impressed.

"Did you know that the Falls started flowing at the end of the last ice age?" I asked.

"When was that?" Aunt Anne asked.

Tedder moaned.

"Over 12,000 years ago."

Tedder suddenly barfed up macaroni and cheese, soaking unsuspecting Kanga.

"Oh, gross!" I shouted.

"Get away from me," Frank yelped when Tedder tried to hug him.

While Aunt Anne tried to wash Kanga with water from a fountain, the three of us wandered along the side of the river. Tedder had refused to leave Kanga in the car. He was worried somebody might steal her. I doubted it. Kanga stank of partially digested cheese and Frank and I ran away anytime they got close.

A cold high wind blew my hair back, whipping sand against my bare legs. An abandoned magazine blew across the gravel parking pad and tumbled over the edge, where it flew like a paper airplane for about forty feet before disappearing from view.

Aunt Anne returned with her Brownie Hawkeye camera swinging around her neck. She handed a wet Kanga back to Tedder.

"She smells good," Tedder said, hugging Kanga tight and taking a deep sniff of her neck.

"I want to get a photo of the three of you by the sign," Aunt Anne said, backing up to get a good perspective.

"Not with that stinking Kanga," Frank said.

I agreed.

"She's got to go in the trunk when we drive back," I said. "Or I'll barf too."

Reluctantly Tedder placed Kanga on the ground and joined us by the guard railing, leaning over the side. The rail didn't feel very secure. Too much weight and the rail could snap and we'd all be gone, swept into the river and broken into a hundred pieces by the rocks at the bottom of the Falls. Frank tickled Tedder, who giggled.

"That's good," Aunt Anne said, snapping the photo. She stopped a couple out for a stroll.

"Could you take one of me with the children?"

Aunt Anne was coming towards us when a huge wind swirled down from the sky, turning our clothing into a twister of fabric. Aunt Anne's bandana blew right off her head.

"Goodness, that was strong," Aunt Anne said, chasing the bandana.

Kanga.

Tedder turned. Kanga was sitting on her tail like a good kangaroo should when the wind struck, catching her by the pouch, bouncing her up and down across the gravel and then, with a final bounce, Kanga jumped into the river and disappeared over the edge of the Falls. Tedder screamed and I grabbed him just in time to stop him from following her.

Tedder cried for two days and nothing could shake him out of his funk, not even the genuine Indian headdress Aunt Anne bought him at the souvenir shop.

"Shouldn't we look for her?" Tedder asked as we got back into the car.

"I don't know where we'd start," Aunt Anne replied.

Frank and I felt terrible for Tedder and put our arms around him. He'd had Kanga and Roo his entire life. They were like members of the family.

"If you've got to go, that was a pretty exciting way," I said, trying to make Tedder feel better, but he just started wailing again.

Not even Aunt Anne's firm talk about bucking up did any good. Tedder just cried louder.

Two weeks later the boys and I were playing football in a big field behind a fancy new complex in Toronto called The Colonnade. It had a big round staircase that swept out onto Bloor Street. The Colonnade was an architectural experiment, full of shops and apartments, and it even had an ice cream stand. Aunt Anne lived there, and she was upstairs getting dressed for her shift at the hospital. A car horn blasted. I turned and saw Mom leaning out the window, her auburn hair held back by a pretty pink kerchief.

"Were you kids good?" she called, as the car rolled up to a stop. I ran over and gave her a kiss.

"Hi, Dad," I waved. "I've been good. Frank's been bad."

"I have not!" he yelped, trying to give me a kick.

"We've all been good. Even Tedder," I said.

"But there was an accident," Frank said in a low voice as Tedder ran up wearing the headdress. Mom got out of the car and picked Tedder up, giving him a kiss.

"Where's Kanga?"

"She jumped over Niagara Falls and died," Tedder howled, clinging to Mom's neck.

"Oh no! I can make you another one, honey."

"I don't want another one. I want my Kanga."

Mom gave Tedder another kiss. A couple of cars were idling behind, wanting to get by.

"Why don't you come with me," Mom said. "Daddy's got to park the car."

Tedder stuck his face into Mom's hair as they climbed into the car. Tedder sat on her lap. I wanted to sit on her lap and sniff her beautiful hair, but I was too old. As the Oldsmobile took off, Mom put a hand on the roof to steady herself. The tail of her pink kerchief flew like a flag against the clear blue sky.

Two days after we got home, Mom hired an interior decorator. I went into Frank's bedroom to get his opinion. He was lying on his bed reading a book called *Hockey is a Battle*.

"Don't you think it's strange the way Mom's renovating the living room?" I asked.

"She likes decorating."

"But why hire the lady?"

Mom always made these decisions herself. She took months to pore over colour samples, flip through magazines and make everyone crazy with swatches of fabric and photos of furniture, but now she hired a professional. Why the rush? And then there was Dad and money. He was always crying poorhouse. It worried me. Frank put down his book.

"What's going on with you and Kenneth?"
"What do you mean?"
"The kids at school are talking."
"What are they saying?"
"That you're going steady."
"Who said it?"
"Some of the guys."
"Don't you dare tell Mom."
"What are you going to do?" he taunted.
When I raised my hand and made a fist Frank knew I meant it.

That autumn the whole neighbourhood glowed like the inside of a big, red oven. Nature looked how my body felt: sometimes as red hot as the changing leaves, but then icy and cold like the wind. Kenneth kept asking me to go into the bushes. So far I'd said no, but I couldn't say no forever. The workmen's truck was parked in the drive. They were finishing the broadloom installation.

The side door banged open and Mom appeared in a blue housedress, carrying a spade. I followed her around the back towards her garden. Everything else was fire and light, red and yellow, as the leaves of Mom's maple trees fluttered down. Like Granny Gillespie, she'd planted a line of trees along the side of the property when she got married, but they weren't nearly as tall as Granny's giant spruces. Mom sat down in the garden. There was dirt under her nails. I'd never seen dirt on my mother's hands before. I asked her where her gloves were.

"They're too bulky. Help me."
"What about my good clothes? Shouldn't I change first?"
Mom patted the earth. "Don't bother. The light will be gone soon."
I knelt down beside her.
"I want to separate the plants and spread the roots. Oh dear. The irises have really multiplied haven't they?"
"I guess so."
"You don't like gardening, do you?"
"Not really."
"You will one day."
"I don't think so."
"My girl. Always got to have the last say."
"So do you."
Mom laughed. She had a smudge of dirt on her cheek. She looked pale. I reached out to wipe the dirt away.

"Are you feeling okay?"

"Just a bit tired. I've been out here all afternoon."

The plants had been cut back, rotting leaves and stalks piled neatly in the corner. Mud spattered the front of Mom's housedress. The dirt made me uneasy.

"What can I do to help?"

"Dig me some holes near the back of the fence."

The spade mouthed into the earth, the ground already a bit harder from the cooler nights. Mom shook the dirt from the plants, carefully separating the roots as we quietly transplanted the flowers. When she brushed her auburn hair away with the back of her hand a ray of golden light illuminated her face.

"Did I ever tell you about where your father proposed?"

"No."

"He drove me up to the top of a high hill near Granddad's farm. The earth fell away in all directions. It reminded me of heaven."

"I think Niagara Falls is like heaven."

"Not for me – all that noise and crashing water."

"I like noise."

Something in the garden caught her eye. She leaned over.

"Look at that," she said, yanking a withered beet out of the ground. "I missed some of the vegetables. Mother would have said, 'Laura Gillespie you wasteful child.' We grew up in the Depression, you know."

I knew. I didn't like beets and was happy if some of them were dead.

"I should have taught you how to can."

"What?"

"Preserve. My mother taught all of us how to do that."

"You can buy that stuff now."

"It was something nice to do together."

A train hooted in the distance. Mom glanced up, looking into the distance.

"Those were the only times I really got to know her – your Granny. We were always so busy working. Do you understand?"

I didn't, but I nodded anyway.

"There was never any time for anything else. You fed the hired hands breakfast, did the dishes, milked and then gathered eggs. Once you'd done that you'd have to cook a big supper for the men, and then you went to bed and then it started all over again. When I was about your age I decided my life was going to be better than that." Mom shivered. "Your grandmother thought it was shameful."

"Really?"

"It was the only real argument we ever had. She said I was trying to rise above my station."

"I can't see Dad out in the cattle pens," I said.

Mom laughed. "I'm being silly."

She carefully tapped the earth down with her trowel. "How do you like your friends?"

"They're okay."

"Just remember, Maddy. A person is judged by the company they keep."

"Betsy and Sandy are nice."

She nodded. "Are there any boys?" she asked.

"No." I prayed that she couldn't tell I was lying again and that Frank hadn't talked.

"Good. You've got plenty of time for that."

She finished burying the bulb.

"And if you're going to smoke, promise me you won't do it on the street."

"I don't smoke," I protested. Could she smell the tobacco from Frenchy's on my coat? Frenchy's was a hamburger joint where the older kids hung out, and I'd started going there with my friends after school.

"I know you're not smoking, honey. It's just that if you ever do, please don't do it in public."

She reached for my hand. "And please promise me you won't spit on the street…and that you won't say ain't."

"Okay."

This was scary. What was going on? Mom brushed some hair out of my eyes.

"I'm awfully proud of you."

I knew I wasn't supposed to, but I couldn't stop myself. I hugged her. I hugged her harder than I had in years. I hugged her the way I did the first day of school when I didn't want to leave home. I hugged her the way I did when I got sent to church camp. The way I hugged her whenever I felt scared, only this time she didn't push me away and tell me I was too big now. This time, she hugged me back.

Mom knew exactly what she wanted and, while it must have cost a fortune, the renovation was beautiful. The wallpaper was off-white with a faint raised moiré stripe, and the green broadloom reminded me of the sea. When the movers finally left and the last vase was positioned, Mom sank into her new pale green sofa, tossed her right leg over the left and proudly looked around. The main floor was perfect.

Several nights later there was a flurry of activity outside my bedroom door.

"Teddy! Get up!"

It was Mom. I peered out and saw her bolting down the hall in her mauve dressing gown. Dad stumbled out of their bedroom in groggy pursuit. Frank appeared. There was a sound of rushing water. Tedder stood in his doorway rubbing his eyes as Mom flew down the stairs.

"Did somebody leave a tap on?" she cried.

Mom stopped at the bottom of the stairs, her hand clamped over the newel post, madder than I'd ever seen her, including the time I said "holy cow" in church. Water poured out of the ceiling onto the sea green broadloom. A pipe had cracked. The rug squished between our toes. Something Mom couldn't control was boiling up inside her when suddenly out rolled the biggest "GOD DAMN!" I'd ever heard. I wondered if the house would split in two.

The broadloom eventually dried out and we didn't even need to change the under-padding. The carpet man said we were extraordinarily lucky. Mom kept sniffing for mould.

"Do you want to go to the fairgrounds?"

Kenneth was walking me home from school. A series of dark clouds were gathering in the west and creeping across the sky, beginning to blot out the sun. Winter was nearly here. I'd recently turned thirteen.

"I'm cold."

Kenneth pulled my hand. "Come on, it'll be fun."

I followed him up the dirt road towards the ball diamond. We climbed the boards and sat at the top where Brad had carved "Brad and Betsy forever" into the seat. Kenneth pulled out his penknife and started scratching "K + M" into the wood. Nobody had ever carved my initials into anything before.

"We've been going steady for a long time," he said, giving me a sly look.

It hadn't been that long. The sky was turning black and a drop of heavy rain struck my forehead.

Night Town

"I don't want to get wet."

We bounded down the boards and jumped to the ground. The sky opened and the thunder clapped as the rain turned to hail. Taking off across the horse track that circled the ball diamond, we ran into one of the sheds that housed the animals for the Sterling Fall Fair. There wasn't much inside. Just some old bales of hay, an empty cigarette pack and a couple of crushed 7Up cans. Kenneth guided me towards the bale, pulling me down beside him.

"We'll go as soon as the storm passes."

Hail drummed on the metal roof and the shed smelled of manure. Kenneth leaned over and kissed me on the cheek. I turned and then he kissed me on the lips. We'd made out before with Brad and Betsy, but this was the first time we'd been all alone. Kenneth wasn't as shy as he used to be.

"Do you like it?"

I wasn't sure, but I couldn't say that, so I said I liked it and he kissed me again. The thunder was getting louder, the hail pounding the roof like fists. Kenneth put my hand in his lap and something moved in his pants. When I tried to pull my hand away he held it fast. Something was wiggling.

"Do you want to touch it?"

Leaping to my feet I ran for the door, out into the battering hail, through the slippery mud and bolted out onto McKenzie Street, running home to my mother as fast as I could.

She wasn't there. Ruth told me and the boys that Dad had to take Mom into Toronto for a while.

"Why?" Frank asked.

"You'll have to ask your father." Ruth looked uncomfortable. "Why don't you kids watch some television? I'll get your supper on."

We watched everything we wanted that night. Mom would never allow us to watch that much television. By ten, Ruth had tucked the boys into bed, but I wanted to wait up for Dad. Ruth went into the office to catch up on paperwork. Sometime near eleven I heard the car door slam and Dad walked in.

"What are you still doing up?" he sighed.

"Where's Mom?"

"She's going to spend a bit of time at Aunt Anne's. A couple of doctors at the hospital want to examine her, and it's easier if she's there."

"Doctors?" I asked, suddenly concerned. "What's wrong with her?"

"There's nothing to be worried about. She's going to be fine."

Dad, still in his overcoat, turned on the TV and sat down beside me.

"I'll be going now, Dr. Barnes," Ruth said, sticking her head through the door. "Come on, Maddy, let your Dad alone. It's time you get to sleep," she added, putting on her gloves.

"Ruth's right. You get up to bed. It'll be morning before you know it."

He gave me an absentminded kiss. Reluctantly, I left the room and climbed the stairs. The front door closed behind Ruth as Irv Weinstein asked, "Do you know where your children are?" I wondered what Mom was doing. Normally people didn't need to be near a hospital unless they were really sick.

"We get to eat Sloppy Joes every night," I said. "And watch all the TV we want."

Sandy said I was lucky. Her mother would never go for that. Betsy, Sandy and I were crammed into our booth at Frenchy's. Kenneth and Brad sat at the counter. When Kenneth turned and flashed his sly dog look I turned away. I was worried about his uncontrollable urges and didn't want to be alone with him. Brad glanced at Betsy with a secret smile that made her beam. She stuck her left hand out, placing it on the table. There was a silver signet ring on the wedding band finger, which officially meant going steady.

"It's beautiful," I said. Secretly, I was jealous and wanted one too. The signet was engraved with "B&B". That meant undying love and you'd be together forever. A ring like that would make it acceptable to touch a penis.

Mom had been gone for weeks and we rarely saw Dad. When he wasn't seeing patients, he spent all his time in Toronto and got home really late. One night I decided to wait up. The boys were always asking me about Mom and I wanted to know too. Christmas was coming, and the television announcer said Rudolph the Red Nosed Reindeer would be on TV the following week. When I heard the door open, I got up and flicked off the set.

"Hi, Dad," I said, walking into the foyer.

"Hello, honeybunch," he replied, automatically placing his fedora on the hat rack. Mom had trained him to be neat in the house.

"How's Mom?"

"She's in the hospital."

I thought she was staying with Aunt Anne. "What's wrong?"

"She's going to be fine."

"We should go and see her."

Dad just shook his head. "It's not going to help if you get yourself all worked up."

"I'm not worked up. I just want to see her."

"Mommy just needs plenty of rest." He looked at his watch. "Isn't it time for you to get to bed?"

"Okay," I said, trudging up the stairs.

Something didn't feel right, but I knew my parents wouldn't lie to me and I was probably worrying for nothing. Sometimes people simply needed a hospital stay to get things straightened out. Dad said it was occasionally part of the cycle of life.

"Look who's here!" Aunt Anne called, opening the front door. It was the night before Christmas.

Dad helped Mom over the threshold. She stood in the hallway in her good tweed coat while Tedder and Frank jumped all over her, making her promise she wouldn't go away again for a long, long time. She was too thin and her skin was paler than the new walls.

"How's my Maddy?" she asked, smiling tiredly.

"We've set up the tree just so. Come and look," I said, pulling on her hand.

Frank, Tedder and I had especially selected the tree from the lot downtown and dragged it all the way home ourselves. It was a tall, bushy pine with warm welcoming branches. The scent filled the entire downstairs and made the whole house feel jolly. We'd spent the day decorating the Christmas tree the way Mom liked it. You couldn't see the electrical cords behind the twinkling lights, and we hadn't just tossed on clumps of tinsel. Every single shiny silver strip hung perfectly straight, and the ornaments were positioned so they balanced.

"Tedder made the angel for the top," Frank said.

Tedder beamed up at her, his arms wrapped around her legs. "I think you'll really like it, Mommy."

"I just need to lie down for a bit," Mom said, putting her hand on Dad's arm, signaling it was time to go up to bed. "I'll look at it tomorrow."

Dad helped her up the stairs.

"Santa's coming," Tedder sang. "You better be up in time."

The next morning Frank and I tore down the stairs to see what was under the tree. Tedder was speeding around the living room on a new red tricycle with a big bow on the bars. All the other presents were wrapped, and Frank and I were both desperate to see what we got. Aunt Anne arrived in her housecoat carrying mugs of steaming hot chocolate.

"Where are they?" Frank asked, curiosity getting the better of him.

We weren't allowed to open our gifts until Mom and Dad came down. Tedder swooped around the room on his tricycle in accelerating circles.

"It's time they come down!" he squealed.

"Go and get a broom," Aunt Anne said.

I got one from the hall cupboard and Aunt Anne turned it upside down, striking the ceiling with the wooden handle.

"It's time to get up!" she yelled.

"Get up, get up, get up!" we all called as Aunt Anne kept banging the broom.

Finally we heard Mom and Dad coming down the stairs, but when we saw her enter the living room all the joy blew out of the day. She collapsed on the sofa, put her feet up on the new coffee table and tried to smile, but all she could do was wince. Poor Mom, she must have been feeling really bad. Tedder gave her a gift to open, but Dad had to do it instead. After we'd finished quietly unwrapping our gifts, Mom went back to bed. She said she'd be down for Christmas dinner, but she never returned. All day she just lay beneath the green satin eiderdown, and every time I poked my head in to say hello, her eyes were closed.

Kenneth came over the day after New Year's. Frank answered the door. I peeked out from the living room. Kenneth was wearing a new coat and looked spiffy.

"Maddy?" Frank called sweetly. Then he yelled, "It's your boyfriend!" I rushed out of the living room and scowled at him.

"Would you please leave?" I hissed.

Frank sauntered by, returning to paint a model boat.

"Hi," I said leaning up against the newel post, trying to look nonchalant.

"Hi," Kenneth replied, staring at the floor, shifting his boots back and forth as bits of wet snow and mud flecked off onto the new broadloom. I wanted to tell him to stay on the rubber matt, but didn't dare.

"It's nice outside," he said nervously.

"Yeah," I agreed, looking through the window. It was miserable. The sky was leaden and there was a good foot of snow on the ground.

"Do you want to go for a walk?" he asked.

"Where?"

"How about down by the gully?"

We were sitting on the big rock at the bottom, banging our boots against the stone. Clods of white snow fell out. Kenneth was nervous. He had his hand in his pocket. What was in there? I prayed it wasn't the penis.

"What have you got there?"

Kenneth pulled out a pretty little white box with a red ribbon and handed it to me. Carefully I opened it. Inside, on a bed of white tissue, rested a silver signet ring just like the one Brad had given Betsy. I couldn't believe it. Somebody had given me a ring. I pulled off my mitten.

"Will you put it on?"

Kenneth slipped it on the ring finger of my left hand. It was a bit too big and wasn't engraved, but I didn't care. I had a ring. Glancing at me for a split second, he darted in for a kiss. His tongue probed around in my mouth, striking enamel. Kenneth was trying to French me! I unclenched my teeth, closed my eyes and was letting his tongue slide in when I heard her.

Mom was standing at the top of the hill screaming my name. Her mauve dressing gown, now much too big for her, was clutched around her body, and her skin, white as chalk, stood out against the flat grey sky. She wasn't wearing a coat. She hadn't taken the time. Mom must have heard us downstairs and followed us across the field. She wasn't even wearing boots.

Mom called again as the wind tore open her housecoat. I didn't know whether to run up the hill or head toward the horizon running as far and fast as I could. Kenneth jumped off the rock. We both shook with cold and fear. My mother looked terrifying up there, so skinny, like a white scarecrow that might take flight and swoop down, plucking out our eyes. She raised her arm and pointed her finger down at me, the mark of ultimate damnation.

"Laura!" Dad's voice.

Coatless as well, he swept her up in his arms and glanced down at me, then turned his back and they vanished.

Kenneth pulled his toque down over his ears. "I didn't know your Mom was sick."

"She's not sick!"

He tried to take my hand, but I didn't want anyone touching me. I didn't want to talk. I told him to go. Everything was still. Everything except the wind.

I stayed there on the rock. My head was cold. I hadn't worn a hat. But I was too scared to go home. What Kenneth said about Mom being sick. I started to breathe fast. She wasn't sick. She was just having tests.

The Oldsmobile was gone but there were other cars in the driveway. Dad must have left on an emergency house call. Maybe they wouldn't be so mad at me if I entertained the patients.

"Mom?" I called, opening the door and kicking off my boots.

The living room was empty. Tedder's Hot Wheels track roped around the legs of the new coffee table. A bright yellow truck lay on its side. Nobody answered.

"Mom?" I called, even louder this time, walking slowly up the stairs.

The phone in the office rang, breaking the silence. I could hear Ruth's voice in the background.

"Dr. Barnes's office, please hold."

I was still scared and knew I was going to get it, but I wanted to see Mom anyway. The bedroom door was closed. Without knocking I quietly turned the knob. The unmade bed was empty and Mom's eiderdown comforter lay in a pool of green on the floor. Leaning down I picked it up and buried my face in the satin, but the scent of Joy was gone. Something sweet and earthy had replaced it, a fleeting smell like the garden after all the flowers had died.

"Mom?" I called again.

I walked into Frank's room. He was doing homework.

"Do you know where Mom is?"

He looked up from the books. His eyes were red and puffy. He'd been crying.

"Dad took her back to the hospital…and it's all because of you and your boyfriend."

"It's not my fault!" I yelled.

It was Mom's fault. She followed me out into the snow. If she'd stayed in bed and drank her fluids then she'd get better. Dad always said that was the ticket, though sometimes you needed antibiotics. Why did he take her to the hospital? What could they do that he couldn't? The kiss, it had been a French.

Aunt Anne returned that evening. Frank, Tedder and I were lined up on the sofa, and Aunt Anne sat opposite us. I stared at the design of the moiré wallpaper.

"Ruth is going to stay with you kids," Aunt Anne said.

"Where's Dad?" Frank asked.

"He's going to stay with your mother."

"I want Mommy," Tedder whined, clutching Roo to his chest.

"She can't be here right now," Aunt Anne replied.

"Why can't you stay?" I asked.

"Because I need to be with your mother."

I couldn't read her face. It was as blank as Granddad's after Granny died.

"Will you be alright?" she asked.

We all nodded. I was still staring at the wallpaper.

"Can we do something?" Frank asked.

I could see his agitation, fingers wriggling like snakes.

"Behave the way your mother would want," Aunt Anne replied, her eyes shifting to me.

Ten days passed. I barely slept. Every time I closed my eyes I saw Mom up on the hill. Kenneth had told everyone that Mom was sick.

"What's she got?" Betsy asked.

We were down in the rec room, practicing some new dance steps.

"Some kind of flu."

It had to be that or the mumps. Maybe pneumonia. She was awfully thin. Sandy asked when she was coming home but I didn't know. Every couple of days Aunt Anne arrived to check on us and bring letters from Mom. They were full of the usual stuff: Was I being good? Did I do my homework? Was I being a help to Ruth? But there was never anything about her and the tests, and never once did she mention Kenneth. I tried to read between the lines, looking for clues like Nancy Drew, but there was nothing to find, or else I wasn't smart enough to figure it out. I felt so scared and mad too. She was punishing me for the French.

The phone rang upstairs.

"Maddy," Ruth called. "It's your aunt."

"Hi," I said, sitting at the dining room table, staring out the window, the pale green receiver clenched in my hand.

The world outside was white. The chain link fence was nearly buried in high drifts of snow and I could see past Mom's garden, beyond the gully, all the way to the railway tracks. Aunt Anne didn't speak.

"Are you there?" I asked.

"Yes, dear."

"How's Mom?"

Aunt Anne was quiet again and then she cleared her throat. "Would you like to come and see her?"

My heart fluttered with hope, but then fear clamped itself around my chest, squeezing like a band of steel. So hard I couldn't catch my breath.

"Why doesn't she just come home?"

"She can't," Aunt Anne replied.

Ruth banged a pot in the kitchen.

"I could come and get you right now," Aunt Anne said.

I didn't answer. I couldn't.

"Betsy and Sandy are here," I said, staring at Mom's fence. "They're staying overnight," I lied.

"Oh."

"Why doesn't Mom just come home?"

The air hung like a blanket – air that still smelled faintly of fresh paint and wallpaper glue. I tried hard to keep that smell fresh in my mind. If I didn't let it go, then Mom would come back and start decorating something else. Maybe we could do my room together.

"I better go," Aunt Anne said.

She cleared her throat again, then the line went dead. The dial began to hum and then Betsy yelled up from the basement. I hung up and ran down to my friends.

There were no more letters or health updates that week. Neither Aunt Anne nor Dad came back to the house. Just the odd phone call to Ruth to make sure everything was all right.

"Can I talk to Dad?" I asked, but Ruth just shook her head, placing the phone back in the receiver.

"Maybe next time," she said, picking Tedder up and carrying him into the office. The patients kept arriving, even though Ruth told them that the office was closed for the time being. Everyone asked the same question.

"When's he coming back?"

Mothers bouncing sick children on their hips, old farmers doubled over with rheumatism, and even Florence arrived one afternoon complaining of her gut ache.

"When's he coming back?"

I tried to talk her through it, but she needed Dad's magic pills. He was gone, and as each day passed I tried harder and harder to push the scary thoughts out of my mind, but they kept appearing like thought bubbles in the comics: "Batman raced to the cavern. Maybe Robin had been kidnapped by The Joker." "What if Mom isn't coming back?"

"Go away!" I told the thought bubbles, but that didn't always work, and at night, the bubbles were the worst. I never knew what they might say.

The boys and Ruth were asleep, but I was wide awake in the little spare gabled room that overlooked the church. After Mom left I started sleeping there. I couldn't bear my own bedroom because the window overlooked her garden and the gully – the gully where she'd seen the French. Two single beds rested on either side of the window. There wasn't enough room for a dresser, just two tiny bedside tables with driftwood lamps Mom and I had made. I ran my fingers over the driftwood. It was still smooth. Mom and I collected the wood down by Lake Erie, sanded the bases and sealed the wood with shellac. They were as nice as any lamps in the store. There were no slivers. We'd done a good job.

The little room was cold. I pulled the quilt up under my chin. A sudden blast of wind struck the side of the house, making me jump and rattling the shutters as a cold draft seeped beneath the windowsill. The storm windows were still out in the garage. Mom had forgotten to get the yardman to prepare the house that winter. Another blast hit the house. I got up and looked out the window to see if the shutters were still intact. Maybe they'd snapped off.

The trees twisted, bare branches swinging like skinny arms. Our metal garbage can had fallen on its side and was rolling across the driveway. A line of red started to peek over the edge of the horizon when suddenly everything went still. The garbage can stopped rolling. The trees relaxed. I opened the window. The wind was gone and it was peaceful. I could smell the air, brisk and fresh, when the phone rang out like an alarm. I shut the window and hopped back into bed. Ruth stumbled out of the spare room, her body shifting in the dark hall. The band of fear was back. I tried to breathe.

"Hello," Ruth said, picking up the receiver. "Oh no," she said, letting out the tiniest cry. "Yes," she said, over and over. "Yes." She put the phone down and quietly walked towards my room.

I lay down, closed my eyes and pretended to sleep. Ruth paused in the doorway and I heard her uneven breathing, little jagged gasps catching in the back of her throat. Then she turned away, her footsteps getting softer and softer as she walked down the hall and descended the stairs. Then the wind resumed its wild dance; the shutters banged and the shingles threatened to rip themselves off the gables.

The wind eventually settled down but I didn't. I lay there staring straight up, watching the day begin to spread itself across the ceiling, getting brighter and brighter. The band of steel remained, clamping tighter and tighter. A car pulled into the driveway, the front door opened, then closed. Ruth must have been waiting in the foyer. Her voice mixed with Dad's, getting louder as they climbed the stairs. He told Ruth to wake the boys as he entered my room and sat down on the other bed.

"Maddy," he said, his voice trembling. "Wake up."

Dad was still in his hat and coat. His pants were wrinkled and he hadn't shaved in days. Sitting up, I swung my legs over the side of the bed and put them on the cold maple floor. Somehow the chill took a bit of the terror away, but it came right back when Dad looked at me. His face wasn't blank. It was full of pain. So deep there was no bottom. I didn't go to him.

Frank and Tedder stood in the doorway. Ruth was behind them. Tedder climbed into Dad's lap, rubbing the sleep out of his eyes. Dad wrapped his arm around him and Frank sat down beside him. The band squeezed.

"How's Mom?" Frank asked.

"She's with the angels," Dad said, one hand stroking Tedder's hair, as the other found Frank's hand. His voice shook.

"Where did the angels take her?" Tedder asked.

"What do you mean?" Frank interrupted, his jaw clenching and unclenching.

She was dead – that's what he meant. There was a hangnail on my right thumb. I pulled at it and made it hurt.

"I was with her. She was peaceful. There was no pain."

Then Dad looked straight at me, meeting my gaze, but I turned away. It had to be the kiss. He turned back to the boys.

"The door opened and an angel came in, and the angel took her to heaven."

Frank started to cry.

"I want her back," Tedder said.

He was crying too. The three men of the family sobbed as Ruth stood out in the hallway, not wanting to intrude. I sat straight-backed, staring at the church and the red dawn. I didn't cry. I wouldn't – no matter what – I wouldn't cry, for fear I'd be swept away by the tears or swallowed up by the terrible bubbles. No. I sat on my bed, pressing my feet into the cold, cold floor. No.

Aunt Anne arrived a few minutes later. She burst through the front door, flew up the stairs and into my room, swooping the boys up into her arms, kissing them on their cheeks, telling them their mother loved them and that we'd all get through this together. Her clothing was as wrinkled as Dad's, but she wore that face that said, "March on! We're strong. We can get through this." Dad stayed where he was, in his hat and coat, with Tedder in his arms. I got up and walked past them all, down the hall and into the bathroom, locking the door behind me.

"Maddy," Aunt Anne called after me. "Maddy!"

I turned on all the taps so I couldn't hear. The shower poured down and ice cold water splashed out, soaking the good chenille mat. I didn't care.

"Maddy!" she called again, knocking at the door. "Let me in."

I didn't answer. I stepped into the shower in my nightgown. Standing under the rushing water, I opened my mouth as wide as I could and thought about all the men who rode barrels over Niagara Falls. They'd all drowned, the barrels smashed into bits by the rocks. The cold prickled my skin and rushed into my ears, like shards of ice slicing into my body. I couldn't hear a thing. How did the men feel as they flew along the Niagara River, and what was it like when they struck the rocks?

The doorbell chimed. The boys and I were dressed in our Sunday best. Aunt Anne told us it was our job to answer the door. It felt as if everyone in the world was coming to our house that day. I opened the door. The lady whose little girl had been killed on McKenzie stood there, clutching a Corning Ware casserole dish. So did all the women standing beside her. Endless casseroles and tubs packed with precooked food.

"Would you please come in?" I asked, opening the door wide.

When they looked at the three of us they all burst into tears. "You poor motherless children," said the lady with the dead girl.

The others dabbed their eyes with embroidered handkerchiefs, passing into the kitchen to drop off the casseroles and then joined all the other friends and neighbours in the living room. Frank and I started carrying in dining room chairs for the overflow of mourners, while Tedder sat on the fireplace hearth clutching Roo.

I heard one of the women say, "Did you even know she was sick?"

"Nobody did," another replied, glancing at me.

"Where's Dr. Barnes? The children shouldn't be all alone."

Dad had disappeared when I was standing in the shower the morning before. Ruth said he just got in the car and drove away. He still hadn't returned.

Aunt Anne arrived, pushing Mom's mahogany tea trolley into the living room. It was covered with an assortment of Mom's favourite brightly painted teacups. "Can I get any of you coffee or tea?"

"Oh, no," a lady said, rising to her feet. The other women did the same. "You'll need your time alone," she added.

They left behind a mountain of food that covered the kitchen counters and spilled onto the dining room table. Aunt Anne couldn't make enough room in the fridge, so she pulled all of Mom's Tupperware containers down from the top shelf over the sink.

"There's no point in letting good food go to waste," she said, automatically transferring spoonful after spoonful of scalloped potatoes and macaroni and cheese into the clear plastic tubs. She attacked some noodles stuck to the bottom of a pan. "It's important to get it all."

Snapping the lids into place, I wanted to ask what had happened to Mom, but I didn't dare since I was the one who had kissed Kenneth in the gully.

Aunt Anne pushed up the sleeves of Mom's black cashmere sweater. There wasn't enough time for her to go home and change, and Aunt Anne needed something decent to wear. Since Mom's slacks were much too long, Aunt Anne had been forced to wear a skirt. Other than church, it was the only time I ever remember her wearing one. Her pale legs looked exposed in the light. The only sounds in the room were the slap of the spoon and the snap of the lids, coupled with the uneasy sight of Aunt Anne's bare legs.

"I'm sorry."

"What on earth for?"

Then I grabbed her, hugging her as tightly as I could as the Joy washed over me and I remembered the softness of her hair.

"It's all my fault."

"It's nobody's fault."

The harder I hugged, the more Aunt Anne's body stiffened and the harder I hung on.

"Maddy!"

"Where's Dad?"

"I don't know."

"Maddy. Let go."

I clung even tighter.

"This is no time to let emotion get the best of us," she said, wrenching herself free. Seizing me by the shoulders, Aunt Anne held me firmly at arm's length and, like the determined nurse she was, administered the Gillespie family medicine:

"Now make yourself useful, run those tubs down to the freezer and meet me in your parents' room."

It was quiet in the basement. The big, white freezer was full of frozen meat wrapped in brown butcher's wrap. The cuts read 'Roast beef,' 'Chuck,' 'Prime Rib,' 'T-Bone,' 'Stewing' and 'Flank.' Once a year, Mom asked Granddad for a side of beef. He'd personally select the animal and have it sent to the slaughterhouse. Once the animal was butchered, Granddad would load the meat into the trunk of his Lincoln and drive it over to our place.

"Be darned if it doesn't fill the whole thing," he'd say, marveling at the storage space his big sedan provided. "I could fit all you kids in there," he'd say, running after us, threatening to put us inside and close the lid.

Granddad could make sense of this. He'd know what to do. He'd tell me what happened. I moved the rib roasts to the side and tossed a couple of rigid chickens into the bottom of the freezer, placed the still faintly warm casseroles on the upper rack, then went upstairs to look for Aunt Anne.

I found her in Mom and Dad's bedroom in the middle of their enormous walk-in closet. Dad's side was a snarl of socks and shoes, with pants and jackets dangling haphazardly from big wooden hangers. Mom's side was perfectly organized, with clothing ordered according to season and function. Sunday suits were followed by slacks, sweaters, blouses and dresses; formal wear was near the back, with footwear lined up neatly beneath. Mom's good quilted housecoat hung on a hook. Why didn't she take that to the hospital? She must have been in a terrible hurry. She must have been wearing the mauve dressing gown – the one she was wearing at the top of the hill.

Aunt Anne was rifling through Mom's clothes. "What do you think your mother would like?"

"What?" I asked, confused by the question, but comforted by the smell. Standing on the threshold of Mom's closet was like walking into her arms. I wanted to tear every dress and slip from their hangers, roll up the sweaters, throw everything into a heap on the floor and lie there, drifting away in the smell that had surrounded me my whole life. But I didn't. Aunt Anne wouldn't approve. I would come back later when I was all alone.

"What do you think she'd like?" Aunt Anne repeated.

"I don't understand."

"To be buried in."

Neither of us spoke. The doorbell rang and I heard Ruth answer it.

Aunt Anne looked at me. "Your father isn't up to it, so I thought you'd like to help."

"Where is he?"

"Maybe this," Aunt Anne said, selecting a good navy Sunday suit.

"No." I walked into the closet, towards the formal wear.

The blue suit wouldn't do. I reached out and selected the gold dress Mom had bought especially for a New Year's Eve party that she never attended. We'd driven into Toronto to Eaton's in the early fall and I'd helped her pick it out. The saleslady said that Mom was as pretty as any model. Mom said she didn't think so.

"And just as slim," the saleslady added.

Why hadn't I noticed how much weight she'd lost? If I'd noticed, maybe I could have done something to stop it.

"Do you have any shoes?" Mom asked. While the saleslady rushed out, Mom asked me what I thought.

"Do you think it's too showy?"

"I think you look beautiful." And she did. The golden satin shimmered as Mom slowly turned on top of a round pedestal that rested in front of the dressing room mirror. The saleslady returned with a pair of golden shoes and a matching evening bag. Mom put them on, walking down the corridor of mirrors, turning to examine her silhouette from afar.

"I'll take it," she said. When the saleslady turned away, Mom took a look at the price tag, grimaced and, giving me one of our secret smiles, added, "Your father will kill me."

"She liked this," I said, thrusting the gold dress at Aunt Anne.

"It's much too good to be buried in," she said. "It's still got the price tag. No, we'll give this to charity. Help me pick out something else."

"No!" I said. "This is what she wanted! She would want to wear this!" Aunt Anne was about to give me a lecture about sassing back, but for some reason she stopped. The gold shoes sparkled. I snatched them up, handing them to her.

"And with these," I added. "I want her buried in her new shoes."

The funeral clothes were ready and we were all packed to go to Granddad's, but Dad still hadn't returned.

Aunt Anne told Ruth she was going to take us up to the farm. "When you hear from him, tell him where we've gone." Ruth and Aunt Anne had been whispering in the kitchen about how arrangements needed to be made, but Dad was missing.

"Where's Daddy?" Tedder asked, pulling me by the sleeve.

"I don't know," I replied, yanking my arm away. "Stop asking."

Frank and Tedder had been pestering me about Dad all day, and the longer he was gone the more irritated I became. I didn't know where he went. Tedder turned away and wandered off. I felt awful. He was only a little boy.

"I'm sorry, Tedder," I said, going after him. "Dad just needs a little time on his own is all. You know how you feel after you cut your knee."

Tedder nodded. "You need time to cry. And then a Band-Aid."

"That's right," I said. "We're going to go to Granddad's house."

"Will Buster be there?"

"I'll make sure Granddad ties him up nice and tight."

Tedder took my hand as Aunt Anne picked up Mom's white Samsonite suitcase. "Have you kids got your good clothes?"

We all nodded.

"We better leave Dad a note," Frank said. "In case he wonders where we are."

"I already did," Aunt Anne replied. Of course she did. "Now let's get going."

We walked into the farmhouse foyer, but everything was still.

"Where's Granddad?" Tedder asked, undoubtedly worried about getting his pinch.

The living and dining rooms were empty, but we finally found the whole family sitting in the kitchen, even the men. The only ones missing were Dad and Granddad. The women silently prepared salads and sandwiches for fellowship after the funeral. When we entered they all rose.

One of the twins said she was sorry and suddenly burst into tears. Her mother passed her a handkerchief and told her that crying didn't help. I was afraid to start in case I never stopped.

Hugh swept Tedder up in his arms and onto his shoulders. "Do you want to go for a ride?" He turned to the other boys. "Let's go check on the cattle."

Happy to escape the death house, the boys nearly ran out of the kitchen.

Aunt Anne sat down, turning to the adults. "They did everything they could."

Who were "they" and what did they do?

"It was just beyond their control," she added.

What was beyond their control? How did a case of the mumps turn into something like this? I looked around the kitchen.

"Where's Granddad?" I asked.

"He's busy in his office," Aunt Anne replied. "It's best you leave him alone."

I didn't pay any attention and just walked out.

Granddad's office was at the end of a long, oak-paneled hall. Its walls were covered with family photographs. There were framed photos of glossy cattle pinned with red ribbons proudly declaring Wilton Gillespie winner of the Royal Winter Fair. There were pictures of

Granddad holding silver cups, as well as ones of Mom and her sisters, young girls no older than me, showing off their yearlings at the 4H club. There was even a photo of a bashful looking Granny as she cut the opening ribbon at the local fall fair. There they all were, all together – the whole family – only now the youngest was gone.

Granddad's heavy oak door was shut, but a line of yellow light shone out from beneath, and I could hear the radio. The evening cattle futures were on. We were never to bother Granddad when the door was closed, but I had to see him.

He was sitting in his black leather desk chair, the one that spun around while he picked up one of the three black phones, barking out orders to ranchers in the west, making deals with meat packers in the east and talking to the railway men about schedules. Always on the go my Granddad, never still. There was always a man to talk to, a deal to make. Not tonight. Tonight he was collapsed in the chair, head in his hands, staring at something in his lap. I crossed the room. He hadn't heard me. Mom's university graduation photo rested in his lap. Granddad moaned low like an animal in pain. I reached out and touched him. His shoulders flew back and the photo fell.

"What are you doing in here?" he asked, furiously swiping the back of his hand across his eyes.

"I'm sorry," I replied, backing up in fear.

"Where are the boys?" he asked, picking up the photo and placing it on the desk, face down.

"They're out with the cattle."

"Did your father bring you?"

I shook my head.

"Where is he?"

"I don't know."

"Sit."

I sat in the big wing chair opposite the desk while Granddad's fingers drummed the back of Mom's photograph.

"We've got to be strong."

His fingers stopped. I thought my ears would pop.

"Do you understand?"

"Yes." But I didn't. "Granddad?"

"What is it, Maddy?"

"What happened to Mom?"

He didn't say a word. The cattle futures had given way to the crop report. Spring wheat was going to fetch a good price.

"There's no point dwelling on that," he said. "Now go and help – " He almost said, 'Your mother.' "Go and help your aunts."

The house was black. Everyone had gone to bed. Aunt Anne put me in Mom's old room. The clock ticked. I couldn't sleep. The thoughts in my stomach scared me. I'd never had a nightmare this bad. There was nothing to compare it to. The feelings in my stomach were hot and prickly and they'd started to grow. I could feel them rolling through my body and into my bones. If the heat got into my head…I opened the window wide and lay down on the floor in my nightgown until I was so cold it hurt. The door opened. It was Aunt Anne. She'd come in to check on me.

"What are you doing?" she cried. "Let me get you back into bed."

Aunt Anne shut the window and buried me in a pile of blankets. The weight of them felt like earth. Tears hung on her lower eyelashes defying gravity, but she wouldn't let them fall. She wouldn't let the emotion take hold. This was what Granddad meant by being strong. We didn't hug because it would have been too hard. It was best to push the pain aside. That horrible, hot, endless ache would sweep you away and make you crazy. There could be no talking about it and no thinking about it. Mom was dead, and she wasn't coming back.

The moment Aunt Anne closed the door I pulled off all the blankets and opened the window again. I lay down on the floor and let the frigid air do its work, make me numb, preparing me to be strong for the funeral the next day.

I had just finished putting on the last dress Mom had made me when there was a knock at the door. I opened it. Dad stood there, shaking in his dark suit.

"Where have you been?" I asked.

"Driving."

I took his hand. "It's time to go."

We walked down the hall. I looked over the banister. Frank stood at the bottom of the stairs with the rest of the relatives milling around the foyer, a slow moving sea of black. Aunt Anne was knotting Frank's tie while Granddad stared out the window – his white hair a stark contrast to the darkness of the day. Dad stumbled. Heads turned as the relatives looked up at us, curious eyes darting like crows in the barn.

It was just as drab outside. The world shrank as clouds of fog floated down, engulfing the fields, then the silo and finally everything beyond the cars. The boys and I waited beside the Oldsmobile. Granddad and Dad stood next to the long black hearse having a serious conversation. Uncles and aunts were already loaded in the hearse, and the cousins had been loaded into matching black Lincolns. Granddad kept gesturing towards the hearse, but Dad shook his head no. Finally he placed his hand on Dad's shoulder, but Dad shrugged it off and walked back to our car. He opened the back door and the boys slid in. I was confused.

"Aren't we going with Granddad?" Aunt Anne had told me we'd be travelling with Mom's body. That was the way things were done.

"We're going to take our own car," Dad replied, turning over the engine. "That's the way I want it."

I climbed in beside Tedder. The hearse went first, followed by the line of Lincolns and finally our Oldsmobile. Staring up at Granny's giant spruces, I wondered if she and Mom were together watching. Tedder took my hand as we followed the black cars into the fog.

Even though it was only about twenty yards ahead, the fog made it hard to see the tail lights of the last Lincoln, just the odd flicker of red to let us know we were on track. It didn't really matter – Dad could have found his way to the church blindfolded. That was where he and Mom had been married and where we'd been baptized. He admired the minister and loved debating scripture with him. The Oldsmobile slowed down and Dad flicked on his indicator.

"You're going the wrong way," I said as the car swung left into the fog. Tedder squeezed my fingers.

"You should never rush a left turn," Tedder whispered.

"Be quiet," Frank said, never once taking his eyes off the back of Dad's head.

"Where are we going?" I asked, but Dad didn't reply.

The Oldsmobile picked up speed, bouncing along the gravel side road. We were flying blind, but it felt as if we were travelling up, up into the sky. The boys were silent. Then Dad started to cry. Could he see the road through the tears? We struck a pothole and the Oldsmobile bucked, pulling hard towards the left. Tedder's fingers dug into my wrist and we both held our breath. Another car could be coming and we'd never see it. We'd be wiped out in a crash. Maybe

Mom was waiting. We could go to heaven as a family and maybe Dad was trying to take us there.

The Oldsmobile pulled out of the fog and into the sunlight. We were near the peak of a giant hill. Countryside rolled away on all sides like swells in the ocean. The spire of the church poked through the sea of fog below. I knew where we were. This was the place Mom told me about – her idea of heaven – the place where Dad proposed.

Dad stopped the car, got out and sat in the back. We all squeezed together to make room, but he didn't turn to face us. Instead he left the door wide open, staring at the fields and sky.

"I've got to put my feet on the ground," he said, his good black shoes rooted in the snow. He wasn't wearing galoshes.

The fog crawled up the hill towards the car, but the church spire still stood like a beacon. All of our relatives were down there and we weren't. The funeral must have started. None of us said a word. We sat there like the three monkeys: see no evil, hear no evil, speak no evil.

"You don't want to go the funeral, do you," he said.

It wasn't a question. Dad was crying. The car was cold. We all shivered but didn't dare ask for heat. My little brothers looked up at me. I was the oldest, but I didn't want to make things worse. Tedder didn't understand, but Frank's expression said it all. Everything was my fault and now I couldn't even get us to the funeral.

"Mom would rather you remember her the way she was," Dad said. "Don't you think so?"

"I guess," I replied.

If Frank had a gun he would have shot me.

"Good," Dad said. "We made a good decision."

What kind of a decision was that? We hadn't known she was dying and now we didn't get to go to her funeral. Dad got up and walked down the hill into the field. The fog swirled around his legs as he slowly disappeared.

"Where's Daddy going?" Tedder asked.

"He'll be back," Frank said. "We just have to wait."

And so we watched as Dad walked the foggy field, vanishing and then reappearing, while everyone else said goodbye to our mother.

We didn't even go to the burial. Dad drove us back to Granddad's house instead.

I was in the billiard room throwing the enamel coloured balls across the table as hard as I could. Nobody was back yet. The blue ball bounced off the green felt bumper, flew up into the air and rolled across the wooden floor. Frank was outside pounding pucks into a net by the side of the barn. Tedder sat on the stoop in his snowsuit with Roo sitting beside him. I couldn't tell if he was crying. The fog had finally lifted, but snow was drifting down. It was a dreary day. A lousy day. I couldn't remember the last time it had been sunny. I knew I should be taking care of Tedder, but I couldn't make myself move. My mind would say one thing, but my heart another. Dad was upstairs lying down. I knew for sure because I kept my eye on the car, and that was why I missed the Lincoln.

"Theodore!" Granddad roared.

I didn't hear him arrive. Just saw the black car out in the drive after the shout. Frank dropped his hockey stick. Tedder was still sitting on the steps, his head tilted up, mouth open, staring as the aunts ran past him, up the stairs and across the veranda – black veils shrouding their faces. Hugh swooped Tedder up in his arms, carrying him out towards the barn. An uncle grabbed Frank by the arm, the two of them spinning like dancers in a half turn. I tore down the hall into the foyer.

"Where the hell are you?" Granddad yelled.

He stood there, white hair on end, wild, the black overcoat thrown open, red-faced with fury. I'd never seen Granddad so mad and I'd never heard the word "hell" before. Not in my family. The aunts flew in behind him.

"Dad!" they cried when they noticed me standing in the doorway.

Granddad grabbed the banister. "Where is your father?" he asked, his voice a bit softer at the sight of me. My mouth wouldn't open.

"Where is he?" Granddad asked, a lot louder this time.

"We won't have raised voices," Aunt Anne shouted.

I was too scared to defy him and just pointed upstairs. Granddad was halfway up when Dad appeared at the top – hair a mess, jacket and tie askew.

"She was their mother," Granddad said. "She was your wife!" he yelled, his finger pointing right at Dad. "What kind of a man are you?"

For a moment it was quiet and then Dad replied. "The children didn't want to attend and I thought it was best."

"You thought it was best?" Granddad yelled and was about to continue when the radio went on full blast.

An old big band song, the kind Mom and Dad used to dance to, filled the foyer. Aunt Anne was up the staircase by now, pinning Granddad against the oak-paneled walls with her bare hands, telling everyone to settle down. Dad came down the stairs, past Granddad and Aunt Anne and told me to pack my bag. It was time for us to go home. It was a miracle Granddad didn't punch him.

The house was dark. I reached in and flicked on the overhead light. Dad carried Frank and Tedder up to bed. They'd fallen asleep in the car. I walked into the living room, dropping my coat on a chair. Ruth had dusted and vacuumed. The green broadloom was perfectly smooth. There was no evidence of the parade of women in pointy high heels tramping across the broadloom, bearing casseroles and sympathy. It was as if they'd never been there – a ghostly visitation.

I sat down on the sofa and turned on the television. Mobs of angry teenagers were picketing the White House demanding the President stop the war in Vietnam. Walter Cronkite said that never in the history of the United States had the youth led such a wave of protest. Someone set a straw doll of Richard Nixon on fire and the crowd roared as flames licked the sky. The news shifted to a local story about an arsonist in Buffalo. Where was Dad? He should have put the boys to bed by now.

Mom's oak sewing box sat on the floor beside the sofa. She liked to relax doing embroidery when the old black and white movies were on and always said that she was "simply mad" about Clark Gable.

"But don't tell your father," she'd add.

I opened the box and looked inside. A starched, white pillowcase, clamped into a metal hoop, held a cluster of bright red roses with fine green stems. We'd been working on this together. It was another one of Mom's attempts to get me interested in womanly skills.

"You have to be careful, Maddy," she said, as I forced the red thread up through the starched cotton and drove it back down. "It's a cross stitch. You have to bring the needle back down on the opposite side."

I didn't like embroidery. "Can we watch Frankenstein?"

"You have to follow the pattern."

When she took the hoop out of my hands our fingers brushed. I touched her gold university ring. Mom never took it off. I shimmied across the sofa, burrowing into her side. She was wearing a black turtleneck, matching slacks and a strand of pearls. Carefully, she undid my mistake.

"I hate patterns. It's way more interesting to invent my own design."

"If you don't follow the pattern all you get is a mess," Mom replied, putting the pillowcase into the box and closing the lid.

This was the first time I'd seen the pillowcase since then, and I picked it up, burying my face in the fabric, but Mom's smell was gone. There had to be something left. Desperately, I pushed even more deeply into the stiff cloth when something sharp stabbed my cheek and a drop of blood fell. Mom had stuck the needle with the long red thread into the fabric for safe keeping. The drop of blood began to spread, seeping into Mom's fine green stems. The stain would never come out. Another thing I ruined.

"Maddy."

Dad stood in the doorway. I placed the pillowcase back into the sewing box and closed the lid.

"It's time for bed."

"Let's watch the news." I said, patting the sofa beside me. I wanted to be with him and maybe if we were alone we could talk. But Dad just shook his head.

"Brush your teeth," he said, turning away. I got up, turned off the TV and followed my father up the stairs.

I hung up my good dress, slipped into my flannelette nightgown and brushed my teeth. The doors to the boys' rooms were closed, but Dad's was still ajar and the lights were on. Pushing the door open, I walked in. He was doing exactly what I'd wanted to do the day before. He was sitting on the floor of their closet with Mom's clothes all around him, crying so hard he didn't even hear me. He looked like a bomb had gone off inside him.

"Dad?"

He jumped up and stepped back. "Why aren't you in bed?" he asked, shaking his head, trying to find his bearings.

I moved towards him. "I love you, Dad."

"I love you, too," he replied. Then he turned me around, walking me towards the door.

"Dad," I said, trying to turn around to hug him, but he wouldn't let me close.

"We've got to get some sleep," he said. "Things will look better in the morning."

Then he kissed me gently on top of the head, pushed me out into the hall and quietly shut the door behind him. When I reached out for the handle, about to turn it, the lock clicked. I sat on the floor, my back up against the wall, waiting, but Dad never came out.

CHAPTER THREE

We were out of school for two weeks. When I came back somebody new walked through the doors. Somebody who had lost the most important thing in the world and had no idea how to get it back. My brain felt like a balloon suspended on a long piece of string, floating down the hall, propelled by my rack of bones body. Every fragment felt disconnected, like the anatomical skeleton dangling in Dad's office, clickety-clack clickety-clack. Betsy and Brad were talking by her locker. He laughed at something she said. It was so good to see my friends.

"Hi, Betsy."

Betsy stopped smiling. Brad backed up.

"I'm sorry about your Mom," Betsy said and looked at her feet.

"Thanks."

Brad grabbed Betsy's arm, pulling her down the hall.

"We've got to go."

I was desperate to do something, anything that would trick reality, even if only for a moment.

"Do you want to go to Frenchy's after school?" I called. "My treat."

"Can't," Betsy replied and they ran away.

All the other kids acted the same way. One day in the washroom a girl I barely knew saw me come in. She gaped and ran out the door, her soaking wet hands leaving tiny pools of water behind her.

Betsy and Sandy were supposed to be my best friends and Kenneth had given me a ring. One recess when I was sitting on the swing by myself, he started towards me, but some kids pulled him back, whispering something in his ear. He gave me a sad look and walked away. That afternoon I went over to his locker and dropped the ring through the metal slots in the door. I could hear the silver as it bounced and clattered, striking the bottom. I didn't have a boyfriend anymore.

There was no one to talk to. Aunt Anne told me to "soldier on" and Dad retreated to the office. He started seeing patients at eight in the morning, worked straight to midnight and the next day started all over again. One morning I found him asleep on an examining table with an open bottle of pills on the table beside him. The same pills Mom didn't want to take the night of the dance. They were called Valium. While Dad splashed cold water in his face and brushed his teeth, I straightened his tie. He needed a shave.

"Dad?"

"Hmmm?" Barely there.

"Nobody at school will talk to me."

"I'm sure you're exaggerating."

He filled a Dixie cup with Listerine and began to gargle.

"They hate me. And I don't know why."

"Give them some time, they'll come around."

No they wouldn't. Dad threw the paper cup towards the overflowing wastepaper basket, but it bounced off the top and onto the floor. That was another thing that was slipping away. Mom's beautiful orderly house was becoming a pigsty.

"And don't forget," Dad said, turning. "We've got church this weekend. There's a guest preacher."

I took a deep breath. "I'm not going."

Now he paid attention. "What do you mean?"

"I'm not going to worship a God who killed my mother."

When Mom was alive the house was clean and we had good food to eat. She kissed us goodnight and told us that she loved us. Now she was gone and it was as if Dad had followed her. I had to wake him up, make him see that we were still there and needed him. We stood there staring at each other. Eventually somebody had to blink.

"If that's what you've decided," he said. "You're a big girl now."

Ruth was still at the nurse's station doing paperwork, muttering about how her new husband was going to kill her for coming home late again. Tedder slept on her lap while I leafed through a record club catalogue, checking off the boxes for records I wanted.

Ruth's eyebrows shot up. "Does your Dad know you're ordering those?"

Ruth knew Mom didn't want me listening to rock and roll.

"Sure," I replied, slipping the order card into the pile of outgoing mail.

"Are you telling the truth?"

"Yes," I lied. Lying didn't bother me much anymore. The grown-ups lied so why couldn't I?

Tedder woke up, snuggling into Ruth's neck.

"Tell your father I've gone home. I'll finish up in the morning."

I could hear Ruth walking up the stairs to tuck Tedder into bed. A messy stack of magazines rested in the window well. Since nobody would talk to me, I'd spent the last couple of months reading Dad's subscriptions, learning about the real world.

The latest issue of *Newsweek* said there was a youth revolution going on. Young people were fighting with their parents and "the establishment" trying to "make love not war." They took drugs to "tune in, turn on and drop out." I wasn't really sure what that meant, but it was clear that the adults hated what the hippies were doing and claimed that drugs were becoming a serious problem. And then it came to me. I had a dispensary full of them.

I pulled *The Compendium* off the dispensary shelf and looked up Dad's nerves pills. Valium could be used to treat depression, but it was especially effective in dealing with anxiety. The book said that if a patient had been agitated for a long period of time Valium could be helpful in returning them to a more balanced state. Dad pushed his way through the dispensary door, searching for urine sample bottles.

I closed the book. "What's LSD?"

"What?" Dad asked, looking at me as if I were speaking Chinese. "Where's Ruth?"

"She had to go home," I answered. "It says here that the hippies are dropping pills called LSD. Do you have any in here?"

"Dropping?" he asked.

"What's LSD?"

"It's illegal dope," he replied, looking at his watch. "Have you done your homework?"

"It's all finished." Another lie.

"You'd better get up to bed anyway. It's getting late," he said, finally locating the sample bottles. "I'll come in and kiss you goodnight."

The light was still on in Frank's room, so I just walked in.

"Don't you ever knock?" he asked.

"Frankly, don't you ever stop studying?"

I sat down on his bed, examining a model of the Santa Maria that he was building from scratch. A finished model of the Pinta sat on a shelf over his bed. Frank was fascinated by Columbus. Maybe he wanted to sail away to a new land. I couldn't blame him.

"What do you want?" Frank asked, his nose wedged even deeper into the geography book. "I've still got another chapter to go."

"Why are you working so hard?"

Frank set his pencil down. "Because that's what Mom would expect of me. And maybe it'll make Dad happier."

"You're such a suck."

He jumped up. "You're a selfish jerk!"

"Why are you mad?"

"It's *your* fault Mom's dead."

I pushed him. "No, it's not."

He shoved back. "Then why did she die?"

"I don't know."

But I did.

"She died because she was out in the snow. She was out in the snow because of you and your boyfriend." He started to cry. "I heard Dad. They were talking when he carried her into the house. He kept saying she had to take care of herself. She said you were her little girl. He said she shouldn't be out in the snow in her condition. Then he took her away in the car and she never came back."

Now I was the one who was crying.

"It's not my fault!"

Frank picked up his book.

"I didn't mean for it to happen, Frank."

But he just sat down, wiped his eyes and started to study again.

I walked down the hall and into my room, put on my pajamas and crawled in between the cool sheets. The bedside lamp was on so Dad could find his way. The clock ticked as I watched and waited, but he never came up to kiss me goodnight.

Sometime after one I quietly got up, closed the door and opened the bedside table. There was only one thing the aunts didn't find when they spirited all of Mom's stuff out of the house, and it was hidden in the drawer behind a bunch of books. Mom's magical bottle of Joy.

I lay down and turned off the light with the Joy resting on my chest. Being oh-so-careful, I gently removed the heavy stopper. Moonlight struck the crystal as the genie silently rose out of the bottle.

My eyes closed and Mom appeared, turning every head on the street; that beautiful, long neck and the deep colour of her hair. I could see her dancing around the living room using the dust mop as a partner, when something started happening. The memories began to degrade, like bits of Dad's home movies that had been overexposed to light, or records that skipped, interrupting the song. I replaced the stopper and tucked the bottle away. The Joy was a powerful potion that had to be handled carefully or it would lose its power, and I'd lose my way back to Mom.

"Can you please turn that down?" Dad asked.

"In-A-Gadda-Da-Vida" was playing full blast on the stereo. We were having burgers and cherry Kool-Aid in the living room while Dad was trying to watch the evening news. Young American soldiers in Vietnam were encountering a terrible device called the Bouncing Betty. The announcer explained how it worked. It was safe when a soldier stepped on Betty, but the second he removed his foot Betty shot out from the ground and exploded, blowing the soldier clear out of his boots. The lucky soldiers died, but there were a lot of crippled boys being sent home to veterans' hospitals. Some of them had joined the hippies to protest the war.

Tedder was trying to cut into the hamburger bun with his spoon. "Do you want some help with that?" I asked.

"No, thank you," Tedder replied, as the spoon slipped, knocking his glass of Kool-Aid off the tray and onto Mom's sea green broadloom. Instinctively we all jumped to our feet, petrified that the red punch would stain, but then we stopped. Who would care? Only Mom. Out of habit, or maybe it was respect, Frank ran into the kitchen and got a damp cloth. He was on his hands and knees, trying to get the stain out when Aunt Anne unexpectedly walked into the living room.

The boys were promptly tucked into bed and I was sent to my room to do homework, but instead I perched at my old spying spot at the top of the stairs. Dad and Aunt Anne were out of my sightline, but I could hear snippets of conversation.

"This is no way for children to live," followed by, "Laura wouldn't want this," and, "You need some help."

When they came towards the foyer I had to run back to my bedroom.

"Don't think I can't hear you Madeline Anne!"

Quietly, I closed my eyes and padded off to bed. Aunt Anne was going to come and stay with us. At lease things would be kind of normal.

Two days later there was a knock at the door. A girl of about twenty with a brown bowl cut stood there clutching a suitcase.

"Allo? Lookink vor doctor."

"That's around the side of the house. But my Dad isn't taking any new patients right now."

The girl shook her head. Her English was terrible.

"My name Rika," she said. "I am here vor verk."

"Dad, she can't cook."

Dad was sitting at the head of the table pretending to read the morning paper while Frank and Tedder were staring at slices of white Wonder Bread slathered in suspicious brown goo.

"Vat is matter?"

"It's fine," Dad replied with a gentle smile, as Rika excused herself.

She had just served us another breakfast of chocolate sandwiches. Rika was an even worse cook than I was, she didn't even know how to operate the washer and dryer and never cleaned dishes properly.

"I can take better care of the family than she can!"

"I don't want you doing the housework. You've got school to think of and fun to have."

"But Dad, she's no good!"

"Give her a chance," he said, finishing his chocolate sandwich and getting up to go to work. "Your mother would want you kids to enjoy yourselves," he added as he disappeared.

Frank, Tedder and I stared at the sandwiches. There was no way we were eating that.

More new records arrived in the mail. Clutching them under my arm, I approached the smokers' wall. It had taken every bit of nerve I had, but I had to lure my friends back and the records were the best bait I could think of. Betsy and Brad stood in the middle of a big group of kids. We'd had a good spring rain earlier that day and pools of muddy water pockmarked the football field. Betsy lit a cigarette. I didn't know she was smoking. Taking a deep breath, I walked into the centre holding Janis Joplin out in front of me like an Indian with a peace offering.

Everyone stopped talking and looked at the album cover. Brad pulled back, but Betsy didn't. She was intrigued.

"I've got a whole bunch more. You want to come over and listen?"

I slowly held up each record so everyone could get a look. The crowd moved closer. Somebody oohed. A couple of kids muttered, "Cool." They'd never seen these records before.

"Betsy!" a girl shouted.

The crowd turned. A scowling girl stood near the back, her fists shoved deeply into her coat pockets. The same girl who had run out of the washroom with soaking wet hands because she was afraid of me. The other kids nervously giggled. The girl darted in and out of the milling crowd, getting closer to me and then abruptly pulling back.

"Stay away from her," the girl said, yanking her hand out of her pocket and pointing her finger at me. "You know what will happen. You'll catch cancer."

Silence fell. My face throbbed and my heart started to thump with raw anger. The records fell into the mud. My heart pumped something up into my throat, something I'd never felt before.

"You better shut your mouth," a strange voice said. It was my voice, but a deep scary me that I'd never heard before.

The girl got closer, putting her hand over her mouth making a finger mask.

"My mother said your mother died of it and everyone knows you only get cancer if you deserve it," the girl said, looking at the pack of kids surrounding us. "Or," she added, "if you've been around people who've had it."

"You are such a liar!" I screamed, grabbing the girl by the lapels, smashing her back into the brick wall.

Mr. Thom, the principal, rushed across the field and arrived just in time to hear the end. He seized the girl by the arm and gave her a really good shake.

"That is an ignorant thing to say. You apologize right now."

The girl's face flushed. She hated me and I hated Sterling. I hated every kid I'd gone to school with for the last eight years. I didn't belong there. I turned and ran.

I ran across Main Street, past Comfort's Diner and down McKenzie. It was raining again. A neighbour who was taking out the garbage waved at me. I could barely see him, I was crying so hard. Dad was just getting out of the car when I tore up the driveway.

"Everyone's saying that Mom died of cancer. Make them stop, Dad. Please make them stop lying!"

Dad took me by the shoulders. "It's true, honeybunch."

It couldn't be. Only bad people got cancer. People who deserved it. Rain bounced off the hood of the car.

"Why didn't you tell me?"

"She didn't want anyone to know."

A car pulled into the driveway with headlights so bright that Dad's glove flew up to shield his eyes. Mr. Thom got out and asked me if I was all right.

"I'm going inside," I replied.

Ruth was gone and the office was empty. I sat down at the desk, watching Dad and Mr. Thom through the window. They were both getting soaked, probably sharing other secrets I knew nothing about. I picked up the phone books, smashing them down as hard as I could. Did the relatives know about the cancer? Maybe that's why Granddad didn't come to our house anymore. He had no time for sickly things. I didn't care if I caught it. It would be better to be dead than live through this. I yanked open the drawer to toss the phone books inside. Random bottles of medicine rolled around. The mess was making me crazy. Everything was out of order. I picked up a bottle – one of Dad's restricted substances. An engine turned over outside. I hastily put the pills back where they belonged as Dad walked in.

"Mr. Thom says you gave that girl quite a push."

"What happened to Mom?"

"She got sick."

"But how? How did she catch cancer?"

"It's not something you catch. It's a disease of the body. The cells turn on themselves."

"But you don't get it unless you do bad things."

"That's not true."

"Then why did Mom hide it?"

"Because she didn't want people to know."

"Why?"

"Because they might be afraid."

"Why?"

"Because cancer has a stigma."

A stigma. That's what I got at school.

"Was she ashamed?"

He didn't answer. He wasn't telling the truth.

"Was it because of me?"

He gave me an odd look.

"Because of that…that day on the hill. Did that escalate the disease?"

Dad always told me how important it was to keep illness at bay, and that meant staying in bed and keeping warm.

"I don't think so."

If cancer didn't follow the rules that meant it wasn't my fault. I swallowed.

"But it probably didn't help either," he said.

So it was my fault. If I hadn't gone out to the gully with Kenneth. If I'd only stayed home and been good. Dad rested his hands on my shoulders, fingers shaking.

"Don't worry, honeybunch. Eventually this will all blow over."

I wanted to believe him but I didn't. He stood and then disappeared into the dispensary, followed by the rattle of pills.

Dad's body might have been in the house, but the father I'd known for my whole life was gone. He was in the dispensary gobbling up another handful of Valium. I knew at that moment everything had changed. Dad couldn't take care of me, so I had to take care of myself. There was no room for being a stupid little kid anymore. I had to be tough and strong. I had to grow up.

Pedaling down Main and up Station Street on my way to Wellington High I whizzed by a group of little kids trudging up the hill to Sterling Public. A yellow school bus honked hello as I rode up to the high school. My hand shot up, but I stopped myself. Only twerps waved. A line of buses were dropping off the farm kids. We hadn't had a lot at Sterling Public, but Wellington High got all the teenagers from the surrounding countryside. I dumped my bike on the ground and straightened my dress. It was a stretchy blue mini. My hair had grown long, hanging well past my shoulders. I pulled a compact out of my purse and flipped it open, shaking my hair so the bangs tumbled into my eyes. The blue eyeshadow still looked good. Sandy and Betsy were talking to some other kid. I couldn't see her face, but she had honey-blond hair that nearly touched her waist.

Casually, I strolled over. I'd been working on my walk as well as my hair. The walk was a cross between an easy strut and a bounce.

The strut made me look cool and not too anxious to please. The bounce showed I was a lot of fun.

"Do you think high school is going be hard?" I asked.

Sandy laughed. "Like you ever study anyway."

Betsy, Sandy and I had spent most of the summer together playing my new records and learning dance steps. Betsy asked me if I'd gotten the new Led Zeppelin yet.

"At home," I replied with a promising smile.

"Can we come over?" Sandy asked.

"Sure."

My basement was the new hangout because we could do pretty much anything we wanted. Brad and Betsy made out on the sofa, but when Kenneth tried to pull me down, I ran upstairs. Something inside me had changed and I didn't want to be his girlfriend anymore.

Betsy introduced me to the new girl. Her name was Ginnie Hall and her eyes were cornflower blue. She lived on a dairy farm way past the outskirts of town.

I turned to her. "Do you want to come too?"

"I can't. I have to do chores."

The bell rang. It was time for class.

The four of us were crammed into our booth at Frenchy's. While Comfort's Diner was clean and offered good home cooking at reasonable prices, Frenchy's was dirty and dangerous. The red vinyl in the booths were cracked and the red lettering on the window was chipped and fading away. Frenchy's was run by a short Quebecois woman who chain-smoked and looked like a Grape-Nut. Our gang always went there for lunch. Sandy and Betsy ordered a 7Up and two straws, I asked for a Coke and Ginnie wanted milk.

"You sure you don't want a Coke? My treat." Since I'd started helping myself to the change on Dad's dresser I didn't have to worry about money.

"No thanks."

I pulled a pack of Export A's out of my jeans. It had taken a while to get used to the taste, but I was a fulltime smoker now. I waved the cigarette under Ginnie's nose.

"Want one?"

"I don't smoke."

Ginnie was so innocent. I took a long drag.

"Do you have a date yet?" she asked.

The big bonfire, the social event of the fall, was coming up and Aunt Anne was going to take me into Toronto to buy a new outfit. I was going to get brown Lee cords.

"I'm going stag," I said

Betsy lit a cigarette. "You can't go stag."

Ever since the day in the gully I'd sort of lost my interest in boys, but I couldn't very well say that out loud.

"Kenneth is dying to take you."

"I don't know." I blew another smoke ring. "What about you, Ginnie?"

"Mom won't let me and besides, I've got chores."

Ginnie always had work to do.

I heard the familiar jangle of the bell as the door opened. It was Kenneth, Mark and Dale. Dale got bussed in for school with Ginnie, and Mark was Sandy's new boyfriend. He and his sister lived with their father, a trucker who drank too much. Sometimes Mark came to school with a black eye.

"He's so cute," Sandy whispered.

Mark swaggered by, running a comb through his blond hair. Sandy looked like she was going to melt. Kenneth leaned against the counter, asked for a coffee and gave me his sly dog look. He shouldn't drink coffee. It would stunt his growth and he was already runty. Betsy leaned towards Ginnie.

"Do you have the hots for Dale?"

"No," Ginnie replied, turning to me. "Don't you go out with Kenneth?" She had a milk moustache.

"Sort of," I replied, wiping the milk from Ginnie's lip. She smiled.

It was easier having Kenneth as a sort of boyfriend, but I didn't want to go parking with him. It was all so complicated. Betsy glanced at Kenneth.

"You don't want to get a reputation as a cock tease."

"I never tease him."

"If you tease a boy then you'll get raped and you'll deserve it."

"It's true," Sandy added.

"I'm saving myself for when I get married," Ginnie said.

Betsy said that if they got over excited it was better to jerk them off. What was jerking off? Was that touching it? I wanted to change the topic.

"You guys want to come for a sleepover next weekend?" I asked. "I can show you my new outfit."

Sandy had a date, and as usual Ginnie couldn't, but Betsy was game.

The Toronto skyline appeared. Until recently, the Royal York had been the tallest building in the city, but now two sleek black skyscrapers had zoomed up beside it. Aunt Anne didn't approve. She said that they had demolished perfectly good, solid banks to erect an eyesore.
"But it's modern," I said. I liked anything that was new.
"How's school?" she asked, changing the conversation.
"It's okay."
The car was still. What was there to say? Why didn't you tell me that my mother was dying? I glanced at my aunt's profile. Jaw set, eyes focused on the road ahead. Aunt Anne always loved telling jokes, laughing her silly giggle, but not anymore. She came out for Sunday dinner, but after we ate, she and Dad generally went into the living room for "adult conversation," while the boys watched TV and I talked on the phone.

Nobody talked about Mom, and that was fine with me. Other than the occasional sniff from the bottle of Joy, I'd locked Mom up, and the only time she got out was in nightmares where I couldn't control what she did. Sometimes she crawled out of the grave. Other times she didn't remember who I was, and in the worst one, she left us for another family and refused to come home.

Aunt Anne parked down the street from Eaton's department store at Yonge and College. Shiny new cars lined the boulevard and families bustled by, holding parcels. A boy and girl hippy sat on the sidewalk. The boy had a straggly beard and played a guitar, and the girl had long brown hair parted down the middle. A beat-up guitar case was open in the hope that people would toss in coins. I took a quarter out of my pocket and watched it bounce on the red velvet amongst the pennies.

Aunt Anne stopped walking.
"That's a lot of money to be throwing around."
"It's my allowance."
The guitar player changed tunes and started singing "Hurdy Gurdy Man." The girl was wearing a purple suede vest with fringes.
"I want a top like that."
Aunt Anne gave the girl a Gillespie look.
"I'm going to buy you a pretty new dress."

The dress flew across the room.

"I'm not wearing it!"

Rika was trying to get me into the new dress Aunt Anne had insisted on buying.

"Leave me alone!" I screamed, threatening to cut the dress into a million pieces.

Rika eventually retreated. She had a date that night and didn't want to be late. Lying on my bed, I flipped through a fashion magazine. I'd been certain that Aunt Anne would buy me cords, but she'd insisted that proper young ladies wear dresses. There was no point arguing, so we both clammed up. Aunt Anne marched me into the house and handed the dress to Rika with instructions that I wear it. There was no way I was going to take orders from a housekeeper who barely spoke English. Betsy arrived in the doorway holding her overnight bag.

"Rika told me to come up. What do you want to do?"

"It's back here," I said, taking down a dusty bottle from the top shelf in the root cellar. Our family didn't drink, but that didn't stop some of Dad's grateful patients from dropping off a bottle in thanks for a baby delivered or a wound stitched.

"I thought your parents, um sorry, I mean your Dad," Betsy said, stumbling. "I didn't think your Dad drank."

"He doesn't," I replied, blowing the dust off the label. At least he said he didn't. Who knew what the truth was? "I bet he doesn't even know what's down here."

Dad had stopped working late and started disappearing in the evenings and on weekends. He never told me where he went. After I made sure the boys had gone to sleep, Betsy set a bottle of Coke, the rye and two glasses in front of her.

"Do you have a shot glass?"

"No."

"Okay, well then you pour the rye in to the count of seven and then top it up with Coke."

About four inches of rye sloshed into each glass. I took a sip. It burned my throat.

"That's horrible!"

"Then hold your nose and chug."

Betsy picked up her glass, pinched her nose and swallowed. I copied her. At first I felt as if I was going to barf, but then I started to feel warm and good. For the first time since Mom died the sadness drifted away.

"Again!" Betsy called, pouring us each another drink.

Arms out like an airplane, I flew around the room.

"How do you know about drinking?"

"Dave taught me."

Betsy was so lucky to have an older brother.

"I just love Brad," Betsy cooed, falling back on the sofa. "Don't you still secretly love Kenneth?" she asked, wagging her finger at me, her eyes getting all googly. "He really wants to take you to the fish fry."

I turned on the record player.

"Don't you secretly want him back?" she asked.

No, I didn't. I put the needle on the record. "Let's have another one."

Every time Betsy started to talk about boys I just filled up her glass, and before I knew it the whisky was gone and we were spinning around to "Mama Told Me Not To Come." Turning the volume up full blast, we galloped up the stairs, whooping through the house. Frank came out rubbing his sleepy eyes, complaining that he'd tell Dad that we were making a racket.

"Frankly, I wish you'd shut up!" I yelled, laughing at the top of my lungs.

Betsy and I started singing, stumbling back down the stairs and into the living room, when suddenly she put her hand on the wall.

"I don't feel very good."

I didn't either. The floor was spinning. I felt dizzy and sick. Betsy brought her other hand up to her mouth just as I looked at Mom's sea green broadloom.

"No!"

We barfed all over the house. I threw up in the kitchen sink. Betsy hit the patients' toilet. Then she barfed in the dispensary sink while I hurled into the garbage can. Betsy vomited in the laundry tub as I barfed up in the washing machine. Finally we crawled up the stairs and into Mom and Dad's washroom, puking into the pink his and hers sinks, the pink toilet, plus the matching tub. The last thing I remembered was Betsy crying for her mother, her long black hair trailing with vomit.

There was a knock at the door. Betsy and I looked at one another. We were tucked into my bed in clean nightgowns. I felt awful. Another hard rap.

"Oh man, I'm going to be in so much trouble."

I stumbled across the room, remembering all the barfing and especially the empty bottle of booze. There would be no talking my way out of that. I opened the door. Dad stood there holding a tray with two glasses of pop and some dry toast.

"The ginger ale's flat. It should help settle your stomach."

He handed me the tray, and without another word he turned and walked down the hall. Betsy couldn't believe it.

"Your Dad's so cool. My Mom would have pitched a fit."

I knew better. I could have set the house on fire and he wouldn't notice. I could die and he wouldn't give a shit.

Not giving a shit was my new way of looking at the world. I didn't give a shit what the neighbours thought. I didn't give a shit when Rika threatened to quit because Dad asked her to clean up the vomit. I didn't even care what Aunt Anne thought. The power of not giving a shit was amazing. Every time I turned down Kenneth's invitation to the bonfire it made him all the more determined to take me. He made such a fuss at Frenchy's that there wasn't really a choice. Betsy gave me a look, stubbing out her cigarette.

"You're supposed to go with a boy."

Kenneth and Brad were talking by the jukebox. Kenneth kept looking over at me.

"If you don't that means you're either an ugly douche bag or you're weird."

After everything I'd done to make people like me, the last thing I wanted was for them to think I was weird.

Betsy, Brad, Kenneth and I piled into Dave's Chevy and headed down to Lake Erie for the bonfire. I wasn't interested in watching a fire. I wanted to know where the party was. I'd swiped the last bottle of Dad's booze stash – some sweet homemade wine – and we all pinched our noses and chugged it in the car. The wine wasn't nearly as strong as the rye, but it made me feel safe and I wanted more.

Kenneth and I sat on a log watching Brad and Betsy dig a big hole in the sand for the cooler. Dave was helping the other guys pile driftwood while couples huddled under blankets along the beach. The chilly nip in the air said winter was getting close. One of the boys had a yellow car, and the car doors were open with music blasting out both sides. A girl in a denim jacket emblazoned with a peace sign danced in the sand. It should have been perfect but it wasn't.

Something was missing. Something always was. Kenneth put his arm around my shoulder.

"Do you know where we can get more liquor?" I asked.

"Follow me."

Kenneth took me around back of a dune.

"It's over here."

But there was no liquor – only Kenneth and his grabby fingers. The minute we were away from the rest of the group he started kissing me. I kissed him back because I didn't want anyone thinking I was weird, but I didn't like the way he tasted – like sour Juicy Fruit gum.

"I thought you knew where to get some booze," I said, trying to wriggle away.

Kenneth squeezed me so tight in his arms that I could barely breathe. His breath was hot against my face.

"You want to touch it?"

His penis pushed against the inside of my thigh, and he tried to slip his hand under my jacket to grope my boobs. After Mom died I'd dumped the bras. I'd even ditched wearing underpants. I didn't want anything holding me back or holding me in. The boys liked it. My breasts had grown and bounced when I walked. I could tell they had power. But now Kenneth was the one with the power, and he was starting to breathe harder and harder. Betsy had warned me not to be a "cock tease." If you were going to tease a boy you'd better be ready to go all the way. Well I sure wasn't going to go all the way with Kenneth. I had to get away. I reached out and touched his thigh.

"You want me to?"

Kenneth's eyes flipped open and in a flash his hands dropped as he unzipped his jeans. Fumbling with his underpants, he pulled out what looked like a big, old ugly skin worm. I wanted to laugh, but didn't dare, because Kenneth seemed so proud of it. There was a hole at the top. As he rubbed the skin the worm reacted and the whole thing started to seize up, tensing and getting bigger and bigger. Kenneth's eyes flickered.

"Just touch it," he groaned.

Kenneth grabbed for my hand, but I pushed him and he tumbled backwards, tripping over twisted pant legs. I jumped over the dune, back to the party.

The school bell rang. Kids pulled their coats out of their lockers and rushed for the door. Ginnie and a bunch of other kids were standing outside in a perfect circle in front of the yellow school bus, but nobody was getting on. They stood like zombies, staring at the ground. Ginnie glanced over at me with a funny mixture of shock and fascination and then she looked back into the centre of the circle. Mark's little sister was lying face down in the dirt with her hands underneath her body. She was pumping up and down on her hands, which were tucked beneath her crotch. I didn't know what she was doing, but it was obviously making her feel good. Everyone stood quietly and watched. Nobody laughed or teased. And then she started to moan. A teacher arrived, breaking through the circle and snatched Mark's sister up with an angry yank.

"Disperse!"

Nobody moved. The teacher's face was red. Mark's sister had a strange smile. She didn't apologize. She just turned and wandered down the road. The teacher didn't know what to do, so he started yelling.

"Country children get on the bus! This isn't a show! That girl needs help!"

Ginnie and I looked at one another.

"That was weird," she said.

"No kidding." I threw my book bag over my shoulder. Kids filed onto the bus. It was time for Ginnie to go.

"You want to come out to my place?" she asked.

I was surprised. Ginnie had been to my place for lunch and stuff, but I'd never been invited to hers before.

"You could stay for supper and my Mom could drive you home. That is, if it's okay with your father."

"Oh it'll be alright. I'll just call from your place."

I followed her up the stairs. The bus smelled like old gum and lunches.

The Hall farm was on two hundred acres of prime land. The tilled earth, dark and loamy, stretched from the concession road to a large stand of trees that marked the end of the property. The barn was freshly painted and sparkling white, a sure sign of a prosperous farm. You can always tell a farmer's fortunes by the state of his barn. Spic and span meant there was enough money for a frill like paint. Faded and drab sent the message that there was no money for fix ups. Holes in the roof meant the bank was getting ready to foreclose. Everything about the Hall place said good crops and healthy cattle. Both the barn and the house were white with green roofs and green trim. New shutters framed the windows and a deep green door welcomed you inside. Ginnie swung open the wide screen door. It snapped shut behind us. The kitchen smelled like Mom's cooking. Good food. Not Rika's chocolate sandwiches. Ginnie called out to let her mother know that she was home. This was a happy home. Ginnie asked me if I'd like anything to drink.

"Sure," I replied, slinging my books on a chair by the door.

They'd just struck the wood when Mrs. Hall entered the room. She was an enormous woman with a jet-black beehive and pumps. Her hips were round and her calves strong and shapely. Poured into a skimpy black dress with big jangly earrings, Mrs. Hall was way too fancy to be a farmer's wife. If my mother were still alive she would have been very polite in Mrs. Hall's presence, but once we were in the car she'd have said, "Mrs. Hall is overdone." It wasn't as if she wasn't nice to me, but there was something definitely scary about Ginnie's mom. The moment Ginnie said she'd brought me home for dinner Mrs. Hall chucked me under the chin and said that she'd put in some extra turnip. Then she jabbed me in the stomach, saying that I could use a bit of fattening up. I flinched. I didn't want to be fattened up. I smiled at Mrs. Hall and thanked her for the invitation.

"What time is your father expecting you home?"

"Oh jeeps! We haven't called him yet," Ginnie cried, pulling me towards the phone.

I knew there wouldn't be a problem. There never was.

Ginnie and I hung out all that fall and winter and she even got me a Monkees record for my fourteenth birthday. For the first time in my life my father forgot, but my little brothers didn't. They had Rika bake a cake and we all sang. Mom said birthdays were our own special day and important to celebrate, but Dad just forgot. Betsy and Sandy weren't much better. They'd vanished into boyville and we only saw them in class. Kenneth still asked me out, but after a while he gave up and just mooned at me with his cow eyes. Ginnie was more fun than I first thought and it was nice spending time at her place, even though her mother made me do chores.

"Don't you girls come back unless both baskets are full," Mrs. Hall said, handing us each a wicker basket.

"Yes, Mrs. Hall," I replied, always very careful to be polite.

Mrs. Hall was taking fresh, white sheets down from the line. Mom used to do that, and they always smelled like the wind.

The henhouse was located in a white clapboard shack corralled by a new green fence. A proud orange rooster stood on the gate and crowed. Ginnie and I walked down the path with baskets over our arms. It was late April and the weather was unseasonably warm.

"Watch your head," Ginnie said, ducking as she entered the coop.

Ginnie began gathering eggs. It looked easy enough. I reached towards the chicken, but the second I touched the feathers the bird's beak came down on my hand with a vicious peck, drawing a tiny bead of blood.

"Hey!" I yelled.

The hens started clucking. I backed up towards the door, but Ginnie told me to follow her and watch closely. When the chickens settled down she told me to try it again.

My hand still stung. "I don't think so."

"Chicken?" she asked, tickling me.

"No. I just don't want to get pecked to death."

She tickled me again, making me wriggle and laugh.

"I'll protect you. Don't you trust me?"

"I don't know. You've got killer chickens."

"Give me your hand."

Ginnie grabbed my hand and stepped close behind me. She smelled like sunshine and grass. My body went warm and my head was swimmy.

"Let me guide it."

A red hen looked up from her nest.

"You have to be really quick. If they don't know what's happening, they don't miss the egg. Ready?"

"Okay."

Together our hands thrust forward, under the feathers, and then the warm egg rested in my hand.

"Don't break it," Ginnie whispered in my ear.

The white egg nestled in the palm of my hand.

In a half-hour we'd filled both baskets and were walking back up the lane towards the house.

"That was fun," I said.

The sky glowed red with the embers of day.

"I'd like to do it again."

"This Saturday Dad's going to burn the brush on the back forty and I've got to help. Do you want to come out in the morning and stay over?"

Mrs. Hall emerged from the front door, her big breasts leveled like missiles.

"Get in the car, Maddy. It's late."

Ginnie and I ran towards the shiny new white Buick.

"Is it okay if Maddy stays over next weekend?"

Mrs. Hall paused. "Your father's going to need you."

Oh no.

"That's why Maddy's going to come out. She'll come in the morning and help for the rest of the day." Ginnie turned to me and smiled. "Right? You'll do the eggs."

"If it's okay with you," I added, smiling my warmest, most polite Gillespie smile at Mrs. Hall. Her lip curled as she considered it, assessing me as she did her home and her makeup. Was there a flaw?

"As long as she pulls her weight," Mrs. Hall said, settling into the driver's side. "Now do as I say and get in the car."

I ran to the passenger door and didn't even realize I'd left my schoolbooks in the kitchen until Ginnie called me later that night. Her place wasn't long distance and when we weren't hanging out together we yakked on the phone. I didn't care about the schoolbooks.

"How are you going to study for the math final?"

I told her not to worry. I didn't care about math. Lying in bed, gazing at the stars, I had a terrible urge to go up into the attic and look out of my telescope to see if I could see Ginnie's farm but I stopped myself. That was a baby thing to do.

Saturday morning I galloped in and jumped on the bed. Dad was still asleep.

"Wake up!"

He pulled the covers up and over his face. "The Halls won't mind if you're there after lunch."

I hit him with the pillow. "Come on. Get up!"

Dad got dressed, prepared a cup of instant coffee and we got in the car, heading out the back concession road. I was so excited. Dad took a sip from the mug and looked over at me.

"How are things at school?"

Since when did he ask about school?

"How are your friends?"

Like he cared. "Fine."

"People out here can be a bit backward..."

I looked at the clock on the dash. It was already a few minutes after nine and Mrs. Hall might not let me stay if I didn't pull my weight.

"Can you please hurry Dad? I don't want to be late."

The car picked up speed. He took another sip of coffee.

"I'm going to stay in the city this weekend. There's a dance in Toronto."

"What kind of dance?"

"A doctors' dance," he replied, a smile spreading across his face.

The Olds pulled into the drive. Mr. Hall's field truck was out by the barn. They hadn't left yet, which meant I could still burn something. I set my suitcase on the front porch and ran down the lane.

Ginnie and I sat on the humming wheel wells in the rear of Mr. Hall's cherry red pickup. The truck roared across the field so fast I thought we might flip. Mr. Hall was a tall, quiet man with short grey hair, neatly shorn about the ears. He always wore clean overalls and a snappy blue fedora, but the devil got a hold of him when he drove. Mr. Hall struck a hole. I bounced off the wheel well. Ginnie grabbed me by the waist and pulled me down beside her, holding me tight.

The pickup up squealed to a stop. Mr. Hall told us to gather all the loose brush from the edge of the bush and collect the branches that had drifted over the fields. It was crucial to get everything off the ground because a loose stick could damage a harrow or a plough, so farmers took special care of their fields. Ginnie and I threw armload after armload of brush into the flames, watching the embers fire up into the bright blue sky and then float back down to earth. It was a red hot day and pure hell by the fire. Sweat rolled down my back and I thought I was going to pass out. I'd never worked so hard, but Ginnie was barely winded. She just moved ahead of me, sweeping the branches up into her arms and tossing them back into the fire. She was whistling and teasing me about being a city slicker.

"What?" I yelled over the fire. "My grandfather is one of the biggest cattlemen in this country."

She poked me in the stomach. "You're soft."

I laughed, pushing back, "We'll see who's soft."

I started to tickle her and we dropped our branches and began to wrestle. Ginnie fell down, pulling me with her. We were rolling around in the earth when her Dad picked us both up by the belt loops, telling us to stop horsing around.

It was a little after one when we'd finished burning the brush and gathering eggs, and I was starving.
"Do you girls want to go for a picnic?" Mrs. Hall asked. "You could take Maddy down by the pond. It's a nice afternoon."

The Hall cow pond was at the far end of the property. A herd of Holsteins grazed under a stand of maples to avoid the midday sun. Ginnie and I finished eating and started tossing rocks into the water, trying to sink a lily pad.
"You want to go for a swim?" she asked.
"It's too cold."
Ginnie stripped down to her underwear. Her bra and panties were both white with tiny pink flowers.
"Are you sure you don't want to come in?"
"No."
"The cows don't use it other than to drink. It's too deep," Ginnie said, stepping in. "Are you afraid?"
"I'm not afraid of anything," I replied, rolling over on my side, pushing my hair off my face.
I paused, looking deep into the green, searching for a four-leaf clover. There was a splash and then nothing. When I looked up Ginnie had disappeared. Her body glided beneath the surface. When she came up her blond hair was dark and slick. She smiled as I stripped off my clothes.
"Where's your underwear?"
"I don't wear any."

Later we were lying on the blanket looking up at the clouds talking about boys.
"Are you going to get back with Kenneth?"
She ran her fingers through her hair. I leaned over to pull out a tangle.
"He really likes you," she said.
"He likes sex. That's why he likes me."
She sat up.
"You haven't – "
"I would *never* do that. Not until I was married. And besides I don't think I'm going to get married. I plan on having adventures."

"I bet you will," Ginnie replied quietly, falling back down, looking up at the sky.

I sat up. I had a great idea. "You could come with me. We could go to Australia."

She smiled. "I couldn't leave the farm."

I fell back down. It was true. Every bit of Ginnie was tied to this place. She was like Granddad. They'd take her away from Wellington County in a box one day.

"I'm going to have a life before I die," I remarked to myself and to Ginnie.

"You're not going anywhere soon, are you?" she asked, her fingers reaching up to tuck a tumble of damp hair behind my ear.

"This is what you call an ensuite," Mrs. Hall said, giving me a tour of the master bedroom. "It's French for bathroom."

Mom had put one in years ago, but never gave hers a name.

"It's lovely."

We passed a guest room, a playroom and a small office where Mrs. Hall did the farm books. Ginnie's and her sister Victoria's rooms were on the third floor. It reminded me of climbing the stairs in Granddad's house. Ginnie's room had a four-poster spindle bed, thick blue carpeting and matching drapes. There was a dresser and not room for much more. I slipped out of my clothes, into my nightgown and under the sheets, moving next to Ginnie. I wanted to feel her next to me. I didn't know why, but I thought I'd go crazy if I didn't.

"You girls get to sleep!" Mrs. Hall called up the stairway.

"Okay, Mom!" Ginnie called back, turning off her bedside lamp. "Are you tired?"

"Not really."

I stared at the ceiling, thinking about how Ginnie would go to sleep and the night would end. There had to be a way to make it last.

"You want to play a game?" I asked.

"Like what?"

"Why don't we try sleeping with our heads at the foot of the bed? We can see how it feels."

"Okay."

We swung our bodies around and tried out the new angle.

"What do you think of the ceiling from down here?"

"It's pretty good, but the light will be in my eyes when I wake up," Ginnie replied. "Let's lie across the bed."

Our legs hung over the edge of the bed and we both laughed. Victoria yelled for us to be quiet. Ginnie got out of bed and padded over and quietly shut the door. When she got back in I had another idea.

"Why don't we roll up and down the bed?"

"Who's going to go first?"

"No, we'll roll together. Like we're one person. Want to try?"

There was a pause in the dark and then Ginnie said, "Okay."

I put my arm out and she rolled into me. I could feel her whole weight pressing down on me, the sweetness of her hair and the smell of fire on her skin. I gasped for a second and then we started to slowly roll. Fourteen-year-old legs and arms and nightgowns wrapped around. Two bodies rolling as slowly as they could because when it ended it would be time to go to sleep. When it stopped I was lying on top of her, looking down. I could see her eyes wide open in the near blackness. I knew it wasn't right, I knew it was supposed to be with a boy, but I couldn't help myself. I kissed Ginnie before she could say no and then she kissed me back. We didn't take our clothes off. We didn't need to.

I was addicted to Ginnie Hall, and for one incredible summer I think she was hooked on me too. We never talked about what we did, but the moment the lights went off, we were in one another's arms, rocking our bodies until they exploded. Then we'd fall asleep in a happy rumpled heap and wake up staring at each other. I would have been happy if I died then. It was like swimming in a cloud or floating in the softest grass. It felt like nothing I could compare it to, and I couldn't get enough.

That Labour Day weekend Ginnie and I drove into Toronto with her parents to see the CNE. Mr. Hall was showing cattle in the Coliseum and Mrs. Hall was off to the Better Living Centre. Ginnie and I were on the Alpine Way Sky Ride, a series of tiny primary-coloured two-seater cars that ran along suspension wires criss-crossing the entire fair. Our car was canary yellow with matching plastic seats. People lined up beneath us to play a giant wheel.

I stood up and pointed. "There's the Crown and Anchor! When we get down, let's spin it." The movement made the car rock.

"Mom says they're rigged and that I'm not to waste my money."

Ginnie was likely right but it still might be fun. The only games I'd ever been allowed to play were Fish and Bobbing for Apples. A little boy ran up the midway holding a gigantic blue bear while somebody dressed like Sir John A. Macdonald tottered by on a pair of stilts. The line-up for the Flyer stretched all the way around to the back of the rollercoaster. Cars slowly rattled their way to the top and then screams rang out as the riders plummeted down the steep vertical slope, brakes squealing as the cars ricocheted around the terrifying turns and began to climb again. Ginnie squeezed my hand.

"Should we go on the Flyer next?" she asked, plucking a tuft of pink cotton candy from her cone.

I didn't buy any candy because I was too nervous to eat. I'd brought a gift for Ginnie, something special that showed her how much I loved her. The most precious thing I owned lay in the bottom of my purse. Could I do it? Could I give it to someone else? Our car stopped, suspending us over the Better Living Centre. Ginnie leaned over, looking down over the milling crowd.

"I wonder if Mom's still in there."

I put my hand in my purse stroking the cool cuts of crystal.

"I've got a present for you."

I pulled the bottle out of my bag and handed Ginnie Mom's bottle of Joy.

Her eyes widened. "It's beautiful."

She quickly kissed my cheek, making my stomach skip. "Thank you," she said.

"I'm glad you like it."

"But it's open."

"Why don't you try some on?"

Ginnie removed the stopper, and just like Mom, she dabbed a bit behind her ears and the tiniest drops on the insides of her wrists. She thrust her wrist towards me. I closed my eyes and breathed it in. What was the word? Swoon. I nearly did. Then the little canary car lurched back to life.

I don't remember the details of the day, just the scent of Joy as Ginnie and I rode the Polar Bear Express, lost all of our change in the Salt and Pepper and ate so much peanut brittle we thought we'd get sick. We crammed into a photo booth and mugged for the camera, laughing at the strip of silly photos that slid out of the machine, and then we got in and did it again. There were times that day that I thought Mom was with me. It was a mirage. The sun, the sounds and the smell. Oh, the smell. I'd see Mom's face, but then it changed into Ginnie's. My beautiful Ginnie, who I loved more than anyone else in the world.

At seven o'clock we met Mrs. Hall in front of the Coliseum. Mr. Hall was in the parking lot getting the car.

"Did you girls have fun?"

"The best."

Mrs. Hall sniffed the air.

"What's that smell?"

Ginnie thrust her wrist beneath her mother's nostrils. "It's perfume, Mom. Maddy gave it to me."

"Let me see."

Ginnie removed the bottle from her purse. Mrs. Hall's gloved hand snatched it, holding it up to the light.

"This is half empty. Where did you get it?"

Please give it back, Mrs. Hall, please give it back. "It's from my family."

She removed the stopper, took a sniff, and then gave me a very strange look.

"This is French perfume. Expensive French perfume is something that a man buys a woman. It's not an acceptable gift from a girl."

"But, Mom – "

"No buts. Maddy, I'm afraid you're going to have to take this back."

"Please Mrs. Hall, it's just something small."

"No."

"I want Ginnie to have it."

Mrs. Hall thrust the bottle at me. I put my palm up to stop her, but our hands collided and the bottle slipped. I tried to catch it. So did Ginnie. But Mom's prized possession, her bottle of French perfume, smashed, shards of crystal shattering across the red brick steps.

"Oh, Maddy," Ginnie said. "I'm so sorry."

Once it was free from its bottle, the Joy began to evaporate.

"That's a shame," Mrs. Hall said, looking down. "But you shouldn't have put up such a fuss." She took her daughter by the arm. "Come along, Ginnie, we've got to meet your father."

I wanted to get down on my hands and knees and smell the Joy before it disappeared, seeping forever into the stone and air. But I couldn't do that. I followed Ginnie and her mother back to the car.

After that, things began to change. One night, after we shut the door and crawled into bed, her sister called, "What's going on in there?"

Ginnie's breath quickened in the dark.

"Nothing," she replied, her lips an inch from mine.

"It sounded funny. What are you doing?"

Ginnie's body stiffened through the bed clothes. She got up and opened the door. Opened it wide and left it there.

"We're not up to anything."

Ginnie hopped back into bed. I whispered to her to shut the door, but she just moved closer to the wall.

"Go to sleep," she whispered.

"I want to kiss you," I whispered back, snuggling in tight beside her.

"Stop it."

"Why?"

"This is supposed to be with a boy."

"Do you want to do it with a boy?" I asked into the black, petrified of the answer.

"I don't know."

She rolled over and pulled the sheet up tight to shut me out.

Betsy and Sandy started asking questions too. It was late November, after I turned fifteen, another birthday that Dad forgot. Betsy was quizzing Ginnie over by their lockers.

"What's going on with you guys?"

"Nothing," Ginnie replied, way too defensively.

Betsy gave her a funny look.

"Dale was wondering if you'd like to double with us. We're going to the drive-in this Saturday."

Ginnie looked over at me. I violently shook my head no. We were having a sleepover. "Sounds like fun," she said.

I ran after her, finally catching up by the bus line. "Why are you doing this?" I yanked her out of the line.

"Let me go. You're making a scene," she said.

"Just give me a second."

I pulled her towards the basketball hoops. This was bad. She was slipping away. "You don't even like Dale. Why are you going with him?"

I tried not to be pathetic, and tried really, really hard not to cry. I cared about Ginnie way more than she cared about me.

"I've got to go."

She turned away. I yanked her back and a bunch of kids looked over. I didn't care. I didn't give a damn what anybody thought. But Ginnie did.

Her voice dropped really low. "This isn't normal. I don't want people talking about me," she said. "And I don't think you should come out to my place for a while."

I burst into tears in the middle of the schoolyard.

"You're my friend. Aren't you my best friend?"

I was thinking what it was like to be Mark's sister, driven to get down in the dirt. I would have done that for Ginnie. I wouldn't have cared what anybody said. But one look at her face and I knew that if I didn't back off she'd be gone for good. The bus driver honked and Ginnie ran up the stairs. The yellow school bus kicked up gravel as it pulled out of the lot. Ginnie sat at the back, her beautiful long blond hair draping over a seat. Dale sat beside her, sliding his arm around her. It was worse than being kicked in the stomach by the biggest horse in the world.

"Dad?" I poked my head into the waiting room. Nobody was there. The office was closed and the Oldsmobile was gone. I walked into the kitchen. Rika was finishing up the evening dishes.

"You late vor supper," she said, not looking up from the suds.

I wasn't hungry anyway.

"Where are the boys?"

Rika set the frying pan in the dish rack.

"You know this is virst time I hear you ask about them?"

She had to be lying.

"You know Vrank is captain of baseball team and Tedder is in Cubs?"

I didn't. I'd seen Tedder wandering around in a costume, but I hadn't thought to ask. He always wore weird things. Rika pulled a pot out of the hot, soapy water.

"You are bad, selvish girl."

"Leave me alone," I replied, walking out of the kitchen, down the hall and into the office.

The light in the dispensary was still on. Rika was just being mean. None of my friends played with their younger siblings. It wasn't something that you did, but I used to. Sure Frank and I fought, but we also played catch and loved building rocket ships out of giant cardboard boxes strung with Christmas lights.

The latest copy of *TIME* magazine lay on the metal counter. It was another issue devoted to the youth drug culture. There was a picture of a teenager injecting drugs into the hollow of his arm. The writer talked about how the counterculture had begun with peaceful protests and marijuana, but there had been a nasty shift to hard drugs and riots. There had been a hard shift in my world, too.

The Compendium said it would take about fifteen minutes to feel the effects of Valium and recommended taking one. I took two and wandered down to the rec room. At first I felt floaty and light, but then I just passed out on the sofa with my clothes on. Nobody noticed that I'd slept down there that night, even though the TV was blaring. While the Valium really knocked me out, it didn't help with how sad I felt when I woke up the next morning.

"Hi," Ginnie said, walking towards me.
 I turned the other way. It was hard, but I knew the only way to get her back was to ignore her. Nobody wants you if you need them. They only want you if you don't. Kenneth stood by the water fountain. I walked over, bent down and took a few little gulps of water while he stared at my boobs.
 "Are you going to the drive-in this weekend?" I asked.
 "Do you want to come?"
 I shrugged, chewing on a strand of hair. "It depends. Can you get anything to drink?"
 Kenneth's head bobbed up and down.
 "Mark's got his dad's car. We can pick you up at eight."
 Ginnie was at her locker, pretending not to watch.

Mark was so short he needed to sit on a phone book to see over the steering wheel, and he didn't have a driver's license but I didn't care.
 "You want a drink?" Kenneth asked.
 Sandy had mixed up a batch of Purple Jesus. That's when you saved all the heels from your parents' liquor bottles and mixed them in with purple Kool-Aid. It tasted horrible but had a real kick, making the thought of Ginnie being with Dale fade away. Tearing down the two-lane highway, we chugged the liquor and laughed. About a mile away from the drive-in Mark pulled over and told Kenneth and me to get out.
 "Why?" I asked.
 "We're getting in the trunk," Kenneth replied.
 Mark didn't have any money for tickets so Kenneth and I were going to be smuggled in.

"But we'll freeze in there."

It was early December and I didn't bring a coat.

"I'll keep you warm," Kenneth smiled.

"Can I have another drink first?"

"After we get out," Kenneth replied.

I followed them to the back of the car. There were a couple of lawn chairs in the trunk already, making it cramped and uncomfortable. Just before Mark shut the lid I caught Kenneth's glance. He had that horny look on his face and a bulge in his pants.

"No way." I wasn't touching his penis in the dark.

"If you do, you don't have to touch it again all night."

This was gross. I could smell his Juicy Fruit breath, and he kept trying to grab my hand and put it on his crotch.

"Please?" he whimpered, begging.

Right then I wondered if Kenneth and I were so different. I would have been crying for Ginnie to touch me.

"You promise you won't tell?" I whispered, reaching into the black, feeling for the cloth of his jeans.

"Never, ever," he gasped, promising over and over, so desperate and pleading.

My fingers traced up towards his crotch. I could feel him fumbling for the zipper, trying to yank it down. I didn't feel so grossed out anymore. I felt sorry for Kenneth and I felt sorry for me.

"You can have all the drinks you want."

Mark honked to warn us we were near the gate. My fingers closed around Kenneth's penis. It was rock hard. He tried to grab my hand to pump it, but I wanted to do it myself. Harder and harder I pumped. Up and down and up and down until he let out a tiny moan. Something felt wet. Then the trunk opened and for a moment, all I could see was stars.

"Where's the liquor?" I asked, hopping out and pulling a lawn chair with me. I wanted a good seat for the show.

By the time I saw Ginnie I was totally polluted. The ground rolled when I walked, making me giggle. I threw my arm around Kenneth's neck and slid up against him for support. Ginnie and Betsy were coming back from the girls' washroom by the concession stand.

"How's it going?" I slurred.

Ginnie frowned. She didn't like me being with Kenneth.

"Where's your coat?"

"Where's Dale?" I replied, pulling Kenneth even closer.

He didn't mind being used, but then again, he probably didn't know it either.

"He's back at the car," Ginnie said. "I didn't know you were coming."

"We're here with Sandy and Mark. We got a bunch of drinks. You should come over."

Ginnie quickly said, "No thanks," but Betsy thought it sounded like fun.

Brad and Dale arrived.

"Hey, you guys want to party? Sandy's got really good Jesus," I added, with a grin at Dale that read pure dare.

Dale slung his arm around Ginnie's shoulder. "Sure."

I dumped the pop on the ground and filled the concession paper cup with liquor. We were all crammed into Mark's car. He and Sandy were making out in the front seat beside Betsy and Brad. Ginnie and Dale were in the back beside me and Kenneth. Kenneth had his hands all over me, and it was making Ginnie crazy. She just kept looking out the window to see if anyone was watching. Betsy took a big drink from the cup of Jesus and laughed, handing the cup to Brad, who belted it back.

"That burns! What's in it?"

"You don't want to know," I said, handing some to Dale.

"I don't think we should be drinking," Ginnie said.

"Oh come on, it's Saturday night. Let's have some fun."

"Chug it, Dale!" Betsy yelled. "Chug! Chug! Chug!"

Dale didn't have a choice but Ginnie refused. I proposed another round. The first round was kicking in and we were all feeling good. The cup passed around again. Betsy and Brad started making out harder. I took another gulp and kissed Kenneth. Dale put his arm around Ginnie and tried to get closer, but she threw open the door and announced that she was going home. Dale tried to follow but I jumped out first, telling him to wait in the car.

"Hey, wait up!" I called, staggering after Ginnie. "What's wrong?"

She was upset. "When did you start drinking?"

"It's just about having fun. I thought that's what tonight was all about, having fun with boys." I tried to pull her around, then lost my balance and started to fall. Ginnie caught me.

"Are you and Dale having a good time?"

"No."

"How come?"

"Because I'd rather be with you."

That would have made me happy, if only Ginnie didn't look so sad.

Dad was out. Rika and the boys were asleep. I sat on the metal counter in the dispensary reading the *Diagnostic and Statistical Manual of Mental Disorders*. The book said that people attracted to the same sex were called homosexuals or lesbians and their sexual interests were "toward sexual acts not usually associated with coitus, or toward coitus." What was coitus? Then it said "homosexuals performed sex under bizarre circumstances such as in necrophilia, pedophilia, sexual sadism and fetishism." Necrophilia was dead people. I threw the book down. Ginnie and I weren't deviants. We were like secret sisters.

The Purple Jesus had worn off and I needed something for pain. The *TIME* magazine with the syringe on the cover said the best drug was heroin, but Dad didn't have any of that. *The Compendium* said that heroin was an illegal substance that was derived from the opium family, which was related to morphine. There wasn't any morphine, but I knew where to find synthetic substitutes – Dad's restricted substance drawer.

I went into the nurse's station and dug out a bottle of Dilaudid – little pink pills that Dad prescribed for extreme pain.

"Maddy?"

Footsteps down the hall. I dropped the bottle back into the drawer. Dad walked in as I stood up, shutting the drawer with my leg.

"You're home early," I said.

"You're up late," Dad replied, eyes down, leafing through the day's mail. "Did you have fun tonight?"

"It was okay." I felt myself sway as I crossed the room, leaning into the door jamb for support. "I'm going to bed." I turned and walked out. "See you in the morning."

"Honeybunch?" Dad called, poking his head through the doorway.

I leaned against the wall to steady myself. I was way drunker than I thought.

"Are you free next Friday? I want to take you to a recital at Aunt Anne's church in Toronto. A friend of mine is singing."

I was about to complain, but now that I was up and moving around I was seeing double and knew I might start slurring again.

"Okay."

Dad smiled. Waving goodnight, I turned, praying he'd do the same, and thankfully he did, because when I took the first step I lost my balance and bounced off the opposite wall.

"Are you alright?" he called.

"Oh, yeah."

Dad parked in the lot at the side of the church. My bare legs stuck to the vinyl of the car seat. Aunt Anne had called earlier that day and asked me to wear my new dress.

"I hate dresses."

"Do this for your father."

"No."

"Then do it for me."

There was no point fighting.

I followed Dad into the church and we took our seats near the front. The church's chancel had been transformed into a forest with wigwams and a fake lake. It must be something about cowboys and Indians. Aunt Anne slipped into the pew beside me.

She seemed nervous. "Don't you look pretty?"

I shrugged.

"Where are your nylons?"

Pantyhose? No way.

"At least I wore the dress."

Aunt Anne nodded and patted my thigh. "Thank you for that."

She leaned over to say hello to Dad. The program said we were going to see a musical.

"Where's Isabel?" Dad asked.

"Backstage."

Isabel? The lights dimmed and a colourful boat, carrying a fat man in a stovetop hat, sailed across the stage and landed in Indian territory. Placing his hand over his heart, he was singing about the brave new world when a tall, handsome woman dressed like an Indian princess stepped out from behind a stand of oak trees. She had an enormous voice, and her presence swamped the stage, dwarfing the Indians, the Puritans and even the boat. Dad's eyes lit up. I hadn't seen him smile like that since Mom was alive.

"Is that your friend?" I whispered.

He nodded.

"That's Miss McAllister. I've asked her to marry me."

There were platters of sandwiches with the crusts cut off, pickled beets, purple punch and raspberry tarts. The United Church Women cleared away empty plates and cutlery. Aunt Anne was talking to some of her friends from choir while Dad and I stood beside the coffee urn. Dad took a sip.

"How can you marry somebody else?" I whispered, numb with shock and fury.

"Miss McAllister is a very fine woman."

He took another sip and smiled at a man pouring a cup of coffee. We stopped talking until the man left.

"Have you forgotten Mom already?" I hissed.

"Of course not."

I pulled him towards the wall, my voice rising slightly. "I don't want a new mother."

Aunt Anne glanced over. The Indian lady, Miss McAllister, came out from behind the stage, still in costume.

"Isabel!" Dad called.

She made her way towards us through a crowd of admirers.

Dad turned to me. "I want you to meet her."

"But Dad – "

And she was there, extending her hand.

"You must be Maddy. I'm Isabel. Your father does nothing but talk about you kids."

What was I supposed to say? I never heard about you, but there's no way you're marrying my Dad.

I shook her hand. It was steady and no nonsense.

"I'm sure this is a bit of a surprise," she said.

Dad stood behind me. Miss McAllister still had me firmly by the hand and wasn't letting go.

"I would have preferred we do it privately but your Dad thought..."

Dad squeezed my shoulders. "Maddy loves surprises, don't you honey?"

Aunt Anne arrived. "Isabel, the show was terrific."

"How do you two know each other?" I asked.

Miss McAllister laughed. Aunt Anne slipped her hand through Miss McAllister's arm.

"We've been friends for years. We sing together in the choir."

"If it wasn't for your aunt, I never would have met your father."

I looked at Aunt Anne. Traitor. Miss McAllister let go of my hand and kissed Dad lightly on the cheek.

"Did you and Maddy have time for supper before the show?"

Dad picked up a sandwich from the platter and took a bite. "I thought we'd eat here."

"Honestly, Ted, you need to take better care of yourself. Are you hungry, Maddy?"

The man in the stovetop appeared, sweeping Miss McAllister away for cast photos, taking my father with her. I turned to face Aunt Anne.

"How could you?"

"Give her a chance."

I didn't say a word all the way home. The minute we got in I tore out to the dining room and picked up the phone.

"Who is this?" Mrs. Hall asked, sounding sleepy.

I looked at the wall clock. It was after midnight.

"I'm sorry, Mrs. Hall. Can I speak to Ginnie, please? It's really important."

"I don't care how important it is, Madeline. You're not to call here at this hour ever again."

She slammed the phone down as Dad came in, undoing his tie, a desperate look on his face.

"Did you like her, honey?"

I couldn't believe he'd even ask. "She's not very pretty."

He ignored me.

"And she sure doesn't have Mom's figure."

"She's got a perfectly nice figure."

"Have you kissed her?"

A look crossed his face as if he'd been caught cheating. "That's not your business."

"When are you going to tell the boys?"

"When the time's right." He dropped his tie on the table and walked up the stairs.

When I heard Dad's bedroom door close I opened the drawer and fished out the Dilaudid. Little pink pills rolled into the palm of my hand. I looked up the side effects. Nausea. I didn't want to spend the night puking. *The Compendium* recommended Dramamine so I took two Gravols. Next, the dosage needed to be determined – one two-mg capsule for extreme pain. I decided on four. *The Compendium* noted that Dilaudid could also cause "twilight sleep." That sounded nice. While I waited for it to hit, I thought about Mom and that day in the garden. Her hair, the red and golden strands, how they turned white gold in the summer sun. Miss McAllister's hair was mousey. Dull. Plain. And then I started to dissolve.

My fingers and toes disappeared, followed quickly by my arms and legs. I felt my jaw and face slacken, and then the brain relaxed as if it was surrounded by thick cotton batting. For the first time in a long time I forgot to be on guard, waiting to see what horrible surprise would tumble out of the sky. After a while, I stood, wondering if I might fall down, but I didn't. Drifting through the dispensary like a ghost, I trailed my fingers across the paper labels on brown bottles, stroking the stainless steel counters, pushing through the swinging door and up onto the cool vinyl examining table. I felt nothing. No pain or joy. My worried, always clucking, Henny Penny brain suddenly muzzled, now as still as a boat on a calm lake. I sat up after three in the morning and knew I'd found an escape hatch.

Every day different pills went in and the pain went out. I didn't tell my brothers about Miss McAllister, but all my friends felt sorry for me. Mrs. Hall didn't. We were peeling potatoes for supper.

"It will do you some good to have more supervision."

"But she's not my mother," I replied. "I've only met her once."

"Your father could have handled the whole thing a lot better, but what's done is done. And you three need a mother," she said, as a long twist of potato peel dropped into the bowl.

"I told you, she's not my mother."

It was that loud voice again. The voice that sometimes just escaped. Mrs. Hall set the knife on the counter. I was mad and I didn't care.

"And she's not going to tell me what to do!"

Ginnie's face went white. Mrs. Hall was big and bossy. Just like Miss McAllister. She quickly removed her apron, hanging it on a hook.

"Time to take you home."

I looked at Ginnie. It wasn't time yet, but Ginnie didn't say a word. Head down, she kept peeling. I didn't want to leave. It was horrible at home.

"I'm sorry. Please don't send me home."

"Ginnie, get Maddy's coat," Mrs. Hall said, cutting me off.

Ginnie dropped the knife and ran. My pea coat was on the dining room table. Her mother sat me down and took my hands, holding them fast. I started to cry.

"I won't let you drag Ginnie into anything. She's a good girl and I don't want you influencing her."

"Please," I said. "Please don't make me go."

Mrs. Hall removed her car keys from the hook. Ginnie handed me my coat and opened the door.

A couple of months later Dad cleared his throat and nobody paid attention. We were waiting for dessert. Tedder was dressed in a goalie mask and red and white leg pads. He'd recently taken up goaltending and Frank took shots on him out in the garage. Every night we heard thwack, thump, whump or a scream, depending on where the puck hit Tedder. Dad cleared his throat again, tapping the water glass with his spoon.

"I've decided to remarry. You children need a mother."

"Mother?" Tedder asked, as some potatoes fell out of his mouth.

I kicked the table so hard I thought I'd broken my foot. Dad hadn't mentioned Miss McAllister since that night, and I'd hoped, no, I'd prayed that she'd gone away.

"I thought your sister might have told you."

Frank looked at me across the table.

"The lady's name is Miss McAllister and she's coming here with Aunt Anne." He glanced at his watch. "They should be here soon."

Dad shoved his chair back and got up and left the room.

"Who is she?" Frank asked.

"I don't know."

Frank could see I knew something and looked away disgusted and confused. Feeling guilty, I went up to my bedroom and flipped up the mattress. Bottles of pain medication, tranquilizers and barbiturates were scattered across the top of the box spring. I washed down a handful of codeine tablets and lay down on my bed, waiting for the pain and fear to disappear. The leaves on the willow began to rustle and twist. They were so lovely, like the green fields of tall wheat blowing in Granddad's fields. The doorbell rang. Dad's heavy feet echoed through the still house as he strode down the hall. A series of voices followed. Aunt Anne rapped on my door. Slowly I sat up on the side of the bed and got dressed.

A filmy, skintight, black rayon dress barely covered my bum, and the thick streaks of jet-black eyeliner were crooked, but that was on purpose. They went well with the messy smudges of dark blue eyeshadow. My eyes were glossy from the codeine and I slid into some black slingbacks. Swerving down the hallway, I went over on my ankle twice before reaching the landing. Frank was down below talking to Aunt Anne and Miss McAllister. Aunt Anne beamed at Frank as if he was one of Granddad's prized steers. Tedder, still in his mask, stood back in the shadow of his bedroom door, silently taking in the whole proceedings. Miss McAllister made a visual sweep of the house.

"Hello, Maddy," she called, her voice echoing up the stairwell. It wasn't a friendly voice like Mom's.

"Hi," I replied, making my way down as she ascended. The scent of her perfume arrived before she did. It wasn't Joy. She checked me out, looking at my hair, which was hanging in my eyes, my makeup and especially my dress. Her eyes said she didn't like it. Good. After eyeballing me she passed by and went over to Tedder. He instinctively pulled back even further into the gloom.

"Is this Theodore?"

"His name's Tedder," I blurted out, but she ignored me, thrusting out her hand and keeping it there until Tedder took it.

"Do you like oatmeal cookies?"

Tedder nodded.

"Good. I made a batch today," she said, pulling him out of his bedroom and into the hall. "Let's have one while we all sit down and talk." Her other hand reached for his mask. "And I think we'll take this off."

We were all in the living room. I tried to balance a teacup on my knee while Miss McAllister passed around a plate of cookies. Tedder, his dark hair standing up on end, looked naked without the mask.

"Your father and I feel that it will be best for you children if we move to Toronto."

"No!" I said, louder than I should have.

"Maddy," Aunt Anne replied in a warning voice. "Hear this out."

"Why do we have to move?" Frank asked.

"Because I've never lived in the country and your father and I have decided that it would be best for everyone if we started with a clean slate."

"There are just too many memories in this house," Aunt Anne said. "It wouldn't be fair to Isabel."

Fair to her. What about us? While Miss McAllister talked about schools, Aunt Anne told Frank and Tedder about the ball diamonds and hockey arenas in Toronto.

"What about the chickens?" Tedder asked.

Miss McAllister laughed, passing him another cookie.

"Your aunt and I will make certain you get up to your Granddad's to see the animals."

"But I'm used to seeing them all the time," Tedder replied.

After they left, Dad said it was time for a family powwow. He leaned forward on a chair. The three of us were lined up on the sofa with Tedder in the middle, the metal goalie mask back on and clapped tightly over his face. I think Frank was holding his breath. I wanted to disappear into the dispensary and take every pill in the place.

"Why do we have to move?" Frank asked.

"Because we need her," Dad replied.

"No we don't," I said. "We're doing just fine on our own."

Why did Aunt Anne bring Miss McAllister here? I'd never forgive her.

"You've got to be very, very good, or else Miss McAllister will go away," Dad said, his fingers clamping onto his knees to stop his hands from shaking. Severe shaking often came before a nervous collapse. I remembered that from a book. Frank bit his bottom lip. A Frank way of saying, "Be quiet."

"Where would she go?" Tedder asked.

Dad didn't answer. Instead he just slumped over, staring at the back of his hands. For the first time I noticed his wedding ring was gone.

"So do we understand one another?" Dad asked, glancing up.

"Yes," Frank said.

Dad tapped Frank and me gently on the thigh and pinched Tedder's toe. "I've got some paperwork to finish up," he said, rising to his feet.

The minute Dad was gone, Frank whirled around on the sofa.

"This is your fault. If you weren't always getting into trouble, then Dad wouldn't have to go out and find us a new mother," Frank yelled, shooting across Tedder to give me a hard shove. I was about to push him back when Tedder screamed.

"I don't want a new Mommy!"

Frank and I stopped. Tedder never raised his voice. Then he started to cry.

"It's okay, Tedder," I said.

"Don't worry," Frank added, trying to pull up the hockey mask, but Tedder held it fast.

We both put our arms around Tedder's shoulders.

"Do you want me to take shots on you?" Frank asked.

Tedder nodded and waddled out the door in his goalie pads. Frank followed. He always tried to do what was expected of him. Well I could take my shots too. I was going to fight.

A couple of days later the whole family had an appointment at the dentist's office in Eltonville. Dad asked me to be home by three thirty. He asked me twice.

"I've got late patients coming in and I've got to be back," he said.

"Okay," I replied.

But I didn't go home. The moment the yellow buses were gone and all the teachers had left, I started toilet papering the entire school. Tissue banners hung from the trees as I wrapped the bike racks like mummies and climbed up on the roof rolling balls of toilet paper. A horn honked. I walked over to the edge – so close my toes poked out. It was Dad. I put my hands on my hips. He pushed his hat back. Frank and Tedder were in the back seat of the car, looking through the window.

"Madeline!" Dad called, waving for me to come down. "We've got to get going."

I ran to the other side, giving him no choice but to climb up. Dad stood on the roof. The ribbons of white toilet paper rippled in the wind, wrapping around his legs. He glanced at his wristwatch and then at the horrible mess.

"We'll have to come back later and clean this up," he said, walking towards me. "Let's go."

"No."

He tried to snatch my sleeve, but I ducked, running to the other side of the roof. "I hate her!"

"You don't even know her." He walked towards me, fists clenched. He was mad and that was good.

"I don't want to!"

"This isn't your choice."

We'd see about that. I started to hum.

"Does she sing to you the way Mom used to?" Then I began to sing their song. "Gonna take a sentimental journey..."

His mouth went crooked and then he moved, charging across the roof, kicking up a cloud of gravel and asphalt. My foot stepped back, but the roof was gone, nothing there but air. My arms spun. The Oldsmobile was right beneath.

Dad grabbed me, pulling me back, holding me fast in his arms. I wanted to hug him and hold him close, but spat out the lyrics instead.

"Sentimental journey home. Never knew my heart could be so yearny."

"Stop it!"

I wriggled away, breaking free from his grasp.

"Don't you get yearney for Mom anymore? How could you forget her so soon?"

He was panting so hard his chest heaved up and down.

"Have you forgotten the way she smelled? The way she smiled? The way she laughed?"

Then he slapped me across the face.

We got in the car. My upper lip had started to swell and bleed. It really hurt, but I wanted Dad to hit me again. At least he knew I was alive. Instead he just sank behind the wheel, twisting the key in the ignition.

"Why are you doing this to me?" he asked. "Why?"

We drove home. I glanced in the rearview mirror, touching my lip. The boys sat silently in the back seat, too scared to ask what happened, and then Dad started to cry.

I sat on the counter in the dispensary while Dad applied ice to my swollen lip. He was still crying, apologizing over and over again, muttering that he wasn't the kind of man to strike a fifteen-year-old girl. His crying scared me, and the fear made me mad.

"Stop crying."

He didn't. Couldn't.

"I'm sorry."

I didn't care that he was sorry. I didn't care that he was upset. Somebody had to stop this terrible mistake.

"Granddad always said you were weak."

That slowed the crying.

"That's why you're marrying that woman. Because you're weak."

He wiped the tears away.

"You're going to treat Miss McAllister with respect."
"No I won't."
"Yes you will."
Then he slammed his palms down on the examining table and left.

I might have to go to the wedding, but at least Ginnie and I could be together. I sat at my desk, spraying good cologne on a sheet of fancy writing paper, while Ginnie lay on the bed.

"They'll never know," I said, waving the paper around.

Ginnie didn't look so sure. "I don't know. My Mom always figures everything out."

The plan was for Aunt Anne to think I was staying at the Halls and for Mrs. Hall to think that Ginnie was staying at our house under Aunt Anne's supervision. Everybody approved of Aunt Anne because she was so strict.

I turned to Ginnie. "Don't you want to spend one last summer together?"

"Yes..."

"This way we can. And nobody will know."

Using Dad's special fountain pen, I began to write:

Dear Miss Gillespie,

Mr. Hall and I would be most pleased if Madeline could stay with us while Dr. Barnes and his new bride will be away in Europe. This will give the girls a chance to enjoy the summer and perhaps help ease the transition for Madeline. Rest assured we'll keep her busy gathering eggs, milking cows and helping out with the housework.

Sincerely,
Mrs. Roger Hall

I handed Aunt Anne the letter later that week.

"You seem awfully preoccupied with that girl," Aunt Anne said, carefully examining the note. There was something about it that intrigued her. She sniffed the edges for cologne.

"She's my best friend. Didn't you ever have a best friend?" I asked.

Aunt Anne looked up over the top of the note. "It's important that we have a lot of friends in life. Not just one."

"Betsy and Sandy will come out for hay rides and stuff."

"Will there be boys?"

"There won't be any stupid boys!" I said, starting to get agitated.

"Maybe I should call Ginnie's mother." Aunt Anne's nurse's instincts were kicking in. I had to calm down.

"I just want to have my last summer with my friends."

She looked at me, then down at the note. Nothing had been the same between us since she brought that rat into our family.

"Please."

"As long as you call me and check in regularly."

The wedding happened on a hot day in downtown Toronto. Frank, Tedder and I sat beside Aunt Anne in the front pew of an enormous church that was as big and fancy as a castle. The floors were made out of white marble, and the pews were long and dark. Voices echoed as people talked. Giant stained glass windows loomed, featuring Jesus at all the different stages of His life. Frank was staring at a man with white hair playing the organ.

"Where's Granddad?" he asked.

"He had to stay home and take care of the cattle," Aunt Anne replied.

I coughed. We hadn't seen Granddad since Mom's funeral. When I told Dad that the freezer was getting low, he said he'd get the butcher to fill it up. When I told Aunt Anne that the meat was nearly gone, she said that it would be one less thing to move, and when I called Granddad to tell him we were low, he said he couldn't talk. None of the other relatives had come either. The white-haired organist began another song. The classical music was beautiful and Mom would have loved it. I pictured her listening and laughing as Dad covered his ears, claiming he could do a much better job on his ukulele.

The bride's side of the church was loaded with professional women like Aunt Anne and Miss McAllister. Lines of light wool suits and brightly coloured summer dresses filled the pews, every head displaying a grand hat. They bobbed as the women chatted and then turned to see who was arriving next. The men were scarce. Frank kept glancing at them until Aunt Anne told him to stop.

"I'm not staring," Frank replied.

Aunt Anne fanned her face with the program. "Gad, it's heavy in here."

The organ paused.

"There's your father," Aunt Anne whispered, jabbing me in the ribs. "Sit up straight."

Everyone looked up. Dad and his best man, who was a friend of Miss McAllister's, entered from beneath a wide marble archway. The wedding march began and everyone looked down the aisle, everyone except me. I was watching my father.

"He looks terrible," Aunt Anne whispered.

She was right. The wedding suit that had fit a month earlier now hung on him like a sack. It was the first time I'd really looked at him since Mom died. He'd aged years, had gone from being a solid guy with a great big grin, to a skinny stick with hollow, desperate eyes. I tried to catch his attention, to smile at him, but he wasn't looking at me. He was smiling at Miss McAllister, who was crossing the threshold to take his arm. He was trying so hard to please. His legs wobbled, but the shaking stopped when she touched him. She held him up. Dad needed her and he didn't need me.

Aunt Anne drove me and Tedder back to the house. The streets were motionless, as if everyone in Sterling had vanished. Our driveway was empty. The practice closed, the patients gone and Rika had taken a position with another family. The movers would come at the end of the month. Even Ruth had moved her stuff, but she'd sworn she'd be back to say goodbye.

"Are you sure you don't want me to take you out to Ginnie's house?" Aunt Anne asked. "I don't like leaving you here all alone."

"I've still got to pack. Mrs. Hall will pick me up before dinner," I replied. "Besides, you've still got to take Tedder."

Tedder was going to stay with relatives and Frank was already on his way to camp. I turned to give Tedder a quick hug goodbye but he grabbed me, holding me tight.

"Come with me," he said, his little brown suitcase resting on the seat beside him.

"I can't."

"Please."

"You be a good boy," I said, pulling away. "I'll see you soon."

I stood in the driveway waving goodbye until the car disappeared over the hill. Walking up the sidewalk, I went over all the details for my romantic evening. I'd hidden fresh flowers in my room, was going to put candles in the candelabra and lay out Mom's good china and silver flatware. There would be a roast of beef, potatoes and peas for dinner and then we'd go up to my room.

When I opened the front door and stepped in Ginnie was already there. My Ginnie was sitting on the bottom step of the staircase. She couldn't wait to see me either, because she'd forgotten her suitcase.

"Where's your bag?"

She stood up. Nervous. "Mom changed her mind."

No no no. I walked towards her. "Maybe you can come tomorrow?"

"I can't come over at all."

"Why?"

"Because I told her."

Ginnie told her mother about our secret plan to spend the summer at my house. That meant we'd never be alone again. I'd move away and never hold her. Never again, for the rest of my life. Everything was ruined. When she opened the door I started to cry.

"But I love you."

"I'm sorry."

And the door shut and my Ginnie was gone.

I was all alone. No patients ringing the doorbell saying how sorry they were to be calling so late but the baby was really sick. No Frank flying down the stairs with his baseball mitt. No Tedder racing his Hot Wheels around the living room floor. No Mom, beautiful Mom, kissing me on the end of the nose, saying how proud she was of my straight A's. No Dad holding me tight, telling me I was his Maddikins. Nobody left in that great big house where our family used to live. I ran down the hall and into the dispensary.

The Compendium recommended 50 mgs of Demerol for extreme pain. I'd seen Dad inject enough patients to know how to fill a syringe. I drew back the liquid, tapping the glass lightly whenever an air bubble appeared. They could stop your heart or make your brain explode. Next I scrubbed the inside of my arm with an alcohol swab and picked up the syringe. The needle pricked the skin. I shoved the steel into my arm and drove the plunger down and everything tasted of metal.

"You're nuts!" Sandy squealed.

I waggled the syringe at them. "Do you want to shoot up?"

Betsy shook her head. "I'm scared of needles."

"How does it make you feel?" Sandy asked.

"Like heaven."

It was true. I'd spent three hours adrift in the Demerol, but when I came down I wanted to go back up. I didn't want to be alone, so I'd called my friends.

"I think I'd rather take pills," Sandy said.

"Me too," Betsy replied.

I poured a handful of Dad's blue tablets into the palm of my hand.

"These are Valium."

"Mother's little helper," Betsy said.

"That's right."

I dropped two tablets into Betsy's hand. Sandy was looking at a bottle of yellow capsules.

"What do these do?"

"They make you bounce off the walls."

"The yellow reminds me of Mark's hair. How many do I take?"

"Two."

I dropped them into her hand, shoving the bottle in my pocket.

"Why didn't you tell us about this before?" Betsy asked.

"Because I'm telling you now."

I showed them the Demerol bottle. 50 mg didn't kill me, so why not 100? The girls sat on the counter, eyes like searchlights, watching me fill the syringe.

I stood up. "Let's go downstairs and party."

Sandy took a swig from a bottle of whiskey she'd stolen from her father.

"When are the pills going to hit?"

"About ten minutes."

A clear drop of Demerol clung to the end of the needle and then slowly fell onto my skin.

Betsy closed her eyes but Sandy couldn't look away. Down went the needle – in came relief. The syringe slipped between the cushions as the Demerol rolled over me. My heart slowed and my vision flickered like a television set losing reception. It was hard to breathe.

"Are you alright?" Sandy asked. "What does it feel like?"

I sunk into the sofa as all the bad feelings disappeared.

"Fantabulous."

"You're crazy," Betsy mumbled, lighting a cigarette. The smoke hung like a thundercloud.

There was a bang upstairs. I ignored it. My neck muscles went slack and my head fell back. Out into the calm I sailed, bobbing far, far away. Ginnie...My head lolled. Ginnie...I tried to sit up. What was Ginnie doing standing at the bottom of the stairs? Was she real? Betsy offered her a drink and Ginnie yelled something, turned and ran up the stairs. I called for her to stop.

"Let her go," Betsy giggled.

I staggered after Ginnie, yanked open the door and out onto the veranda. She was halfway down the drive.

"Come back!" I yelled, tumbling down the stairs, landing on the asphalt, cutting my hand. Ginnie spun around.

"My mother was right. You're damaged!"

I got back up.

"Is this what you do when you're not with me?"

Her lower lip quivered. Was she going to cry? Did she care somewhere in there?

"Stay away from me. Just stay away. I never want to see you again!"

With all of her strength she shoved me, so hard that I fell back on the sidewalk, striking my head on the concrete. She didn't even stop to see if I'd cracked my skull.

The water woke me up. Sharp, cold and stinging it slapped my face. Betsy was passed out on the floor. Sandy was sprawled across a chair. I was on the sofa. There were two empty liquor bottles on the table and an ashtray loaded with a mountain of butts. The sofa was drenched and squishy. I swiped my hand through my hair. Aunt Anne was standing there with an empty bucket wearing the worst nurse's face I'd ever seen. How much did she know? I had no idea. How did I get down here? Did she find me on the sidewalk? No. I remembered crawling through the dewy grass.

"Get dressed," she said evenly. Way too evenly for this kind of mess. Betsy moaned. Sandy growled for us to be quiet.

"What time is it?" I asked.

The doorbell rang.

"That will be their parents," Aunt Anne said, turning and going back up the stairs.

Oh no. I gave Betsy a kick. Where was the syringe? I stuck my hand between the cushions. Thank God. The barbiturates were in my pocket.

"Get up!"

The doorbell rang again – three quick angry blasts.
"Get lost," Betsy replied, putting a pillow over her head.
"Your Mom's here."
"What?"
"So is Sandy's."
"Oh shit," Betsy said, as their mothers followed Aunt Anne into the rec room.
"Get your shoes," Betsy's mother said, grabbing Betsy by the arm.
Sandy's mother saw the empty liquor bottle and gave her daughter a cuff across the back of the head. "You won't be coming here anymore."
Up the stairs the girls went, rank and file, heads bowed, followed by their furious mothers. Aunt Anne stood at the bottom of the stairs, arms crossed, still wearing the impenetrable nurse's face.
"Change your blouse," she said.

Aunt Anne gripped the wheel as the Ford bore down on the asphalt. It was like travelling in an ambulance without the sirens. Hard rain battered the cornfields. The windshield wipers threw off the water, only to have it gather again. A horn blared. A well-dressed woman in a hat stared at me as the Ford tore by. Water streamed down the window. Aunt Anne's head turned. The nurse's face was gone. The blood drained out of it, pure fury, Granddad rage.
"I go out to the Hall house to get you, and Mrs. Hall tells me that you're not there. No, it was some kind of ruse you and your friends cooked up so you could drink all summer."
So Ginnie hadn't told her mother about the drugs. Aunt Anne didn't know.
"I'm sorry."
She picked up speed as the rest of the traffic slowed.
"What's wrong with you?" she asked, her palm striking the wheel. "I do everything I can and you just throw it back in my face. And Isabel, I told Isabel that you were a fine girl."
"But Aunt Anne – "
"No buts. You've gone too far this time. You've disgraced yourself. You've disgraced your mother's memory. She'd be so ashamed of you."
I wanted to yell, but I bit down on my tongue instead. How dare she say that? She was the one who disgraced Mom's memory by bringing that woman into our lives.

"Don't you have anything to say for yourself?"

I didn't reply. If I told her what I really thought I would be the one disgracing Mom's memory. Mom tried to live life like Granny Gillespie. "With grace and a quiet dignity." The more I thought about it, the madder I got. But I wasn't going to yell. I stared out the window, watching the trees change to truck stops and then to power towers and then houses until finally we were in the city. At the hospital. The same hospital Mom died in. Toronto General. Aunt Anne pulled into the lot. The parking attendant gave her a ticket and she set it on the dash.

"Your father's been in an accident."

I followed Aunt Anne through the glass doors of the Emergency Department, pushing past the gurneys, jostling through the sick and crying, the bloody and the broken, up to the nurse's station. A pretty nurse not much older than me sat doing paperwork, her uniform neatly pressed. She had long blond hair like Ginnie's pinned neatly under a bright white cap. My jeans had green grass stains from crawling across the lawn the night before. When we reached the desk the nurse looked up.

"Anne," she said, rising to her feet and hurrying out from behind the counter. She took Aunt Anne's elbow and began to steer. "He's this way."

The two nurses walked down the hall in front of me, heads together, softly exchanging information. I couldn't hear a thing. The din of the emergency room faded away as we passed through scratched steel doors into a different area of the hospital. It was all so sterile and white. My heart started to thump. I wondered if it was the morgue.

"Can I see him?" I asked and the fear jumped.

"Not right now," Aunt Anne said, pointing me towards a metal chair. "Just sit over there and wait."

The nurse and Aunt Anne went into a room, closing the door behind them. I looked around. There weren't any magazines. The hallway was too quiet. I tapped my jean pocket. At least I still had the barbiturates. I got up and started to pace. What was this place? My gut pumped up fear and spit. Aunt Anne had told me to wait. Where was Dad? I walked over to the door Aunt Anne had disappeared behind and placed my hands on the cold steel. I could hear voices. Softly, oh so gently, I pushed it open and heard a man's voice.

"His wife told me that Ted disappeared into the bathroom of their hotel room."

I pushed open the door a crack more. A man sat on the edge of a desk. I didn't recognize him, but he was obviously a doctor and he knew Dad. Aunt Anne and the nurse sat in chairs.

"He'd been gone a long time so Isabel knocked at the door. No answer. Then she opened it. Ted had rigged his belt to the light fixture and stepped off the edge of the tub."

Aunt Anne's hands went up to her mouth. I closed my eyes and swallowed.

"Is he dead?" Aunt Anne asked.

The doctor shook his head. "Isabel grabbed him by the waist and held him up. I don't know how she did it for so long. Security heard her screaming all the way down the hall. If she'd let go, he'd be gone."

"How is he now?" Aunt Anne asked.

"He was extremely agitated when they first brought him in, but I've got him sedated. Ted's concerned about the prospect of losing his new wife. If there's anything you can do…"

Aunt Anne nodded.

"Can I see him?"

"Of course, but let's keep things positive," the doctor replied. "And we'll need to keep him here for a while."

Hearing the chairs shift, I backed up, and right into somebody standing behind me.

"What are you doing here?" Miss McAllister asked.

She was still wearing her blue going-away outfit. She looked exhausted, and I couldn't tell if she'd been crying, but if she had, she was over it. She looked…firm. Yes, that was the word, *firm*. My back was against the door. Miss McAllister wasn't moving, so neither was I.

"Is it true?" I asked.

"Your father is a very sick man."

My heart was going so fast. "You've got to help him."

"I don't think I can."

She was still wearing her wedding band. This time something in her voice wasn't quite so firm.

"He loves you."

"This isn't about love," she said. "I know what you did. Anne called me and told me how you lied." She shook her head. "I can't do this. It's too much."

She'd held him up. Held him up when he wanted to die. I thought of the things I'd done. Called him weak. Made him cry. This was likely my fault too.

"If you stay I'll be good."

Miss McAllister stared at me – looking clear through.

"No you won't."

If she left he'd do it again. I knew this much was true. I had to do something to save my Dad. She couldn't go or he'd be dead.

"I swear I'll be good."

"And if you aren't?"

"I'll go away. But don't *ever* tell Dad you were going to leave. Please."

That would break his heart.

"Do you promise?"

"I promise."

The door opened and Aunt Anne appeared. "Do you want to see your father?"

"Miss McAllister should go in. He wants to see her," I said, returning to my seat.

"Maddy," Miss McAllister said. I looked up.

"Yes?"

Aunt Anne was standing right beside her.

"I would never ask you to call me Mom, but I'd like it if you'd call me Isabel."

I nodded. Isabel followed Aunt Anne inside. The stainless steel door closed behind them. This was the mental ward.

CHAPTER FOUR

My coat landed on the floor as a pot banged. Something fishy was burning. Isabel must have been trying to make her tuna casserole again. An upright piano stood beneath a colourful painting of Algonquin Park that had been in her family for years. Orange and yellow leaves blew from the branches of nearly barren trees. The rest of the landscape was stark. All of Mom's new modern furniture was gone, replaced by McAllister family antiques. Without taking off my shoes, the number one rule in Isabel's house, I walked down the hall. My room was in the basement.

Isabel called from the kitchen, "There's a letter for you on top of the piano."

I ran across the room. Maybe it was from Ginnie. I'd written her every single day since we'd moved and never gotten a word in reply. The envelope was covered in red hearts.

"Madeline."

Isabel stood in the doorway, staring at my feet, a glob of mushroom soup stuck to the front of her apron. I stomped over to the foyer and kicked off my shoes.

"Who's that from?" Isabel asked.

"It's private."

"Hang up your coat."

Stuffing the letter into my back pocket, I threw my coat on a hook in the closet and headed for the basement.

"How was school?"

"Horrible."

Closing the door, I ran down the stairs, tearing open the letter. It was from Betsy. Ginnie had never written me back. Her mother must have been intercepting the mail. I stuck my hand under the mattress, rooting around for pills. Before we'd moved I'd taken any kind of painkillers or tranquillizers I could find. There were so many pills in the dispensary that nobody would notice a few bottles gone, but now there weren't many left.

I swallowed a couple of Librium and started reading. Betsy said the teachers were a pain and school was a bore, but there was a dance coming up and she wondered if I could bring some acid. I'd sort of told her that I'd made a ton of friends and that I'd already dropped acid. They were both lies. I hadn't found any acid and I hadn't made any friends. The kids were spoiled rich snobs and some of them called me a bumpkin.

My eyes skipped over the words. If I could get to the dance then I could see Ginnie. If she saw me she'd remember how much she loved me. There was a knock at the door. Nobody was allowed in my room. It was one of the few laws on my side.

Frank banged at my door. "DINNER!" he yelled.

We all sat around the McAllister oak dining room table. Frank dropped a knife and the sound ricocheted off the walls. The room needed a rug. A slightly charred tuna casserole sat in front of Isabel. I took a spoonful of peas and was about to set the bowl down when Isabel told me to use the trivet.

"What's that?"

"It's that square pad. It keeps the bowl from marking the wood."

"The Leafs are going to take the cup," Tedder said, spearing a pea with his fork.

"No way, the Habs have got it," Frank replied.

The boys were completely immersed in hockey and their new public school. They'd both made friends and, as Isabel said, "were blending in nicely."

"How's school going?" Dad asked.

I shrugged. I wanted to go down to my room.

"Your father asked you a question," Isabel said, stabbing one of Tedder's runaway peas before it rolled off the table.

I looked at Dad. He was just a smear of his former self. He took up space, ate meals and drank coffee. He rarely asked questions. I took a bite of casserole.

"It's all right."

"Have you made any friends?"

"Not really," I replied, wondering what he thought of Leaside. I didn't know if he liked it or not.

"Maybe if you joined the Glee Club," Isabel said, passing the carrots.

Frank burst out laughing. "Can you see Maddy at the Glee Club?"

"What's a Glee Club?" Tedder asked.

"It's a perfectly lovely occasion for young people to get together and sing," Isabel replied. "And Frank, if Maddy wants to go, you shouldn't make fun."

"Oh come on, Mom," he said. "That's the most ridiculous thing I've ever heard."

And there it was. The first time anyone had called her Mom. Tedder stopped playing with his peas. The oak gleamed and the room stilled. Even the echo fled. Dad caught my eye and held it until I had to look the other way.

"Is it okay to call you that?" Frank asked, knife and fork clenched in either fist.

"I'm very happy that you did," Isabel said. "And there's nothing ridiculous about Glee. I made some of my best friends there."

"Can I be excused?" I asked.

"You've barely touched your dinner," Isabel replied.

I pushed my chair back. "I'm not hungry."

"Suit yourself."

The boys picked up their conversation about hockey. "Do you think you'd ever buy us season's tickets, Dad?" Frank asked.

Dad chewed, not paying any attention.

"Ted?" Isabel said.

Dad lurched up in his seat. "I think we should wait on that a bit."

"Come on," Tedder cried.

"How much do they cost?" Isabel asked.

I got up and walked over to the basement door. When I looked back I couldn't help but think how peaceful and normal the scene seemed without me. Even Dad was more relaxed. Mom wasn't the only ghost. Welcome to family life in Leaside.

The school bell rang and everyone tore out of the classroom. Keeping my head low, I headed for the girls' washroom. The school was old and the halls felt like a tomb, long and narrow with dark wooden wainscoting and ancient grey lockers. Overhead fluorescent lights, trapped in wire cages, gave off a steady angry buzz, and there were lots of red fire bells and big institutional clocks. I'd only been there a couple of weeks and the kids in the hall still stared at me. It was like being back in Sterling when Mom had to make my friends for me because I didn't know where to start.

Night Town

I pushed through the washroom door, locked the cubicle and had just sat on the toilet when a group of girls walked in, passing by the slit in the door. They were all dressed in pastel skirts: pale yellow, baby blue and pink with matching knee socks, white blouses and black penny loafers. There was a flash of red in the centre. I recognized the girl from geography class. She was popular like Betsy, only more like a movie star, and the whole school seemed to be under her spell. When she laughed, everyone laughed. When the boys walked by, they stumbled. The girl wore a short, pleated red skirt, and a tight white blouse with a button-down collar. Two red barrettes pulled the black hair out of her eyes and her teeth were whiter than clouds. I stared through the crack, being careful not to be seen or heard. The pretty girl made me nervous. She applied a layer of lipstick and smacked her lips.

"I'm telling you, she's lez be friends and go homo."

I stopped breathing and leaned forward.

"No way!" squealed the girl in pink.

"Yes way," replied the girl in red.

Astonished laughter as the girls brushed their hair, giggled and talked about how sick lezzes made them. Someone said that if a lez ever pounced on her she'd call the police. I hugged my stomach, praying that they weren't talking about me. I already suspected I might be a lez, but had no idea how anyone else could tell since I didn't even know for sure myself.

The talk in the washroom had unnerved me. I was walking quickly down the hall with my head low, opening a new pack of smokes and didn't see her until I ran into her. The pretty girl in red was standing in the middle of the hall.

"I'm sorry," I said.

"I'm Mary," she said. "Do you have a cigarette?"

I gave her one and she smiled at me.

The smokers' wall was near the exit doors, but Mary wanted to go somewhere private, so I followed her across the football field to the back fence. Fresh white lines had just been painted on the field and the grass was perfectly cut. Everything in Leaside was like that, the lawns manicured and maintained by vigilant husbands, out every night raking the leaves. Every house was identical, row upon row of two-storey brick houses with brass knockers on the front door. Isabel said that Leaside was "the ideal place for professional people to live." I hated it.

A group of football players stopped their scrimmage to watch Mary cross the field, pulling every eye in her direction. She stopped walking and placed her hand on my elbow, moving closer, like we were best friends sharing a secret.

"Where are you from?" she asked.

"A village."

"Like in a fairy tale?"

I didn't want to talk about Sterling and pulled away.

"I know they call you a bumpkin," Mary said, giving my elbow a squeeze. "And I'm going to make them stop."

Mary could do anything at school – she had ultimate power. When we reached the back fence, she leaned against it, placing the cigarette between her lips.

"Can you light the match? I'm afraid of fire."

The yellow flame licked. Mary took a long draw and a smoky O floated out of her mouth.

"How did you do that?" I asked.

"With my tongue and my lips."

She had the most beautiful mouth. I wondered what her lips felt like. "Show me."

No matter how many times I tried, only jagged puffs came out. Mary laughed, reminding me of Ginnie, although Mary was a lot more grown up.

"You're funny."

That's what Ginnie used to say.

"Hey Mare!" a boy called. He was a tall, good-looking guy with dark hair and a varsity football jacket. He waved. Mary didn't.

"I've got to go," Mary said, dropping the cigarette. The ember glowed in the dirt. "That's Tim. He's my boyfriend. And you," she pulled her fingers through the ends of her black hair. "You're cute. We should double date sometime."

I thought of Kenneth and the drive-in. "Or we could just go to a movie, you and me."

A smile. "You *are* funny."

And then she left and all the excitement was gone.

Frank's door was shut. I knocked.

"Can I come in?

"I'm studying." Frank was bent over a book at his desk. His bed was made and the room was neat. "What do you want?"

I handed him the envelope and a sheet of paper with Ginnie's address. "Can you write this address on the front?"

"Why?"

"Ginnie's mother is intercepting my letters."

"You should make some new friends."

"Don't you miss Pete?"

Frank and Pete had played together since they were little.

"Yeah, but I don't sit down in the basement and write him every day of the week."

"How do you know that?"

"Mom told me. Ginnie's mother called."

Isabel had no right talking about me behind my back.

"Everyone thinks it's strange how you act about Ginnie. They say that you're fixated."

I closed the door shut behind me and walked down the stairs. I wasn't fixated. I missed Ginnie and that was normal. Pretending that you didn't care about people or miss them, now that was weird.

Dad was stretched out on the sofa with his feet up on the coffee table, scanning the business section. He used to read the comics. I sat down beside him and put my head on his shoulder. He still smelled the same, like medicine and aftershave.

"How's the new practice?"

He grunted that it was fine.

"Betsy asked me to a dance back home. It's my birthday weekend and that would be the best present ever."

Dad dropped the paper and said we'd have to ask Isabel.

"Please, Dad. She doesn't understand. I miss my friends. I miss everything." I looked up at him. "Don't you?"

He wrapped his arm around my shoulder and rested his head on top of mine. "I do."

We sat there for a while, nice and quiet, just me and my Dad, and things almost felt normal until Isabel came out of the kitchen, wiping her hands on a tea towel. "What are you two up to?"

Dad pulled his arm away like we were doing something bad. "Maddy wants to go to a dance in Sterling."

I wanted to yank his arm back around me. No Dad. You were going to let me go. We had an understanding.

"It's time Maddy focuses on the present and not the past."

"Please…just this once," I begged.

"No," she replied firmly.

"Dad?"

He disappeared behind the newspaper wall. "You have to listen to your mother. She makes the decisions around here."

The judge had spoken. I went down to my room and slammed the door so hard the hinges shook.

The classroom was quiet. Everyone was hunched over their desks, frantically answering exam questions. I stared out the window, watching two black squirrels chase each other around a thick tree trunk. The paper in front of me was blank. I hadn't studied, I was going to fail and I didn't care. The only class I liked was biology and only because I couldn't make myself hate it. Mary's white teeth nibbled the pink rubber on the end of her pencil. She must have felt me staring because she looked up. When I couldn't stop the blush, Mary smiled and returned to her exam. A thought bubble appeared. Did Mary like me?

"Did you get the one about the Cabot Trail?" Tim asked.

The leaves bunched up around our feet as the three of us walked across the lawn in front of the high school.

"Who cares about a stupid trail?" I replied, booting through a large pile that the school janitor had just finished raking up. Tim slung his arm around Mary's shoulder. She wore it like a sweater that belonged to her. The janitor scowled as coloured leaves fluttered down around him.

We reached Tim's car, a white Triumph Spitfire that his father had bought him for his birthday, a two-seater convertible with a jump seat in the back. Mary leaned against the hood and applied a fresh layer of lipstick. Two boys in a coupe drove by and wolf whistled. Tim gave them the finger, making Mary smile. Tim's pal Ian walked over. Ian was a big blond football player who was always giving me goofy grins.

"Hi," he said.

"Hi," I fake smiled back.

Mary slipped the lipstick back into her purse and turned towards me. "Want to go out this weekend?"

Mary's mother didn't like Mary being alone with Tim, so she always dragged me along to play chaperone. At first I'd do anything to be close to Mary, but sitting in the jump seat watching the two of them neck was getting really hard, and I don't think Tim liked it very much either.

"I don't think so," I said.

"What if we went downtown?"

Isabel was sitting in the living room wing chair reading a book, little silver half-moon glasses resting on the end of her nose, while Dad stretched out on the sofa having a nap. His mouth was open ever so slightly, just enough to make a little whistle. The boys and I were on the floor watching *The Partridge Family*. David Cassidy was singing, "I think I love you, but what am I so afraid of? I'm afraid that I'm not sure of a love there is no cure for." The doorbell rang and Isabel answered. Mary stood there in a tight white dress and matching shoes. Dad snored. Mary extended her hand to Isabel.

"You must be Maddy's mother. I'm Mary Sharp and I'm very pleased to meet you."

Before I knew it Mary was sitting on the edge of a petit point chair, ankles crossed just the way parents liked, telling Isabel how well I was fitting in at school.

"Even the teachers like her."

Frank burst out laughing. He knew I never did homework.

"What's so funny, dear?"

"Nothing, Mom."

Most of the teachers didn't know what to do with me. The math teacher said he'd never had a worse student. I'd already forged Dad's signature on a failed history assignment the teacher sent home, but didn't know what would happen at Christmas when midterms came back. Mary smiled at Isabel.

"Would it be alright if Maddy came out tonight? Just the two of us going to a movie."

We'd be alone...I caught Mary's eye and the look she returned made my heart skip. Isabel tapped Dad on the shoulder. He rubbed his eyes.

"What is it?"

"Do you mind if Maddy goes out with her friend?"

Dad blinked, looking over at Mary. Slowly he swung his big feet down and sat up.

"So you're a friend of Maddy's?"

"Yes, sir."

"What's your name?"

"Mary."
"When I was a boy we had a horse called Mary."
Oh God.
"Ted!"
"Can I get you a glass of milk?" he asked.
"We should get going, if that's alright," Mary replied.
Isabel nodded, and the moment the door closed, Mary and I laughed, running across the front lawn. It didn't matter what movie we saw, as long as we shared a giant box of popcorn and sat near the back where it was the darkest. We reached the sidewalk and Mary hooked her arm in mine, pulling me down the street, but when we turned the corner, Tim's convertible was idling by the curb. And he wasn't alone. Ian was sitting in the jump seat waving.

"I thought it would be fun if we doubled," Mary said as the Spitfire raced down Yonge Street.
What could I say? I might be a lez be friends and I want to be alone with you more than anything? The overhead sky flew by, black like Mary's hair, as Ian's arm crept towards me. My knees jammed into my chin. There was no escape in the jump seat.
"Are you coming to the game next weekend?" Ian asked.
"I hate football," I replied, twisting the knife.
Ian's mouth fell. "Everybody loves football!"
"I detest it."
Mary turned and smiled, ruffling Tim's hair while I looked the other way. I'd never been this far south. Isabel said that it was where the 'undesirables' lived. Lights strobed, people clogged the sidewalks and a neon sign covered in green lights flashed the outlines of busty women into the night.
Tim pointed at a place called Le Coq d'Or. "They've got niggers in there."
I'd never seen any Negroes, other than in Sunday school books where we learned that Jesus loved all the little the children of the world. A huddle of black men in wide-legged pants and afros emerged from the side door of the club. The tallest one had a long diamond-encrusted cigarette holder. Another one pulled a pick out of his hair. Only it wasn't a pick. It was a knife.
"A little different than your village, huh?" Tim asked, honking his horn. A car up ahead responded in kind. Soon all the cars were honking like geese.

Night Town

I loved it downtown. Men with knives hidden in their hair. Women dancing on signs. I loved the squalor, the noise, the pulsating lights and the way the music rang out of cars and bars. You could get lost down here. Anything could happen. When Tim pulled into a parking lot I felt like I'd arrived.

The front of the building was covered in twinkling white lights. A lush maroon carpet rolled down the front steps past a couple of big urns with ferns. Two drunken men staggered out as Ian and I struggled out of the jump seat, following Tim and Mary across the lot. When Ian tried to take my hand I pulled it away. Climbing the stairs, my heart began to pound, mixing with the drumbeat that punched through the brick wall. A tall man in a frilly white tuxedo shirt, black pants and a red cummerbund held the glass door. He asked the people in front for ID. I didn't have any.

Tim stuffed some bills into the man's hand and the four of us were whisked through the entrance into a long hall filled with mirrors and silver railings. Thick red curtains hung at the end, hiding our ultimate destination. When we reached the curtains Mary stepped forward and, like a circus ringmaster, with a grand flourish, she pulled them back. A nearly naked girl stood on a smoky stage, all alone in the centre of a rowdy crowd of drunken men shouting, "Take it off!"

Mary turned to me. I couldn't hear what she said, but her lips mouthed, "Surprise!"

The stripper shook her shoulder-length black hair, playing with her black bra, garters and stockings. Men tossed money up on the stage, trying to get her to stick her breasts in their faces. Ian and Tim hooted for the waitress to serve our table, as Mary leaned into my ear.

"How do you like it?"

Her breath gave me goose pimples.

"It's cool," I replied.

I couldn't bear to look at the girl, but I couldn't take my eyes off her either. A part of her reminded me of the winning cattle Granddad showed at the Royal Winter Fair. The judges clapped enthusiastically for the finest in carcass class. Flashbulbs popped as red ribbons were awarded to slaughtered animals hanging from hooks. The girl dropped to her haunches, and then I felt the other part of me, the bad part of me that shouldn't be affected by things like this, get hot and excited. Ian ordered a round of something called Tom Collins. It tasted like orange juice and perfume. I flushed it down. The perfume burned but settled the banging in my chest. Ian ordered another round and howled. I chugged the next drink and tried not to look at the stage but it was impossible. The stripper held every eye in the house. With a slow dip, and a sexy spin off came the black silk.

Tim howled again. "Gimme some!"

The stripper shimmied a black boa up and over her breasts until her nipples stood like straws. So did mine. I blushed, freaking out that people could tell what I was thinking. Mary looked at me and then giggled something to Tim. Were they laughing at me? The stripper shook her boobs as one bead of sweat chased another down her slick wet chest.

I leaned towards Mary. "I'm going to go pee." Then I got up and tried not to run.

I was slapping my face with cold water as the bathroom door opened and Mary walked in. Coming up close behind me, I could see the top of her breasts in the mirror – the place where her skin met the white satin brassiere. The sight made me swallow. More slaps of cold water.

"Do you think I could be one?" she asked.

"What?"

She turned me around and dropped into a slow grind. "A stripper."

"I guess so." I fumbled, trying to tear paper towels out of the metal holder.

"I think it would be fun. The power to turn guys on like that."

Mary didn't need to strip to turn guys on. She placed her hands on my shoulders and pulled my face down, so close to hers. "Does it turn you on?"

Mary's tongue rolled slowly over her lower lip, as her hand touched my chest. Fingers splayed so wide they lightly brushed my nipples.

"I think it does," she said, her voice a raspy whisper.

Even though I knew it. I knew I shouldn't. I knew it was bad, knew it was trouble, but I couldn't stop myself. I had to do it. So I did. I kissed Mary Sharp right on the mouth. Then the door opened and a stripper walked in. Mary jumped back, shoving me so hard my tailbone struck the counter, like the sound of a bat hitting a baseball on its way to a home run.

"*What* do you think you're doing?" Mary asked, walking across the room, pushing open the door harder than she had to.

The stripper pulled a tube of lipstick out of her pocket and gave me a funny smile. Sweat dripped through her pink kimono.

"I'd watch out for that one," she said.

Tim's car was parked in front of my house. Mary hadn't said anything but I was so scared I could barely breathe. She and Tim were necking in the front and Mary kept wriggling her body into his and looking back at me, black hair slightly tousled with her lipstick all over the edges of his mouth. Ian made a move to kiss me, but I dodged him and jumped out of the car, walking up the drive. The car door closed and Mary's voice came up from behind me.

"Wait up."

I turned. Mary's silhouette stood against the round headlights. Was she going to tell Dad and Isabel?

"Do you want to go shopping?" she asked.

She knew what I wanted to do.

"I don't think so," I replied.

"I think you better."

There wasn't a choice. If Mary told anybody at school I'd be as good as dead.

A gust of wind blasted through the tunnel, signaling the arrival of the train. Brilliant light flashed up ahead as we roared into the station platform, brakes tossing up sparks, as the train squealed to a stop. Mary and I climbed the stairs at Bloor and St. George, rising from the darkness into the sharp light of day.

The street was busy with cars and students. We were in the university area. A sign directed people to Varsity Stadium. The students were mostly hippies. Boys with long hair and girls wearing beads shuffled along the sidewalks in wide-legged jeans frayed down at the ends, feet clad in sandals and clogs. A guy with a beard sat cross-legged on the ground, playing "Season of the Witch" on his guitar. Mary bought pretzels from a street vendor, and then we sat in a pair of rusted swings in a park across from a tall concrete apartment building called Rochdale. I asked her what it was.

"It was supposed to be co-ed student housing, but it turned into a free love commune." She took a bite out of her pretzel, swinging back and forth. "Do you believe in free love, Maddy? I don't think I do."

Mary wouldn't believe in free love because people would sell their soul for her. Now she had mine and no matter what the price, I had to pay. Somebody shouted. A girl was climbing out a second-storey window in Rochdale and out onto the ledge. She was totally naked, big breasts swinging in the air. A pair of hands tried to pull her in, but the girl just jumped. Mary gasped. I laughed and dropped my pretzel. It wasn't a swan dive, more like a cannonball.

The girl bounced off the roof of a little green car, screaming, "What a gas man!" and streaked back into the building.

There wasn't a mark on her. She could have died but she didn't. I kept laughing, swinging back and forth.

Mary was confused. "What's so funny?

"That was so cool."

Mary still didn't understand but I did. I belonged in this place where girls jumped out of buildings.

"Who did you say lives there?" I asked, taking the swing higher.

"Hippies," Mary replied. "And they sell drugs."

"How do you get in?"

"You walk."

"Where do you go once you get in?"

Mary just shrugged her beautiful shoulders and smiled.

"I don't know," she replied, setting her hand on my arm, stopping my swing. Her fingernail slowly, gently traced my skin.

"But I want you to find out."

The swing chains creaked.

"Are you going to come with me?"

Mary shook her head, pressing twenty dollars into my palm.

"No. You're going to buy me some acid."

Stuffing the money into my pocket, I walked over to the entrance. It was a normal apartment foyer except for a couple of dorky guys sitting behind a wooden table playing chess. There was a phone and a ledger on the table beside them. The elevators stood to the right. I pulled up the collar on my corduroy jacket, dropped my head and pushed the glass doors open. I'd figure out what to do next once I got inside.

One of the dorks asked where I was going. I kept moving towards the elevator.

"You!" he yelled this time.

I hammered my thumb into the call button, praying that the dork would vanish, but he didn't. He grabbed me by the arm, marching me over to the desk.

Night Town

"Do you live here?"
"I'm going to see a friend."
"What friend?"
"Just a guy I know."
"What apartment?"
"I think it's on the fifth floor."
"No name. No apartment. No entry. Those are the rules."

A guy with long curly hair came out of the elevator. He had big round blue plastic glasses and stopped to listen while I tried to reason with the dorks.

"I just want to see my friend. Can't you give me a break? Please?"
I tried flirting. It didn't work.
"Get out."
"Come on, man."
"Get out before we call the cops."
There's nothing worse than a dork on a power trip.

I sat down in front of the building, occasionally glancing at Mary. She was still waiting on the swing and didn't look happy. What would she do if I didn't get her acid? I lit a cigarette. The guy with the curly hair and the blue plastic glasses walked over.

"Tough break," he said.
"Yeah."
"You really know somebody in there?"
"No."
"Then why are you here?"
Mary was still watching.
"I want to buy some acid."
"That's what they're here for," the guy replied, motioning toward the dorks. "They're the Greenies. They're supposed to call the cops if anyone comes in looking for dope."

I was about to run when the guy said, "My name's Steve. Maybe I can help you out."

Steve signed me in as the Greenies sneered. I smiled back and then turned, following Steve to the elevators. There was nothing the Greenies could do. I had a name and I had an apartment number. Then the elevator doors opened to reveal a naked guy and a dog. The guy shouldn't have been naked because he had an unbelievably ugly body, greasy hair and a series of volcanic chin zits. Steve and I got in. The elevator walls were covered in graffiti that said things like "Nobody's faster than Jimmy," "pot on four" and "beer on eight."

"What does that mean?" I asked.

The naked guy scratched his penis while the dog squatted and took a poo. "You want a drink, go to eight. Pot's four and acid, mesc and MDA are on six." Steve lived on the acid floor, in 602. The elevator shuddered to a stop.

The hallway smelled better than the elevator and looked better too. There were all sorts of posters on the walls: Cream, Creedence Clearwater Revival and Led Zeppelin. Somebody had gone nuts with a can of yellow dayglo paint on one of the doors, spraying a giant peace sign. Different strains of music slid beneath the doors as we made our way down the hall to Steve's place. At first I'd been scared, but now I was excited.

Steve's room was painted deep purple, a beaded curtain covered the window and two car seats acted as chairs. He opened the bottom drawer of a desk covered in candles and incense and removed some funny looking sheets of thick white paper covered in green frogs, each one the size of a postage stamp.

"What do you want?" Steve asked.

"What have you got?"

"Froggy blotter."

What was that? I nodded like I knew.

"How many do you want?"

"How much?"

"Two bucks a hit, but if you buy more than ten you get them for a buck each."

An idea formed.

"Give me twenty."

I could give Mary ten and keep ten for myself. She'd never know the difference and for once I'd have something on Mary. Steve began cutting frogs out of the heavy paper. There were about a hundred of them with big glassy eyes and toothy grins.

"The blotter comes from Frisco. This shit is nearly pure. Straight liquid from the lab and then chemists take a dropper and squirt it on the frog. Cute, huh?"

"Yeah," I replied as Steve carefully manipulated the scissors.

While he cut out the blotters, Steve told me all about how they made the dope. Its clinical name was lysergic acid diethylamide and had its roots in native plants and mushrooms. Scientists had decided to try it on the brain to cure minor personality disorders and enhance artistic creativity. I couldn't wait to try it on mine.

Mary sat beside me in the subway car, scrunched up against me nice and tight. Her chest heaved up and down. I'd never seen her so excited. "Let's see."

"Not here."

I'd read about narcs, narcotics officers, in one of Dad's magazines. There was a whole new department devoted to catching people peddling drugs, and they dressed like hippies to blend in.

"How many did you get?" she whispered.

My heart thumped. "Ten." Mary's eyes flashed. Her tongue rolled over her red lips. The wet made them glisten. I scanned the subway car for narcs. "You want to try one?"

She squeezed my hand. "The park tonight at seven. Just you and me."

Isabel and I stood at the kitchen sink finishing the dinner dishes. I tossed the damp towel onto the counter. "Can I go out?"

"Where?"

"Mary's house. We're going to study." Sure we were, we were going to study what happened when you swallowed paper frogs.

Frank and Tedder were out on the driveway playing hockey with some of the neighbourhood boys. A little white vase painted in blue flowers rested on the windowsill. The flowers reminded me of Ginnie's eyes. Isabel touched my shoulder. Her hands were bright red from the hot water. Mom always wore gloves.

"Mary's a nice girl."

I think that's what the English teacher called an irony.

"I'm glad you're making friends," Isabel said. "Just make sure you're home by nine."

"Come on."

"Nine thirty."

"Ten?"

"Nine thirty and that's firm."

"Okay. And Isabel..."

She turned.

"You should wear dish gloves. They'll protect your skin."

It was a beautiful evening. Mary was sitting on the bench. "You're late."

I didn't apologize. "Are you ready?"

She nodded. "What do we do?"

"Open your mouth and say ahhhhh."

Her mouth opened, and like a minister giving the Host, I rested a blotter on her pretty pink tongue. The frog faded away the moment it got wet, dissolving in Mary's mouth. I handed her another blotter and put the rest in my jacket pocket.

"Now you give me mine." I opened my mouth and Mary set the paper on my tongue. Chemicals tasted so good.

We were walking down by the river when I started to feel funny. A tingling at the bottom of my spine started to walk, then dance, up the back of my neck. A deep friendly tickle made my whole body rev like a race car at the starting gate. Drops of delicious salty saliva dripped down the back of my throat, making me swallow like mad. Then the river began to hum and sing. I was made of air and Mary's hair glowed. Her irises were gone, eclipsed by big black bowling ball pupils. She laughed so hard, spinning like a top with her arms out at her sides. Light grew and pulsed and my voice sounded far away when I talked, like sound flying down a long concrete tunnel, bouncing and binging and turning into something else when it tumbled out the other end. I started to laugh and couldn't stop. Everything was so incredibly funny. Mary took my arm and we walked towards the river. The sky was still blue.

Sitting by the edge of the water, we took off our jackets and then our shoes, wanting to feel the singing water with our feet. A million years passed while I undid the laces. The eyelets and the laces mystified me. In a millisecond, in a single eyelet, I could see the past and the future, and the lace became a rope that could take me to the centre of the earth. Then I got caught up in the look and feel of the rocks. They were so beautiful. Everything in nature was perfect and for once I completely understood my place in the order of things. I looked up to the sky, past the blue and into the universe. Mary, who was afraid of fire, lit match after match, mesmerized by the flame. I blew one out before she burned her hand. Her hair blew and flew. Mary was laughing and her teeth flashed white into the twilight. I wanted to rub them and feel the porcelain. She took my hand, pulling me to my feet, and we walked into the river together. Mary disappeared beneath the surface, her hair spreading out like a Siren's. I fell on my knees as the water folded over me, baptizing me into chemical wonder. Then the twilight was gone, the sky was black and we weren't in the river anymore. We were lying on the grass with our heads together, soaking wet and cold. That's how I knew I was back on earth.

When we reached Mary's house I pulled the remaining eight hits out of my jacket and handed them to her, but she wouldn't take them.

"I want you to sell them for me," she said.

Then Mary kissed my cheek, a special Mary kiss that could promise unspeakable bliss or the possible detonation of my entire world.

The house was dark as I snuck through the side door into the basement foyer. Everyone was asleep. Good. I was nearly in my room when the hall light flicked on and Isabel's voice rolled down the stairwell.

"Maddy?" She was down the stairs in a shot. "Are you all right?"

"I'm fine."

"Your father finally got to sleep," she said, peering into my face, trying to get a look at me. Her hair was rumpled and her housecoat had been hastily tied. I kept moving. I had dried off a bit, but if she touched me or got a good look into my eyes she might figure out something was up. It was so hard not to laugh. Her face was starting to look like a donkey's.

"He can't be worrying about you."

Now her body was turning donkey too. Hello, Eeyore. I wanted to yank her tail and see if she brayed. I couldn't help it – I started to laugh, making Isabel mad.

"This isn't funny."

Yes it was. This whole scene was a joke. Me living in a sideshow in the middle of a city full of snotty kids, being blackmailed by the high school goddess and saddled with a fake mother. It was far too funny for words. While I tried to get the giggling under control Isabel wanted to know if a girl who broke the rules deserved a nice birthday party. Big deal. I didn't want to celebrate with them anyway.

"You said that you'd behave."

So she was going to throw *that* in my face. The thought made me hot.

"You promised to behave for your father."

That wasn't funny. I'd left my home, all my friends and given up Ginnie. I'd done everything I'd promised. Isabel wagged her donkey hoof in my face.

"One more time, Madeline Anne. One more time and you're grounded."

I stumbled into my room. Fully dressed I fell back on the bed, listening to the big blowhard stomp up the stairs. I was furious. How dare she bring that up? I let my little brothers call her Mom even though I wanted to beat them up every time they said it. I'd been good. I'd kept my end of the bargain and lost everything in return.

It was the weekend of the Halloween dance. The Spitfire idled at a stoplight as two hobgoblins with pointy red hats and fake beards crossed the street. Tim, wearing his grass-stained football jersey revved the engine, trying to act like a man. His hand stroked Mary's thigh, lucky boy fingers pressing into her soft skin. I hated his fingers. There hadn't been even a hint of a possible Mary kiss in over a month, but there hadn't been any threats either. I passed up a stack of bills that Mary quickly counted and tucked into her purse.

"Did you sell them all?" she asked.

"Fifty at lunch. The rest'll go before the dance."

Mary was so proud of herself, convinced that she was getting rich from blackmailing me into dealing her acid, but little did she know I was secretly ripping her off. There was a risk since nobody knew that Mary was in the business, and if we got caught I'd get the blame, but that wouldn't happen. I was smart and knew how to be careful. Tim shot his hand up Mary's skirt. She playfully slapped his hand and told him to stop it.

"You're stoned," he said.

"So what?" Mary replied.

"You're always stoned."

Mary swallowed all of her profits. She took even more acid than me. Tim's hand went up her skirt even higher. Then he suddenly stopped, as his eyes caught mine in the rearview mirror.

"What are you looking at?"

He'd caught me. "Nothing."

Mary started rubbing his neck, but Tim wouldn't back down.

"Why are you always hanging around?" he asked. "Why don't you get your own boyfriend?"

I tried not to blush. The light changed to green, but the car didn't move.

"Or is it a girl that you want?"

"Maddy's my friend and if you don't like it, you can find somebody else," Mary snapped.

The Spitfire shot into traffic and the conversation was over, but Tim was right. I was Mary's puppet. Since I'd started dealing, everyone wanted to be my friend, and even if Mary said I was a lez, all I'd have to say is she was lying and the kids would believe me, because if they didn't I'd cut off their drug supply. I had the kind of power at the school that Mom and Dad had in Sterling, and everyone needed to keep me happy. But Mary, beautiful, mean Mary Sharp held the ultimate power over me. The minute she said "Get in the car" I hopped in like there was an invisible noose around my neck. No matter how badly she treated me I always came back for more.

I was on my way out the door when Isabel called me into the dining room.

"Where's your costume?" she asked.

"Costumes are stupid."

"They most certainly aren't stupid. You need a costume for Halloween. Isn't that right Ted?"

Dad shoveled in a forkful of meatloaf and nodded. He'd put some weight back on, but still acted like a sad zombie. I wanted to ask him if everything was okay, but I never had the chance because he was never alone. Isabel was always standing guard.

"Why don't you go as a hockey player?" Frank asked, taking a bite of potatoes.

"Yeah, right." I rolled my eyes and turned to Dad. "What do you think?"

"Why don't you go as a doctor?"

"Try this on," he said, handing me a pair of green hospital scrubs.

They were too big, but after Dad got on his hands and knees and safety pinned the pants and sleeves, the clothes fit okay. We looked in the mirror together, my Dad standing behind me, his hands on my shoulders, giving me a little squeeze. Zombie or not, Dad did look better. I put my hands on top of his and held them there.

"Dad?"

"Uh huh?

"Do you still think about Mom?

He pulled his hands out from under mine, walked over to the closet and started pulling boxes out of the top cupboard.

"Dad – " I wanted him, needed him, to answer my question, but instead he handed me his old black leather bag.

"A doctor isn't a doctor without a medical bag."

Then he draped his stethoscope around my neck, stuffing the breast pocket with tongue depressors.

"Now don't you look just fine?"

"I guess so," I replied.

I sat at the picnic table at the back of the football field. Ghosts, witches, firemen, cowboys and spacemen were hiding behind trees and tall shrubs, waiting for their acid. When I'd picked it up at Rochdale Steve told me to be careful, it was the strongest he'd taken. I didn't care and took two. The lights at the back of the school were black. That meant no spying teacher eyes. I opened the medical bag, gesturing for the customers to come forward. One by one the costumed kids approached as I pressed purple pills into their palms. Half an hour later we were all inside the gym and starting to get off.

Steve was right. The acid was strong – maybe even bad trip kind of strong. The Leaside lion on the school crest signaled to me while a skuzzy band played "Windy" off-key. A girl galloped around the dance floor, gusting and blowing as hard as she could, while two witches sat on the floor staring at their hands. The math teacher was trying to make the witches stand up when a fairy began to laugh. The wind girl was swooping around, blowing on the fairy's wings. I searched the gymnasium. Mary had to be here somewhere. We could ride out the stone together. Tim was by the stage talking to some of the other jocks. They'd come dressed as murdered football players, faces painted white, clothing soaked in fake blood, with gun shots through their jerseys.

"What do you want?" Tim asked. His voice slurred. Tim wasn't stoned, he was dead drunk and really loud.

"I'm looking for Mary."

"You're always looking for Mary."

Couples stopped dancing and heads turned; the floor rolled under my feet and a crack appeared. The linoleum yawned open as the lion on the school crest snarled at me with yellow fangs. I needed Mary.

"Where is she?"

"She's in the washroom all messed up," he said, in a really pissed off mood. "And it's because of you…"

He poked me in the chest with his finger and I poked him back, right in the centre of the gunshot wound.

"Stay away," he said, pushing my shoulder this time, hard enough to make me stagger.

I just pushed him back and called him a jerk.

"Stay away from my girlfriend!" he yelled, punching me in the face as hard as he could.

This time I didn't punch him back. Instead, I ran off the dance floor, past the female guidance counselor, who tried to stop me, asking what on earth was wrong.

"Mary?" I called, walking into the girls' washroom. My voice bounced around while a million me's stared back from the mirror. Somebody was cooking hamburgers. What was wrong with my face? My eye was turning blue. I wanted to poke at the eyeball with my fingers and try to pull it out. Instead, I pushed open stall doors. "Are you in here?"

A giggle.

"Mary?" I called again, looking under the panels. I found her in the last stall, sitting on a toilet seat, dressed like a princess. Everything was pink, her crinoline, tiara, even her shoes. A cigarette smoldered between Mary's fingers, past the filter, stuck into the flesh, cooking her pink skin…her pink hamburger meat…

I ripped the cigarette out and threw it on the floor. "What are you doing?"

Another giggle and then that Mary smile. "I'm not afraid of fire anymore."

I pulled her to her feet, dragging her out of the cubicle towards a row of sinks.

"The water might sting a bit at first, but it'll help."

As I turned on the water Mary reached out and touched me eye. "You love me," she said, pushing on the bruise.

"How is your hand?" I asked.

"Why don't you kiss me?"

The water was gushing. Mary's fingers were burning. My eye was swelling.

"I know you want to," she said.

"I know I shouldn't."

"But what if I'm asking you to."

I took Mary's face in my hands, my lips touching hers, when the female guidance counselor walked in.

The guidance counselor had me pinned down on the front steps of the school.

"Do you know what you did is unnatural?" her pink gums asked. They were the same colour as Mary's dress. I didn't answer, just sat there in my doctor's scrubs, staring at my feet, trying to tune out the words "pervert" and "mentally ill." The Oldsmobile pulled up and Dad and Isabel got out of the car.

"Your daughter," the counselor said, in a disgusted tone. "Your daughter is seriously disturbed."

I looked down the road, wondering if I should run. Dad told me to get in the car. I followed him while Isabel spoke to the counselor, who wouldn't stop talking. Dad opened the back door for me to get in, and head down, slowly returned to Isabel and the counselor. They were talking so loudly it was impossible to ignore.

"Timothy told me that Maddy's always trying to touch Mary."

I shrunk down.

"Girls are frequently physical with one another," Isabel said.

"Not the way a boy kisses a girl."

Dad looked as if he'd been punched. I touched my eye.

"Keep Maddy away from Mary, or the next time – "

"It won't happen again," Isabel said. She took Dad by the arm and they walked back to the car. Isabel was driving.

The car was silent. I tried to ignore the counselor's words but they wouldn't leave. Banshees and sirens swirled around the car howling, "Pervert!" "Freak!" and "Deviant!"

Dad leaned over quietly and said something to Isabel. I pretended not to listen.

"Maybe it's just a phase," he whispered, looking to her for hope.

I heard, "Boys never come by."

Dad sighed, so long and so sadly, as Isabel took one hand off the steering wheel and reached out to stroke the back of his neck. There was no blaming Isabel anymore. She wasn't the one wrecking our family. It was me.

Dad trudged up the stairs and disappeared into their bedroom as Isabel took my coat and opened the closet door.

"You must be very confused," she said, a soft look on her face.

For a split second there was a human being standing there. A human being that understood what was going on. She didn't yell and scream and call me a freak. She could have made Dad ship me off to the nut house, but she didn't. Maybe I could talk to her about how I felt about Ginnie and Mary. Maybe she could help.

"But I can't have you upsetting your father any further," she said, walking up the stairs. "We'll talk about psychiatric treatment later." And another door slammed shut.

I didn't leave my room the next day until dinner time.

"Surprise!" Tedder yelled.

I'd forgotten about my birthday. The whole family sat around the dining room table singing "Happy Birthday". A pink cake blazed in the centre of the table and gifts were piled by my placemat.

"What did you do to your eye?" Frank asked.

It was black and blue from Tim's fist. Luckily, I didn't have to answer because the doorbell rang.

"Blow out your candles and make a wish," Isabel said, rising from her seat.

There was nothing I wanted that I could have so I just blew out the flames. The boys clapped.

"Does it feel any different being sixteen?" Frank asked.

"Not really."

A man was talking in the living room and then Isabel's voice shot up an octave. My neck bristled. She was always calm. Dad pushed back his chair. The boys followed him out into the living room with me behind.

Isabel was talking to a man a little younger than Dad with dark hair and a stocky build. He was wearing a three-piece suit and held a yellow document. There was a uniformed policeman with him.

"This is Detective Al Hanson," Isabel said, her voice shaking with fury.

"What?" Dad asked.

"We received a call from your daughter's high school. She was selling drugs there last night. We have a warrant to search the house."

The detective looked at me. "Are you Madeline Anne Barnes?" he asked, crossing the room towards me. I backed up into the piano.

"She is," Isabel replied.

"Show me your room."

"It's this way," Isabel said.

Isabel opened the door to the basement. The policeman was tearing my room apart while Detective Hanson interrogated me.

"Where did you buy the LSD?"

"I didn't."

"Two teenagers got sick. Their parents say that they bought it from you."

"They're wrong."

"You're lying."

All the drugs I'd sold or taken flipped through my mind like the cards in a rapidly shuffling deck. I'd sold all the microdots and was positive everything else was gone too. But what if I'd forgotten something? Isabel's face got redder and redder as the police flipped the mattress, dumping desk and dresser drawers all over the floor, tearing through the closet, searching my pockets, looking through books and even checking the vents. They found no acid – only bottle after empty bottle of Dad's prescription drugs.

"Where did you get these?" the detective asked.

"From my father's dispensary."

"Does he know you have them?"

"No," Dad replied.

Dad was standing in the doorway. My brothers stood behind him. Tedder's face said he didn't understand but Frank did. He wouldn't even look at me. The detective asked Dad if he knew some of the drugs were restricted substances. I thought Isabel was going to implode.

"Yes, sir," Dad replied.

"You could lose your license."

"Please!" I cried. "He didn't know. This is my fault. I was the one taking them. They were just for me."

"What about the LSD?"

"I don't know anything about that."

The detective stared at me and I stared back, the two of us, in the middle of the car accident that used to be my room, playing a game of chicken. I wouldn't let him hurt my Dad, but I wouldn't confess to the acid either. I'd just turned sixteen and didn't want to go to jail.

"We'll see," the detective said. He paused. "That's all for now." There was nothing more he could do and he knew it.

"I'll show you out," Dad said, shooing the boys out of the room and up the stairs. The uniformed officer followed. Isabel didn't. She picked up an empty bottle.

"That's it."

"What are you talking about?"

But I knew what she meant. Our deal. The deal I'd smashed into a million pieces.

"It's you or me," she said.

I had to take one last stand. "Then let him decide."

Isabel softly set the bottle on the bureau. "Would you ask him to do that?" Then she left, shutting the door behind her.

Of course not. Dad could never make that decision and I couldn't ask him to. He was as happy as he was going to be with Isabel. So were Frank and Tedder. It was up to me. I was the one who had to go.

CHAPTER FIVE

The sunlight stung my good eye. The black one was nearly swollen shut. I stood at the corner of Yonge and Dundas holding Mom's white suitcase, stuffed with whatever I could grab before I ran away. A stubby man wearing an old fashioned derby hat and a sandwich board advertised for a place called Starvin' Marvin's. Huge posters of topless girls with big boobs were plastered on the walls and windows behind him. Some of the girls proudly cupped their breasts in their hands, while another one licked her own nipple. She must have had a long tongue to do that. The man held a megaphone.

"Come on in," the man barked, bowing deeply as I passed by. "Don't be shy. We've got more girls than you've got dreams!"

Two burly guys carted cases of beer out of an idling truck and into Le Coq d'Or. As the doors opened music slipped out, soul music that sounded the way the street felt: smooth and exciting – the way my future was going to be. Granddad started with nothing and made his own fortune. He didn't cry, all alone out on the prairies wrangling wild cattle. He slept under the stars with yipping coyotes in the hills, built up his herd and then took the cattle to market. That's what I'd do too.

I'd spent all my money at Steve's and my pockets were stuffed with little purple pills. Now I needed to find a new customer base and that wouldn't be hard. The sidewalks were full of hippies and heads. I didn't need anybody taking care of me. I was all grown up.

The scent of patchouli oil drew me up a wide set of red brick steps into a warren of tiny market stalls selling brightly coloured beads, tie-dye skirts and boxes of incense that smelled of travel. Young people panhandled, while others smoked cigarettes and watched the world go by. Strains of sitars mixed with incense and calls of "Girls! Girls! Girls!"

A pretty girl with an oval face and a halo of short white hair stood beside an old man who had a silver brush cut and squatted on his heels. The girl panhandled while the man rolled a homemade cigarette.

"Looky looky, here comes Cookie!"

Was he talking to me? I didn't know what to do so I kept walking.

"Wine's fine but liquor's quicker."

I turned. The man's fingers trembled as tobacco flakes fell.

"And you know what gin does?" he asked. He was missing a few front teeth.

"What?"

"Gin makes you sin."

I smiled as the old man sucked through the hole where his teeth used to be. "I ain't seen you around here before," he said, looking at my suitcase and then at my eye.

"I'm new," I replied, looking at the girl with the white hair, quickly brushing my bangs over the bruise.

"I'm Gabe and that's Lily," he said, jabbing a yellowed thumb at the girl. "Isn't she as pretty as a flower?"

She was. Tall and thin, the white hair ringed her face like a blossom.

"We're together."

Was Gabe her father? He couldn't be her boyfriend because Lily didn't look much older than me. Not wanting to be rude, I didn't ask. Lily stopped a mother and a little girl for some change. The lady rooted in her purse, dropping a coin in Lily's hand. Lily turned to me and said hi. I'd never seen white eyelashes before.

"I'm Maddy."

"Where you from?" Gabe asked.

"Out of town." I didn't want to talk about the past.

"Us too," Lily said, sitting down.

I hung out with them, enjoying the warm sun on my face and the sweet smell of incense mixing with gas, when two older boys arrived, asking Lily if she wanted to smoke a joint. Lily said no, but the boys didn't leave. One had a big nose. His friend wore a smiley face tee-shirt and had a squeaky high-pitched laugh. Smiley Face told Lily that a joint might loosen her up.

Gabe spat on the sidewalk. "The lady doesn't want any."

"Why don't you get lost?" asked Smiley Face.

Lily's ears went pink as she shot to her feet. "Why don't you fuck off?"

It was the first time I'd ever heard a girl say fuck off. Not even Mary said that and Mary said everything. The boys still didn't move so Lily and Gabe left. Smiley Face pulled a lumpy looking joint out of his coat pocket and waved it at me.

"Smoke?" he asked.

"Sure," I replied. I'd only smoked pot a couple of times with Mary and Tim and it always made me cough.

Using Mom's suitcase like a coffee table, the three of us passed the joint around. The weed was so strong I couldn't feel my toes. Eventually the talk shifted to getting higher. The guy with the big nose wanted to go buy acid.

"How many do you want?" I asked.

"You carrying?"

I nodded, ready to dicker the way Granddad did. "What'll you pay?"

"Two bucks a hit," Smiley Face said.

"Make it three and I can help you out."

"Sure."

My hand was already in my pocket when Smiley Face said we should take it into the alley. He was right. It was stupid to deal right out in the open. I was high and not thinking straight. The three of us slipped into the alley behind Sam the Record Man, stepping around flattened cardboard boxes and piles of stinking garbage bags. While I set the suitcase down I noticed black scuffs on the white leather and wondered if they'd ever come off. A rainbow danced on top of an oil puddle.

"How many you want?" I asked.

"We'll take them all."

"Cool," I replied, pulling the bag of microdots out of my pocket. "That'll be $120."

"I don't think so," the big nosed one said, snatching the acid while I grabbed his arm and started to yell.

Smiley Face had the suitcase and was laughing his high-pitched giggle.

"Give me my acid!" I screamed, kicking Big Nose in the shinbone so hard he yelped. "Give it back!"

He punched me in the stomach, fist blowing out all the air, but I wouldn't let go of his arm. Wouldn't let go until a white box whacked me across the head and I fell down, losing my grip. It was Mom's suitcase.

I was back at Steve's door, covered in alley grease.

"What happened?" Steve asked as I walked in and sat down.

"I got ripped off."

"All of it?"

I nodded, rubbing the rising goose egg on my head. It was sore.

"Geez, Maddy. You never keep your whole stash in one place. If you have to travel with it, you hide it on different spots on your body."

I didn't know that, but it was a mistake I'd never make again. "I need you to give me ten hits. I'll pay you later."

Steve frowned. "I don't front."

"Just once?"

"No."

This was bad. I couldn't pay rent if I didn't have money for dope. My stomach growled.

"Can I crash here?"

Steve would help me out. We were friends.

"The old lady doesn't allow it."

Since when did Steve have an old lady?

"I'll sleep on the floor. I don't even need a blanket."

There was a knock at the door.

"What if I clean the place?"

"Sorry," Steve said, getting up.

It was dark in Allen Gardens and the park didn't feel safe, but I was too tired to walk any further. Early winter wind blew leaves across the grass. Shivering, I did up the top button of my shirt, stamping my feet. Smiley Face got my coat when he stole Mom's suitcase. Around midnight I'd walked into a phone booth, nearly calling home, but I stopped myself because Dad would be forced to come and get me, and then Isabel would leave and he would kill himself and it would all be my fault. A golden light glowed in the centre of the park. Maybe it was safe and warm in there.

Pools of light fell from old lampposts that ran along a ropey pathway. I hurried down the path towards the glow, past wrought iron benches, rushing from lamppost to lamppost, terrified of the rattles and scary hisses that came out of the dark. There was a rustle from a bush to the left and then a girl about my age appeared beneath a tree. Leaves and grass were stuck to the back of her hair and her skirt was hitched up around her hips.

"What are you staring at?" she asked, yanking the skirt down.

"Nothing."

The girl pulled a twenty dollar bill out of her brassiere and shoved it into her purse. "I never saw you here before."

"I'm new." It was so good to see another person. Maybe she'd like to sit and visit.

But the girl simply said, "Watch out for the cops," and disappeared into the night.

The beginnings of a dome began to appear in the glow. I ran down the path like Dorothy travelling through the witch's forest in *The Wizard of Oz*.

The glow came from an enormous glass observatory that rested in the centre of the park. Fingers of moonlight broke through a roof of palm fronds, stroking a thick grove of exotic plants before they landed on the ground, transforming the dark green moss into a shimmering carpet. The garden felt warm, alive and breathing, a safe place to spend the night.

But the door was locked. Ducking between a hedge and the glass, I snuck around the side, looking for another way in. Then a sudden rustle and the snapping of a twig, followed by a series of crackles, coming up, racing up fast behind me. I tried to run, but a hand came down, a strong hand clamping onto my shoulder, spinning me around into a beam of blinding light.

"What do you think you're doing?" Squinting, I dodged the glare to see a uniformed policeman. "I asked you a question. What are you doing out here?"

"Nothing."

"Show me some ID."

It was in Mom's suitcase.

"I don't have any."

The policeman grabbed my arm and marched me through the park, over to a cruiser. He opened the front door and shoved me inside. A truncheon rested on the vinyl seat. He got in the driver's seat and picked up his radio.

"What's your name?"

I wanted to lie, but what would I say?

"Madeline Anne Barnes."

He looked me over. "What happened to your face?"

"I walked into a door."

"Did somebody do that to you?"

Tim.

"No, sir."

"Address."

"I don't have one."

"Date of birth?"

I gave it to him.

"Just sixteen, eh?"

"Yes, sir."

"And you figure you're big enough now to be out on your own?"

"Yes, sir."

"We'll see about that."

While we waited for the background check the policeman lectured me all about the dangers waiting for young girls out on the streets at three in the morning. Did I have any idea of what went on in the park after dark? I thought of that girl with the grass in her hair. So that's what she was doing. I'd never do that. The radio crackled to life. A missing person's report had been lodged for me that morning. That meant Dad cared.

"Your mother reported you as a runaway."

Dad didn't even call.

"Let me take you home."

"No."

If I went back home my stepmother would leave and my father would kill himself.

"Don't you think you should at least call them?"

He could take me to prison for vagrancy if he wanted, but I wouldn't put my Dad in that spot, the place where he'd have to pick. And besides, it hurt less not knowing than to find out for sure that he'd choose her over me.

We sat in silence until the frustrated policeman said, "Okay, get going, and don't let me find you in here again."

There was nothing else to do, so I sat on The Steps watching the city wake up. Before dawn everything was quiet except the distant hum of street sweepers and the odd lonely cab searching for a fare. Then the delivery trucks rumbled by, loaded with fresh produce, and office workers began to stream out of the subway, heading for Bay Street's financial towers, and then around ten, the retail shops opened for business. Nobody noticed me, a sixteen-year-old girl in rumpled clothing and a black eye, tucked into the corner of a doorway.

Finally my friends arrived.

Gabe whistled as Lily loped along beside him. She was nearly a foot taller, but still looked like an innocent little kid. When they saw me, they came over and plopped down on either side. Lily asked me where my suitcase was. Gabe patted me on the thigh and then gently pulled my face towards his.

"Did you get rolled?"

He sounded so kind that I started to cry.

"Everything."

"Oh, kiddo," Gabe said.

"Those guys with the weed."

"Fuck me," Lily said.

"No, fuck them," I replied and then started to laugh through the tears. Laughing because I'd said fuck out loud for the first time in my life and because I wasn't alone anymore.

"Are you hungry?" Lily asked.

I nodded.

"We'll get you some breakfast and then you're going to learn how to panhandle."

Breakfast consisted of a loaf of bread and a package of bologna. It cost under a dollar and it fed the three of us. I would have liked some mustard, but there was no money for condiments. Lily wiped her hands on her jeans and stood up, announcing that it was time for class.

"I'm a rich lady," Lily said, pretend sashaying down the sidewalk.

Gabe and I laughed.

"Don't laugh. One day I'm gonna be rich. You just wait and see." Lily kept walking towards me. "So what do you do?"

I approached her with my hand out, eyes cast down. "Excuse me, ma'am, can you spare any change?"

"You're acting too desperate."

"I'm begging for money, of course I'm desperate." I didn't like begging and was worried that I'd see someone I knew.

"When are we getting a bottle?" Gabe asked.

"We're not getting a bottle. Maddy, try it again."

"Do you have any spare change?" I asked.

"Get a job," she said.

"Even a penny would help."

Lily approved. "That's smart."

"That way they don't think I'm greedy."

"Okay, try it on somebody real."

I decided to go for guilt. Lily said nobody wanted to help desperate people, but I'd learned from my Dad that most people wanted to do the right thing. All you had to do was give them the proper incentive, and what was more guilt inducing than the importance of saving a teenaged girl in trouble? An older woman with several shopping bags approached.

"Excuse me," I said.

She walked on by.

"Please," I said, with a little cry. "I got mugged and I don't have any money for the subway."

She paused. "Why don't you call your parents?"

"They're not home."

"Where do you live?"

"Leaside."

She stopped and looked at me.

"Maybe you can give me a ride?" I asked.

"I'm not going that way."

She opened her purse and handed me a quarter.

"Here you go. Now make sure you get right on the train and don't you spend this on anything else. This is hard-earned money."

"Oh no, ma'am." I oozed. "You're so kind. I'll be sure to tell my parents that there are still decent people in the world."

The woman left all puffed up and proud while Lily and Gabe split a gut.

"You're good," Lily said.

Guilt worked, but there was something low about using people and lying. Granddad always said there was nothing more despicable than a liar or a thief, and Mom claimed that misrepresenting yourself was the biggest sin of all. Dealing dope had dignity – begging had none. I needed to get enough money together to start a new stash. After a couple of days panhandling I planned to be back at Steve's.

We finished at about eight, combined our money and headed for the hotel. I couldn't believe it. There'd be nothing left after we paid for a room.

"How are we ever going to get ahead?"

"Some days are better than others," Lily replied.

Hungry and exhausted, I trailed along behind them. My clothes were dirty and I needed a bath.

"Have we got enough for a bottle?" Gabe asked. "I'm getting the shakes."

Lily scratched her ear. "The doctor said you need a break."

"Please, Lily," Gabe begged.

"Lily, please," I added. I could use something myself.

She gave Gabe a kiss on the cheek. "Maybe tomorrow."

I followed Lily and Gabe past abandoned storefronts, pawnshops and shoe shines. Lingerie dangled from the windowsills of crumbling buildings. Alkies were either propped up against brick walls, happily chattering away to one another, or flopped over on the sidewalk passed out cold. Gabe said hello to a couple of guys he knew and asked them if they had any liquor, but they were all empty.

We arrived in front of the hotel. The Warwick, a five-star jewel when big bands used to play, had turned into a skid row flophouse. A poster outside boasted aging burlesque dancers with saggy boobs that reminded me of inflatable dinghies with the air let out. Lily told us to go around back while she got a single room for one. Apparently it was cheaper than paying for three. We hid out in an alley until Lily's white head poked through a third-storey window, waving us up.

Gabe and I snuck up the metal fire escape and climbed in through the window. The ripped drapes had once been expensive brocade and the chenille bedspread had luxurious tassels, but the green was fading away and most of the tassels were gone. Wind blew through a transom where the glass was smashed, and the bed had a deep sway. Gabe flicked on the TV. There was an old western playing. The cavalry sounded the charge. Gabe was still negotiating for a bottle when I fell fast asleep on the floor.

It was the banging that woke me up. "Maid!"

"I'll be out in a minute," Lily called.

Gabe was in the bathroom taking a shower.

"Check out!" the maid called again.

"Give me five minutes," Lily replied, motioning for me to be quiet.

"If you're not, I'll call the manager. I got cleaning to do."

Lily peered through the peephole as Gabe tiptoed out of the bathroom with a towel wrapped around his skinny waist. Soft patches of white hair curled over a pale blue tattoo of a warship that sailed across his chest. Gabe was in the Navy?

There was no time to shower. The maid banged on the door again and while Lily yelled back, Gabe and I crept out the window and down the fire escape.

Night Town

The three of us met up at John's Open Kitchen, a short-order eatery that was once canary yellow with green linoleum floors, but now the walls were caked in grease and the floors were scratched and dirty. The short-order cook was a friend of Gabe's from the old days and he fed us for free.

"He's my buddy," Gabe said, as the cook slapped down plates of French toast. "We were in the merchant marines together."

That made sense. Gabe looked way more like the sailor on the cigarette pack than a Navy man. A gang of skinny kids came in, falling into one of the booths. They were chain smoking and talking loud and fast, yelling for coffee. Lily frowned, saying the diner was losing its class if it was letting speeders in. Speed was on my list of drugs to try, but since Lily didn't approve, I kept my mouth shut and took a bite of toast. It was delicious. I was so hungry I could have eaten all three helpings, but it wouldn't be polite to ask for more. Lily thought that taking drugs was the stupidest thing in the world and, giving Gabe a serious look, went on to say that it was bad enough people drank liquor. He kissed Lily's cheek and asked her for a bottle.

"We're saving for an apartment," she replied.

I had to ask. "Are you guys related?"

Gabe smiled. I'd never seen such yellow teeth. If I didn't brush my teeth soon, they were going to look like his.

"Lily's my angel," he said, softly rubbing her white fuzz.

"I'm not an angel," Lily replied with a sweet smile, getting up to leave for the washroom.

Lily was wrong. Her white halo of hair glowed, and whenever I felt scared she magically made me feel safe. Gabe watched Lily cross the diner with the besotted love of a father.

"She's everything I got."

After thanking the cook for the meal, I went into the washroom to clean up. My hair was matted and the black eye was even worse. Using my fingers I combed through the knots, holding a cold compress of wet paper towels to my eye to reduce the swelling. My breath was sour and my clothes were dirty. I had to find a way to wash them or buy something new. Gabe and Lily went back to The Steps while I decided to try the museum.

A steady stream of yellow school buses transported children in from all over the province. Bright banners blew from the top of flag posts as lines of little kids followed teachers into the museum. I wandered up and down the sidewalk, on the lookout for anyone who would listen to a sob story.

"My eye hurts. I need money to get to the hospital."

"Pardon me, ma'am. I've gotten separated from my school trip and need a nickel to call home."

Sitting on the museum's steps crying worked the best of all.

"What's wrong, dear?"

"The bus left without me. I don't know how I'm going to get home!" I wailed.

"Where's home?"

"Oshawa."

"Let me give you a dollar. That should help, now shouldn't it?"

After three hours I had four dollars, but once I bought some cotton candy and two Eskimo bars from the street vendor who sold balloons on sticks, more than half of the money was gone. My stomach felt nauseous and Lily was going to kill me. Another yellow school bus pulled up to the curb, its doors yawning as teenagers spilled out. Most of them looked bored, like they'd been captured alive and dragged onto the bus against their wills.

Pitching the cotton cone in the trash can, I started walking up to Bloor Street when Dad's Oldsmobile pulled up onto the sidewalk and he jumped out.

"Maddy!"

I thought of the police, Dad's pill bottles, him losing his licence, the counselor shouting "pervert" and now me dirty and begging on the street. I ran.

Dad caught me by the statue of a lion, holding me in his arms. He was still faster. "I've been looking for you everywhere. Are you all right?"

So my Dad *had* looked for me. I tried not to cry, but then I saw the look in his eyes, the dark, lost look he'd had after Mom died. He shook it off but how long would it last? He would try again – he would kill himself if Isabel wasn't there for him, and it would be my fault. Again. I pulled out of his arms and backed away.

"I'm not coming home."

His hands fell to his sides. "Where are you staying?"

"With friends."

"Give me the address so I know where you are."

"It's nothing permanent."

He knew what that meant – transient.

"Let me get you a room."

I started to say no, but he rode right over me. "Let me get you a room. Then we'll get you some clean clothes and take things from there."

I wanted to hug him, but I just said, "Okay."

We drove around the Annex looking at different rooming houses while I nervously leafed through medical journals that had been tossed on the floor. Some of the houses were for university students and wouldn't take anyone who was "between things." Eventually Dad settled on an establishment for young ladies located above a dentist's office. It was an old Victorian with grey shingles and sweeping turrets. I wanted one of the turret rooms because they had round windows and reminded me of Rapunzel locked away in the tower, but they were already taken. My room consisted of a single bed, a chest of drawers, a bedside table with a poodle lamp and a poster of the Eiffel Tower tacked to the wall. The poodle had a pink skirt and matching shade. I put the new clothes Dad had bought me on the bed along with more medical journals.

The kitchen was communal and everyone shared the television. A chubby girl with a scowly face hogged the sofa. There were five boarders all together. The dentist's assistant explained the rules of the house.

"Rent's every Monday. Don't eat anyone else's food." She tried not to look at my dirty clothes. "There's a washer and drier down in the basement, a payphone in the hall and whoever's first at the TV gets their choice."

The chubby girl looked like she lived on the sofa.

"Curfew?" Dad asked.

"Eleven o'clock and we lock the door."

I couldn't complain. It was better than sleeping in a park with monsters.

Dad and I stood in front of the open refrigerator, stocking my shelf.

He glanced over at my face. "How's the eye?"

"It's okay." I didn't want to talk about it and he didn't press.

Dad handed me a carton of eggs. We'd gone out shopping for food and come back with eggs, bacon, bread, chocolate ice cream and salt and vinegar chips.

"Are you sure this is going to be enough?" he asked, glancing into the empty brown paper bag.

I nodded. It was so nice to have him here with me. He looked different, as if he was clearer or slightly more defined. A white handkerchief peeked out of his breast pocket.

"Is that a new suit?"

He nodded. "Do you like it?"

"Spiffy."

"Isabel picked it out."

I slammed the eggs into the keeper.

"Don't break them."

I didn't want to talk about Isabel. "When will I see you again?" I asked. "For rent and stuff."

"If you need money call me at the office."

That meant he didn't want me calling at home. He just wanted me gone.

"Why don't you leave me some just in case?"

Dad frowned. "I'll need to check in and see how you're doing."

"What if you're too busy?"

His hands started to shake as he looked around the kitchen. "I don't know if this is a good idea."

It's not like I could go home. Isabel wouldn't allow it. "What if you forget?"

"Maddy...I wouldn't forget."

His face looked so hurt it made me feel sick. "I might be out looking for a job when you come by. If you leave me money I can take care of it myself."

Silence. I could feel him weighing out what would happen if he brought me home. And then I couldn't help it. "I could always call the house."

Dad's face went fast into fear as he pulled out his wallet and handed me forty dollars. "Make sure you keep it somewhere safe."

I shoved the cash into my pocket. Forty dollars. That's how much I was worth.

We walked into the foyer. *The Mighty Hercules* cartoon was playing on the television in the living room. A centaur was running round yelling, "Daedalus has got Helena! Daedalus has got Helena!"

Dad looked down the stairs. "Do you want to see me out?"

I couldn't bear to say goodbye. "I think I'll stay here. I want to get my room set up."

He grasped the banister and I saw the fear wasn't alone. The sad darkness was with it. I put my hand over his, squeezing it. "It's okay, Dad."

Then he started tearing up. Crying was bad. If he cried he might get sick again, and I had to make him feel better, make him see that he was a good Dad and I was the bad one. No wonder he didn't want me calling him at home. He didn't want me infecting the boys.

I pulled the handkerchief out of his breast pocket and reached out, wiping the tears away. "This is just what I needed to get me back on my feet."

The handkerchief had been freshly ironed.

He blinked through the tears. "Isabel thinks counseling might be a good idea. Might help you sort things out."

Isabel wanted to put me in a mental ward. That was their plan. They wanted to lock me up. I stuck the handkerchief back in his pocket.

"By the next time we talk I bet I've got a job."

"Maybe you could think about school?"

"Maybe...Well I guess I better get my bed ready and stuff."

"I guess so."

We didn't hug, just stood there for an awkward moment.

"If anything urgent comes up, you call the office. I'll be right down."

And then he was gone.

The chubby girl didn't leave the sofa all week. Maybe it was better being in the park or sleeping on the stinky broadloom in the Warwick than lying all alone in my room staring at the ceiling. I'd tried to talk to the other girls in the kitchen, but they were bank tellers or secretaries and we had nothing in common. I didn't belong here, I didn't belong anywhere. There was no point looking for a job because I didn't even have Grade Ten. If Dad's medical journals were right I had a severe mental disorder and they'd lock me up and throw away the key. That was me – a throwaway. Granddad always examined newborn animals, claiming that you "kept the best and drowned the rest." It wasn't mean. It was just practical. You couldn't have deformed animals on a farm because they'd pollute the bloodlines, and soon you'd have two-headed cows and three-legged cats and that was no good at all. I thought of

Hercules's centaur. Everyone loved him. But that was a wonderland. I wondered what Granddad would do with me and started to cry. Here I was, all alone, dumped in a rooming house because nobody wanted me.

The next day I was back at The Steps.
"Look who's here!" Gabe cried. "We got a bottle last night. You missed it and I woulda shared with you Maddy, I really would. Lily's no fun. She don't drink."

I gave him a big hug. He smelled sweet, like whisky and unfiltered cigarettes. Lily pocketed a dollar bill from a businessman and ran happily back to The Steps. She didn't make me feel like Ginnie or Mary, but whenever I saw Lily and Gabe it felt like home.

"What happened to you?" she asked.
"This and that."
Lily lit a cigarette. She never pushed for information.
"Rotten day," she said, counting the money. "We might need to sleep outside."
Gabe negotiated with Lily. "If we got a bottle we'd be warm."
"No bottle."
"You gotta think of my nerves."
I pulled two dollars out of my pocket and gave it to Gabe. It was enough for cheap sherry.

Gabe and Lily waited downstairs in the foyer. Other than the chubby girl on the sofa, the coast was clear. We'd gone through half the bottle in the park, but it started getting cold and since I didn't want to be alone, I invited them back to my place.

"Whaddya doing?" the chubby girl asked, when I started closing the door to the TV room.
"I can't sleep with the noise."
Gabe hiccupped.
The girl grunted, but still didn't get up.
Lily's white head peered up from below and I signaled for them to tiptoe. Gabe missed a step, but Lily grabbed him before he fell down the stairs.
"What's that?" the chubby girl called.
"Just dropped a shoe."
"Get in here," I whispered, pulling Gabe and Lily into my room. "You've got to be quiet."
"Aye Aye!"

I giggled while Lily examined the poodle lamp.

"That's nice."

I think she meant it.

"I like stuff from foreign places."

"I been to France," Gabe said, looking at the poster of the Eiffel Tower.

Mom never made it there but Gabe had. Lily lay down on the floor. I threw her a blanket and gave her my pillow. She curled up and closed her eyes. Didn't they ever brush their teeth or wash their faces before they went to bed? Gabe pulled out the bottle, took a slug and passed it to me. The taste made me gag. We talked and drank for a while.

"What's it like?" I asked.

Gabe took another chug. "What?"

"France."

"They're a bunch of midgets who drink all day."

"Did you see the Eiffel Tower?"

He nodded. "It looked like something on top of a cake. And the people eat giant white asparagus and fancy bacon."

"What about the Louvre?" Mom had always wanted to go there and see the art.

"Ain't never heard of that."

"Where else did you go?"

"Wharf mostly or looking for women."

"How old were you?"

"Long time ago."

"Before Lily?"

Gabe nodded his head, leaning down to gently stroke her hair. "I was young then."

Lily opened her mouth and snorted. We both laughed out loud.

"Sleeps like a baby. Always did."

"How long you been together?"

"I forget."

There was sharp rap at the door.

"Madeline?"

The dental assistant. She wasn't supposed to come upstairs.

"Yes," I answered, trying to sound sleepy.

Lily snorted.

"Do you have guests?"

"No."

Thank God the door was locked.
"I heard voices."
"Must be the TV."
"The television is off. Open your door."
"No."
"Open it."
"Get under the bed," I whispered to Gabe, but it was too late. The assistant opened the door with her passkey and found Gabe sitting on my bed, clutching the bottle of sherry with Lily fast asleep on the floor. She kicked Lily and Gabe out and gave me a warning. If I ever had guests past curfew again I'd be asked to leave.

Well, I didn't want to stay. I took Dad's money, bought another stash of acid and started my business again. Only this time I wasn't going to get ripped off. Unless I knew the customer personally, I only sold one hit a time. Lily kept the money and Gabe held the stash while the customer and I slipped into the alley to complete the deal. If I didn't come out in five minutes, Gabe would arrive and start jabbing the air.

"You pay up or I'll beat the crap out of you!" he'd scream.

But it wasn't the threats of Gabe's punches that scared anyone – it was the sight of this ghostly old man who screeched like a hellhound. One time a girl decided she wasn't going to pay, but when Gabe arrived in the alley and started to howl she dropped her wallet and ran for her life.

The three of us were sitting on The Steps having our usual lunch. I dug into our loaf of bread, pulled out a couple of slices and slapped bologna in between.

"I bought some hash. It's laced with opium."

Gabe got up and did a little jig. "You hear that Lily? Hear that?"

Lily handed him a sandwich. "You're not taking that. Maddy, what are you doing offering him stuff like that? You know he's sick."

Gabe scowled and sat while I took a bite of my sandwich. Since I'd gone back to Steve's I'd dropped mescaline, eaten magic mushrooms, snorted cocaine, and when the opium came in Steve said I could try that too. Why couldn't Gabe and I try it? What was so great about reality? Why shouldn't we escape it if we had the chance? Reality didn't make any sense when there were better, happier places to be. One night I took acid before going to sleep just so I could wake up stoned.

"You're going to get caught," Lily said.

I ignored her.

"And then you're going to go to jail."

"I'm not going to get caught. I'm too smart."

"You're so stupid dealing dope."

Gabe got up and nervously skittered away.

"At least I'm not a beggar."

That made Lily so mad her ears went pink. "No, you're a mess! Stoned every day of the week."

"Who's paying for our room?" I asked, getting angry too. Since I'd been dealing we had a weekly rate with two big beds near the ice machine. The Warwick manager even called me by name.

"Then we'll go," Lily replied, ramming the sandwiches back into the bread bag and standing up.

"No!" I cried, seizing her hand. They were the only family I had left. "I'm really sorry. Please don't go. Please."

"I'm just doing the best I can for me and Gabe," she said, and then she sat down, handing back the sandwich bag. "Want another one?"

"Thank you." I replied, so relieved they didn't leave. We didn't talk, just silently chewed. My breath came out in icy puffs. Winter was nearly here. Lily shivered.

"We're going to need warm coats soon," I said.

"I can buy them."

I gave Lily a gentle shove. "I never said you couldn't."

For a girl who begged, Lily had a lot of pride. We watched our breath some more and then she sighed.

"You're right. Begging's horrible. I just don't know what else to do."

A man in an expensive wool overcoat was approaching. Lily applied some orangey lipstick and fixed her white hair. Lately she'd started applying makeup, trying to look older.

"What did you do before?" I asked.

"We had a place but then we lost it."

"Me too."

A couple of times I almost called Dad at the office to tell him that I'd moved out of the rooming house, but I couldn't make myself pick up the payphone. It was easier to get high and pretend he never existed.

The man in the overcoat had nearly reached us. Lily rose as one of my regular customers, a high school student, arrived. He wanted five hits of acid for a dance the coming weekend.

Coloured pills rested on my palms like planets strung across the universe.

"So I've got blotter, sunshine and microdot. They're all two bucks a hit."

A tiny clear square sat in the centre. "This is windowpane. It's four dollars."

"Is it worth it?" the guy asked, practically salivating.

"It's the strongest I've ever sold."

He started handing me the money.

"Madeline!"

Dad was in the entrance to the alley. My customer took off, but Dad didn't. He just stood there staring at my hands, my hands stuffed with drugs and money. I shoved them into my pockets, but it was too late, he'd seen everything.

I'd never seen my Dad that mad. Not even on the roof at the school. This was different and way worse. He walked towards me. "Did you take my money to buy drugs?"

I shook my head.

"Don't lie." His voice shook with fury. "You're not making clear decisions. I'm taking you to the General for an assessment. Aunt Anne knows a doctor."

A psychiatrist, that's what he meant. A psychiatrist for the "lez be friends." He was going to lock me up. He tried to take my arm, but I backed up.

"Get away from me."

"Just somebody to help you sort this through…"

"Through what?" I was going to make him say it. "Through what?"

His voice dropped. "The homosexuality." Then he dove for my arm.

I shoved him and ran past Gabe, who'd just arrived in the alleyway and started to scream. Dad was screaming too, his yells mixing with Gabe's as he called for me to stop. I didn't. He was close behind, keeping up. I ran against the red light at Yonge and Dundas. Right into the traffic, thrown up onto the hood of a blue car that screeched to a stop so short that I got tossed right back down onto the asphalt. Something hurt but I just leapt up and kept going, running like the devil was chasing me. But when I turned around it wasn't the devil. It was my Dad, standing in the centre of the street, his hands high in the air. And then, like giant wings collapsing, his arms fell. He stopped, and I knew right then that he would never run after me again. He was finished. I turned and kept on running. Running from the fact that he hated me and running from the fact that I hated him too.

CHAPTER SIX

"Whoa!" the huge man yelled as I ran into him, nearly knocking us both to the ground. "Where's the fire?"

The man was older than me, at least ten years, and wore a white shirt, wide striped tie, dress pants and carried a maroon briefcase with brass hasps.

"Sorry," I said, panting. I couldn't catch my breath.

"Sit down."

He guided me to a stoop. I was shaking. He sat down beside me and put his arm around my shoulder. "Put your head between your legs."

"I'm okay."

I wasn't. I felt sick and dizzy. Dad could be after me with the police or men with straitjackets from the mental hospital.

"You're hyperventilating. Put your head between your legs."

He grabbed me by the back of the hair, gently pushing my head down.

"Now just breathe. Breathe," the man repeated. "Concentrate on your breath. One…"

I tried to follow his advice. The big guy's voice was so low it was more like a purr. He softly rubbed my back, and by the time he counted to sixty I'd stopped panting.

"Thank you."

"What's your name?"

"Maddy."

He put out his hand and I shook it. It was strong. "I'm Vic. Want a drink?"

I glanced around, scared. "I'm underage."

"Don't worry about that," Vic said as we stood up. "I know every bartender in town."

Nearly naked, yellow neon girls flashed as we passed through tinted doors into the Zanzibar – a cavern of thick smoke, stale beer and brassy mirrors. An announcer's voice trumpeted over the loudspeaker, "Gentlemen, give it up for the lovely lady!" as "You Shook Me" began to play.

The black stage curtain parted and a girl dressed in a white cowboy hat, sparkly bra and glittery panties strutted into the circling spotlight, shaking her tits. Clapping was sparse because there weren't a lot of customers at that time of day. Only regulars perched on stools in front of the main stage, nursing warm beer. A waiter in black trousers and a crisp white shirt rushed over the moment he saw Vic.

"What can I get you?"

"Two Zombies, George," Vic replied. "Is that okay with you?"

"Sure." I didn't know what a Zombie was.

Vic waved at a guy sitting at a booth near the back. I couldn't see very well, but I thought I also saw a girl through the smoke.

"You crazy fucker, get your ass over here!" the guy called.

Vic tossed the maroon briefcase down on the vinyl seat. The other guy, only a few years older than me, was leaning back in the banquette with his feet up on the table. My aunts would have pitched fits at that kind of behaviour. The guy had the most beautiful hair I'd ever seen on a man. Thick, black and glossy, it tumbled onto the shoulders of his black leather coat. He reminded me of a raven. A sulky girl in a yellow halter top, short jean skirt and platform sandals sat beside him. She had curly brown hair and lips the colour of raspberries. The guy asked Vic if he had any news.

"Not yet," Vic said, telling me to take a seat.

"This here's Cope and his old lady Charlene. Meet Maddy."

Cope's eyes twinkled like pixies' as Charlene wrinkled her nose. Vic said he had to make a call and left.

Empty glasses and ashtrays overflowing with brown cigarette butts covered the table. Charlene started peeling the label off her beer bottle. Vic's waiter friend George arrived with two tall glasses topped with plastic pink parasols harpooning bright red cherries. I took a sip. It tasted yummy like the tropics. I slurped it all down.

Cope shoved the other Zombie at me. "Vic won't drink it anyway."

The Zombie made me feel relaxed, and it wasn't gaggy like Gabe's cheap liquor.

"You the new old lady?" he asked.

"We just met."

Charlene lifted the edge of the green label, and I thought if she was careful, she might be able to tear the whole thing off in just one pull.

"I only ask because you'll be disappointed in the cock department," Cope said, rubbing his crotch. That magic pixie smile again. Charlene looked down at the bulge and slapped Cope's hand.

"You're a pig. Can't you ever leave it alone?"

"Speed makes me horny," Cope replied, adding, "I'm not like Vic. He can't get it up."

Kenneth's was always up. I glanced at the briefcase. Was speed in there? I'd always wanted to try it. Dad's *TIME* magazine said you didn't get physically hooked on it. There was no physical withdrawal.

"So what do you do?" Cope asked.

"Acid dealer."

"Never seen you around," Charlene said.

"Street."

"Oh," she said it like it was low life or worse.

"What about you?" I asked.

"Methamphetamine," Cope replied proudly, taking two long puffs and then stubbing the smoke out on the top of butt mountain. "Me and Vic are runners. You want another drink?" he asked, picking up my empty glass.

"I do," Charlene interrupted, dropping the label in the ashtray.

"Does it make you hallucinate?" I asked, as Cope signaled George for another round."

"What?" Cope asked.

"Speed. Does it make you see things?"

"Only if you don't get your sleep. It's a clean drug."

A new dancer came out on the stage.

"Coppers know you?" Cope asked.

I shook my head. "I'm careful."

"You don't look like a dealer," he said. Then the stripper caught his eye. "Look at that!" Cope yelled, jumping to his feet, thrusting his hips at the stage. "How about me baby? You think you could take it all?"

Charlene yanked on his arm, telling him to sit down.

"What's wrong with showing a little appreciation for a wonder of the world? What do you think, Maddy?"

The girl's boobs were bigger than her head. Her eyes swept across the faces in the crowd and then they lighted on me. She smiled and before I could stop myself, I smiled back. Cope caught the exchange and jabbed me in the ribs.

"Look at the way they stand up like jelly moulds. I'd mount those babies if they were mine. I'd build them a shrine," Cope said. Then he turned, tweaking Charlene's nipples. "Yours are getting saggy. You better start wearing a bra."

"Fuck off."

"So what do you think, Maddy?" Cope asked.

"What?"

"The girl."

I glanced the other way.

"Oh, come on, I saw you smiling at her."

I looked back at the stage and then down at the table. "She's okay I guess."

"She's more than okay." He pulled my chin up. "Look at her. You don't see them that fresh too often."

When I went beet red Cope jumped.

"I think Vic's new *girlfriend* is wet for the dancer!"

"I am not!"

Cope threw his hands up in the air like I had a gun on him. "What's wrong with pussy bumping? That's my favourite kind of action. Right honey?" He kissed Charlene's ear. "It's a whole new scene and I think it's hotter than fuck. What could be better than watching two girls go at it? Or better yet, you ever have a ménage Maddy?"

I didn't understand and was too scared to ask. He stuck his tongue out and then rubbed his crotch. "Ménage à trois. Two girls. One guy. Very liquid."

I didn't want to have sex with a guy and didn't want to see any liquid.

"Or it could be two guys, one girl. For the more adventurous man."

"You're a pig," Charlene said.

"I'm a sexual adventurer."

"I'm a free spirit," Charlene replied.

"I don't care about that stuff," I said, as George arrived with two Zombies. "I'm only interested in business."

"Really?" Charlene asked.

I nodded, sucking on the straw while Cope stuck his face down Charlene's top, telling her breasts that they were the finest specimens in the whole wild world.

Charlene corrected him. "It's *wide* world."

"Not with me, baby. With me, everything's wild."

Then he started talking to her breasts again. Charlene pretended she was mad, but I think she liked it. I liked Cope too. Sure he was a pig, but he was the first person who talked about girls being with girls like it wasn't something perverted that belonged in a mental hospital.

Vic walked back into the club, straightening his tie while his eyes scanned the place. Satisfied no one was watching, he squeezed into the seat beside me, and with a grin that could split the moon said that Hermann had scored. Cope and Charlene yelped in unison, thrusting their fists into the smoke like triumphant gladiators.

"You want to come along?" Vic asked.

Dad might still be looking for me and I could always come back later when it was safe. "Sure."

Vic tossed down a twenty and didn't even wait for the change.

A maroon Ford Mercury waited on a side street. Cope strutted towards the car, flicking the long tails of his black leather coat like a peacock showing off its plumes. He and Charlene climbed into the back seat and Vic told me to get in the front. There was a yellow parking ticket under the windshield wiper. Vic snatched it up and tossed it into the back seat. There must have been a hundred of them back there acting as mats. Old coffee cups were wedged between the dash and the windshield. Vic rammed an eight track into the holder, shoving the silver gear shift into drive as T. Rex's "Bang a Gong" boomed out of the Mercury's windows. He put the pedal down and we burned rubber up Yonge.

Taking a hard right on Gerrard, the car blew over the tall viaduct that spanned the Don River. Shallow and murky, it snaked down to the lake through a snarled valley of high grasses and the twisted remains of abandoned grocery carts. Charlene tossed her cigarette butt out the window and asked Vic why I was there.

He looked at me, then stretched his arm across the back of the seat like he was reaching, but it was up to me if I wanted to get caught or not. It reminded me of the sex game with Kenneth in the trunk of the car – a bit of me for a bit of whatever Vic wanted. Cope said Vic couldn't get his penis up, so that meant I could control things. Sliding across the seat, I snuggled up beside Vic. He kissed the top of my head, wrapping his big arm around me, squeezing me tight.

"She's mine," he replied.

And from then on it was like we'd always been together.

"Hermann runs speed with the Paradise Riders," Cope said, as we hit the Danforth.

"We're the bag men. We run dope to street dealers," Vic added.

Charlene filed her nails. "Hermann's just tracked down a new chemist in Quebec."

"He cooks the meth and most importantly," Vic said, handing me a lit cigarette, "the RCMP don't have a lead on him yet."

Cope leaned over the front seat and honked the horn. "As soon as a lab is up, the narcs usually know within a month or two."

"Hermann's smart. He's always ahead of the law," Charlene said, a dreamy look on her face.

"But he's mean," Cope added. "You don't want to get on his bad side."

Vic said that you had to have brains and muscle if you were going to be successful in the dope racket and Hermann had everything covered. Charlene talked about Hermann like he was a superhero – the Batman of speed. But there was something in Cope's tone that made me wonder if Hermann wasn't more like The Joker.

We cruised around lower Riverdale in the Mercury for a good half-hour, making sure we didn't have a tail. Next we got out and walked down the streets, checking out cars containing strange men who looked as if they didn't belong there.

"How come we've got to do this?" I asked.

"Undercover narcs," Vic replied.

Uniformed cops had occasionally come by and threatened to arrest me, Lily and Gabe for vagrancy, but Vic and Cope were being followed by an entire branch of the police force. It was thrilling.

Once Vic decided it was safe, we walked into an alley that led to a long line of garages. Cope banged on a scuffed metal door about a third of the way down. A muffled male voice asked who it was.

"Cope."

The voice said to come in by the side.

It was the strangest garage I'd ever seen. There was no lawn mower, hedge clippers or toboggans. A checkered sofa was shoved under a narrow window and a fridge buzzed loudly in the corner. A well-muscled guy with cropped blond hair, jeans, a tight white tee and polished cowboy boots sat in the centre of the sofa, closely examining a bag of sparkling white rocks.

"That's Hermann," Charlene whispered, getting a slight catch in her voice.

Hermann reminded me of a snake coiled on a log – tense and ready to spring. Another man, burly with a bald head, kept throwing a knife at a dart board. Then he'd walk over, pull the knife out and do it over and over again. He never missed the bullseye, and I never got his name.

Hermann opened a cigar box on the coffee table, removing a syringe and spoon, and filled the syringe from a glass of water. The needle reminded me of Dad's Demerol. Like a scientist, Hermann dropped several white rocks into the spoon, carefully dousing them with water and mashed the speed into a paste. Other than the steady thump of the knife, it was quiet like church.

Once the rocks dissolved, Hermann tore a tiny bit of white filter from a cigarette, dropped it into the speed, placed the needle on the filter and drew up the liquid. He wrapped a thick belt around his bicep, holding it there until the middle vein in the crook of his arm popped up. Once the needle had slid into the skin, Hermann pulled back on the plunger and a ribbon of red backed into the syringe. I'd never seen Dad do that and I'd seen him administer lots of shots.

"Why is he doing that?" I asked Vic in a whisper.

"It's called flagging and you do it to make sure you're in the main line. Otherwise you can get an abscess and rot your arm off."

I'd read about mainlining in Dad's magazines. It was the big vein that junkies used. Hermann drew back a bit more blood, let go of the belt and pushed the plunger down. After a moment his face flushed and the odor of chemicals shot out of his nose – that and the smell of green apples.

"Fuck, yeah," he said, eyes closing. When they opened, they settled on me. "Who's *that*?" he asked, pointing the empty syringe.

"She's with me," Vic replied, wrapping his arm around my shoulder.

Hermann stood up, walked over to Charlene and started chewing on her ear lobe. Cope didn't look very happy about it, but Charlene did. I wouldn't like it. I wouldn't like sharing my girlfriend one bit.

"There are a lot of dealers in the joint because they trusted chicks," Hermann said, giving me a nasty look. He started licking Charlene's neck like she was a popsicle.

Night Town

"Do you want to fix?" he asked. It wasn't a question, it was a test.

"Sure," I replied, figuring a fix was a hit.

"Fill the bowl."

I sat in a straight-back chair, carefully setting a couple of rocks in the spoon. I smiled at Hermann, hoping to make friends, but he didn't smile back.

"More," Hermann commanded as his hand travelled up Charlene's skirt.

There was already more speed than Hermann had taken.

"You got a problem?" Hermann asked.

"No," I replied.

I reached out, dropping two more rocks in. Hermann pulled Charlene down onto the sofa. Cope looked out the window as Vic nervously glanced down at the spoon.

"That's a lot."

The knife hit the bullseye. Thump.

"I want to make sure she's no narc," Hermann snarled.

"It's fine," I said, my palms sweating as Hermann mixed the liquid.

Vic wrapped the belt around my bicep and Hermann filled the syringe. I wondered if it wasn't too much, but instead I focused on the needle tearing through the skin. Hermann flagged and the moment my blood appeared Vic let go of the belt. But Hermann didn't take it nice and slow to see how I'd feel, which I'd read is what you should always do with any kind of drug. Instead, he injected the whole mixture into my bloodstream, pulled the needle out and threw it on the table.

The rush rumbled through me like an earthquake. It started in my toes and blasted up through my body, pounding out of the top of my shoulders, a detonating chemical cannon that threw me off the chair flat on my back on the floor. The smell of fresh green apples forced all the oxygen out of my chest. At first my heart was beating so fast I couldn't hear it, but then it came back, getting slower and skipping and stopping and starting and skipping. I sucked little shallow gasps, but no air came in so I gave up. The room was covered in a dewy white glow and everything was white like heaven. I wondered if I was dying. If I was, I'd be happy. I'd be with Mom.

Settling into the perfect silence, I floated up and away until suddenly a giant squall of air pushed me down, kicking me out of heaven, crash-landing me back on the floor in the garage. Vic's mouth was pasted on mine, giving me mouth to mouth. Charlene and

Cope's faces were ashen. Hermann laughed, saying it was the closest O.D. he'd ever seen. I just smiled and asked for more.

"Maddy," Vic said, tapping me lightly on the cheek.

The bald guy with the knife was gone, and Cope and Vic had weighed their buys and were ready to leave. Hermann was expecting other runners. Charlene got up from Hermann's side and walked over to Cope.

Vic rested his hand on mine. "Do you want to come with us?"

He might have been a lot older, but Vic was sweet and he'd take care of me. I could make myself kiss him and stuff, but there was no way I was putting out like Charlene. If things got out of hand I could always just leave. Besides, there was nothing to worry about as long as Vic was stoned, and from all the speed in his briefcase, we were going to be stoned for a long, long time.

The Mercury crawled by a long row of art deco motels clustered at the edge of the lake. Each one was painted white with boldly coloured metal trim. Blue, pink, orange and green vacancy signs flickered from the roofs. The strip was once a prime tourist attraction, but times had changed and so had the clientele. Vic pulled in under a red neon seahorse that wore a matching neon saddle. The Seahorse manager didn't care how many of us slept in the room. He just took the money and tossed Vic the key.

Our room was on the second floor, with two double beds covered in orange blankets and drapes that didn't close. The TV hardly got any stations, but that didn't matter. We just shot up again and again, staying up all night endlessly talking, solving the mysteries of life; and then, holding hands, we walked along the stony lakeshore, watching the waves roll over each other as the final star went out and the rim of the horizon revealed a beautiful band of pure pink.

When it was time to sleep I took off my clothes and lay down in Vic's arms, curling up on his chest. He fell asleep instantly, the soft skin of his penis brushing against my thigh. I didn't want his penis anywhere near me, but I was afraid to move away for fear I'd wake him. That was something I hadn't considered. Maybe Vic would wake up and have ideas like Kenneth. What if I was the first one up and out of bed? My mind worried and planned while I listened to Charlene and Cope's sex sounds. They sounded like animals, pulling and pushing, groaning and begging. The sheets shifted and the bed jumped.

Vic tightened his grip and snorted. I tried to pretend he was Ginnie, but that didn't work and besides, we never slept like that. As soon as we finished rocking back and forth Ginnie always rolled away, pulling the sheets up under her chin and went to sleep. That was because our love was sick. I caught myself on the word love. What Ginnie and I had shared wasn't love, it was an affliction. Slowly I reached my hand out, settling my palm on Vic's chest. It was furry like Dad's.

Vic dropped me off in front of The Steps and I told him I'd meet him at the Zanzibar. I hadn't seen Lily and Gabe in over a month and needed to check in. I leaned over the back seat to grab Vic's tweed coat when he grabbed my boob and squeezed it.
"Hey!" I said, pushing him away. "That hurt."
"You just need more practice. Give us a kiss."
Cope told me Hermann had been teasing Vic, saying he was a neuter with a frigid old lady who was ripping him off. He grabbed me by the scruff of the neck, yanking my head back. "Open your mouth."
"People can see."
"You're my old lady. Open your mouth."
I tried not to gag and pretended that I liked it until he let me go.

Lily was panhandling while Gabe sat on the stoop watching a couple of guys install a billboard on top of a building. The sign read "The Green Door" and offered topless body rubs. A tubby, partially naked guy stretched out on a cot while a pretty girl in a bikini rubbed his body. How disgusting. At least I was getting free speed, and all I had to do was kiss Vic and make pretend moan sounds when he grabbed my tits. Although lately things had started to get tense, and I was worried Vic was looking for a whole lot more.
I sat down beside Gabe. He was losing weight and had a black eye.
"What did you do to your face?"
"Fightin. And I woulda won if the cops didn't break it up. Looky looky, Lily. Our Cookie's come home."
I hugged him hard as Lily walked over. Gabe's teeth chattered.
"Where you been?" Lily asked.
"Here and there."
She sat on my other side and gave me a quick squeeze. "You're too skinny."
"Got too much to do. No time to eat."

Lily pushed up the sleeves of Vic's coat. "Your arms look like sticks."

They were white and kind of skinny, but that was because we rarely went out in the day. And besides, I felt great. I didn't need to eat or sleep. My mind burned energy like the sun. When Lily saw the track marks she slapped me on the side of the head.

"What the hell is this?"

"I'm into something way better now. Way more lucrative."

"Like what?"

"Speed."

"Asshole."

Lily thought speeders were scum, but she was wrong. We were doper royalty. It reminded me of doing house calls with Dad. Every night Vic, Cope, Charlene and I drove all over the city delivering bags of whiz to street dealers. When we knocked on the door, speeders fell over themselves ushering us in. They offered us drinks and cigarettes. One of the speeders even called Vic "Sir." Gabe shivered. I reached out and rubbed his hands.

"So where are you staying?" I asked.

"Hotels," Lily replied.

I didn't believe her. They were sleeping outside. It was January and they didn't even have winter jackets. I wrapped Vic's scarf around Gabe's neck and pulled ten dollars out of my pocket.

"For a bottle?" Gabe asked, making a grab, but Lily snatched the money first. Gabe wasn't as quick as he used to be.

"For coats. You can get them at the Goodwill."

Lily's pride didn't like it, but I made her take it. "If you're going to stay out here, you've got to stay warm."

"Okay," Lily said. "But I'll pay you back. I mean it. I'll pay you back."

That was the last time I saw them that winter.

The pockets in the pants were deep – 1940s pleated dress pants, the kind that Granddad wore – and I liked the feel of the starchy white cotton shirt. Men's clothes belonged on my body, plus they helped hide my curves.

My fingers shook trying to force the buttons through the little holes. It had been nearly a day since our last hit and Vic was out trying to score. There'd been some big busts lately and supply was scarce. At least we had an apartment.

"Why do you dress like a guy?" Charlene asked, pulling on a skimpy blue dress that barely covered her bum.

Charlene and I had gone shopping for spring clothes at the Salvation Army and were playing dress up to pass the time.

"Maddy likes girls," Cope replied. He was stretched out on a nubby brown sofa, leafing through a *Playboy* with his hand down his pants.

"No I don't," I said. What I wanted to ask was, "How do you know?"

The coffee table was covered in Cope's collection of girlie magazines. Every month he bought *Hustler* and *Playboy* and we compared centrefolds. Charlene took off the dress, dropped it onto the floor and reached for a skirt. Charlene had the most amazing tits. Her nipples were bright pink but she had no areolas. I loved it when the nipples got hard. Cope turned the magazine sideways and looked at the picture.

"Girls are hot. Especially girls who go both ways, right Charlie?"

"I like guys," Charlene replied, pulling up her skirt and turning to me, "Will you zip me up?"

I tugged the zipper into place while Cope watched. Charlene might have been a slut, but she was a sexy slut and I loved watching her parade around naked.

"Let her rub your tits," Cope said.

I backed away.

"Don't be scared," he said. "Rub her tits. You want to don't you?"

I looked at Charlene.

"Go ahead," Charlene said.

"No," I said, but I didn't back up anymore.

"It's okay with me," Cope said.

I worried he was masturbating, but didn't look. Charlene walked closer.

"Give me your hands," she said.

I raised them in the air and Charlene took them, placing them around her boobs. The skin was so soft to the touch and when I rubbed the nipples they sprang up.

"That's enough!" Charlene said.

I pulled my hands back. "Was that too hard?"

"That was too good," Cope laughed.

Charlene pulled a tight tee-shirt over her head and tucked it into the top of the skirt, but that didn't settle down those nipples of hers.

They poked through the fabric like they were waving hello. My fingers remembered how they reacted and they wanted to say hi right back, but then the door opened and Vic came in, tossing his maroon briefcase on the sofa.

Cope clicked open the brass hasps, took out a small baggie of speed and went over to the kitchen table. Charlene ran for the water, fits and spoons, and I was about to join them when Vic grabbed me by the arm, staring at my pants.

"Make me a drink."

While I poured him a rye and water, Charlene and Cope were already dropping speed into the spoon and starting to fix.

"Aren't we going to do a hit?" I asked, worried that Cope and Charlene would take it all. There wasn't much speed in that bag.

Vic chugged the rye in one gulp, slamming the glass onto the coffee table. "I want to fuck."

He shot a hateful look at my men's shirt and then reached out, ripping it open so hard the buttons popped, flying across the room like hail. Hermann must have been teasing Vic about me again.

"Sure," I said, kissing his neck. "But let's fix first."

"Now!" He swept me up in his arms and carried me across the room, kicking open the bedroom door with his boot.

Cope dropped his fit and gasped "good shit," as the smell of green apples blew through the room.

Vic caught the scent and froze in the doorway, staring down at me. "Just one and then we fuck."

I kissed his cheek and said, "Yeah, baby."

Cope was right. It was probably the best speed I'd ever had. Charlene and Cope vanished into the bedroom and Vic had opened a bottle of rye and started taking the TV apart. Speeders always get busy with electronics because the drug makes you super smart, like space monkeys in laboratories. There was only one problem. When you came down, you'd forgotten how to put things back together again.

While Vic tinkered, I stood in front of the open window, hands deep in my pockets, watching the streetcars rattle up and down Broadview. Across the river, the skyscrapers glittered, the CN Tower standing between them like a skeleton sentinel. Newspapers said it was going to be the highest freestanding structure in the world. To me, it looked like a naked Eiffel Tower or the Tower of Babel, a story I heard in Sunday school.

Thousands of years ago God's children decided to build a tower that stretched all the way up to heaven. They claimed they wanted to go and worship Him, but secretly they wanted to prove they were smart enough to get up there. Once the tower was built, the children started to climb and God, hidden behind His fluffy white clouds, glared down, getting madder and madder. How dare they? His children thinking they were clever enough to climb to heaven? He was of the air and they were of the earth. He was of everything and they were of nothing but clay.

Then God raised His fist and down it came through the clouds, smashing, lashing, bashing rocks and mortar, and the tower came crashing down. Most of the children died in that fall, but the ones who didn't were determined to rebuild. But when they started, something strange occurred. The children used to speak the same language, but now they all spoke in foreign tongues. They no longer understood each other, the communal knowledge was lost and God's children could never build another tower to heaven again.

Yellow light fell on my face. Night had passed while I was high, dreaming about the Tower of Babel. Was it noon yet? Hot breath settled on my neck, making the hairs prickle. It was Vic. I hadn't gotten up first and snuck out to get our morning coffee. Now Vic was down from his trip and standing behind the chair, hands clamped hard on my shoulders.

"Why are you always looking at Charlene?"

Traffic travelled up and down Broadview.

"Hermann says you're queer."

"What do you think?" I asked, thinking of Charlene's naked body.

"I think you need to be taught."

I stood up and turned to face him. The sofa bed was pulled out. Something else I'd missed while I was out of it.

He pushed me towards the bed. "Come on."

"I'm too high."

Vic shoved me down on my back and crawled on top. I was only wearing a tee-shirt and men's trousers.

"You're always too high." I tried to roll away, but he had me pinned and started undoing my pants. "I've always been good to you."

"Can't we just cuddle instead?"

"Haven't I always been good to you?"

Vic hadn't shaved and his beard was scratchy. "This is how you say thank you," he said, yanking down my pants. "This is how it works."

"Get off me," I said, starting to fight.

Vic just laughed at the kicks and punches, pushing his body down on mine, forcing my legs open with his thighs.

"This is how you pay."

I clamped my legs together but he just wrenched them open.

"Please, Vic," I whimpered, but that didn't work either. He told me to be still and with one hand squeezing my tit, he started kissing me. His mouth was covering mine when I felt him tear into me. It felt like red. I screamed, it hurt so bad, but then he just shoved his hand over my mouth and told me to shut up – shut up and enjoy it. Back and forth, in and out he went. I could barely breathe, his hand was clamped so tightly over my mouth. How long did it take? This is what the other girls did for free drugs. I tried to think about Charlene naked and how it was business, but Mom appeared instead. The time I kissed her – kissed her right on the lips and then felt the bump. The innocent little bump. I pushed her face away.

Vic was going faster now, breathing really hard, when Mom returned again. Only she was larger and clearer this time, and she wouldn't go away. All giant, like at the movies, standing on the top of the hill with no boots on, in her mauve dressing gown, watching Kenneth French me, screaming my name, pointing down at me, yelling at me to stop.

My hands flailed, punching Vic, slapping him as hard as I could, but he just kept drilling into me. Back and forth, back and forth, like my body was just a doll.

Mom kept screaming. The dressing gown flapped in the high wind, her chalky skin and no boots, no boots on in icy snow, and then something popped in my brain – a baby. This couldn't happen, would *not* happen to me. Not Madeline Anne Barnes. My hand reached for the bottle of rye on the side table, grabbing it by the neck and brought it down as hard as I could, smashing into the back of Vic's head, in the place Dad called the occipital lobe.

Vic was out scoring, Charlene was getting dressed and Cope sat at the kitchen table in his Jockeys. He still had a nice body for a speeder, tight and muscled. Cope had just finished washing his hair and I was trimming the ends. He was like a girl that way. Every day he washed his hair, conditioned it and blew it dry. Snip went the scissors as another lock of black hair fell.

"Vic raped me."

I told them I bashed his head in and they both laughed. I think Cope kind of admired me. There was something in his expression. I didn't mention that I'd been a virgin. Nobody would believe it and besides, there was no point dwelling on yet another thing that was gone forever.

"What am I going to do?"

Charlene gave me a look. "Sex for drugs is the way it works," she said, turning to Cope. "Like it or not. Isn't that right?"

Cope grunted something about Vic's manly pride as I opened the scissors.

"I won't do that, can't do that," and the blades seemed to snap themselves shut, making Cope jump back. "But Vic said he'd kill me if I hit him again."

What I didn't say is that if Vic ever tried touching me again, I'd be the one doing the killing. He was never going to get his pig hands on me, no matter what the rules were. Cope could tell I was serious because the room got so still until Charlene couldn't stand the quiet anymore.

"What's an occipital?"

I resumed cutting Cope's hair. "It's part of the brain. It lets you see."

"How do you know about that?"

"Read it."

"You're weird," Charlene said. "You should stay away from Vic. He did time in the pen for assault."

So that's why he was older than us.

"Don't you ever want to quit using and go home and read about occipital shit?" she asked.

Even if I did, that door was closed and locked up tight. Dad wouldn't let me back into the past and speed controlled the present and future. Charlene smacked her lips. I liked Charlene, even though all she talked about was how badly she wanted to get balled.

"I'm sick of this shit. But my old man hates me more than my mother loves me," she added, getting up to go to the bathroom. "He'd beat the crap out of her if she stood up for me. So I'm stuck."

I knew what that was like. There was a mental hospital waiting for me. Charlene shut the bathroom door as I set the scissors on the table. The haircut was done.

"Maddy," Cope said. "You know how it works. Chicks put out. Guys take the risks."

I looked at my friend straight in the eyes.

"I can't...and I think you know why."

Cope picked up his hand mirror. "You did a good job," he said, admiring the cut. "Let me give you something."

He rummaged through the closet and pulled out a red cowboy shirt. It had white mother of pearl snaps and white lassos that roped across the back. He tossed it to me.

"For real?" I asked.

Cope nodded, pulling on a pair of jeans. I buried my face in the cloth. The shirt was so soft and faded. I loved it.

"Thank you."

Cope slipped on a clean shirt, checking out his reflection again. "It's okay to be into girls, you know."

I didn't say anything.

"You ever love anyone?" he asked.

I nodded.

"Some chick?"

I nodded again. "But she didn't love me back."

"I know what that's like."

Was he thinking about what Charlene did with Hermann? Business rules or not, that would hurt so much. Cope ran his fingers through his hair, slipped on the leather coat and flicked the tails. "Come on, let's go."

Hermann and Gabe had the same stomping grounds. John's Open Kitchen was home to alkies and speeders, a place for them to eat a cheap meal or nurse a coffee. Cope and I sat in one side of a vinyl booth while Hermann sat in the other, staring at me with his crazy rabies eyes.

"Girls aren't runners."

"That's stupid," I said.

Hermann's eyes narrowed. "You calling me stupid?"

"No. You're the smartest guy I know. It's the rule that's dumb – "

Cope broke in. "That's why it's so brilliant. We've had a lot of heat lately." He poured a steady stream of sugar into his coffee. "Not only is she a chick, the cops don't know her, and she looks like she just walked out of a church for chrissakes."

Cope took a sip of coffee and spat it back into the cup.

"This would expand your territory. Make you the biggest dealer in town."

Hermann grabbed Cope by the lapels, yanking him over the table, index finger nearly up a nostril. "She's your responsibility?"

Cope nodded. "And you handle Vic."

Hermann released Cope's lapels. By the time we left, Hermann had taken all the credit for the idea. I had a job and Vic never touched me again.

CHAPTER SEVEN

I took two buses across town to make sure I wasn't tailed and circled the block three times checking out suspicious cars for undercover narcs. Once I was satisfied everything was safe, I jumped the neighbour's fence and walked across the yard. While other runners used cabs or personal cars, I flew across the city in subways, streetcars and buses. That was my own personal touch. Narcs would never be looking for a sweet faced girl in a blue and white sailor shirt riding the TTC.

The speeder house where Hermann had been crashing the past month was a wreck. Two windows were broken and an old sofa with the stuffing punched out was thrown on the back porch. Mom would have called the house a "civic embarrassment" and enlisted the United Church Women to engage in missionary work and clean it up.

I took the key out of its hiding spot in the drainpipe and opened the back door. The living room was full of beaten up chairs and cushions. The kitchen table was in the dining room, covered with glasses of water, the odd broken fit, spoons with used filters and the residue of dried up speed. I climbed the stairs and walked down the hall, past bedrooms with mattresses covered in twisted sheets. Milk crate coffee tables covered in candle stubs cast wild light on the ceiling at night. One of the speeders had a guitar and used to jam till dawn, but Hermann didn't let him play anymore because he thought the music would tip off the cops. Hermann had never been what Dad would call stable, but things had gotten a whole lot worse since he'd turned paranoid.

I peeked in. Hermann was sitting in a chair by a second floor window, staring through a slit of a heavy brown curtain. A suitcase rested by his feet. Charlene said she'd heard Hermann had a gun, but I never saw one. He looked like he could use some sleep. I'd been there every day and he hadn't moved from that chair in a week. I rapped lightly on the door jamb and Hermann jumped.

"Don't sneak up on me," he snapped, still staring out the window. He leaned down, pulled four ounces of speed out of the suitcase and told me to deliver it to an address on Main. His eyes never left the street.

"I've never been there before."

"You got a problem?" he asked, turning to glare at me with his rabies eyes. He'd been chewing on his lower lip, making it bleed.

"No."

"Then do the fuck what you're told," he said and turned back to the window.

The buyer, a scrawny girl under twenty, answered the door. I couldn't get a good look at her because she kept the house dark. I followed her down the hall and into the living room. A pot of tea sat on an old coffee table beneath a floor lamp with a fringed shade. The house smelled of weed and something else – something that reminded me of the root cellar in Granddad's house near the cistern. Roots, dirt and the faint aroma of decay.

"Grab a chair," she said, going into the kitchen.

It took a while for my eyes to adjust to the gloom. The girl came out holding a glass of water and two spoons.

"Let's do a taste."

"I've got to get back."

It was late. Hermann was waiting for me.

"I'm spending a lot of money."

True. I pulled an ounce out of the bottom of my purse. Hands shaking, the girl tore open the bag and filled her spoon with white rocks. I prepared my fix, tied off and hit up. The good feeling rolled in, the feeling that washed everything else away. I closed my eyes. When I opened them the girl was stabbing the needle into her arm, trying to find a vein. The syringe was full of blood and speed and she was starting to cry.

"The vein's dead. The fucking vein's dead."

I went over, knelt down and reached for the syringe. "Let me help you."

She released the syringe but yanked her arm, hiding it away. "Use the other one," she said, sticking her right arm out.

Her arm was so skinny I could see the blue arteries pumping like oil fields. Using my belt I tied her off and hit her up. Once the speed hit, the girl stopped crying and she slumped back, eyes closing as she entered amphetamine orbit. I glanced at her arm. Green puss oozed out of a swollen hole in the centre. No wonder she couldn't find a vein in that mess. It was a furious abscess, her body revolting against all the crap she'd been pumping into it. A body that had simply had too much poison and was starting to rot away, piece by piece. I'd never seen real gangrene before, but I'd seen the photos in Dad's medical books and knew that if she didn't get antibiotics soon, she was going to lose her arm. I told her what I thought, but she didn't want to talk about it.

I dry heaved into the toilet bowl. That girl was so revolting. She had no dignity at all. Stabbing a syringe into raw meat like that over and over again. If I hadn't helped her she would have shot up in the back of her knees or maybe tried the jugular vein. Cope told me he saw a guy do that once. I didn't believe him then, but now I did. That girl would have stuck a needle in her eye if it meant getting the speed.

There was nothing to vomit so I pulled down my jeans and sat on the seat, trying to pee. Lately it had started to hurt but I had to go. Waiting for the urine, I examined my legs. They weren't much more than bone. Since the pee wouldn't come I stood up, stepping onto a beige scale. The needle bounced around and then settled, but it couldn't be right. When I left home I weighed about 140 pounds and now I was down to ninety. I did it again. Same result – ninety pounds.

Who was I to judge the rotting girl? Mom would have called me a hypocrite. The girl and I were exactly the same. That was the smell in the house – the stink of rot and death. She was going to die and so was I. It was just a matter of time before I flamed out in an overdose or got busted and thrown into prison where a bull dyke would murder me. The weird thing was I didn't know if I cared. All I knew for sure was that I was on a train hurtling through darkness, I didn't know if I'd survive a jump, and if I did, where I would land. One thing was certain: there'd be nobody there to catch me. Those arms were long gone. I lifted the washroom blind to get some light but the sun was down.

Yanking up my jeans, I tore back into the living room. "It's dark out. Hermann's going to be pissed."

I pulled the rest of the speed out of my purse and asked for the cash.

"I don't have it."

"Oh shit," I said, stuffing the dope back into my purse.

"I'm good for it."

"Do you know what Hermann will do to me if I show up without his money?" I cried, snapping the purse shut. "I'm going to be in so much trouble."

"Wait. Just wait!" she was already on the phone. The whirl of the dial.

"I don't front," I said, hand on the door knob.

"It's Cope," she said, passing me the receiver.

He told me to give her the speed and meet him back at the house.

"Are you sure?"

"Positive."

Cope had seniority, so I handed the girl four ounces of whiz and headed back to Hermann.

Slipping through the back door, I ran down the hall, past a boy in the dining room, who glanced up from his spoon and told me that I'd better have a good story.

"He's been up there screaming for you."

Scared, I climbed the stairs and found Hermann still peering through the slit in the curtain, talking to himself.

"I see you out there. You think you're so smart, but I'm smarter."

I cleared my throat. Hermann spun around.

"Where the fuck have you been?" he yelled.

"The buyer wanted a taste."

"Give me my money," he said looking back out the window, sticking his hand out. His fingernails were filthy.

"I don't have it."

My heart pounded in my throat because I could see what was in his lap. Charlene was right. Hermann had a gun.

"It's coming," I sputtered.

Hermann pointed the gun at me. "Get your ass over here."

There wasn't a choice. He would have shot me in the back if I ran. I walked across the room, standing before him. Hermann grabbed my wrist and yanked me down into his lap, ramming the cold metal barrel up against the side of my head.

"How stupid do you think I am?" he yelled into my ear, so hard my brain clanged.

I took a breath and kept repeating in a quiet voice, like the one Dad used with the lady who got up on the roof after her husband died, "Everything is fine, the money is coming."

But Hermann wasn't listening. The barrel of the gun, the icy metal, kept sliding between the hair and skin on my temple.

His breath quickened as he whispered, "You fucking bitch. I knew from the beginning that you were a narc."

Right then I realized I should have taken a chance with the bullet in the back because he was going to pull the trigger anyway.

"So this is it," I thought, staring at a single spot on the wall. "My time to die."

Was Mom scared when her turn came? When the angel came into her room, was she ready to go and escape all the pain? Where was my angel? I had one when I was little because she used to come and visit me, but now I was no good and she'd gone away.

Hermann cracked me in the cheek with the butt of the gun and said crying was for weaklings. He kept looking through the slit in the curtain, rambling on about how there was this van across the street, which had been there all day. Something was coming down. I started to sweat through the tears. The end of the gun barrel slid across my temple. Hermann turned and looked at me, totally insane in the face and then cocked the hammer, hissing that he knew I was the one who turned them in.

"Please," I moaned, trying to get up and run away.

His free hand grabbed my hair, holding my head fast to the gun, while his finger squeezed down. It was time. I closed my eyes and thought of Mom, Dad and the boys. As I took my last breath, I realized I didn't want to die.

Then there was a shout, running feet and the metallic click of the trigger as the bullet fired. Its energy swept by me like a falling star.

Cope had pushed the gun away from my head. The bullet ricocheted off the wall and into the ceiling. Hermann and I hadn't heard Cope, but we all heard the explosion of glass and wood rocketing up from downstairs as the front door crashed down.

Cope flew out the window and onto the roof. Hermann tore down the back stairs and I hid in the back of the clothes closet as the narcs stormed up the stairs, through the bedrooms and finally into Hermann's room. I held my breath, trying not to breathe or move. The bed crashed as it was flipped.

"Shit," a man's voice said. "He's gone."

Footsteps headed towards the hallway. They were leaving. I closed my eyes, silently thanking God, when the door handle turned over and light spilled in. Hands pushed back heavy coats on the railing and there was Al Hanson. The same cop who'd come to Dad's house to bust me for selling acid.

"Who do we have here?" he said, pulling me out.

I said nothing as the happy narcs started rifling through my purse and pockets. Their happiness didn't last long because there was nothing to find. The rotting girl had been my last stop and she took everything I had.

"Give him up!" Al yelled as his fist hit the desk. The files jumped.

I wouldn't. I couldn't. I was too scared. I sat in the metal chair beside Al's desk. We were in the police station. Speeders who were holding more than a quarter ounce were lined up on benches waiting to be booked. Everyone else had been let go. Cope was slumped up against the wall, his black leather coat wrapped around him like feathers, his beautiful glossy hair hanging down, shrouding his face. They picked Vic up at a pool hall with two pounds of meth in the trunk of the Mercury. There was still no sign of Hermann.

"Do you want me to call your parents?"

The threat didn't scare me. Nobody would come. "Go ahead."

"Do you know what Hermann'll do to you if he catches you?"

Yes I did and I stood a lot better chance if I didn't roll over. "I don't know anything."

And the cops didn't know about me. I'd been so good covering my tracks that the narcs had never fingered me as a runner. Too bad the same wasn't true for Cope. They'd been following him for nearly a year. Al slammed Hermann's priors down on his desk. I saw the list: arson, theft, drug dealing, assault with a deadly weapon and rape. He'd never been successfully prosecuted. I wasn't going to be their dead stool pigeon. The cops would have to get Hermann on their own.

"Get her out of here!"

Charlene and I went to sentencing in Old City Hall. The courtroom, long and wide with wooden wainscoting and marble floors, was packed with nervous users shifting in their seats, waiting to see what happened to their dealers, their source to the one thing they loved and needed. Tall oak doors at the back of the room swung open and Cope, Vic and the other guys who'd been charged shuffled out in shackles and handcuffs, surrounded by armed guards.

"He looks terrible," Charlene said.

She was right. Cope tried to smile, but I could tell he was scared. Someone had cut off his beautiful hair, and he was swimming in a suit that was way too big for him. Cope reminded me of Dad on his wedding day.

The judge, dressed in a long black robe, emerged from his chambers as the bailiff called, "All rise."

I did, out of habit and respect, but the other speeders remained in their seats.

Al recommended the judge deliver maximum sentences because of the severity of the crimes. The street dealers got two years each. Vic got five and Cope would have too, but since he didn't have a record the judge handed down three. I thought Charlene would die, she was crying so hard until a young woman with a baby in her arms shot to her feet.

"Please, your honour!" she cried. "I need my husband to provide for me and my baby."

"What?" Charlene shouted, as Cope shrank into the prisoner's box. "You bastard! You told me you loved me!" Then she went even crazier and took off her shoes, whipping them at Cope.

The judge slammed down the gavel, warning Charlene to settle down, as the court was adjourned and Cope was dragged off to jail. Al picked up Charlene's shoes and brought them over.

"You should have given him life," she said.

"If it was up to me I would."

Then he turned to me. "Have you seen Hermann?"

"No," Charlene replied. "And if we did we'd run the other way."

Al handed me a card. "If you change your mind call me."

I stuffed it in my pocket, but there was no way I'd ever call. Nobody screwed with Hermann. I just wanted to drop out of sight and prayed he forgot all about me.

Charlene and I walked out of the courtroom onto the steps of Old City Hall. Everything was different now. My best friend was in prison, Hermann was missing and a long drought was on. The choice was simple. It was time to quit.

We had no access to downers or money for booze so we spent that day tearing through the flat, pulling every pocket inside out, hunting through coats, turning drawers upside down, rooting through garbage cans, looking for the dregs of any old speed we could find. I slit plastic baggies open with a razor blade, scratching away any white film that hid in the corners or clung to the sides. Charlene doused used filters with water, trying to coax out even a single hit. There wasn't enough to properly get us off, but it kept the monsters at bay for a day. After that, we stepped off the edge of an endless chemical run into the nightmare of a full out crash.

I sat at the window staring out a crack in the blind, just as paranoid about Hermann as he used to be about me. Shapes on the street constantly shifted. Mailboxes transformed into goblins and normal pedestrians turned into trees that twisted into ladders that stretched up to our window. Then Hermann was climbing the rungs, face in the glass, gun in his hand. Charlene sat in a ball on the sofa, rocking back and forth and crying. We couldn't survive like this. We'd been strung out too long.

The next day I was knocking at the door of the rotting girl. Maybe she had some left. I kept glancing around, terrified that Hermann was watching. I'd taken the subway across town and run up an alley behind Main. Nobody answered. I sniffed at the door jamb. The rotting girl might already be dead or Hermann might be in there with his gun. My whole body shook with need. I looked up and down the street, knocking even harder until I heard a rustle coming down the hall. The door opened a crack and an eye peered out. The chain was on.
"Can I come in?"
The rotting girl weighed the idea. I could see her mind say no.
"Please."
The chain dropped, the door opened and the girl pulled me into the foyer. Making sure the deadbolt was on, I followed her down the narrow hallway into the dark living room. A bag of speed sat on the coffee table. My heart jumped. She still had some left.
"I can give you a hit but that's all. I don't have enough to sell."
The white rocks glistened as she squirted water into the spoon. I swallowed, already imagining the smell of green apples and feeling the rush, the Niagara Falls-speed rush that swept me away. I sat down, waiting, watching her mash the meth and thought of how many hits I'd done over the last nine months and how I didn't remember most of it, because everything had all been the same. Days of nothing but speed and needles, floating up and flying around in the clouds of drug heaven and then crashing down, punctuated by painful hours of desperate, screaming need.

Speed was all I wanted anytime, anyplace, anywhere. That's all there'd been. That's all I was now. It wasn't heroic or death defying and it certainly wasn't cool. I'd been such an idiot – a stupid, blind asshole. Cool is the last thing I was. In fact, I wasn't really anything but dead while still technically alive and walking the earth. Dad would have said this was the behaviour of a parasite in suspended animation. The girl's hands trembled.

"You want me to hit you up?" I asked.

She nodded, handing me the syringe. I wouldn't look at her arm. The smell was worse. I tied her off and asked for a favour. She nodded, anxious for the syringe.

"You got any downers?"

"The shelf in the bathroom."

She stuck her arm out. I could see where she'd been stabbing at it, trying to mainline with her left hand and missed. Little abscesses bubbled and the surrounding skin was scabby.

"You might want to try your wrists."

"Blown out." She gave me a wry smile. "Hurry up." She'd been pretty once.

So I did. The intoxicating scent of green apples rushed out of her nose and my heart skipped and my body begged me to stay, but I dropped the fit on the table, went into the bathroom and cleaned her out of every downer she had in the house, everything except a bottle of blue Valium. If the rotting girl ever decided to come back to earth she'd need something to soften re-entry. I closed the front door behind me. It was time to get normal.

A rectangle of white light woke me up and I could smell eggs. I really had to pee. Getting out of bed, I scratched my head. My hair was itchy, but the paranoia was gone. How much time had passed? Charlene was sitting cross-legged on the sofa eating a huge helping of scrambled eggs and watching *General Hospital*. That meant it was after three o'clock. I rubbed my eyes.

"How long have I been asleep?"

"A day and a half," Charlene replied, taking another big bite of egg.

We were down.

My jeans struck the tiled floor as I sat on the toilet seat, but the moment I started to pee I howled. The pain felt like rubbing alcohol splashed on a burn. Doubling over, clutching my stomach, I tried to breathe through my nose. When my bladder emptied the pain stopped, but I had no idea as to the cause. There was no blood on the toilet paper or in the urine. I scrubbed my face and hands. It must have been some kind of bug.

My stomach growled and I felt shaky. "Are there any eggs left?"

Charlene shook her head, shoveling the last forkful of food into her mouth. I poked my head in the fridge. There was a loaf of bread and a pound of bacon in the keeper. I dumped all the bacon into the frying pan. I couldn't remember when I'd ever been that hungry, and by nightfall Charlene and I had devoured every morsel in the house.

Charlene sat in the window chain smoking, glaring out at the skyline.

"He has a wife," she said, tossing her butt out the window.

I sat on the counter trying to figure out what to do. It was no minor bug. I was running a high fever.

Charlene turned to me, so sad. "I loved him, you know."

"Since when?"

"Since always."

"Me too," I replied, stroking the soft red fabric of my cowboy shirt.

Charlene began pacing the room. Clip clop, clip clop, her wooden wedges struck the hardwood floor. Her hair was greasy and stuck down on top and she had a funky smell. Charlene needed a bath. I probably did too. My jeans were filthy.

"I want more food," Charlene bitched. "I don't think I've had anything to eat in over two years."

We both laughed. I couldn't remember my last real meal either. In fact I couldn't even remember how long I'd been stoned. All I knew was that I was going to be seventeen soon, and that meant I'd been out on the street nearly a year.

"Now all I can think of is food," Charlene said, slapping her stomach. "And I'm going to get a big fat belly and you know what? I don't give a shit because I'm never fucking another guy."

"I give you a week."

She sat down beside me and took my hand. "Can you be a virgin again?"

"I think once it's gone, it's gone."

"You're hot," she said.

I smiled at her.

"I'm serious, Maddy, your hand is hot."

There was a loud knock at the door. We stared at each other.

"I know you're home."

My hand went up to signal quiet, but the landlady didn't go away. She opened the door with the master key, hair twisted into a sloppy beehive and an apron tied around her waist.

"I want you girls out."

Charlene reminded her we were paid up for another week.

"There was a strange character asking for you last night."

"What did he look like?"

"Blond. Cowboy boots. Not the sort I want around my house."

Hermann.

"What did you tell him?"

"I told him you'd moved weeks ago."

"Did he believe you?"

"I don't know, but I want you out."

In less than five minutes, Charlene and I were on the street with everything that we owned stuffed into two green garbage bags.

Charlene's garbage bag landed on the sidewalk. "That bitch should have given us back the rent."

Steady drizzle was threatening to turn into a full out late summer storm. Lily and Gabe were nowhere around. The newspaper boy who always worked The Steps had just sold his last paper. He couldn't have been more than fourteen and I always wondered why he wasn't in school.

"See Lily around?" I asked.

The boy pointed up the billboard for The Green Door. "She got a job."

Charlene glared at the sign. "Whore house? No way."

"I'm going to borrow some money," I said, stepping out into traffic.

A horn blared. Charlene flipped the car the finger and reluctantly followed, dragging the garbage bag behind her.

The lime neon sign at the top of a tall, rickety staircase read: "The Green Door." Faded pin-ups of topless girls covered the walls on either side. Inside the body rub lounge there were sofas, a couple of puffy chairs and coffee tables with tin ashtrays and girlie magazines. A sign reading "Rules of the Management" hung over the manager's wicket.

The rules were: "No Extras, No Touching the Girls and Money Up Front." I wondered what extras were.

A pretty girl lay on the sofa. She lit a cigarette and asked me if I wanted a rub.

"No, thank you," I replied, trying not to sound judgmental.

The girl had green hair with green eyes, green fingernails and wore ripped black pantyhose, fake black eyelashes and angry swipes of thick black eyeliner. She was stuffed into a bright green bustier and mini skirt.

"Sit," she said and I dropped down beside her, grateful to rest. My brain felt light, but my body was heavy.

Charlene remained on her feet, hands on her hips. "Who are you?"

"Helen," the girl replied, blowing a thick plume of smoke at Charlene. She was about eighteen. Helen took my hand and held it.

"You're hot."

I smiled weakly.

"You're scared," she added.

"No I'm not," I lied, yanking my hand away.

"I don't believe you."

There was something kind in Helen's voice beneath the edge. A pudgy middle-aged guy with mousy brown hair appeared in the wicket. He was wearing a short-sleeved beige shirt with a white pocket protector. Leaning across the counter, he rubbed his hands, grinning at Charlene. He practically had no lips.

"I'm Ivan. Pleasure to meet such lovely young ladies such as yourselves."

Charlene glowered. I told him we were there to see Lily.

Ivan looked at the clock on the wall. "Should be out any minute. Unless of course things go over," he said, rubbing his hands even harder.

Helen started humming "Ziggy Stardust".

"David Bowie's a fag," Charlene said. "The Eagles are a real band that writes real music."

Helen turned to me. "Your friend's a no taste fat cow."

Charlene dropped her bag to the floor. "Listen, bitch."

I reached out and touched Helen's bare shoulder to stop her from getting up. I didn't have the strength to stop a fight.

"We just need some money and we'll go," I said.

Helen's skin was soft.

While Charlene grumped around the lounge like a Presbyterian church lady, I tried to change the topic, asking Helen about David

Bowie. Obviously fascinated, Helen sat up straight, crossed her legs and launched into a speech about glam.

"Everyone's either asexual or bisexual."

"What about you?" I asked.

A puff of smoke came out. "I used to be gay, but now I'm asexual. Working here will put you off sex for life."

Sure Helen had green hair, but she was definitely pretty. Was she really gay? And what was the real colour of her hair?

"You'd be kind of cute if you cleaned yourself up," she said.

The downstairs bell jangled. Ivan poked his head out the wicket. "Sit up straight. Somebody's coming." Footsteps thumped up the steps. "Hurry up," he whispered, scowling at Helen.

Helen repositioned her tits in the bustier, leaned back and posed. A couple of men arrived in the room, looking for a body rub. One smiled eagerly at Charlene.

"Pig," she hissed, snatching up her garbage bag and heading towards the stairs.

I didn't know what to do. I felt too sick to stand, but Lily was still with her customer. I grabbed my bag of clothes and followed Charlene.

"Wait a minute," Ivan said. "If you need a job, come back. I can always use new talent and the pay's good."

Helen was still reclining on the sofa as a man perched on either side, staring at her tits. She gave me an easy smile, while her boobs powered that room like a nuclear reactor.

"I can't believe you'd talk to *that*," Charlene snapped, walking backwards up Yonge Street with her thumb out. "We'll go and see a friend of mine. She'll take us in."

But nobody stopped so we had to walk all the way in the rain. When Charlene's friend saw us in the doorway, dirty, soaking wet, with garbage bags in our hands, she knew she'd never get rid of us. She knew we'd eat her food, drink her booze and probably rip her off, and she would have been right.

"I'm sorry Charlene. The old man's home," the girl said, nervously looking over her shoulder.

The door was open, and down the hall a bunch of guys were drinking beer and playing cards. Every once in a while somebody shouted, "Get your ass back in here!"

When the girl closed the door in our faces Charlene finally lost it. She stood out in the front yard and whipped the garbage bag in circles over her head screaming about Cope breaking her heart and how everybody screwed her over and she never ever got ahead. That was it. Even if her father beat the shit out of her, she was going home to see her mother. There was no way she was going to work in some body rub parlour and whore herself out.

"No fucking way!" Charlene screamed as I sat and waited for her to calm down.

While Charlene yelled I checked my pulse. It was fast and jumpy, probably came from coming off the speed. The irregularity would eventually pass. After about ten minutes Charlene had worn herself out and she'd come up with another plan.

"We can stay with my cousin. She won't turn us away. Let's go."

It took nearly three hours. Past diners and late night cab stands and wrecking yards full of snarling, white-fanged dogs crashing into rusted chain link fences. Charlene kept throwing away pieces of clothing to lighten her load. Every one she discarded was accompanied by some swearing about Cope. He must have given her everything she owned.

By the time we reached her cousin's apartment building we were both ready to drop. She pressed the buzzer. Nobody answered. She pressed it again. Nothing. Charlene didn't have any angry tears left. We hung around waiting until a couple of kids came out. We snuck in behind them, took the elevator to the ninth floor and walked down to apartment 917.

Charlene knocked and softly called out, "It's Charley. Let me in." But nobody opened the door. Charlene pulled what was left of her clothing out of the garbage bag and made a pillow for herself on the floor and told me to do the same. "We'll just rest our eyes for a bit," Charlene said, dropping onto the carpet. "And then I'm going home. I swear to God I'm going home," she mumbled.

I sat beside her and nearly lay down. I sure wanted to, but something inside me couldn't. If I did I might not get back up. I knew by now I was running a really high fever and if I didn't take care of myself I would be no better than the rotting girl, sitting alone in that house waiting to die. I had to pull myself up, force myself up and keep moving, because there was no way my life was going to end dead on the floor of an apartment hall. I kissed Charlene on the forehead and told her to take care of herself.

"Watch out for Hermann," was the last thing she said before she fell asleep.

There was a payphone at the corner. I had a nickel left. Clickety-clack it fell through the mechanism into the coin box and the line came to life. I dialed the number by heart.

"Hello?"

It was so good to hear Aunt Anne's voice.

"Hello?" she asked again.

I swallowed. "It's me."

"Maddy! Are you all right?"

"I'm really sick."

"Where are you?"

"Do you promise you won't call Dad?"

A truck rumbled by.

"Do you promise?"

Another truck. A horn blast. I could almost hear her thinking.

"Okay. Yes. Where are you?"

I looked up at the crossroads. "Pharmacy and Eglinton."

"You stay put. I'll be right there."

The line went dead. I sat down in the phone booth and passed out cold.

CHAPTER EIGHT

The glass box shook as somebody tried to force open the folding doors. I shoved back, feet braced against the other side, trying to stop whoever it was from getting in.

Aunt Anne's face appeared behind the phone booth glass. I pulled myself up and opened the doors. She put her arms around me and pulled me out, hugging me so tight I could barely breathe. The back of her hand touched my forehead.

"I'm going to take you to the hospital."

I wrenched free, backed up and stumbled over the edge of the curb onto the road, clutching the garbage bag to my chest. "No!"

I'd run and she knew it. "All right. But you're coming with me."

I lay in a bed of blankets and pillows in the back seat, watching the clouds race by. We'd left the buildings behind, heading into the country. The sky was black and the smell of late summer blew in through the open windows. Fall would soon be here. My back ached. I moaned. Aunt Anne reached over the back seat and gently stoked my hair. Clutching my stomach, I tried to focus on the steady hum of the tires until I fell asleep.

Someone carried me up a flight of stairs. There was a faint smell of manure and something familiar and I thought that it had to be a man. If it was Granddad, he'd be so disappointed in me. I tried to ask, but was freezing with fever and too tired to open my eyes. Aunt Anne said she was going to call the doctor. A door opened and I was set down on a bed, covered in a blanket and then sleep passed over me again.

I woke up in Mom's room in one of her old nightgowns, my skin-and-bone arms exposed to the light. The only contrast to the white was the shameful sight of the red track marks that ran up and down my arms like vicious bites. Aunt Anne and a doctor stood at the end of the bed talking. Every so often he glanced at me and frowned. I crossed my arms and looked around. My running shoes were under the chair.

"Where are my clothes?" I sat up, alarmed. "I had a garbage bag."
"They need to be washed," Aunt Anne replied.
"Where's Granddad?"
"Out west buying cattle."
The doctor opened his black medical bag. "She's going to need a drip for two days. Once I get you set up, can you manage it?"
Aunt Anne nodded.
"What's wrong with me?" I asked.
"Pyelonephritis."
That's why my back hurt and the urine burned. An untreated bladder infection had invaded my kidneys. Dad always said how important it was to nip things in the bud, but I'd let it fester. There hadn't been enough baths and sometimes I sat on freezing concrete stoops for hours waiting for buyers. The cold had passed into my bladder and travelled up to my kidneys. The doctor pulled an IV pouch and plastic tubing out of his bag while Aunt Anne rigged the bed spindle to support it. He sat down beside me and gave me a stern, mean look. His bedside manner was horrible. You were supposed to make the patient feel at ease, no matter who they were or how you felt about them.
"How long have you been sexually active?"
"I'm not," I cried.
Aunt Anne flushed and looked away.
"If you're going to have multiple partners, you'd better use birth control. The next time it could be syphilis. Give me your arm."
Then he snatched it – pulling it out like a weed. And there it was. The stabbed-to-death-by-a-million-needles ruined arm. Proof that everything he thought was true – the drug whore was home to leech from her decent family. The doctor stuck in the needle, taped down the tubing, hooked up the drip and told me to stay put for forty-eight hours.
"After that, take these for another ten days," he said, setting a bottle of antibiotics on the table. "Do you have any questions?"
"No."
"I'll walk you out," Aunt Anne said.
The door shut behind them, and I lay there lassoed to Mom's bed, listening to the IV drip, truly wanting to die.

I rubbed my eyes. Aunt Anne was in the process of removing the IV. Her hair was wrapped up in a kerchief and she wore faded green overalls. A plate of scrambled eggs and toast rested on the bedside table. Two days had passed.

"Are you hungry?"

"Yes, please."

I sat up, while she placed the plate in my lap. The eggs were delicious. How did I go for all that time without appreciating food?

"How are you feeling?"

"Better." I took another bite. "Thank you."

Aunt Anne ripped off the tape and quickly removed the needle, swiftly applying cotton batten and a Band-Aid. I pulled my arm up to hide the marks, but she yanked it back down.

"What have you done to yourself?"

My appetite left as shame took its place. I set the plate back on the bedside table.

"I'll never do it again."

And it was true. I'd never touch speed again. But there was something else, a crucial error that needed correcting.

"That doctor was wrong."

"About what?" she asked.

"I never had sex with a man."

Aunt Anne rolled up the tubing and put the IV bag away. She didn't know how to respond so she picked up my pillow, pounding it back into shape.

"That's your business. I don't need to know."

There it stood – as strong as ever – the unspoken, unbreakable family creed. Everyone expected to stand in their solitary silos, silently bearing their pain all alone, never saying a word about how they truly felt.

"I have to go down and check on a pregnant heifer. That's why I brought you here."

"You have to believe me. I didn't have sex."

Aunt Anne gently pushed the hair out of my eyes, tucking the strands behind my ears.

"I believe you," she said, kissing my forehead. "Now get some rest. We'll talk about all this later."

The door closed, but a little crack appeared in Aunt Anne's silo, letting out a tiny beam of light.

It took a good week before I felt well enough to pull on Mom's housecoat and get out of bed. I wandered down the stairs, through the kitchen and out the back door. Aunt Anne was in the orchard, up on the ladder harvesting apples. Her apron was full.

"How's the heifer?"

"Late, but I don't want to bother the vet until I'm sure we need him. No point wasting money."

Laundry flapped on the line as Aunt Anne climbed down. My jeans danced in the wind with Cope's red cowboy shirt. There was a tear in the sleeve.

"I was thinking we'd go into Steadman's in a few days and buy you a new dress."

I spun in a fury. "I am not wearing a dress!"

Aunt Anne started to laugh. She was teasing me. I laughed back.

"Here," she said, kneeling as the apples gently rolled out of her apron and onto the grass. "Put these in the bushel basket."

She climbed back up the ladder as I sat down and picked up an apple, sniffing the skin and took a bite. I'd never noticed how sweet and genuine they smelled, so different than the chemical green I tasted after I'd done a hit. Cattle lowed and the air was clean. One of the hired hands was out in the southern pasture combining corn. The remaining golden tassels rippled in the wind. The grass between my fingers felt cool and I let myself breathe. I felt safe.

"Your mother and I used to pick apples every summer. But most of the trees have been chopped down now."

"How come?"

"People don't need to preserve as much, what with all the grocery stores."

Things were sure different since Mom and Aunt Anne were girls. I thought of Lily and Helen at The Green Door. Things had changed so much.

"Did you eat apples all winter?

She nodded.

"Didn't you get sick of them?"

"It's all we had."

Like me and Lily and Gabe living on bologna sandwiches. Aunt Anne dropped another apron full of apples onto the ground. I picked one up and took a bite. My tongue prickled it was so tart. The apples would make delicious pies. Aunt Anne climbed back up the ladder in her work pants. Mom always wore a housedress when she worked outdoors.

"You never wear dresses."

"I did."

"Why don't you anymore?"

"I never liked the way they felt."

"Then how come you always made me wear them?"

"I wore what my mother told me to wear until I was living under my own roof."

"I live on my own, so I guess that means I can wear what I want."

"I suppose so."

I put another apple in the basket.

"There are other women who don't wear dresses. It doesn't mean there's anything wrong with them," I blurted out.

"That's right."

"Do you know any?" I wanted to talk about Ginnie and Mary, but I didn't know where to start.

Aunt Anne cautiously examined an apple. "Yes. And they were all fine woman, but they didn't always have the happiest lives. Just because God makes you a certain way doesn't mean you have to act on it."

"What if you want to?"

She stood on her toes and reached even higher. "Darn, the worms have gotten to this branch." She snapped it off at the base and several spoiled apples tumbled down.

"Isabel told me what happened at your school."

More shame sliding down my throat as Aunt Anne climbed down.

"I certainly never supported your father's idea to put you in a hospital. And neither did Isabel."

So Dad was the one who wanted to lock me up.

"Your father just didn't know what to do with you. It seemed like the only solution at the time."

"And now?"

"I don't think you need to worry about that. As you said, you're on your own and you're making your own decisions."

All by myself.

"How is he?"

"Your father? A lot better. His birthday's coming up."

I knew that. He was going to turn forty-five next week. Old.

"And the boys?"

"Frank's determined to be president of the student council and Isabel is teaching him how to debate."

I smiled at the thought. Frank would put the entire school on schedules to improve their grades. I placed the last apple in the basket. It was full.

"And Tedder?"

"He's got a little dog."

I wanted to be happy for them but I wasn't. I was jealous for what they had and I didn't, and I hated myself for feeling that way.

The next morning Aunt Anne was gone. A note on the kitchen table said that she was in the stall with the heifer. I slipped into a pair of overalls and a flannel shirt. I still wasn't too steady on my feet, but it felt good to be outside again even though the weather was changing. A strong wind skipped across the yard from the east, blowing chunky tufts of straw and hay. I was wearing a pair of old barn boots. Charlene would get a kick out of this. I wondered what she was doing and hoped her mother kissed her when she opened the door and prayed that her father didn't beat her up. Maybe they welcomed her back into the family with open arms. But that didn't seem likely. How could they welcome her home after what she'd done? Parents could never forget the speed and the bikers and the sex. Or maybe Charlene lied and they never found out. A loose piece of sheet metal rattled on the roof of the chicken coop as a rooster scurried by, its feathers blown back into an elaborate red ruffle, clearly annoyed by the weather. I approached the concrete stairs to the pens, walked down and opened the iron hasp. The cattle lowed.

It took a moment for my eyes to adjust. The pens, built into the thick stone foundation of the barn, were dark and cool. Shapes milled as the herd shifted. A light swung back and forth near the rear. The pregnant heifer must be there. The yearlings stood, watchful behind sturdy white bars and railings, tags stapled onto their ears as I made my way past. Granddad tagged the cattle so he knew how old they were and where they came from. Fat cattle, the ones ready for slaughter, shoved their heads through the bars, eagerly chewing on the feed the hired hand had shoveled into their troughs earlier. They ignored me as I walked by, mindful of one thing, gobbling up mouthful after mouthful of food. For some reason I thought of Lily and the body rub parlour and the men who trudged up the stairs.

The light was closer. Aunt Anne was in the stall with the pregnant heifer. The heifer couldn't have been more than a year and her eyes were wild. One of the hired hands was holding the animal's head. I couldn't see his face. Aunt Anne's hand was up the heifer's bum, taking her temperature. The heifer lowed and kicked.

"Whoa," Aunt Anne said, quickly backing away.

She removed the thermometer and hopped over the railing to read it in the light.

"I'm going to call the vet," she said, walking quickly down the concrete walkway. The hired hand kept holding the heifer's head, talking to her in a soft voice, trying to keep her calm. I climbed up the slats, swinging easily over the side and sat on the top of the railing.

"Glad to see you're feeling better," the man said, stroking the hair between the heifer's eyes. Her black nose glistened and foamed.

"Hugh?" I asked, squinting into the dim.

"Maddy," he replied, wiping his hands on his pants.

He looked like a young Granddad. Tall and strong in a worn checkered shirt, green work pants and barn boots. His hair was starting to go as white as Granddad's and it stood up just as straight.

"Did you carry me up the stairs?"

"Uh huh," he replied.

"Thanks."

I didn't get down and he didn't come over. The heifer milled listlessly in the straw, shifting the weight of her baby back and forth on her hooves, trying to find some comfort. Hugh was a grown man, but I didn't feel like a grown woman. I felt like the same scared little kid standing out on the barn beam years ago.

"Are you working here?"

He nodded, hand-feeding the heifer some mash, murmuring, "Shhh girl. Shhhh."

We were quiet. I wanted to know if his mother and dad approved of him farming. What about school? His parents had always wanted Hugh to go to university.

"How long?" I asked.

"Long enough," he replied, pulling out a deck of smokes. Hugh lit one and was about to return the pack to his breast pocket when he waved them at me.

"Want one?"

The old warning. Never smoke in a barn.

"Sure," I replied, hopping down and walking over through the straw and manure.

He tossed me the pack. I'd never smoked in front of family. My stomach chucked. The nicotine didn't mix with the penicillin. I took another puff as Hugh took a long draw. The smoke disappeared up into the wooden timbers as he looked at me.

"Where have you been?"

"Toronto."

"I hate that place."

Farmers and cattlemen took it upon themselves to hate everything that came out of the city. What would he think if he knew what I'd been doing? It would certainly shock him.

"You make yourself any friends?"

"Some."

What would Hugh think of Gabe and Cope?

"Get a job?"

Did running speed count?

"Not really."

"Doesn't sound all that great to me."

"It's okay."

"If you say so."

He took a final drag as the fire licked down to the filter.

"Does you being back mean that you're finished making a spectacle of yourself?"

The remark struck like a whip. Hugh broke up a bale of hay, kicking straw all over the cattle pen.

"Granddad's been worried that you might have damaged yourself."

I took a deep drag, reaching out to stroke the heifer. Damaged. So that's what they thought of me. A piece of perfectly good fruit that had rolled off the table and bruised itself. A cracked vase or a car that had been in a head-on collision and didn't drive quite right anymore. Who would want that? Not my family. They didn't want anything that was less than perfect. The heifer moved to the other side of the pen. To everyone else I was just a spectacle – a damaged freak. I was stupid to have felt safe. I didn't belong here. I wasn't part of this tribe anymore.

Hugh dropped his cigarette into the pen, the burner fizzling into the dung. There was a clang as the outside door swung open. Aunt Anne returned.

"The vet's on call," she said. "Hugh, you'll have to stay with her, and when it's time come and get me. Come on, Maddy. You need some rest."

"Good to see you," Hugh said, pouring some water into the heifer's trough.

"You too," I lied.

I didn't want to sleep.

"Then make yourself useful," Aunt Anne said, sitting down at the kitchen table. "We'll make your grandfather some pies." A big blue bowl full of apples sat before her.

Rain streamed down the windows, turning the world outside into a wet green blur. The wind picked up speed, moaning as it hurled itself around the house. The sound made me shiver. I opened the cutlery drawer to retrieve the paring knives. Everything was exactly the same: the knives, the forks, the sterling serving spoons and the big butcher knives. A bouquet of spatulas stood in a colourful jar by the sink. All the same bowls lined the cupboards, the bowls that had been there for as long as I could remember. I traced my fingers through the deep cuts in the wooden counters, the cuts Mom and the sisters had made learning how to cook. Everything was the same, everything except me. I handed Aunt Anne a knife and we began shaving long curlicues of red peel away from the fruit.

"You're awfully thin."

"I'm fine," I replied, trying to focus on the peel instead of what Hugh had said.

I had nearly finished four apples when the wind hit the side of the house so hard I jumped.

"You're not used to the weather," Aunt Anne said.

Was that a criticism?

"Your grandfather should have a man look at the shutters and the eaves. The house is getting older."

Neither of us spoke.

"How is he?" I asked.

"Like the house," she replied.

Then she went quiet again. Maybe I didn't have the right to ask about Granddad anymore.

"Will you get the pie plates?"

I pulled two out of the cupboard on top of the refrigerator. The last time I'd helped make pies I had to stand on tiptoe. Now I reached the pie plates easily. When I turned around Aunt Anne was staring at me. She had eyes like Mom.

"You remember where everything is."

How could I forget? I might have been gone for a while, but that didn't mean I'd forgotten the rest of my life.

"Fetch the lard."

I got it from the butter keeper. The moment I handed it to her, Aunt Anne seized it as if she was possessed, vigorously greasing the pie plates.

"I don't need to know where you've been, what you've done, that business with your arms. But I want to know what you're going to do now."

She slammed the pie plate down and started greasing another. The word flood flowed.

"You're young. You can make different choices. You don't have to keep making the same mistakes over and over again." Her skin was flushed, her eyes bright and focused. "Get me the board and the rolling pin. Oh, and the flour. Don't forget the flour."

I retrieved the baking board and pin from their spot behind the knives and the flour from its bin beside the fridge. When I turned back, Aunt Anne had stopped.

"Your mother made a mistake."

"What?" I sat down, setting the flour in front of her. Mom never did anything wrong.

"Mind you, she didn't mean it."

I'd never seen Aunt Anne so upset.

"You've got to believe me, Maddy. She didn't mean you children any harm."

Then she resumed kneading the dough in the bowl. Plop went the dough onto the board. She ran over it with the rolling pin as if she was trying to kill something.

"But she had no business doing that. She had no business keeping the cancer from you. You were old enough. You needed to be told. I kept saying, 'Laura, she's a young woman. She needs to know. She needs to spend this time with you. It's the only time she'll have.' But she just wouldn't hear of it. Your mother wouldn't hear a word. Not one word. Did you know that?"

Then Aunt Anne started to cry, and Aunt Anne never cried because crying was weak. "She forced your father. She forced me. 'Not one word to the children, Anne. Not one word.'"

"Please don't cry."

She rubbed the tears across her cheek, mixing with a dusting of flour.

"She refused to believe it. Right up until the end, she refused to believe she could die. She had other things to do."

So Mom didn't hide it on purpose. She just didn't believe it could happen, that she could actually die. Maybe Mom and I were the same

Night Town

after all. I thought God wouldn't kill me because he wanted to torture me, because I was so bad. Mom thought God wouldn't kill her because she'd spent her whole life being so good. That was the deal. If you lived a decent life, God would take care of you. But then He broke it. What a shock that must have been. "No Laura, you're dead. Sorry about that." Then a thought flew in like a plane hitting a mountain. If that was true, then Mom's death wasn't my fault. It was God's.

"You've got to forgive your father. It was your mother's choice. I've never seen a person as shattered as your father after your mother died."

"I was there too."

She looked at me and took a breath. She looked out the window and then back at me.

"What happened to you is everybody's fault. You're our cross to bear."

I touched the marks on my arms and felt the tears in my eyes when the back door opened. Hugh stood there while the rain poured down all around him like Noah's Ark.

"She's in labour."

The stall was gloomy. The heifer was on her side. Hugh was at the rear. I cradled the heifer's head in my lap. Her thick tongue lolled out, hitting my hand. It was warm. Her eyes were black and full of fear. Aunt Anne reached into the vagina, up past her elbows. Her hands and arms had disappeared. A coiled chain lay on the floor of the pen.

"The calf is turned around," Aunt Anne said. "I can't get the head."

The heifer mooed and kicked, striking Hugh in the side. He fell back in the straw, holding his gut and breathing hard. Had he broken a rib?

"Are you all right?" Aunt Anne asked.

Hugh nodded grimly, holding down the heifer's legs. Aunt Anne pulled her arms out. They were covered up to the armpits, soaked in blood and mucus. There was a metallic smell to it that mixed with the earth and manure. The heifer lowed again, her head jerking in my lap. Aunt Anne picked up the chain. They were going to have to pull the calf out. Aunt Anne's arms and the chain disappeared into the heifer again.

"Pull!" Aunt Anne yelled. She held down the heifer's legs as Hugh tugged.

The heifer mooed as Hugh strained, trying to keep his foothold. The chain, the bloody chain, was taut. I held the heifer's head as tightly as I could. Her kicks were getting weaker. Hugh grunted, pulling as hard as he could, his boots digging for a toehold as he slid through the blood.

"It's coming!" Aunt Anne cried.

I stroked the heifer's head. "You're a good girl," I whispered. "You're strong."

"Once more, Hugh!"

As he pulled, the chain shifted and then an enormous mass of blood and mucus followed. The calf had been born. The heifer's sides heaved in and out, empty of her burden. Aunt Anne rapidly cleaned out the calf's mouth and nose so the little creature could breathe. Slowly, the calf rose to its feet and tottered around in the straw, moving towards its mother for some milk, but the heifer just lay on her side. It wasn't unusual for a heifer to have problems with her first birth, but if she didn't get up and move around, she ran the risk of turning toxic.

"Come on," I said, gently pulling the heifer behind the ears. "You've got to get up."

"Up!" Aunt Anne commanded. Locks of her red hair had spilled free from the kerchief and her overalls were soaked in blood. "Up!"

Hugh even wrapped the chain around the heifer's neck, but no matter what we did, the heifer just lay there. She had no interest in mash or water. When I ladled some into her mouth, it just drained out the other side.

"Is she going to be okay?" I asked.

I didn't want to cry. I wouldn't cry. There was no point in it. Aunt Anne swiped the hair out of her eyes, patting the heifer's side.

"We'll have to wait for the vet."

The heifer died before he arrived. Aunt Anne and I sat in the kitchen drinking tea.

"Your grandfather is going to be upset."

As selfish as it was, I didn't care about Granddad's feelings. I wanted to talk about my mother. This was the first time anyone had talked about what happened, and I wanted to learn everything I could before the door slammed shut again.

"You should have *made* me go."

I clenched my fists, wanting to hammer her with questions and make her cry. I wanted everybody else to cry – to pay. Aunt Anne set the teacup down, as if she was anticipating a punch, and for a second I wanted to. But it wasn't her fault. It was my mother's. Why didn't she tell me? I would have gone to the hospital if I'd known. I could have helped.

Then I remembered the call. The time Betsy and Sandy were in the basement and Aunt Anne phoned. She wanted to come and get me. I knew in my heart, deep down, even then, what was going on, but I'd just pushed it away. I was as scared as Mom. And just as certain that nothing bad could possibly happen. I wanted to drive my fists down on the table and scream louder than the storm, but I just stuffed it down, forced the feelings back where they belonged. Get down, get down! You're not safe to let out. Leave me alone! Go away!

Then the little voice in the well called up to me, the voice that sent me to the dispensary, "But she was your mother. She was your mother, and you loved her more than anything else in the world."

Aunt Anne just stared into her teacup.

"It was never about love, Maddy. She just couldn't face goodbye."

The rain was letting up and I needed some air. Mud sucked at my boots, trying to root me as I trudged across the yard, up the hill towards the hay mow. When I yanked back the big wooden doors a flock of pigeons swooped down through the dark air out into the night. My hands shot up to protect my face, remembering the crows, but now it was only pigeons and doves, cooing as they blew past. The mow air was humid and heavy, closed in by tall towering walls of hay, grain to fatten the cattle that lowed in the pens below. I reached into the gloom for the switch. A ladder leaned against the wall. The same ladder Dad ran up that night I was out on the beam. It could have tipped and he could have fallen, but he went up to save me anyway. That was then.

I climbed the ladder, walking through the scattered straw and twists of twine, toward the edge where the mow met the beam, and glanced down. My stomach lurched, it was so high. If I had fallen I would have been dead or crippled, my back or neck snapped. No wonder Mom and Dad had been so terrified. Seeing their daughter up on that beam in a nightgown, holding a rifle, and then jumping, tumbling through the air, falling into her grandfather's outstretched arms. I'd done it for the thrill, to make a point to Granddad that I was as good as any boy, but now I realized the seriousness of the game. The bar had been set. After Mom died, I'd started jumping all the time. I jumped into the dispensary, then into Rochdale and finally into a world with Hermann, guns, cops and drugs. Like Dad stepping off the edge of the bathtub, I'd just kept jumping and eventually I was going to die.

"Now that's a moment that went down in family history."

Hugh was down below with his hands on his hips, legs spread wide and head tipped back.

"The spectacle's first appearance," I replied.

"Oh, I don't know if it was the first. You want to see the calf?"

We leaned over the rail, watching the calf sucking at the teat of a surrogate cow.

"Do you think she even knows that isn't her mother?"

"As long as she's getting milk, she's fine."

"So they just forget."

Hugh nodded. "A dog will wait a while, but then they forget too."

"What happened to Buster?"

"Granddad had to shoot him. He started killing chickens."

"That must have been hard on him. He loved him."

Hugh spat. He loved Buster too, but he'd never admit it.

"Did he get a new one?"

"New what?"

"Dog."

"Lots of cats, but no dogs. Claims he lost the appetite."

The little calf stopped sucking and began to wander around, checking out the pen. Its steps were no longer as tentative. Hugh hopped in and made a bed of straw.

"How long you staying?" he asked.

"A day or two."

"You going home then?"

What home? I sloshed a bucket of fresh water into the cattle trough.

"Isabel brings Frank and Tedder out to visit."

Why was she doing that? "Is she still putting on airs?"

"Not so much. I think we made her nervous at first."

It was hard to imagine Isabel scared. Hugh climbed out of the pen and leaned the pitchfork against the wall.

"It's late," he said.

It was. We walked out of the barn, across the yard and into the house. The rain had finally stopped. Hugh opened the screen door.

"You might want to give her another chance. She's not as bad as you think."

The next morning I took the final antibiotic. Aunt Anne and I were standing in the hall foyer looking at Granny Gillespie's prized crystal chandelier. Light bounced around the oak-paneled walls and up the stairwell. Every spring Mom and I used to wash the prisms in big buckets of soapy water and then polish them until they were brilliant. The lights still danced, but they didn't seem quite as bright. I ran up the staircase to the top and leaned over the banister as far as I could. A thick layer of dust had settled on the prisms.

I called down to Aunt Anne, "Mom used to say, 'If they gather dust, they don't sparkle.'"

"I remember."

Hanging onto the banister I blew as hard as I could, watching the dust motes twirl and spin in the sunlight until they finally disappeared.

Aunt Anne and I sat cross-legged on the foyer floor in our work pants surrounded by the prisms, plunging the crystals into soapy water, then cleaning and polishing them. I'd stripped the chandelier bare, being careful not to drop any on the way back down the ladder. Hugh was out in the distance on a bright green and yellow John Deere tractor, pulling the fertilizer behind him. White mist sprayed out of the fertilizer's long tubes, fanning like confetti and settling on the bean crop to prevent it from getting the blight. I dunked another prism into the suds.

"Hugh said Isabel brings the boys out here."

Aunt Anne nodded, rinsing a prism in the clear water.

"She wants them to keep ties to your mother's people."

"Why?"

"She understands the importance of family. She always wanted one."

"Then why did she wait so long to get married?"

Aunt Anne polished another prism, gingerly setting it down on one of the white towels we'd spread out over the oak floor.

"She was. To a fellow she met at university."

"Did he die?" Maybe that's what she and Dad had in common.

"No. He divorced her. She couldn't have children and he wanted a family."

I plunged another prism into the bucket. "So…so he just threw her out?"

"That's a bit simplistic, but it's pretty much what happened."

What a horrible thing to do. I remembered the girls in Mom's bridge club talking about how a barren woman was a useless thing. Apparently it was shameful and meant you had no worth. That seemed stupid to me then and even more so now. Everyone had worth. Isabel must have felt terrible being thrown away like that.

A car horn honked in the yard. There was the sound of voices. Then somebody started banging at the kitchen door.

"Anne!"

It was Isabel. I jumped up. She'd let herself into the house and was coming down the hall.

"Don't go," Aunt Anne said, but I was already on my feet and halfway up the staircase.

"Who are you talking to?" Isabel called.

Fiercely, I shook my head.

"Just myself," Aunt Anne replied, still cross-legged on the floor.

I could see Isabel from the top of the stairs, but she couldn't see me. She was wearing a red tweed suit and carrying a large shopping bag. There was no mistaking it. Isabel McAllister was radiating happiness. She dangled the bag in front of Aunt Anne.

"You silly goose. The boys and I would have helped you with the chandelier. But we can't today. I've got Teddy's birthday present and I need you to hide it."

She set the bag on the floor. Aunt Anne removed a cardboard box. A Royal Doulton figurine of a doctor rested on a bedding of white tissue. The doctor held a little bottle of pills.

"Teddy will love it. Where is he?"

"He's out in the car with the boys. I need you to keep it until the party because he'll just snoop around until he finds it."

I crept down the hall towards the tall window at the end that overlooked the front yard. Granny Gillespie's giant spruces still stood guard. Dad was leaning against the Oldsmobile, his fedora pushed back on his head, reading the paper while the boys played baseball on the grass. A little black and tan dog ran back and forth between them. Frank popped a fly. Tedder's mitt went up in the air as he ran backwards to catch it. The dog followed. I hadn't seen Frank in nearly a year and he was getting tall. Blond bangs flopped in his eyes. Tedder jumped, catching the ball in midair and then rolled onto the grass. When he came up the ball was still in the glove. The dog licked his face.

"Dad!" he yelled, throwing the ball towards the car. "Catch!" Soon Tedder's little boy voice would crack.

Dad looked up and caught the ball just in time.

"Come on!" Tedder called.

Dad tossed the newspaper into the back of the car, took off his suit jacket, rolled up his sleeves and walked out onto the grass, telling Tedder to play outfield and he'd pitch. Frank wiggled his hips, taunting Dad, teasing that he threw like a girl.

"Your father does not throw like a girl!" Isabel called as she came out. She grabbed Frank's mitt, kicked off her shoes and ran out on the lawn. "Let's show him what you've got!"

Dad spit in the palm of his hand, did a ridiculous windup and threw. Frank swung as hard as he could, but the ball flew past him and bounced off the grass. The dog caught it, giving the ball a shake. Isabel cheered and Dad's laugh rang up through the trees, flew around the barn and across the fields. It was long and true. Aunt Anne's hand touched my shoulder.

"Let's tell them you're here."

"No."

"Why not?"

Because my father was happy, the family was whole and there was absolutely no room on that team for a speed freak dyke like me.

"Once they're gone, I want to take the next train back to the city."

Stone parapets stabbed a bank of clouds in the distance – the place where Dad had graduated high school. He'd been the top of his class, valedictorian and voted the most likely to leave the farm forever. Dad's graduation certificate had hung on the wall in the office in Sterling, right beside his medical license. It was hanging in Leaside now.

"You can still stay."

No I couldn't. Aunt Anne and I sat on a bench at the station waiting for the train. An enormous white-faced clock with sweeping black arms indicated it was nearly seven. A garbage bag of clean clothes rested on the platform between my feet. Aunt Anne wanted to lend me a suitcase but I'd refused. A whistle sounded in the distance, the seven p.m. to the city.

I stood up. "That's my train."

"Here," she said, thrusting some cash into my hand.

"Thank you."

I felt like a beggar again and wouldn't have taken her money if I hadn't needed it so badly. As I shoved the bills into my pocket the train pulled into the station, throwing up clouds of spark and steam. A man lit a cigarette. The purser hopped down from the middle car, and travelers began lining up to hand him their tickets. When I picked up my bag Aunt Anne snatched my hands.

"Maddy, please stay."

Her fingers held on tight, not letting me go. For a moment I so wanted to. Then I thought of them playing on the lawn, a perfect family like we'd once been. There was a balance to our lives back then, a delicate natural balance that couldn't be disturbed or else it would implode. Look what had happened when Mom died. It was hard to imagine how something so strong could ultimately be so weak. Dad was better now, the boys were happy, and if I went home – kaboom! Bits of a fine family scattered all over the manicured lawn. And how could it not? I was a dyke. That's who I was. That's who I'd always been, and I wasn't going to bring pretend boyfriends home for roast beef dinner and then play race around the back seat of a car while they tried to make out. The thought of it made me sick. I wanted to meet a girl. No, I had to meet a girl – a girl who wanted me just the way I wanted her. I needed to get on that train and find out who I truly was.

"I'm sorry, Aunt Anne. I just can't."

Her fingers relaxed as she released me.

"Promise you'll call if you need me."

"I'll be fine."

The conductor whistled.

"Last call for Toronto. All aboard!"

"Promise!"

"I promise. Thanks for taking care of me."

Then the whistle sounded and the train hissed as the engine gathered steam. I ran for the railway car, handed the purser my ticket and flopped into an empty seat, determined not to look back, but I couldn't resist. Aunt Anne stood on the platform in her work pants and flannel shirt waving goodbye. I smiled and waved back, but the second she was out of eyeshot I began to cry.

CHAPTER NINE

"Follow me," the manager said, expertly navigating through the customers to a booth at the back. The clatter of dishes and loud conversation was deafening. Murray's was one of the busiest eateries in town, crammed with hungry university students lured in by cheap but tasty food. I'd seen a sign in the window advertising for a waitress and came in to apply for the job. The thought of cleaning up dirty dishes was a drag, but I had to start somewhere.

"I don't have any experience, but I'm a quick learner."

The manager took a sip of coffee, thoughtfully stroking his beard as I quietly nudged the bag of clean clothes under the table. Had he noticed? I had to find a place to stow my stuff.

The manager drummed his fingers on the table, taking another sip.

"And I'm a hard worker," I added.

"Alright," he said, setting down the mug. "We'll start you bussing and take it from there."

I thanked him and shook his hand. He told me to come back in the morning.

"Without the garbage bag," he added.

The sidewalk on Bloor was busy with shoppers and students. Murray's was located on the main floor of the Park Plaza hotel, across the street from the museum, the same museum where Dad had found me begging. I had a job, now I needed a place to stay. Rooming houses were close by, but I remembered how lonely they were – another place I didn't fit. Rochdale was just up the way. Maybe someone was looking for a roommate. At least I'd be with people I sort of knew.

Everything had changed. The dorks were gone, replaced with intimidating bikers who, like trolls under a bridge, demanded a toll to travel up into the tower. The rest of the lobby was packed with people there to watch *Deep Throat*, a movie starring some girl called Linda Lovelace. Posters claimed she could perform erotic feats no one in the history of cinema had ever achieved before. The man's name was Harry Reems, and I overheard somebody say that his dick was a fake.

"How can it be a fake if he gets a hard-on?"

Rochdale felt so different than that first day with Mary. Back then it was all about peace and love, but there was nothing peaceful about bikers and *Deep Throat*. A dog started humping another underneath the poster when someone threw hot coffee on them and laughed. The bitch howled. There was no way to see who burned the dogs because the crowd was so thick.

A short guy, who must have been one of the owners, pushed his way through. "Why'd you do that?"

"Because I wanted to."

There was something familiar. The movie crowd, spooked by the howl, began to mill and shift. A biker in Paradise Rider's colours stood by a coffee urn, holding a Styrofoam cup. At first I didn't recognize him, but when he looked up, there he was and he'd seen me too. Hermann dropped the cup and started punching his way through the crowd. I dropped my garbage bag of clothes and ran.

Halfway across Bloor, dodging cars and trucks, I turned. Hermann was gaining. Pushing through people, I bolted into an alley, leaping over piles of trash, splashing through puddles and out onto University Avenue. A yellow cab idled in front of the museum. Hermann was still behind but I'd made up a bit of ground.

"Yonge and Dundas!" I yelled, jumping into the cab, locking the door behind me.

"You got any money?" the cabby asked, casually slinging his arm over the front seat.

I slammed down the lock on the front passenger door just as Hermann's pulled on the handle. Furious, he smashed his fist onto the windshield.

"You don't want that guy in here!" I yelled. "Go!"

The cabby squealed into traffic while Hermann thumped the trunk, waving for another cab, screaming and shaking his fist. I asked the driver to roll up his window. I didn't need to hear what Hermann was saying. I already knew what he'd do if he caught me.

The meter read $1.55. I handed the driver a tip.

"Don't tell anyone where you dropped me."

I slipped into the doorway of a closed camera shop and tried to breathe. Once I caught my breath I peeked out. No Hermann. Head down, I walked down the street, running up the stairs of The Green Door. Ivan wasn't there, only Helen and Lily sprawled out on sofas reading fashion magazines. Helen was wearing thigh-high rhinestone boots and a glittering silver lamé halter top, and this time her hair was blue.

Lily jumped up, searching my arms for needle marks. When she saw they were clean she actually kissed me. Lily doled out affection like my family. Rare and spare.

"Hermann's after me."

Lily wasn't happy anymore.

"Who's Hermann?" Helen asked.

"You don't want to know," Lily replied, snatching her purse. "I'm taking the rest of the night off."

"Ivan's not going to like it," Helen said, rubbing her hands back and forth, copying Ivan. "This is a serious job ladies, with serious responsibilities."

Even though I was scared, Helen made me laugh.

"What goes up, must come down," she added.

I didn't get the joke, but Lily roared. "Tell him I'll see him tomorrow. Come on," she pulled me out the door. "We've got to get Gabe."

I hid behind a rusted dumpster near the parkette where the alkies hung out, trying not to think about rats. A Harley roared by. Gabe was surrounded by a cluster of his drinking buddies – rumpled, boisterous men with round, bright cheeks and noses red with exploded capillaries. A tall Indian named Big Man opened a bottle of Aqua Velva, the blue aftershave lotion the winos drank when they didn't have money for real liquor. I tried it once, and it made my head knock when I walked.

Lily was trying to talk Gabe into coming home, but he kept yelling "No!" trying to snatch the Aqua Velva. Big Man swatted him out of the way. Lily grabbed Gabe's arm and he slapped her. Not hard, but enough to attract unwanted attention.

I darted out. "Hey buddy! How's it going?"

Gabe looked at me. At first he wasn't sure who I was.

"Cookie?"

My eyes bounced around like ball bearings in a pinball machine. A sedan slowed, familiar speeder faces staring through the cracked windshield. Somebody pointed. I turned, hiding my face.

"Yeah, it's Cookie. I've got a bottle."

The other winos perked up. Gabe wrapped his arm around me. His breath smelled like rubbing alcohol.

"Just for me, right?"

"That's right. But we gotta go."

Gabe roared, "I got women, and I gotta bottle!"

"Get outta here," Big Man said, spitting on the pavement. "I'm sick of your face."

Gabe got feisty, waving his fists, but Lily and I each seized an arm, pulling him away.

"I got women!" he crowed back as the three of us hurried up the street. "And I gotta bottle!"

Lily closed the bedroom door and walked into the living room. She'd saved enough to rent a large one bedroom in a sprawling new apartment complex called St. Jamestown. St. Jamestown was built to attract young swinging singles, but the elevator had been full of immigrants and their children.

Lily and Gabe's unit had a panoramic view of Lake Ontario. Lights from bobbing oil tankers flashed against choppy whitecaps. Lily had decorated the apartment with modern furniture. Everything was as white as her hair: the sofa, chairs, walls and broadloom. A large photograph of a sexy woman holding a vacuum cleaner hung over the sofa.

"General Idea," Lily said. "One of my customers sells modern art and he said it would be a good investment."

Lily was buying art?

"You should take Gabe to Emergency."

He'd vomited blood nearly all the way home. Lily kicked off her shoes, massaging the balls of her feet.

"I think you've got enough of your own shit to deal with."

Same old Lily. Nobody could take care of Gabe except her. I sat down beside her, patting my thigh. My legs felt thicker and stronger. I'd put some weight back on thanks to Aunt Anne's cooking. Lily swung her feet into my lap while I rubbed between the toes.

"Have you ever seen Hermann around The Green Door?"

"Never."

"Yonge and Dundas? Anywhere downtown?"

"Nope."

That was good news. Still, it was stupid dangerous for Hermann the way he'd been out in plain sight at Rochdale. Sane, careful Hermann would never have done that.

"You can stay with us. But you have to pay food and rent."

Aunt Anne's money wouldn't last long and I couldn't go back to Murray's.

"And you'll have to share the pullout with Helen."

Helen was definitely pretty and we'd be sharing a bed. She said she was asexual but nobody really gave up on sex. That would be impossible.

"Maybe she can show me around the scene."

I didn't even know what a gay bar looked like.

"Does that mean you're admitting you're a lezzie?" Lily asked.

I absolutely hated that word. Lesbian. It sounded like some kind of fungus. 'You've got a nasty case of lesbian. You should get some cream for that.'

"I'm a dyke," I replied. That word sounded strong.

Lily wriggled her toes and stretched her arms. "I don't care about sex. I want to buy a house."

I stopped massaging her toes. "That's so weird."

Lily stopped wriggling her toes. "Why?"

"You're too young."

She snatched her feet out of my hands and sat up. "I want a home."

"Why?" I asked, looking around the apartment. "This is beautiful." Mom would have approved.

"I want a real home. And a house is a home." Then her face clouded over and she stopped talking. Lily did that sometimes. Just shut down and there was no turning her back on.

"I'm going to bed. Do you need a toothbrush?"

I nodded.

"There are extras in the linen cupboard and a couple of tee-shirts."

"Okay, 'night."

Lily had extra toothbrushes? I pulled out the sofa, put on a borrowed tee-shirt and turned off the lights.

The lock tumbler clicked. Helen slipped into the room and began to quietly undress, shiny rhinestone boots toppling over. There were no blinds – only Helen's naked silhouette flickering against the lights of the city. I turned on the lamp.

"Did you make a lot of money rubbing old pervs?"

Helen pulled a tee-shirt over her head. "Were you staring at my tits?"

"No." Yes I was. I sat up and lit a cigarette. Helen brushed her hair.

"I thought you might be Hermann."

Helen set the brush on the glass coffee table. "Is he really that bad?"

"Worse."

She walked towards the bathroom. "Then why don't you turn him in?"

Water rushed as the bathroom taps turned on. Clearly Helen had never had a gun held to her head. She walked back in, drying her face. Without any makeup Helen looked young, vulnerable and sort of sweet.

"If you're too scared to go to the cops, why don't you just go home?"

She sat down beside me and lit a cigarette as I stubbed mine out. Helen had curvy legs. I lay down, hoping she'd take the hint.

"I don't want to talk about it."

"Why don't you just go home?" she repeated.

"Because I can't," I snipped. "And will you please put out that cigarette? I need to get some sleep."

Helen gave me a "you're so strange" look, but put out the smoke and fell onto her back. I switched off the light and could smell her perfume.

"So what are you going to do?" she asked.

"Sleep."

"You can't just lie around all day."

"I'll get something." I didn't much like the hint that I was lazy.

"Do you have money?"

"Yes."

"I don't believe you. What kind of job are you going to get with Charles Manson after you?"

"Who asked you?"

"Don't get all bitchy." Helen rolled onto her side, looking at me. "If you could get a job, what would your dream job be?"

"Is your dream rubbing pervs?"

"Fuck off," she replied, rolling away.

Now I rolled towards her, jabbing her in the ribs. "I mean it. Why are you doing it?"

"I'm saving for a professional makeup kit. I want to work in the movies."

That made sense. Helen was obviously into transformation. Every time I saw her she looked different. I moved closer, thinking about the time I cupped Charlene's boobs.

"I bet you'll be good at it."

The room stilled as Helen's breath slowed.

"Were you really gay?" I asked, shifting my thigh near hers. "Before you went asexual."

She moved her thigh away. "I thought you were tired."

"How did you get rid of it?" My hand lightly brushed hers. "The gayness."

She pulled her hand back. "I have better things to do with my life."

Than love? Maybe somebody hurt her like Ginnie. Or maybe it was rubbing the men.

"Have you ever been to a gay bar?"

"Of course."

"Will you take me?"

"No."

I touched her arm. "You asked me what my dream was. It's to go to a gay bar."

"What a stupid dream."

"Come on. I want to meet a girl."

"Maybe," she replied, sounding fuzzy, nearly asleep. "When it's safe…"

I fell asleep smiling. I knew Helen liked me because she never moved her arm.

I sat on The Steps disguised in Helen's blue and white polka dot dress and a bright red cardigan. Three weeks had passed and my money was gone, but at least there'd been no sign of Hermann. Helen had done my makeup that morning and laughed the whole time while Lily giggled. Only Gabe understood the indignity. He sat beside me rocking back and forth like an abandoned ship. He must have lost twenty pounds since I first met him and had taken to cocking his head the way dogs do when they're trying to understand. The doctor at the emergency room warned Lily that Gabe had suffered a lot of brain damage and advised treatment, but Gabe wouldn't go and Lily didn't want to press the point.

"You got any money for old Gabe?" he asked, giving me his sweetest smile.

I shook my head as Gabe picked up a smoldering cigarette someone had just thrown away.

"Don't," I said, knocking it out of his hand. "You don't know where it's been."

Gabe just picked it back up. His spiky white beard had yellowed and milky clouds floated over his eyes.

"Can you see okay?"

"Better 'n ever."

He probably had cataracts. Two girls dressed in McDonald's uniforms walked up the street. A new franchise had opened and a HELP WANTED sign hung in the window. My job at Murray's would be gone by now, and besides, I couldn't work out in the open. Eventually somebody would see me and tell Hermann. Dad always told me to keep my options open, but most of mine were closed.

"Looky looky!" Gabe chirped when the girls came near.

The girls glanced at each other and hurried past. Who were they to look down on us? Mom would have thought working at some fast food joint was no better than being chained to a stove, cooking for hired hands. A sigh slipped out.

"Why so blue?" Gabe asked.

"Money."

Gabe smiled and stuck his hand out, palm up. I shook my head.

"No more begging."

"Pogey?"

I shook my head. No way I'd go on welfare.

"That's what it's there for."

"Never!" I said, snatching the butt out of Gabe's mouth and throwing it onto the street again.

"Jeez, you and Lily's got more pride than Queen Elizabeth." Gabe pointed at The Green Door. "The money's good and it's respectable."

No it wasn't, but there was no choice. At least I'd be tucked away at The Green Door – safe from sight. A truck rattled by. Lily said nobody from the street ever went up there. My gut knew it was shameful, but no one would ever find out. It would be my secret. And besides, all things being equal, wasn't it better to rub men for money than end up dead?

The dingy rub room was painted blood red and dimly lit by a series of flickering red candles. Dad would have called the place a fire hazard but Ivan said it was all about ambience. Naked except for a towel wrapped around his waist, Ivan hopped up on the bed and lay face down on a single mattress that stood on a tall platform with wobbly wooden legs.

"First warm it up."

A line of slimy lotion shot into the palm of my hand. It smelled of coconuts and pine needles. I tried not to focus on what was happening and think about girls.

"Not too much. That stuff ain't cheap."

It sure felt cheap to me. I slapped the lotion across his back and some squirted on the fitted white sheet.

"You're not greasing a pig here."

"Sorry."

"Rub the shoulders. Ah, that's nice. Now take it down a bit. Trail your fingers over the skin, and it never hurts to talk. Guys like to hear a girl's voice when she rubs him."

"What should I say?"

"Not so loud. More like a purr and just don't talk about yourself. Nobody cares about that."

That made sense. It was like being in one of Dad's examining rooms, visiting with his patients. There were even red screens to change behind, only rather than slipping into a medical gown, I'd be taking off my top. Isabel never had to rub men to survive.

"Not so rough."

"Sorry."

Ivan flipped over. I warmed more lotion in my hands and rubbed it onto his furry chest, pretending to work a stain out of a carpet.

"Most of the guys will want you to rub their stomachs so they can stare at your tits."

"And if they try and touch them?"

"Back up and tell 'em that you don't do extras."

I nodded while I massaged, thinking about Dad playing ball on the lawn.

"Don't pull on the nipples. They're sensitive."

"Really?"

I thought men only cared about their penises.

"You've got a way to go, but you've got good hands. Now let me rub those tits."

I put my hand out. "Five bucks."

Ivan slapped his gut and sat up. "You've got the job."

Ivan walked me back into the lounge. A girl with a huge red afro and hooped earrings sat in a puffy chair, jotting something into a ledger. Helen and Lily were talking about the newspaper boy, the one I used to know from The Steps, who'd recently been murdered. We all cried when we heard about it. His body had been found behind a dumpster at the back of another body rub parlour. The cops said he'd been sexually abused. How could anybody do something like that? He was only a kid.

Helen looked up, flashing me one of her looks. "My, my, my. Look who's here to rub old pervs."

"Shut up," I replied.

"Let's keep it ladylike," Ivan said, turning to the girl with the afro.

"I'm Cindy," she said, with a smile that revealed a golden tooth.

Cindy went back to decoding her ledger while Helen and Lily explained the schedule. There were two shifts, noon to six and six to midnight, and depending on the day sometimes up to six girls working.

"There's more guaranteed action at night, but the creep potential's higher," Helen said.

Lily advised me to get a steady roster of clients and service them during the day. Cindy looked up to make sure Ivan couldn't hear.

"Deal dope on the side," she whispered.

"What do you sell?"

"Downers and junk. You want some?"

"No, thank you." I'd given that up.

The rules were simple. The john – that's what the customer was called – entered the lounge, looked at the ladies and selected one. The girl would slowly stand, smile seductively and take the john's arm, walking him over to the manager's wicket. From there Ivan would count the money and tell us what room was free.

"And you go behind the screen and strip down," Ivan added.

"They're about the titillation factor," Helen said. "The longer it takes for you to take off your top, the more revved up they get."

Lily agreed. "It's like a mini striptease."

"But you can't hide back there. Remember, the clock is always ticking," Helen said, looking over at Ivan. "'Cause if you do, he'll dock your pay."

The girls were responsible for changing the bed after each rub. There was a laundry hamper in every room, usually situated near a lone straight-backed chair. Helen thought that Ivan had stolen the chairs from some restaurant and made the bed frames himself because they swayed whenever a fat john hopped up.

"This is a topless rub. Don't take off your panties," Ivan said.

"I don't want to take off my underwear," I replied, already more than a bit nervous about the idea of taking off my shirt.

Ivan turned on the downstairs speaker so the guys could be lured upstairs by "Brown Sugar" or "Angie." He said the Rolling Stones were an aphrodisiac.

"It's your job to show up clean and presentable," he said, leaning out of the wicket. "I don't want no whores working my place. I've got a reputation to think of. And wear something that shows off your titties."

We'd been working for four hours and only Cindy and Lily had been busy. Lily was up at Ivan's wicket with another john.

"If the rub costs twenty and I get five, that means I do six rubs a day at five bucks a rub and I'll bring home thirty dollars. I'll bank the money and retire after a couple of months."

"I haven't retired yet," Helen said, looking into a compact and applying a thick layer of eyeliner. Her green eyes locked on mine. The red thunderbolts she'd hennaed onto the sides of her blue hair reminded me of Zeus. "The only way you do that is if you do extras," she added, glancing towards Lily.

Lily was pulling the john by his tie, leading him out the door and down the hall.

"What are extras?"

Helen looked at me through a veil of false eyelashes. "Are you serious?"

I hated it when Helen acted as if she had all the experience in the world. "Yes – "

She crossed her legs – time for a lesson. "There's hand jobs – that's five bucks."

That's what I'd done to Kenneth.

Helen mimicked peeling a banana, opened her mouth and slowly brought her lips down over her thumb. "A blow job's ten."

"Gross."

"A full out fuck is twenty and around the world is forty."

"What's around the world?"

"That's the whole works. Plus," she said, pointing at her bum.

"No way!"

I opened a worn copy of *Hustler* to look at the centrefold. I'd never let anybody put anything up there. The *Playboy* girls reminded me of naked cheerleaders, but the *Hustler* women had boobs that looked as if they'd been pinched too often. I shifted towards Helen.

"So when are we going to the gay bars?"

When she didn't answer I moved even closer, fingers creeping across the back of the sofa until my arm settled around her shoulder. Helen looked at my hand, picked it up and flicked it off.

"You said you'd take me out for my birthday but you didn't," I complained.

I'd recently turned seventeen, and Helen bought a yummy chocolate cake and everyone sang. The downstairs door jangled, followed by a tentative shuffle of feet. Springing back from Helen, I held my breath as footsteps padded up the stairs. A tall, bone thin man wearing a beat-up black fedora poked his head around the door.

"Come on in," Ivan waved from the wicket. "We won't bite. Will we, girls?"

I sat up straight and tried to look welcoming but my legs kept squeezing themselves shut. Helen stretched out like a lazy tabby. The man stood in the doorway as if suspended in a magnetic field while Ivan ran out from behind the wicket.

"Why don't you meet the ladies?" Ivan asked, guiding the man in. Reluctantly, he allowed himself to be steered. "This is Mercedes," Ivan said, indicating Helen, "and this is…"

"Isabel," I replied, remembering that you needed a fake name to protect your true identity.

The tall, thin man suddenly realized he still had his hat on. Embarrassed, he snatched the fedora from his head and bowed. At least he had good manners.

"Who would you like?" Ivan asked.

"What?"

He was as new to this as I was – a virgin customer.

"Which one of our lovely ladies would you like to give you a relaxing massage?"

Helen readjusted herself on the sofa to look appealing, which was easy because she was incredibly sexy. I just sat there in my red cowboy shirt looking like a dog. Smiling as sweetly as I could, I asked the man how he was. That's what Dad always did to break the ice. He smiled nervously at both of us and then took Ivan aside to wrangle over the price.

"How much?" the man mumbled.

"Twenty."

"What do I get?"

"You get a slow sensual rub from one of these lovely young ladies."

"Are they naked?"

"Topless," Ivan replied. "And as you can tell, they're both very well endowed."

The tall thin man snuck another peek. I grinned like an idiot, while Helen swung her boobs around. It reminded me of a song Aunt Anne used to sing: "How Much Is That Doggie in the Window?" The man pointed.

"I'll take Isabel."

My breath shot out in short anxious blasts when we reached the top of the stairs and walked down the long, narrow hallway. The red walls were covered with faded pin-ups, and some of the loose floor planks bounced when we stepped on them. The tall, thin man was close behind me, clutching his hat like a bouquet of flowers. I pushed open the door and saw the screen, the lotion and the bed.

"Take your clothes off, hop up on the bed. And cover yourself with a towel."

The tall, thin man sat down, hat firmly clenched in both hands. "I don't want to get undressed."

We looked at one another for a moment.

"I don't do extras."

"I don't want you to."

"Then what do you want?"

Was he a creep? My heart thumped.

"There's nothing I appreciate more than a healthy young body." The hat bobbed up and down, shifting from hand to hand. "I want to watch you take your top off."

He stood up, removed a ten dollar bill from his wallet and set it on top of the sheet.

"And I want you to make it nice and slow."

He bowed his head and sat back down, waiting for my answer. How did this fit into hand job, blow job, straight screw, or around the world? Helen didn't say anything about this.

"You can't touch me."

"I don't want to touch. I want to watch."

"But I'm supposed to rub you."

"Do you want to?"

"Not really."

"Then why not just take the money?"

Looking at the bill on the cot I considered the deal. I really didn't want to touch him and this way I wouldn't have to. We'd already spent nearly five minutes and that meant I only had fifteen to go. What was worse? Touching his body or showing him my boobs? If I rubbed him he'd see my boobs anyway so I was actually making ten dollars for free. Fifteen, when I counted in my commission.

"Okay." I snatched up the money and stuffed it into my pocket. "But you have to stay right there," I added, backing up a wee bit. "You can't move a muscle."

"Do you have any music?" he asked.

I turned on the speaker from downstairs and "You Can't Always Get What You Want" rolled into the room. Slowly I undid the white snaps on Cope's old red shirt while Mick growled. Thinking of Ginnie, I leisurely slid the fabric down over my shoulders, remembering the times we kissed in her bedroom as the sun came up. The red cotton teased over my back, slipping down and sliding over my breasts as the man set his hat on the floor and grabbed his knees. Looking down, I lightly touched my nipple and it sprang up. The tall thin man was breathing like Kenneth in the trunk of the car.

As I swung my tits, he began to submit to the spell. I felt like Fernando the Amazing Hypnotist at the Sterling Fall Fair. Fernando swung a golden pocket watch and the subjects slipped into a hypnotic state. This was about power, and mine was absolute. Earlier I'd been really scared, wondering if I could take my top off in front of strange horny men, worried that they might attack me or maybe I'd turn into a pillar of salt like Lot's wife. But this was different. My body was the boss in this room, not the men, and as long as I didn't think about what was happening, everything would be fine. My body performed in this secret world, but my heart and soul were locked away like the ballerina in my music box where I'd crank the brass key, open the lid, and as the music played the dancer spun around. When the music finished I pushed the ballerina down, shut the lid and put the box away.

The music ended and my cowboy shirt lay around my ankles – a pond of red fabric on the floor. I stood there in the middle of the dimly lit room, my breasts exposed to a faint breeze from the open window, while the tall, thin man stared at me.

"Thank you," he said and got up, crossed the room and walked out, shutting the door behind him.

"You're a whore," said Helen, queen of the universe.

"I am not. I'm trying to save some money just like you."

I tugged at the neck of my new Crime of the Century tee-shirt, looking for Hermann, now more a habit than anything else. Gabe had watched the streets for nearly two months and never saw him, so gradually I'd come out of hiding.

Lily, Helen and I were at the Zanzibar playing Pong and drinking Zombies while a gorgeous girl swung around a brass pole, her long brown hair sweeping the stage floor. Lily twirled the little pink parasol while a white computerized ball bounced across the lime green screen.

"What do you say, Lily?"

"I think as long as you get paid it's good."

Lily took a furtive sip. "Tell me if you see Gabe."

If Gabe knew she'd been drinking he'd start chirping, "What's good for the goose is good for the gander."

George arrived and set down another round of brightly coloured Zombies. He was the same waiter Vic and Cope had introduced me to.

"Hey, George, if you do hand jobs are you a whore?" I asked.

"Do you like it? Does it turn you on?"

"No way."

He switched the ashtrays, placing a clean one in the centre of the table. "You're only a whore if you like it. There was a girl where I grew up who you could find out in the bushes by the Esso station any Saturday night with her toes in her ears. Now that's a whore."

"Does that mean I'm not a whore either?" Lily asked. "Even if I go a little bit further?"

"Same rules. If you enjoy it, you're a whore. If you're not, you're a businesswoman."

Lily slapped the table. "See?"

Helen was wrong.

George placed a Zombie and napkin in front of each of us. "The drinks are from the gentleman by the stage."

The tall, thin man sat alone. He was a tool and die maker from St. Catherine's who lived with his mother, and he had become one of my regulars. After the first time with him I'd made a secret deal with myself. I'd never blow the guys or have sex with them, but what was wrong with helping Mother Nature fulfill a man's natural urges? Sometimes when I was jerking a man off my head sent down alarming thought bubbles, but my body said, "Stop worrying, think of the money." I chugged the Zombie and told my mind to shut up.

Lily waved to him. "That's the way to make good money."

"That's the way to become thoroughly fucked up," Helen said, taking a sip. "There are some things you just can't justify. No matter how hard you try."

"Is that why you went asexual?" I asked. "I don't get how you could just turn yourself off."

"I'm asexual because I can't sell my body for money and then go home to someone I love."

"Why not?"

"Because it will fuck up the love and fuck up your head."

"But love's supposed to be free," I said. "And if so, why not share it?"

"If you share your body, you're making love a commodity."

"You're sharing your precious tits," Lily said, javelining her pink parasol into the ashtray. "You're no better than the rest of us. You just think you are."

"I'm not sucking them off."

Lily stared back. "We're just trying to get ahead Helen. Why do you always have to run us down?"

Now Lily's feelings were hurt and Helen's back was up. I dropped a tip on the table for George.

"Let's go," I said. "Ivan's going to wonder where we are."

Helen had to be wrong. I was just jerking the men off to save for a better life and Lily wanted to buy a house. How could that be bad?

The tall, thin man pulled the door shut behind him. With winter here, it was chilly in the rub room, time for cheap Ivan to turn up the heat.

"How's your mother?" I asked.

"She's got arthritis in her toes."

"Make sure she elevates her feet."

The tall, thin man didn't take his usual seat. Instead he shoved the bed across the room.

"Is there anybody downstairs?"

Warning crawled across my stomach as he started jumping up and down on the floor.

"No."

Ivan was dragging trash to the dumpster and the other girls were busy with customers. If he tried to kill me nobody would hear.

"What are you doing?" I asked, trying to calm down.

The tall thin man had always been nice to me. He took off his jacket, folded it and set it on the floor, then off came his shoes, pants, shirt, socks and underwear. One by one, they were neatly folded, and added to the pile of clothing. Next he removed a twenty dollar bill from his wallet, placed it on the bed and sat down in the chair, stark naked, staring at me while I stared at the money. A police siren screamed in the distance.

"What do you want?"

"I want you to do jumping jacks with no bra, and no panties."

"That's all?"

And it was. The tall, thin man jerked off to twenty minutes of naked calisthenics while I jumped up and down to "Tumbling Dice."

Lily brought home pizza, but Gabe just stood in the window, watching the freighters out in the lake, hands thrust deeply into his pockets. He wanted to go to the Dominion. The Dominion was an alky bar where Gabe's buddies hung out.

Lily set the pizza box down on the glass coffee table. "You're not supposed to be drinking."

Gabe turned to me and Helen. "You want to take old Gabe out for a beer?"

"Sorry," Helen said. "Lily's house – Lily's rules."

Gabe grunted, turning back to the window. Lily came up behind him and tried to hug him, but he walked away. Gabe wasn't the same happy guy anymore. I grabbed two slices of pizza, handing one to Helen.

"Want to go out?"

"No."

Frustrated, I chewed on the crust. "You swore. You swore that when it was safe you'd take me to a gay bar."

"I didn't swear."

"You promised."

"I didn't promise. I said maybe."

"I guess your maybes aren't good for much."

Helen picked up another slice of pizza and took a bite.

The cab pulled up in front of a commercial building at the corner of Gerrard and Carlaw, a tough part of town near a railway overpass. The building was long and low with grey brick walls and a Canadian flag draped over the door. Pickup trucks, a yellow Chevy Nova and a couple of old Pontiacs were parked to the side. It reminded me of the tall, thin man's description of a tool and die shop.

"This isn't a bar. It's a garage."

"It's The Blue Jay. It's a hall," Helen said. "The dykes rent it every Saturday night."

A couple of women wearing men's pastel polyester suits passed us by.

"Why don't they just open a bar?"

"The cops are always trying to shut them down. Liquor licenses, underage drinkers. Anything to put them out of business." We reached the entranceway. "Plus, when the straight guys find out there's a dyke bar on the block…"

They'd get drunk and decide to show the dykes what a real man was. Helen yanked open the door. Country music twanged.

"Have a good time," she said.

I told her that dumping me wasn't part of the deal, but Helen wouldn't budge.

"You wanted a gay bar. You got a gay bar," she said, shoving me through the door.

A barrel-chested woman with a silver brush cut, wearing a three-piece men's suit sat behind a red card table. Her hands rested on a steel cash box. She looked so much like a man that I'd never have known she was female if her hands weren't so small.

"Two bucks."

The woman didn't appear to have any breasts. What happened to them?

"Two bucks!" she repeated, getting pissy.

"For what?" I asked, trying not to stare, searching for any sign of tits.

"Admission."

I passed her the money. Maybe she wrapped them in tensor bandages to flatten them down.

"How many tickets?"

"What?"

Patrons were bunching up behind me.

"Are you a retard?" she asked. "Beer tickets."

"Two."

While the dyke made change I looked around. Faded red and white bunting hung from the ceiling. Hurricane lamps threw up flickering candlelight and the tables were draped in red and white gingham. Stackable chairs lined the wall. Mom would have said it was tacky and backward – the kind of show hillbillies put on.

Dykes in men's pastel suits and rented tuxedos foxtrotted with fancy ladies dressed in frilly skirts, high heels and puffy beehives. Others sat around the gingham-covered tabletops drinking beer and pounding their fists. Some of the frilly ladies sat on the dykes' laps, playing with their ties, running manicured fingernails through brush cuts and oily ducktails. The candlelight was so low I ran into a chair. The women on stools, if you could call them that, turned, giving me suspicious looks. They knew I didn't belong and so did I.

The bartender's stiff jeans were hiked up under her tits, held in place by a thick black leather belt, the kind Granddad wore. A pack of green Export A's peeked out of the breast pocket of her tee-shirt and her hair was slicked into a rigid jellyroll. A blue tattoo of a Hawaiian girl wearing a purple lei swayed on her bicep. The bartender grinned at me the way the customers at the body rub did.

"What'll it be, sunshine?"

"A Blue."

Too scared to sit I leaned against the wall, watching the crowd. Nothing seemed real. Frilly ladies flitted around the candlelit room like country and western fireflies while the dykes, thumbs shoved through belt loops, strutted through the smoky haze. A pool cue cracked against the side of an old billiard table and the dykes roared. Another one put money in the jukebox and a Hank Williams song began. The dykes rose, swaggering across the dance floor, bending gallantly to ask the ladies to dance, and when the ladies consented, they pulled them to their feet, sweeping them out onto the worn linoleum floor. One dyke picked her girlfriend up in her arms, and as the frilly lady kicked her heels in delight somebody touched my arm.

"Dance?"

The bartender was standing in front of me, a cigarette dangling between her lips.

I ran out the door. Helen was sitting on the curb. She jumped up. "That was quick."

I stormed by her. "That was mean."

"Butches and femmes. Butches and femmes," Helen sang, skipping along behind me, thoroughly enjoying herself. "You did say you wanted to go to a dyke bar."

I sped up. "Some friend."

Helen ran after me. "I wouldn't have left for real. I would have come and got you."

A couple of butches climbed out of a car. One of them looked at me and horked. I started to cry. I'd never find a girl. Helen turned me around.

"Hey, I'm sorry. It was a joke."

"Not funny."

She touched my cheek. "I mean it. Don't cry."

A red and yellow streetcar pulled up. Helen grabbed my hand, yanking me up the stairs. We sat in the back and stared through the window, watching more butches walk into The Blue Jay. Once the streetcar pulled into traffic they vanished from sight, but I couldn't stop thinking about them.

"What are they?"

"Stone butches. They act like men in every way."

"Why?"

Helen pulled out her compact to check her lipstick. "Because that's the way they are. They don't even get naked because they don't want to spoil the illusion that they have dicks."

"So they hump the femmes with their clothes on?"

"I guess so. I do know they don't use dildos because that would be fake."

Why did everything have to come down to penises? The streetcar's wheels squealed as the doors hissed open. A couple of punk rockers got on, giving the driver a hard time about paying their fares. They were obviously new to the scene, trying to look tough, but they weren't. You could tell by the way they stood. The girl was probably wearing her father's red suspenders and the boy's black Doc Martin boots were still new and shiny. Just like his recently shaved head. Why did everyone need a costume?

"Why do the femmes dress like that?"

Helen shrugged. I lit a cigarette even though it was against the rules. The streetcar crossed the Don River, following the tracks up Parliament, towards John's Open Kitchen. Was Hermann in there? I didn't duck. The driver yelled for whoever was smoking to put out the damned cigarette as I took another drag. The punkers looked at me like I was okay. I didn't want to be okay to them. I wanted to be okay to a pretty girl.

Helen took the cigarette from my hand, took a puff and dropped it onto the floor. "You're right," she said, her hand settling lightly on my thigh. "I shouldn't have taken you there. It was mean."

I didn't want girls like the ones in that horrible Blue Jay place, and there was no way I was going to spend my life dressed like John Wayne. What was I going to do? I'd have to move to another city, but I didn't have any money. After rent, food and clothes, there was never anything left. I always spent it all.

"Where did you meet girls? I mean before you went asexual."

Helen reached up and pulled the bell cord. The bell rang and the streetcar stopped.

Disco pounded down as Helen and I climbed the stairs to a club called Jo Jo's. Guys leaned against the railing and walls, drinking Labatt's 50 beer, playfully grabbing each other by the ass. Two boys tugged one another down the stairs out the door into the alley. I asked Helen where they were going.

"Sex in the bushes."

"In the winter?"

"Yeah."

Wouldn't you get cold and dirty?

Helen and I entered the club. There were sofas, club chairs and a long mahogany bar with a polished brass rail. The dance floor was raised, covered in brightly lit tiles flashing primary colours that pulsated with the music. Jo Jo's was nothing like The Blue Jay. Jo Jo's had style.

Most of the guys were dressed the same: skintight Levis 501s with folded cuffs and yellow construction boots, checkered work shirts with rolled up sleeves to show off Popeye biceps and multicoloured handkerchiefs dangling out of their back pockets. They wore their hair short and moustaches long. Helen signaled for a couple of beers while I asked her why they all dressed the same.

"Clones. They want to look like sexy blue collar guys."

More costumes.

"What's that?" I whispered, pointing at the handkerchiefs, not wanting to sound ignorant.

"Red means S. Black means M. Yellow means water sports and pink just means gay," Helen said, ordering two beers. "That way if a trick is cruising them, they know what the guy's into."

I looked at the yellow handkerchiefs. Water sports? Older men dressed in black leather motorcycle jackets and chaps leaned against the bar, eyes peering out from beneath black motorcycle caps, cruising coy boys who slithered by.

"When you're too old to be a clone, you become a leatherman," Helen said.

"That's weird."

A leatherman hissed, "Then get the fuck out."

"We've got as much right to be here as you," Helen said loud enough so everyone at the bar could hear. She turned to the bartender. "Isn't that right?"

The bartender, a cute clone, nodded, setting down our drinks. New gay bars were opening, busy gay bars filled with younger patrons who refused to hide who they were. To bump up cash flow, the owners were integrating dykes and fags. The older homos didn't like it, but they didn't have a choice. Things were changing and it excited Helen who started talking about the power of being out and being proud.

"I thought you were asexual," I said, not really wanting people to know about me. My sex life wasn't their business. It was private, between me and my girlfriend.

"Just while I'm working at The Green Door," Helen replied. "Then I'm proud to be gay again. You'll get into it, Maddy. I promise. It's infectious."

I knew all about infections and didn't want one. I didn't care about the politics. I wanted Jo Jo's for girls. There were a couple of cute ones up on the dance floor, and sure, the rest of the women were young and fairly butchy, but at least they were dressed in jeans, tees and motorcycle boots instead of the polyester suits. There were hardly any frilly femmes. Thank God. The femmes freaked me out more than the stone butches did. The music was different too, and when David Bowie screamed, "Wham Bam Thank You Ma'am!" Helen asked me to dance. A golden rope around the dance floor held us in the ring. For once Helen didn't talk – we just danced song after song with other gays. None of us were pretending to be straight. We were who we were and nothing ever felt so free.

Then the floor tiles began to vibrate in gold and the music slowed. My hair was slick with sweat and I felt like I was on the Yellow Brick Road. Helen and I stood – awkward because the song was slow – but when I took a chance and put my arm out, Helen moved into me, settling the side of her head against my neck.

Halfway through the song, the beat picked up and the bass boomed. We seized each other by the hands and spun, heads thrown back, faces tilted up to the mirrored disco ball that flashed diamonds of dazzling white light. We whirled in endless laughter until something crashed, the record skipped and an enormous butch in a checkered shirt jumped up from her table, grasping a beer bottle by the neck.

Helen's grip tightened. "That's Easter. She's the meanest dyke in the city."

The bar went eye of the tornado quiet as Easter glared across the bar. Then, lightning fast for a fat woman, she shot up onto the dance floor, pushing us aside and vaulted over the rope, nearly landing on top of a table where another butch held a girl's hand.

"You've been fucking my old lady!" Easter bellowed, smashing the beer bottle and lunging.

The other butch flipped the table to avoid getting a slice of glass in the face. Beer bottles started to fly. Glass shattered. One girl turned to run away. Another girl tripped her. Down she went. When she came up, she sprang – all claws and spit. Energy rippled through the bar. A couple of fags shrieked, "Dyke fight!" and dashed for the door, while one by one the women got caught up in the spirit of the brawl.

Helen and I tried for the exit, but the stairwell was blocked with runaway fags, so we pushed through the crowd, heading towards the bathroom. A beer bottle bounced off my back and Helen nearly got punched in the face but we made it. The bathroom was filling with scared dykes hiding in stalls, locking doors behind them. Easter staggered in, hand to her forehead, blood seeping between her fingers.

"Let me see," I said.

"Fuck off."

I grabbed Easter's hand and pulled it back from the gash. The wound was deep and nasty. I told Helen to go tell the bartender to call an ambulance and get me a bunch of bar towels and a bucket of ice. I soaked paper towels in cold water and told Easter to keep it tight against the wound.

"You're going to need stitches."

"I don't want no stitches,"

"That's your face and you're going to take care of it."

And so it went. Helen returned with ice, towels and bandages, playing nurse while I tended to other wounded dykes. Most of them weren't really all that tough. A few cried. Easter even agreed to go to the hospital. A chubby young woman in a denim jacket and green checkered shirt asked me where I learned how to do this.

"My Dad's a doctor," I replied, looking carefully at her cut. "If you keep an eye on this you shouldn't need stitches. But make sure you change the dressing every morning and if it gets red or inflamed go to the hospital."

The living room was cold and there were no extra blankets. Helen shivered. The apartment was dark and quiet. Lily was out looking for Gabe. Harbour lights flashed in the distance.

"You were really good at that."

Everything I'd learned from Dad just came back.

"Your father's a doctor?"

I grunted. She wanted to ask how a doctor's daughter ended up working at the body rub, but for once Helen had the good sense to keep her mouth shut.

"How about yours?" I asked.

"Baker."

I couldn't imagine Helen anywhere near a kitchen. All she ever did was order out.

"Where?"

"By the airport."

"What does your Mom do?"

"I don't know."

How could she not know what her mother did?

"Does she take care of the house?"

"She never took care of the house. Go to sleep."

Pillows were fluffed and adjusted as quiet lay down again.

"Does she work?"

Helen sat up, light blazing on.

"I don't know! She left years ago and my father is still waiting for her to come back."

"I'm sorry."

Helen shut the light off and flopped back down. "What are you sorry for? It's not your fault. Go to sleep."

We lay there for the longest time, but too much had happened for my mind to slow. I'd been to two gay bars, seen a dyke fight and danced all night with Helen. Even a slow one. Especially a slow one. How could she dance with a girl all night if she was asexual?

"Helen?"

Nothing. I tried counting boats in the harbour. It didn't work.

"Are you asleep?"

A rustle.

"Can I ask you something?"

Sigh.

"As long as it's not about my mother."

Why didn't Helen want to talk about her mother? I guess a runaway mother was worse than a dead one. At least the dead one didn't have a choice.

"How come you're asexual?'

"Because I am."

I rolled over to face her.

"I mean it. How come?"

She rolled towards me, eyes only inches from mine.

"I already told you."

"Tell me again."

Something in her was weakening; her resolution wall was falling down.

"Because you can't have sex with men and love women at the same time."

"Why not?"

"Because it will fuck up the love."

"But we're not really having sex with them."

"If we were lovers, could you jump up and down for that pervert and then come home and get into bed with me?"

"Yeah, why not?"

"Because it's not right."

Helen was wrong. I was just jerking them off to try to save up for a nest egg. She wanted to buy a makeup kit. How could that be bad? Helen squeezed my hand and rolled onto her back.

"Let's go to sleep."

Helen's head rested on the pillow, eyes closed, pale skin glowing white in the night. She looked like Sleeping Beauty who needed only one thing to be brought back to life, and I had to do it. I leaned over and kissed her, and then Helen's lips parted and she kissed me back.

My heart flew around my chest like a bird as Helen took my face in her hands and kissed my lips, my nose and each of my cheeks. I could see her face. It wasn't in the dark like Ginnie. Then Helen pulled me close and her tongue touched mine. They danced and I made love to a girl that night, her fingers twisted into my hair, pulling my face deep inside her. It wasn't a perversion. It wasn't sick. It's who I was, and I knew it in my heart that it was right.

We didn't leave the apartment for two days, only getting out of bed to eat or use the washroom. Lily said we were offending Gabe.

"You ain't offending me," Gabe replied, sitting down in the chair to watch as Helen quickly pulled the sheets up under her chin. "Reminds me of the time we got hookers on the ship."

"I'm taking you out for breakfast," Lily said, pulling Gabe to his feet. "And Ivan wants you both back today," she added, slamming the door behind them.

I rolled over, resting my head on Helen's belly as she stroked my hair. We did need to get back to work, but I didn't want to leave.

"Let's go in tonight," I said, kissing her belly.

"What are you going to tell him?" Helen asked.

"It was a bug and now it's passed."

She leaned down, kissing my forehead. "You know, we don't have to give notice. It's not like Ivan would give us any." She ran her hand over my breast. "Let's just stay in bed."

I rolled away, confused. "What are you talking about?"

"Quitting. My makeup kit is pretty much done. What do you think you'll do?"

Hold on. "I never said I was going to quit."

"You intimated."

Big vocabulary. "No I didn't. I don't have any money. What do you think I'm going to do?"

She jumped up and started smoking. "You knew how important this was to me and you lied!"

"I didn't lie." But I sort of did. I knew Helen's guard was down after all the dancing, but I thought if we made love she'd give up on the silly asexual business. Boy, was I ever wrong. Helen took her gayness very seriously.

"I should have known," she said. "You lied to get me into bed."

"I thought you changed your mind."

"Because you're so hot? You're just like one of the johns."

Oh that was low. I punched the pillow. "What am I supposed to do?"

Helen and I ran up some stairs of a government building, ducking beneath the awning. She'd decked me out in some of Gabe's old clothes: a pair of ripped pants about three inches too short, a moth eaten coat and wrapped a tensor bandage around my wrist. Hard pellets of sleet began rocketing out of the sky.

"Tell them your boyfriend beat you up and you're afraid for your life and you can't go home. Better yet, tell them that you've got a baby to think of."

"What if they want to see it?"

"Tell them that you and the baby are starving and have nowhere to live. They've got to give you money. That's their job. They're the government. Then we can figure out what you want to do."

Two ladies ran up the stairs behind us, arm in arm, likely to keep from slipping. The shortest of the two glanced up, her hair was red. I pulled Helen around so the ladies couldn't see us.

"What are you doing?"

I hid my face and ducked, facing the wall. "That's my aunt."

Helen tried to turn but I held her fast. She didn't like it, but she didn't move. We huddled together, while Aunt Anne and the lady talked by the doors. I could only hear bits of what they were saying, but obviously they were friends. Aunt Anne said something about them having dinner later that night at The Plaza. The other lady, a nice looking woman with short blond hair and a dark trench coat, squeezed Aunt Anne's hand, telling her to have a nice day, and then Aunt Anne hurried back down the stairs – presumably on her way to the hospital. Her friend disappeared into the building. The same building I was going into – the Welfare Office.

Helen pulled away. "Why didn't you introduce me?"

I gestured at my clothing. "Like this?"

"She's an old dyke."

"No she's not." Yes she was. I thought back to our conversation in Granddad's kitchen about how you don't have to act on the impulses, and how women who do don't always have the happiest of lives. Maybe Aunt Anne was acting on them, only she was acting on them in secret. Maybe she had no choice.

"Are you ashamed of being gay?" Helen asked.

"No." But I still worried they might lock me up for being a pervert. I knew I was gay and it was good for me, but I wasn't too sure about the rest of the world. The rest of the world thought we were sick. It was safer to keep it private.

"Want some company?"

"No." Welfare was shameful enough already. I didn't want Helen to see.

"Tell them your boyfriend beats you up. That always gets extra money."

I was way more concerned about running into Aunt Anne's friend than I was in getting the money. She might work in the Welfare Office. I thought about leaving but didn't have another choice. Not if I wanted Helen. She walked down the street, disappearing around the corner as I reluctantly followed an older couple into the building.

The sign over a desk read: INFORMATION. A woman sat behind it. Relief – she wasn't Aunt Anne's friend who might know my name, or at the very least might know Dad's last name, and make the connection. She'd call Aunt Anne who'd come over there and see me dressed in rags, begging for money.

The woman behind the desk handed me a form and pointed to a room on the left. "Take a ticket, fill this out, bring it back and wait. Someone will call you shortly."

The room was crowded. Young couples, broken men, disheveled women and confused immigrants sat in a room full of pale pink chairs. The walls were plastered with ad posters for Manpower and other ads encouraging young people to seek careers in the trades. Two little kids bounced a red and white striped rubber ball back and forth.

The form asked for name, age, prior work experience and current place of residence. I couldn't put down The Green Door and there was no way I was putting down my experience in Dad's office, so I checked off "None." "Married?" No way. "Willing to relocate?" Not really. Not with Helen and me being together. Doing the best I could, I returned the form to the lady, who brusquely told me to set it in the tray. I went back to the waiting room. The clock ticked. An hour passed. There were no magazines. The tensor bandage was making my wrist sweat, but I didn't dare take it off.

I couldn't stop thinking about Aunt Anne and her friend standing together on the steps. All they got to share was a secret little squeeze, not even a kiss on the cheek. That didn't seem right, but that's the way it was. When I looked back up at the clock, another half-hour had passed. Aunt Anne's friend had to be a social worker. Aunt Anne's life had always been about helping people, so of course she'd pick a girlfriend who did the same thing. I wondered what it was like for them when they went out for dinner or to the theatre or out with friends and family and nobody knew what they shared. Some people might suspect, but they'd never say it out loud.

"Madeline Barnes?"

A thin woman in a tweed skirt, striped shirt and sturdy shoes stood in the doorway holding a pile of folders. She wasn't Aunt Anne's friend.

"I'm your social worker, Mrs. Allen. What did you do to your hand?"

I'd forgotten about the tensor bandage. "Just a sprain. Nothing to worry about." I'd decided not to go with Helen's advice about being beaten up.

"Come this way," Mrs. Allen said, ushering me into a large room filled with small brown cubicles. She sat at her desk and examined my file. I took a seat and stared at the carpet. It was industrial grey and had a few coffee stains.

"You don't have any skills."

"No," I replied, wanting to scratch the bandaged hand. This was so humiliating.

"What would you like to do?"

A man in another cubicle looked up from his work. The fluorescent tubes made his skin look green.

"I'm not sure. I don't want to do just anything."

"It's hard to get anything other than menial work when you don't even have Grade Ten," she said, looking at what I'd written down about my education. "Why didn't you finish?"

It felt hot, as if the sun was burning down. "Stuff happened."

Mrs. Allen picked up a beige binder and began flipping through the pages.

"What's that?" I asked.

"Possible places for you to look for work. If we're going to give you welfare, we need to know that you're actively involved in a job search."

Welfare – my entire body felt dipped in shame. Mom would die all over again. Nobody in our family had ever been on the dole. Not even in the Great Depression.

"Can't you get me a job I'd like?"

"Not without any education." She set the binder down. "Would you have any interest in getting your high school diploma?"

"I don't have any money."

"We'd pay for school, books, room and board. But you'd have to maintain a certain grade."

"Really?" recalling what Helen said about dreams.

"We're here to help people get back on their feet. And you're only seventeen. You're still a very young woman."

"Would it be high school?" It would be awful sitting in a classroom with fifteen year olds staring at me, but I'd do it if I had to.

"Adult education."

"When could I start?"

"We'll process your paperwork and give you some money to tide you over. But we're going to need your old high school transcripts."

I didn't have them. Dad did. Another door slammed shut.

Helen was busy with a client, Cindy was polishing her toenails and Lily had gone home early to see Gabe. I threw a magazine on the floor. Ivan leaned out of the wicket shouting for me to pick it up.

"Pick it up yourself. And while you're at it, why don't you buy something new. I've read these ten times."

"You're not getting paid to read. You're getting paid to rub. And since you're slow, go clean the rooms."

"I'm not the cleaning lady."

"I'll pay you!"

My arms were stuffed with used bed sheets and towels. Ivan was right. The rooms were filthy. The doorbell jingled, followed by footsteps. Helen was so mad that I wouldn't call Dad for my transcripts that she refused to speak to me. She didn't understand. Our family was expected to contribute to society, not leech. If you were a leech you were a failure, and if you were a failure they didn't want to see you. You were a stain on the family name and you should go away and be forgotten. I had no dream like Helen, no way to contribute. At least nothing that was possible.

Ivan shouted up from down below. "You've got a customer!"

I tossed the used linen behind the bed, fluffed my hair and lit the candles. It had to be one of my regulars. I wasn't in the mood, but I needed the money. Maybe Helen had saved hers, but I hadn't because I wasn't perfect like little Miss Helen. Heavy boots pounded down the hall. Luckily, I still had one fresh sheet left.

"I'm in the room at the end."

The sheet billowed, slowly floating down. Hermann was standing in the doorway, wearing the same thin smile, thumbs hooked into the top of a shiny PARADISE belt buckle. When I tried to run, he kicked the door shut with his boot and grabbed me by the belt, tossing me backwards across the room. My head basket-balled off the glass as I hit the window, landing on the floor. Hermann stood over me, undoing his pants. The buckle dropped to the side.

"You scream and I'll kill you right now."

I cowered, hands over my head. "I never told them anything."

The teeth of the zipper chattered down. Hermann lifted me up by the hair. I held onto his wrist to keep it from tearing out. Then he threw me again, over the bed and into the opposite wall. My face smashed into the red screen, knocking it over as I flew by. Blood filled my mouth.

"I kept my word."

Then Hermann was on me and I was trapped. He started booting me in the stomach and seized the back of my head. I tried to pull away, but he was too strong. If I screamed he'd snap my neck. He pulled his dick out of his pants.

"Suck it!" He slapped me in the head again and again. "Suck it, you fuckin' dyke."

He drew his hand back, high in the air, fist clenched, about to drive it down, when flames shot up the wall.

The candles had fallen, landing in the pile of soiled bedding. The flames jumped from the cheap cotton sheets and licked up the plywood legs as the bed exploded into a ball of hot fury. It happened so fast, like a barn full of straw. Hermann stepped back as I rolled to my side and up on my feet. Open armed, he lunged at me, but his loosened pants made him stagger. For a moment he lost his balance, just long enough for me to grab the chair and whack him across the head. Hermann roared but didn't go down, and he ran, head down like an enraged bull. Another wild swing of the chair, but this time Hermann got it, tossing it into the fire that was coming up fast, consuming the room. The walls and ceiling were aflame, but Hermann didn't care. He just stood with the inferno closing in all around him and laughed. We were going to die this time. There was no way out. The door was on fire and Hermann blocked the window. Sirens sounded and Hermann charged, throwing me onto my back. The ceiling gave way, revealing a splinter of sky. Snow blew in as plaster and joists came crashing down.

I rolled out of their way, but the main beam landed on Hermann, knocking him to the floor, pinning him like a butterfly. I jumped up and instinctively began to tug on the beam, but it was too heavy. Then

I heard Helen yell. She was still in one of the rooms. More sirens. The window, the only way out, was getting thick with falling snow.

Hermann reached out and gripped my ankle, trying to pull me into the fire with him. I heard Helen scream again as Hermann's fingers dug in so hard it felt as if the bones were going to break. With my free foot I kicked him over and over and over again until he finally let go, and I vaulted over the beam, pushing open the window. As I jumped out, a raging fireball blew, taking the whole room with it.

Fire trucks and police cars were arriving, their swirling red cherries sending beams of light through the snow. Ivan, the other girls and their johns were out front, some of them naked, staring up. Helen wasn't with them. I ran across the fire escape towards the light of the last room. The whole building was on fire.

Helen and the john were trapped in a corner. I opened the window and leapt in, snatching a sheet from the bed and another from the floor, soaking them in heavy, slushy snow from the windowsill. Running through the flames, I tossed the man a wet sheet.

"Run!" I screamed.

Wrapping himself up, he took off towards the window as the wall behind us collapsed.

"Come on!" I yelled, bundling Helen in the other sheet.

"I can't!" she cried, frozen with fear.

Now the room was more fire than air. There was no time for fear. Grabbing Helen by the waist I half pulled and half carried her through the red hot, as the other walls disintegrated into flames.

The whole gang sat on The Steps as plumes of water from fire hoses shot into the sky. It was too late to save the building, but they'd stopped the fire from spreading. As an ambulance attendant applied salve and gauze to my arms I heard a fireman talking to a policeman. They'd found a body inside. Hermann was dead.

"You'll be fine," the attendant said, securing the gauze with a piece of tape. "It's only a slight burn. Just keep it covered."

I already knew that.

He looked at me. "You were really lucky."

Spectators, the so-called good people, stood in the background staring at us. Ever since the murder of that newspaper boy, the public had been agitating. Things they knew nothing about were suddenly front page news, and now they wanted the Yonge Street strip cleaned up. They were so naïve. They had no idea what went on in their city. People talked about Toronto the Good, but I can tell you that if you had the money, Toronto was a sin city where you could buy almost any kind of kink.

CHAPTER TEN

Helen had gone to the only late night drug store for more gauze, but I just wanted to sleep. My cab pulled up at St. Jamestown. I paid the driver and got out. Cindy had just exited the building and was clipping down the sidewalk, lightning fast for a girl on stilettos, especially when the concrete was slick with ice. I stopped. She didn't slow. In fact, she looked upset.

"You okay?" I asked. Cindy lived close by. She must have taken a cab home to tell Lily what happened.

"I'm late."

That was weird. Cindy usually chatted. The apartment door was locked. Lily had an open door policy because Gabe always lost his keys. I dug mine out and unlocked the door. The living room was trashed. Lily's prized General Idea photograph lay shattered, face up on the floor. Somebody had taken a knife to it. The blue goo from Helen's lava lamp spattered the white walls and ceiling. Chunks of glass crunched beneath my feet like broken stars.

Lily sat in the centre of the sofa, heating a spoon full of liquid over a candle. A syringe rested on the table beside a bag of white powder. Heroin. She must have gotten it from Cindy. It made no sense. Lily hated drugs. I sat down beside her as she rolled up her sleeve, hands shaking, crying like a little white kitten tossed out in the snow.

"What happened?" I asked, looking around, wondering who would do such a horrible thing.

"Gabe's dead," she sobbed.

My body went cold.

"Big Man killed him." Lily set the needle in the spoon. The junk backed up into the syringe, as milky as Gabe's eyes.

"Don't, Lily. Don't do that."

"You understand."

I did. I tried to snatch the fit, but she just twisted away, holding the syringe as tightly as if it were a dagger. And then she did it. Lily, who never even smoked a joint because she thought it was stupid. Lily shot up heroin. She'd learned how to do it from watching me.

The syringe missed the table and landed on the carpet as Lily fell back. Holding her close, I rocked her back and forth, feeling her body slacken and her breath slow. Getting stoned kills the pain and takes you somewhere else. I thought it was a place better than life, but that was wrong. When you're high, you're cushioned inside a syringe or bouncing around in pill bottles, separated by glass and plastic. Colours are muted, smells seem faint and feelings don't burn as hot and bright. Drugs don't turn you on, they just turn you down until the lines that uniquely define you simply fade away.

Lily moaned. I kissed her head and lied, telling her that everything was going to be all right. But that would be up to Lily, just as my choices had been up to me. So there we sat, while Lily floated in a medicated wonderland, in the middle of the disaster that used to be her perfect home. The home that she'd just destroyed. Why did she do that? I didn't care if it was rude. I was sick of these secrets and had to know why.

"How did you and Gabe meet?"

Lily lay down, burying her head in my lap. I couldn't see her face – only feel the soft whiteness of that halo of hair.

"He was a friend of my father's.

So Gabe wasn't her dad.

"What about your mom?"

"I never knew her." Lily took a shallow breath and nodded off, but when she woke up she started to cry again, and she told me a story that flowed out in jagged bits.

When she was a little girl, maybe three or four, she lived in an apartment somewhere near the ocean. She said she knew this because she remembered the sound of the sea. Gabe lived in the same building and knew her father, and Gabe used to come and visit. Gabe and her father drank and drank and drank, and when that happened they roared and laughed, but then her father always got mad. He got mad if she spilled her milk. He got mad when she turned on the TV. And then he'd hit her. He hit her all the time.

One night she accidentally knocked over the ashtray, and her father said he didn't want her anymore. Then he opened the window and threw her out. She went high into the sky and flew like a bird until she landed on the pavement and broke her legs. Her father never came down to see what happened, but Gabe did.

She looked up and told me that he picked her up in his arms and ran all the way to the hospital and told her the story of Humpty Dumpty while they braced her legs. Then Gabe took her away.

Lily cried and cried until the room went still. I held her tight. What did they do in that bedroom? What had they done together for all those years? Were they lovers? Friends? I chose to believe Gabe needed a child to call his own and Lily needed a father, because sometimes there's no explaining the unspeakable things we do for love.

A woman's voice answered the phone.

"Dr. Barnes's office." The nurse's voice reminded me of Ruth and I nearly hung up. "Is anybody there?" she asked.

Helen gave me a sharp prod. She was right. No matter what, I had to get those transcripts.

"Can I speak with Dr. Barnes, please?"

"He's with a patient."

Utter relief and total disappointment – double whammy. "I'll call back."

"Can I tell him who called?"

"It's his daughter."

"Please hold."

The phone struck the desk followed by voices. A patient must have wandered in. There could be an emergency. You never knew what might happen in a doctor's office. The line clattered.

"Maddy?" Dad asked.

"Yes."

"Are you all right?"

His imagination probably went straight to jail. My voice tightened. "Do you have my high school transcripts?"

"They're likely down in the basement somewhere. I'll have to ask your mother."

The curly black phone cord scrunched between my fingers. There was no point correcting him. "Could I come to the office and pick them up?"

"You could come by the house."

Now I was good enough? He didn't want me there before.

"I'd rather come to the office."

"Why do you want them?"

"I'm going to go back to school."

A long, slow intake of breath. "That's good news."

I gave him our address and asked him to stick the transcripts in the mail.

"I'll post them tonight."

"Thanks, Dad."

I was about to hang up when he suddenly blurted out, "Why don't you meet me for dinner?"

No. No. No.

"We could go to the Inn on the Park."

Not there.

"I think the mail…"

"For dear old Dad?"

There it was – his sweet voice. And I just couldn't say no.

The bus roared through Leaside, past suburban backyards, snow-covered jungle gyms, shopping malls, kids dragging toboggans up distant hills and parents waiting in cars, while I tried to keep the memories of Mom, Dad, Sterling and the boys locked in the silo where I'd hidden them so long ago. I never planned to let them out, and now here I was with the key in my hand, hurtling back into the pain all over again.

The Inn appeared at the top of the hill in the distance, a large luxury hotel surrounded by acres of parkland. Mom said you could go for beautiful walks in the spring and summer, but I'd only been there once in the winter when the world was white. The bus driver called out Eglinton. I rang the bell, opened the door and stepped into the snow, heading up the long, winding drive to the Inn.

Dad hadn't arrived. There was a bitter chill. I buttoned up the top collar on my coat and sat on a bench beneath the snow-covered awning. The bellhop kept giving me odd looks and I was worried he might ask me to leave. A little girl, dressed for a fancy evening, walked past me with her parents. She wore a red coat, matching hat and gloves with black patent leather shoes and strutted proudly between them, holding onto their hands as if she were a princess.

"Swing me!" she cried. Her mother leaned down, telling her to hush, while her father gave her a tickle. "Pick me up and swing me!" And so then they did, and she laughed as the bellhop bowed and opened the glass doors as the family disappeared inside.

Mom and Dad had brought me there. It was New Year's Eve and we were dressed in our best. I had a new maroon velvet dress, Mom wore a long black gown and a mink stole and Dad looked dashing in his tux. The maître d' ushered us in, past all of the other patrons. Nobody looked as handsome as my family. Heads turned as everyone wondered who that perfect family was. I was so proud – these two grown-ups were my Mom and Dad. We took our seats and the waiter handed me my own menu, not a kids' menu, but an adult menu.

"Thank you," I said, opening it. "What would you recommend?"

Mom smiled at Dad.

"I'd recommend the French onion soup," he said.

"Well then that's what I'll have," I replied, closing my menu. I was only eight and thought I was all grown up. I was wrong.

"Madeline." Dad stood in front of me in his long overcoat with the fedora tilted back, hands thrust deeply into his pockets. We stared at each other for a second that felt like a million years. "I've booked us a reservation."

I rose. We didn't hug or kiss. It wasn't until we shook hands that I noticed he was trembling too.

We followed the maître d' through the restaurant, past tables of well-dressed diners, to a cozy table for two by the window. At least I wasn't wearing my Crime of the Century tee-shirt. My heart pounded while I wiped the palm sweat on my jeans. Dad left his coat and fedora at the coat check, but I hung mine on the back of my chair in case I had to run away. I looked out the window and noticed the frozen fountain standing in a wide shallow pool, covered in layers of ice, and remembered.

"Teddy, we shouldn't be drinking champagne," Mom said, trying to snatch the flute from his hand.

"Nonsense." He moved it higher, out of her grasp. "A sip won't hurt."

I beamed up at him as Dad handed me the flute, the champagne bubbles bursting as they struck the side of the glass. The three of us were standing outside by the frozen fountain listening as the band inside played "Auld Lang Syne". Dad had insisted on the champagne and he'd also insisted that we go outside to ring in the New Year. I could see Mom's breath. "Auld Lang Syne" suddenly came to a halt and the drum began to beat out the countdown as the bandleader called, "Ten…nine…eight…seven…" Mom slipped her arm into Dad's, with me right in between them. I felt her shiver as she squeezed us tight. The bandleader kept going. "Three," he called. The flute felt cold in my hand. "Two…one…" Mom kissed Dad's cheek and smiled at him. "HAPPY NEW YEAR!" And horns honked and streamers flew and voices rang out in the night. Dad turned and kissed Mom right on the lips, in a deep way I'd never seen before. Then they bent down and kissed me. Her cheeks were flushed and she looked radiant. Dad raised his glass to the stars that were more plentiful than all of the bubbles in my glass and declared that our family was going to have a stellar year – no, he wanted to go further than that. He wanted to toast our future, certain that it would be bright and that we'd have the happiest and the very best of lives.

Dad set a manila envelope on the table beside him. They had to be my transcripts. The maître d' handed us each a menu.

"Can I have the waitress get you anything to start?"

"A coffee please," Dad replied. He didn't need the caffeine.

"Coke," I ordered, thinking we both needed hot milk.

I scanned the entrées, unsure of what to order. If it was too expensive he might think I was greedy. Peeking up from the menu I noticed that a lot of Dad's hair was gone and he'd put on a fair bit of weight. But even with the extra weight he looked good. Toronto agreed with him. Toronto and Isabel. As if reading my mind, he pulled a comb out of his pocket and absentmindedly brushed at the remaining black strands. The waitress arrived, set down our drinks and asked Dad if we were ready to order.

"French onion soup," Dad said, looking at me. "If that's all right with you."

I nodded, my fingernails scratching, digging into the white linen. He'd remembered.

"Same for me."

"How are you keeping?" he asked.

"Fine."

I couldn't breathe. Please give me the transcripts. A table of diners near the front started to laugh. I thought of the last time we were here and how happy we had been. The difference between then and now was so stark I felt unsteady, as if the world might tip and I'd fall off.

"Aunt Anne was asking about you."

Maybe Aunt Anne had told him I'd been at the farm and had a kidney infection and had needle marks all over my arms. "How is she?"

"Fine."

"That's good." I looked around the dining room. "Are those my transcripts?"

Dad nodded. My hand reached out, but his fingers dented into the envelope. He wasn't letting it go. Not yet. "Tell me about this school of yours."

I picked up my fork, flicking it up and down to feel its weight. "It's adult education, to finish off my high school.

"How are you affording it?" he asked.

The napkin to the left of the silverware had INN embossed in raised black letters. Shaking it out, I watched the white linen drift down into my lap. Why did I owe him an explanation? Why should I feel so guilty when all I wanted was to go to school? Maybe I was a dirty little dyke speed freak and yeah, I'd done a lot of incredibly stupid and dangerous things, but I did them because I was trying to protect him. He was the adult and should have done a better job. They all should have.

"I don't think it's really any of your concern," I replied, trying to sound as respectful as I could.

Dad looked at me over the cup of coffee. Waves of liquid rolled back and forth in the white china cup, tossing up splashes of black onto his tie.

"Is it legal?"

Of course he'd ask that.

"Yes."

The waitress arrived and set down the soup. A hard crust of cheese floated on the top. I poked at it with my spoon, making the cheese rock back and forth like a raft. My spoon broke through the crust, steam billowed.

"You look well," he said.

"You mean better than last time."

The waitress returned, asking if everything was to our liking. Dad smiled and said something funny. She laughed. He could still be so charming. After she left, Dad methodically unfolded his napkin and placed it on his lap. He looked up at me.

"We had a conversation."

"Who?" I knew who.

"Isabel and I."

"About what?" I knew that too, but I wanted him to say it. I dipped my spoon into the thick soup, quickly brought it up to my lips and swallowed. The liquid burned my tongue.

"About why you left home."

So Isabel told Dad about the deal. Points for the wicked stepmother. I didn't know what to say, so I didn't say anything. Forgiveness was miles off. I couldn't see it on the horizon. Dad took a delicate sip of soup. He ate with great care, the same way he practiced medicine. Why didn't he treat me like that? I dipped my spoon into the soup again, more cautious this time.

"I wish you'd told me," he said.

I wanted to ask him what he would have done, but there was no point. He was too weak. Granddad was right. I stirred my soup, watching bits of onion swirl with the cheese and thought what a coward he was, he'd left me all alone to fend for myself. I took another sip.

No, that wasn't the truth. This was the man who drove through blizzards to deliver babies, who dragged car accident victims out of flaming wrecks, who had run up onto a beam in the middle of the night to save me. My father wasn't weak. He didn't throw me away because of the drugs and the girls. It was something else.

I set the spoon down. "Why did you bring me here?"

He stared back at me. "I don't know."

Yes he did, and suddenly, so did I. He brought me because he missed Mom just as much as I did and he missed me as much as I missed him, but every time he saw me all that pain came back. For both of us. It wasn't about lack of love. That was never the problem. There had always been love, maybe too much love because there was too much pain. Pain that drove me into the dispensary and out onto the streets. Pain that made Dad tie his belt to the light fixture and step off the side of the tub.

He'd stopped talking. I wanted to ask about Frank and Tedder but I couldn't. I'd finally crawled onto firmer ground and I couldn't afford to fall. Watching Lily get lost in junkieland, I saw how close I'd come to the edge and how it didn't take much to drop off. I finished my soup and set the sterling spoon into the white bowl.

"Can I have my transcripts please?"

Dad pushed the manila envelope across the white linen. I folded it and put it in my pocket. He wanted to stay for dessert, but I said it was time to leave.

Dad insisted on driving me back to St. Jamestown. The car was a mess, like always. I sat in the passenger seat, hand on the envelope in my pocket. Tomorrow I'd take the transcripts to Mrs. Allen. The aging Oldsmobile pulled into the round drive, with Dad peering up at the towers. There were nineteen of them in total, standing like a forest of tall white dominoes.

"This is quite the place."

"It's okay."

Dad switched off the engine. "I've got something for you." He dug his wallet out of his trousers and started rummaging around. It took a long time because the wallet, the old wallet Mom had bought him, was now held together by a series of brightly coloured rubber bands. Bits of raggedy paper poked randomly out of the billfold.

One of our neighbours, a young Indian woman wearing a bright blue sari, sailed by, calling hello in a singsong voice. She had a red dot in the middle of her forehead. I waved in return.

"You must meet a lot of interesting people," Dad said, looking at the mark on the woman's face. "What does that mean?"

"It's a bindi. The Indians believe it's the home for wisdom."

"Maybe if I'd had one of those…"

I shrugged, leaning closer to look at Dad's collection of wallet treasures. There was a credit card for every gas chain in North America, loose drug samples, a bunch of coupons for Harvey's hamburgers, plus a recent clipping announcing a car show in the spring. There was a photo of a Studebaker Golden Hawk with wing-like fins on the back and a square chrome grille. She wasn't a traditional car by any stretch, but she was an unusual beauty. Dad handed me the ad.

"Maybe you'd like to go to the show with me."

"Maybe," I replied. We both loved automobiles.

A photo of Isabel appeared. She was getting older. Random swipes of grey swept back from her brow. I didn't want to look at her and was about to say goodbye when I caught a glimpse of an old dog-eared photo in Dad's hand. It was me, grinning like the devil that I was, clambering up the side of the chain-link fence. Mom was behind, trying to pull me off, but I wouldn't let go.

"We couldn't keep you in," Dad said. He took my hand and held it tight. "I tried my best."

"I know."

"I'm sorry," he said, his voice breaking. "I'm sorry I took you away from Sterling. If I'd known how much it would hurt you, I never would have done it."

Shifting even closer, I felt the lightest stubble of his beard brush against my forehead. "It's okay, Dad." He wrapped his arm around me, holding me tight. "We both did the best we could."

We stared at the photo for the longest time, watching Mom smile into the camera. A lock of auburn hair had tumbled free from her red bandana. We all looked so happy. I could smell her Joy in my memory. Dad still smelled of pharmaceuticals and aftershave.

"I miss her so much," he said.

"Me too."

We both kept staring at the picture, trying to will her back to life. It didn't work and it never would.

"Do you remember how much Mom hated that fence?"

He nodded. "But not as much as she loved you. She would have done anything to keep you safe."

I looked at her again, trying to remember every inch of who she'd been.

Dad insisted on walking me into the lobby and right up to the elevator, talking about how different the city was from the country.

"But you know one thing Maddikins?"

"What?"

"No matter where you are, sick is sick, and someone's always going to need help."

The elevator doors opened and Helen appeared. When she saw us her face broke into a wide smile. I thought of "pervert", "damaged" and "psychiatric assessment." My mouth wouldn't open and my face said it all. Helen's smile fell, replaced by hurt. She knew what I was thinking and I knew what she was thinking about too.

"I'm going to the grocery store for Lily," she said. "Do you want anything?"

"I'm okay," I replied.

She began to pass us by and suddenly I knew I had to do it, and I had to do it now.

"Helen?"

She turned.

"This is my Dad. Dad, this is Helen."

Helen extended her hand with a smile.

"Hello, Dr. Barnes."

His face said he knew and my stomach flipped.

"It's nice to meet one of Maddy's friends," Dad said, returning her warm smile and shaking her hand. "How do you two know each other?"

"Work," I said, as strength began to smother fear. I handed Helen the transcripts. "But we're moving in together."

"Your Aunt Anne has had the same roommate for years."

Helen opened the envelope, glancing at the transcripts and gave me one of her looks. "You're going to have to do a lot better than this to get into university."

"University?" Dad asked.

Oh no. Helen had let out the secret dream. One night while we were lying in bed I'd told her. I never told Dad because I knew he would never believe in me.

I reached for the transcripts. "First I have to get through high school."

"You'll do it," Helen said turning to Dad, still holding the transcripts tightly in her hand. "What do you think?"

"You used to be keen on medicine," Dad said, glancing at his wristwatch. "I know it's late but maybe I can buy you ladies a cup of coffee…"

As we walked back to the car I thought about the power of secrets and lies. Mom's decision to keep the cancer to herself was like knocking over a single domino that altered the path of every domino that fell after it. If she had told us she was sick, and if Dad had told me about being so lonely that he had to marry Isabel, who knows…maybe I'd be a different person today. But then again – and I couldn't imagine this – if Mom had told us then I would never have met Helen.

Dad opened the rear door and gave Helen one of his charming smiles. "I hope you don't mind a little mess."

ACKNOWLEDGEMENTS

So many people helped push *Night Town* up and over the hill from a small pebble of an idea into the reality of a finished novel. It began over dinner with my cousin Laurie McGugan when she reassured me that our extended family wouldn't cast me out for writing it. (There are some autobiographical components scattered around the beginning.) Laurie stayed with me for the entire editorial ride and was joined by an army of other readers, who helped birth this book more than they could ever imagine.

Chief among them is my best friend Laurie Finstad-Knizhnik, who has been enormously influential in my choice of profession. An award-winning screenwriter, Laurie ripped apart an early draft of *Night Town* and then, over the course of several months, showed me how to put it back together again in a way that makes the story work. I can never thank her enough for all the precious time and guidance she gave me. I also have to thank her husband Vladimir, who put up with me sleeping on their pull-out couch for weeks at a time.

My nieces Alison and Caroline made sure I stayed true to a young woman's point of view, and Caroline's frankness led to the deletion of an entire chapter, which strengthened the novel immensely. Hester Riches breathed new life into the book when I was ready to put it away.

Many thanks are also due to Darlene Corrigan, Martin Hastings, Teresa Deluca and John McCarthy, who read *Night Town* over and over again, searching for typos and offering constructive criticism and encouraging words. Their unflagging enthusiasm always buoyed me up.

Then Patricia Howard, a retired English professor of mine from the University of Toronto, arrived, rolled up her editorial sleeves and went after grammatical inconsistencies. She also came up with the book's wonderful title. Dr. Howard has had more influence on my choice of career than anyone else. As I recently told her, "I was raised in your lab."

Lisa Garber helped keep me focused with her coaching, Cheryl Nix kept my body moving when all I wanted to do was lie down and cry. Judy Rebick worked her connections and Sally Keefe-Cohen guided me through contract negotiations. My pal and podcasting partner Nora Young shared her wisdom as I wrestled with the decision of whether to venture into the digital world of bookselling or stay bound to the traditional ways of print. Kim Elliott at rabble.ca gave me a venue to blog about my experience of publishing a book at the e-frontier and supported the book launch. Thanks to all of you.

I took a bit of a leap of faith signing on with e-publisher Iguana Books, and Iguana's publisher, Greg Ioannou, took an equally big leap by agreeing to publish this writer's first novel. Thank you Greg, and thanks to all the other wonderful people at Iguana – especially Emily Niedoba, who keeps everything going. It's been a terrific experience, and I have all the confidence in the world in the future of e-publishing and Iguana Books.

The biggest acknowledgment of all I save for my partner Sascha Hastings. Sascha has been with me since the beginning of this journey. Every night I would read her what I had written that day. Sascha edited every single draft and shored me up every time she saw me falling down. Sascha crosses the t's and dots the i's in my life. This book wouldn't have happened without her. I can never thank you enough, Sascha.

And finally, I thank my entire family. You are vast in number and even stronger in spirit. That indomitable Scots Presbyterian character that soldiers on through any tragedy, head held high.

I've written this book for all of you.

Iguana Books
iguanabooks.com

If you enjoyed *Night Town*...
Look for other books coming soon from Iguana Books! Subscribe to our blog for updates as they happen.

iguanabooks.com/blog/

You can also learn more about Cathi Bond and her upcoming work on her blog.

cathibond.com

If you're a writer...
Iguana Books is always looking for great new writers, in every genre. We produce primarily ebooks but, as you can see, we do the occasional print book as well. Visit us at iguanabooks.com to see what Iguana Books has to offer both emerging and established authors.

iguanabooks.com/publishing-with-iguana/

If you're looking for another good book...
All Iguana Books books are available on our website. We pride ourselves on making sure that every Iguana book is a great read.

iguanabooks.com/bookstore/

Visit our bookstore today and support your favourite author.

IGUANA

CPSIA information can be obtained at www.ICGtesting.com
Printed in the USA
LVOW131947300413

331459LV00003B/44/P